Shadow Fade

A Dilettante's Guide to
The French Language
Provençal Culture
& Murder

by

John Stuart Goldenberg

This book is a work of fiction. Names, characters, places and incidents are either the product of the author's imagination or are used fictitiously. Any resemblance to actual persons, living or dead, or to actual events or locales is entirely coincidental.

SHADOW FADE

Cover Designed by
Telemachus Press, LLC

Cover Art:
by Kurt Holmberg

Design by Telemachus Press, LLC
http://www.telemachuspress.com

Visit the author website:
http://www.John-Goldenberg.com

ISBN: 978-1-938701-53-5 (eBook)
ISBN: 978-1-938701-54-2 (Paperback)

Version 2012.10.03

Printed in the United States of America

10 9 8 7 6 5 4 3 2 1

Also by John Goldenberg

Upcoming

With Sincere Thanks:

Madame Monique Deckers
M. Dore Gormezano PhD
M. Mark Lyon
Mitch & Teresse Maloof *et al*
M. Mark Osojnicki
Mme. Jean Shutte
Mme. Ann Zender

Author's note:

The French language appears throughout this book.

Essentially it is the French of markets, restaurants, hotels and bars. What is sometimes referred to as *le Français gouttière* [gutter French]. In other words, the practical living French of the streets. Words are presented with inline translation (as above), hopefully providing an easy uninterrupted flow of the narrative. This is done not to add complexity, but to add clarity and color, and more fully acquaint.

Such translations provide descriptions of words and phrases of interest without method or discernable organization. The only commonality this novel shares with a textbook is paper.

A glossary is appended to further clarify the meaning of certain words (including German, Italian, and even English idioms when appropriate).

The objective of these elements is to portray the amity, crusty wit, and often endearing loopiness of the Provençal people.

And hopefully recount a diverting tale.

To the Gale
Mistress to Chaos and Passion and Time out of Mind.
Lambast and Pummeled unto Heartache and Folly.
To the Mistral.

Shadow Fade is a technical term—equally known as Rain Fade:
The attenuation of a wireless signal triggered by atmospheric events.
Rain, snow, hail, sleet and mist,
Sometimes fog, and their cousins, wind & lightning,
Such elements fade light, clarity, and acuity.
They blanche ink and the information it aspires to convey.
Often they fade hope, faith and purpose.
Even life.
But clouds pass.

Shadow Fade

Shadow Fate

THE COSMOS SEETHE in an infinite tempest of colossal storms and implacable tides. The night sky propagates the illusion of a serene, unvarying and immutable universe.

In reality, colossal forces inexorably draw congruent matter into raging common destinies and we exist in the midst of an infinite and eternal, frenzied tumult. In human terms the ultimate dénouement is, and will likely forever remain, unknown.

From unimaginably infinitesimal quanta to stupendous galactic clusters, the mechanisms are essentially the same. The nature of the force defines the nature of those elements it commands.

Curiously this applies to humans as well, albeit on a scale beyond Lilliputian. Disregarding the alleged caprices of chance, kindred souls seem almost mystically beckoned to the same dark gravity-wells of destiny.

Common lives drawn to common destinies; and sometimes, even convergent geography.

Such ordinations may on occasion be serendipitous. Far too often though, they are ominously malevolent.

This raises a puzzling anomaly.

Evil exists. It walks and poisons and kills and spreads hate amongst us. Yet no *one* is evil. Despite our wickedest acts, no one of us perceives their vile actions as evil. Strangely they are right. Our sins are a function of the actions perpetrated upon us, and accordingly our perceptions.

Therein evil lies.

When did it start?

The genesis of evil?
Why did it start?
Why evil?
Simply the metaphoric anti-matter equivalence to virtue?
Some form of Jhāna cosmic balance?
Or simply a naïf human concept?
Much as the cataclysmic nascence of existence itself:

Forever Unknown

Prelude: Ranny

SHE RECLINED ALONE by the pool. Her nude and tawny mid-summer tan nearly glowed in the brilliant sunlight. Her eyes blissfully lidded.

The icy remnants of her drink melted in a pitcher, shimmering in the afternoon heat. Margaritas. Strong, dry and biting. Unlike the saccharine European concoction, or the insipid mix pumped out in bars across the U.S., she'd learned to make them in Acapulco. Margarita-Mecca. Where incidentally, they were invented by an American lady (Margaret Sames), one Sunday morning late in the winter of 1948. So goes one version of the legend.

~~~~

For such a lovely woman, she was called by a very unlikely name: Ranny.

At first she'd hated that singular appellation, but it was part of her now. As were many things she would have never imagined.

She would have never imagined many facets of her life now. For one, she had been drinking a good deal more than usual of late. Understandably.

A casual observer would assume she was merely asleep, or a casualty of tequila and summer heat. Neither was true. She was simply lost in thought.

Things have changed so much in just a few weeks. I have changed. In part for the better. In part for parts unknown.

I suppose I may be an accessory after the fact of murder, or murders … not to mention suppression of evidence, obstruction of justice, and attempted murder by my own hand. None of which are viewed lightly by the French courts.

I've been frightened. Terrified. Guilty. I've lied. I never used to lie. Ever.

I've taken a lover and I've committed adultery, and reveled in it. I still revel in it. Astonishing.

I've been ruthless in protecting and taking what I want and love. I used to be so … what? Demure? Reserved? Diffident.

People have died. Horribly. But the carnage is ended now. I believe that. And the dead are beyond caring. I believe that too.

I've been in great jeopardy. And I'm still alive.

I came within moments of murdering a man myself.

I'm deeply in love with two men and they love me as well.

I care for them. They care for me. They even care for each other in their way. Not an eternal triangle. More an enduring tetrahedron.

And I've done these things and become all this in just a march of weeks.

And somehow I've never been happier.

Le Massif des Maures

Province is the designation for a legally defined French région [state].
There are presently twenty-two such regions.
Prior to the French Revolution there were forty.
Provence is one such province. Then and now …

THERE IS AN oft-overlooked region in southern Provence known as the *Massif des Maures* (*maa*-ceef *dē marr-rā*). Massif is indeed an appropriate appellation. A massif is a form of huge, graduated plateau, commonly ringed with dramatic topography, as the land fitfully rises and ebbs, ascending to its commanding apogee.

In geologic terms, a massif is a sort of dwarf tectonic plate, elevated by the colossal vulcanic forces smoldering deep in the Earth, or jostled on high by the titanic plates which peregrinate Earth's surface. There are several massifs in France and hundreds around the world. Some of the most dramatic occur in Ethiopia and North America. Many planets and moons demonstrate such marvels, for a variety of reasons. The famous *Face on Mars* is purportedly one such ancient elevation. Other planets stolidly persevere *sans massifs*, or even plate tectonics, cores as old and cold as creation itself, stoically inactive, magnetospheres gone with the solar winds, in eternal geological torpor.

This particular massif extends for some seventy kilometers from Fréjus to Hyères. Or roughly between Cannes and Toulon, in the region called the Var, not far south from the heart of Provence itself, and just at the western extremity of the Côte d'Azur. Or as the British christened it: *The French Riviera.*

~~~~

The Massif des Maures is a striking, eclectic blend of Mediterranean land-scapes. Highland meadows reminiscent of the tawny, windswept fields of Van Gogh and Gauguin and their time out of mind in Arles; skirted by rugged dry-land cliffs reminiscent of Sergio Leone's misnomered *spaghetti* westerns in Spanish Andalusia. A hard-bitten landscape softened by lakes and small rivers and tiny fanciful villages, and dense, windblown forests. This is the domain of the Mistral.

There is some dispute regarding the derivation of the name *Maures.* One interpretation purports it comes from the ancient Provençal word, *maouro,* meaning *dark,* which in fact translates as Moor, bringing to mind the 8th Century Moorish invasions in this area. Another asserts it derives from the Greek, *amauros,* meaning dark or dim. Oddly, although there are some dense woodlands, the Maures are generally neither dark, nor Moorish. Nor does the name bear any commonality with the British Grimpen Moors of *Hound of the Baskervilles* and Dartmoor Prison fame.

Literally: the Moorish—or the Dark—Massif.

In reality, the Massif des Maures is comprised by-and-large of bright rolling highlands. Scored by dusty country roads, spawning towering dust devils in hot, capricious breezes, under a giant sun. Long, precisely etched, afternoon shadows. Blinding blue skies. Grand views cascading down to the sea's jagged coasts, accented by huge rocks and dramatic cliffs. Hearty pines, maple, beech, sycamore, and tough scraggly live oaks mottled with gray-green lichen. Wildflowers by the thousands materialize near magically after summer showers. Bright whites, blues, yellows and reds. Chicory, fire thorn, sweet violet, peony, broom, wild lavender, honeysuckle, jasmine, anemone, thistle, primrose and fragile blood-drop poppies.

Foothills aspiring to mountain-hood rise to the Massif's stunning apex, terminating at *Notre-Dames des Anges* [Our Lady of the Angels], nearly eight hundred meters above the Mediterranean (2,600 feet).

The Maures are famous for *châtaigne* [chestnuts], as well as the increasingly rare *chêne de liege* [Cork Oak], extruding its exceptional fire-resistant, bottle-stopping bark. The Romans donned this obdurate bark as lightweight body armor two thousand years ago in these same hills. Surprisingly, cork was first used by the Egyptians. Although where they found cork in sufficient quantities is obscure. Initially employed as stoppers for clay jars of oil, wine, water and olives, etc., Egyptians moved on to all sorts of applications, as diverse as shoes, ships, roofs and even buoys. Their wisdom was then adopted by the Greeks and the Romans, who innovated uses of their own. But it was the French (Dom Pérignon in the 1600's) who elevated this humble bark to crown of the sparkling essence of the grape.

Sea breezes freshen the Massif at sunrise. Cool and bracing on bright pristine, dewy mornings. Natives claim flowery fragrances from the Îles d'Hyères linger in the dawning freshness, riding the winds from ten kilometers off the coast.

Noontide stands breathless. Hot, flinty and resinous with the cheerful scent of warm pinesap and woodland. The stuff of bees and butterflies and daisies. Warm yellows and satiny whites radiating in the midday sun.

Provençal lunch. An event. Abundant and savory, served on bright terraces overlooking the sea, as well as massive inland promontories. Fresh seafood and meats graced by the olive and aromatic spices. Marjoram, thyme, savory, basil, rosemary, sage, and fennel—what the world refers to as *Les Herbes de Provence*—served up with chilled wines, fresh local fruits, crusty bread and crisp vegetables harvested from farms across the rolling countryside.

Land breezes cool the highlands at dusk bearing moisture from the Rhone Valley. The night air is redolent with the essence of pines, as their needles cushion a muted scrunch underfoot. The winds, spiced with wild juniper, lavender and jasmine. A heady perfume, so intoxicating as to drive Van Gogh himself mad on luminous, starry nights.

As the Massif gently slopes to the east, its lofty woodlands give way to the coastlands at the extreme west of the Côte d'Azur. Coastlands now choked with towns once disparaged as *fleshpots*.

Most notably, St. Tropez.

Decades earlier, only vineries, orchards and quiet fishing villages adorned this coastline—haunted by artists the likes of Picasso and Cézanne—writers the stature of Sartre, Camus, Fitzgerald and Tennessee Williams.

Come the 1950's. 1959 specifically.

And God Created Woman ... who also made Roger Vadim ... who made Brigitte Bardot ... who made St. Tropez ... who made the developers ... who brought the tourists ... who made a mess.

Overnight St. Tropez became the pouty-blonde-bikinied-starlet center of the world. Hitherto charming and euphoric villages emerged as Mecca's of money, glamour, and garish excess.

Not Ms Bardot's fault really. She loved and respected the area and its creatures, but the floodgates were now yawningly agape.

Arabs, Russians, Americans, British, Japanese, Italians, Danes, South Americans and Germans ... even the occasional Frenchman.

Celebrities, politicians, movie stars, billionaires, gangsters, investment bankers, and hi-tech-exec-u-dweebs cumulate aboard massive yachts, trendy restaurants and frenzied nightclubs, parading conspicuous consumption and egregious fashion.

The St. Tropez yacht basin is crammed with multi-million dollar pleasure craft. Many so saccharinely pretentious as to make a seaman's eyes burn and his teeth ache. Insipidly cute names affixed to fantails. Some outrageously fashioned of raised chrome letters, backlit with pink neon and such. Fiberglass confections so ostentatious, mariners shrink from such craft for fear of wrathful sea gods, outraged at such vapid frivolity fouling their briny kingdoms.

Pampered little boys race million dollar toys, terrorizing the countryside at deafening, dizzying speeds. Coveys of bosomy scantily clad beach-baubles at their side.

Tourist beaches, public beaches, nude beaches, gay beaches, private beaches, restaurant beaches, bar beaches, hotel beaches, and on and on ...

Elysium for those derided in earlier times as the *nouveau riche*.

Later they were wheedled as the *jet set*, lauded and deemed glamorous by pre and post pubescents alike.

These days they're just *rich*.

A sweaty, gritty holiday marathon for those of modest means.

A gracious retreat for those with the means and sagacity to seclude themselves in the courtly villas perched in the hills above the summer heat, the manic fray and the interminable traffic.

Restaurants and hotels cater the range from decadent luxury, to discount-bargain-tour-cheesy. Champagne can be had from seven Euros a glass, to Cristal Champagne in some clubs at seventeen thousand Euros a bottle.[1]

In fairness though, St. Tropez does offer excellent restaurants and friendly stylish bars, plunging into to an ebullient nightlife.

The surrounding countryside remains beautifully up-market. St. Tropez is surrounded by some of the most captivating villages and wineries in Europe, epitomizing French country life in the south of France.

---

[1]Author's Note: Cristal Champagne was introduced on the Riviera shortly after WWII, only slightly ahead of the accession of the super rich. While not commonly consumed worldwide, it has long been beloved by the excessively wealthy. A bottle at some clubs may cost in excess of seventeen thousand Euros. Cristal Champagne is one of the quintessential Veblen Goods, or Veblen Commodities with others such as pricy watches, showy villas, enormous yachts, luxury cars, designer fashions, etc. (Thorstein Veblen, U.S. economist, 1857-1929, *The Theory of the Leisure Class*). Veblen identified a specific market segment (the affluent) wherein certain goods actually increase in demand, linearly proportional to their price. The more expensive, the more they are coveted. The axiom being the consumer's perception such goods lent prestige to their owners.

Cristal Champagne (*кристалл* in Russian) was first supplied by Louis Roeder (Official Vintner to the Court) to Tzar Alexander II. Per the Tzar's instruction it was produced in a crystal clear bottle, with a flat bottom (lacking the classical dimpled Champagne *punt*, or *kick-up*). Such design assuaged Alexander's fears of assassination by concealed explosives. Cristal was first marketed outside the Tzar's Court in 1945 and has been increasing in price, thereby its desirability, ever since.

Prelude: David

SEATED AT HIS desk, the view from his window was spellbinding. Cascading flowers, lush greenery, hills and rugged valleys tumbling down to the crystal azure Mediterranean ceaselessly rolling and glittering in the sun. Nonetheless, it barely attracted David's notice. Seated at his desk, injured leg securely propped, he was totally absorbed in fragments of life, some of which had faded over four hundred million years ago. He was methodically classifying, authenticating and re-classifying his finds. Some were poorly preserved and difficult to identify. Others were near perfect. Many quite beautiful. These fossilized bits of unimaginably ancient life gave him pleasure, such as little else in his life, as they had his father and his mother before him, for as long as he could remember. Now that he *could* remember.

He had never been happier, or more comfortable with his life. His was a richly rewarding élan. Science, wealth, a dear friend, and a beautiful Domaine nestled in the storybook valley of Coirón. Most of all, a beautiful loving wife.

It was hard to believe less than one twenty-nine-thousandth of a lifetime—a single day—could cast a shadow so enduring it would vitiate his entire existence. Until now.

No more. An intolerable thorn removed from his figurative mental paw. Thank the fanciful gods of serendipity.

A little bad luck, a tragic stupid accident, serious injury and tortuous death, nearly dying himself twice, and an agonizing catharsis, the love of a good woman, nearly dying yet again, e*t voilà!*

The Lusus was born. Then the Lusus died. Lusus. Devine insanity. A malevolent presence that defies classification. Lusus. With dead, white, unseeing eyes. Green eyes too. But now only David's clear, piercing gray eyes remain.

Things were different now of course. Some might even say *outré* [outrageous].

He'd been called upon to set aside his ego, his pride and his possessiveness. Instead he had to consider the needs of those he loved. And love was indeed the word; and they were now a family of sorts, more and less. He smiled inwardly, at himself, dizzyingly. He had become *ever so* continental.

He would say things were better now. More honest. Benevolent. Trusting and even decent. And they were.

He would say they had found serenity and symmetry. And they had.

He would say he'd been a conventional man all his life. And he was.

Then a pleasant surprise.

Convention was an illusion. A narrow-minded contrivance. A trap. A shackle. A sham. And it was.

So he cast it off. To became a better man. And he was.

He'd hesitantly compromised, bordering on the most sophisticated of European mores. Grudgingly at first. The sour green sapor of suspicion and jealously still resonated on his palate. But understanding was slowly dawning in him. He realized he was neither the master of his fate, his world, or those about him. He was in fact but a functionary of other's needs, as must be every human of true regard. And so he gradually relented. His entente might someday blossom into acceptance, even affection and a new courage of sorts.

Thank the fanciful gods of serendipity.

Coirón sur Mer

UP THE COAST, above the fray, at the south-central limit of the Massif, lies the picture-perfect village of Coirón-sur-Mer.

Coirón is secluded between the towns of Cavalaire-sur-Mer and Rayol-Canadel-sur-Mer (Cavalaire and Le Rayol for short). Most of the village is situated seaside, south of the D559 *Route Departmentale* [county road], just off an artfully landscaped roundabout.

The smaller C121, *Route Communale* [village road] off the D559 entering Coirón is hardly noticeable. Lost in a shady glen. Hidden between two cumbrous hummocks that envelop the narrow road in dark, cool, sun-mottled, gray-green shadow. Easy to miss and uninspiring to explore. In fact, it is the flowery roundabout connecting the D599 with the C121 that engages the traveler's eye, happily diverting the traveler's attention from the innocuous nearby route to Coirón.

Embraced and protected by the foothills of the Massif, Coirón strad-dles a tiny listless river called the *Maure*. The Maure is a tributary of the slightly larger *Mole River*, as it meanders lazily along the coast.

Jade green and mirror smooth, the Maure convolutes and branches through the village, lethargically flowing into the village's fishing port as it rejoins the sea. The 'port' barely accommodates six tiny fishing dinghies.

Nestled within this ancient valley, Coirón is protected and sheltered from the formidable *Mistral* winds that howl down the immense Rhone delta; and the powerful *Libeccio* southeasters thundering out of Italy, spring and fall.

These assorted factors militate to the benefit of the small village. Coirón has been almost totally overlooked by natural forces, as well as human.

Undiscovered, undeveloped, unspoiled, unruffled, un-crowded and unconcerned.

All in all, the quintessential setting for lyric, Provençal life.

Prior to the murders of course.

Prelude: Adam

HE THREW THE wheel to port, unnecessarily albeit instinctively, ducking the boom, coming about smartly, and pointing up. Flawlessly.

I seem to get better at this every day.

I remember when single-handing scared hell out of me. Now, aside from sailing with David, I'd sooner take her out alone. No matter the weather.

His name was Adam MacAfee. Doctor Adam Bradley MacAfee DVM, PhD.

He'd always learned you had to test the limits of your boat. He knew now that really meant testing the limits of her skipper. Damn near any boat could sail, given the right man at the helm.

It was a hot day. He was thirsty and hungry. There was cold beer and sandwiches in the ice-chest, but he took only a beer. He wanted to save his appetites for this evening.

Dinner with his two favorite people. People who had saved him. Knew him. They were more than friends. They had truly saved him. Some form of unorthodox family? Kin? Kinsman and kinswoman? Much stronger than family in some respects. And now they protected him. In many ways ...

When he was a berserker she'd healed him.

Some dreadful thing had summoned a part of his essence from its oblivion. Breathed life into it. Reanimated it. A greater torment than he'd ever endured.

Finally it had died, or he'd killed it, or Ranny killed it. Perhaps even David somehow. However. It had perished. Whatever it was; and he felt no remorse for it. Indeed already it was fading to but a wispy, evil memory. The lingering stench of sulfur when the wickedness has passed.

He certainly felt no sense of loss. More, he felt profound relief. A festering cyst surgically removed by his kith and kin. It had been part of him. But the worse part. A part that would have ultimately killed him.

He felt love and profound gratitude to his surgeons.

His dark carcinoma was gone now, if it ever truly existed.

He was certain.

The wraith of horror foregone.

The one with the eager caprine, golden eyes.

Coirón Natal

COIRÓN WAS FOUNDED by a diffident academic from northern France, roughly three hundred years ago. A gentle man, a widower, and a competent scientist:

Professor Doctor Monsieur André Aron Velleda PhD

Short, stout, huge bespectacled blue eyes, with an enormous shock of steel-gray hair flowing to shoulder length. His graying, stubbly chin was invariably lifted, generous lips pursed, half-smiling, with the buoyant, optimistic countenance of the visionary.

All his life, winter or summer, outdoors or in, regardless of activity, he wore a dark blue suit, waistcoat, stiff collar and cravat. He strode the world as though it were his lecture hall. Shoulders back, hands clasped at his back. A classic Daumierian caricature.

If André were posed a question—any question—a lecture would ensue, whether he knew the answer, or not—a lecture—and the listener would invariably leave enriched.

Throughout his personal and academic life André was revered by family, friends, colleagues, and students alike. One of those exceptional men who never alienated another. Who never lost a friend. Who never found an enemy.

Completing a long career instructing botany at the University of Strasbourg, Professor Velleda migrated to the south of France in the early spring of 1718. His party included his two sons and two daughters, their families, and two life-long family retainers. His adored wife, Sophia, fell victim to cholera the preceding year. André began his pilgrimage on the day of his seventy-ninth birthday. Their pilgrimage was a difficult one, and Doctor Velleda's health suffered greatly. His physical age advanced inordinately, yet his spirit and eagerness remained young and vital, as they had his entire life.

Three hard months later their quest came to its end in a beautiful little river valley opening onto to the Mediterranean.

His eldest daughter, Chantal, faithfully maintained a remarkably detailed diary her entire life. Consequentially, an extensive history of Dr. Velleda's adventures persists to this day. A particularly lyrical page from her diary appears in Coirón's single guidebook.

Today, Coirón's Association Patrimoine & Histoire [Coirón Heritage & Historical Society] houses the complete library of Chantal's Diaries.

After frigid decades in dusty, cavernous classrooms, André sought the sun. Growing, verdurous things. Light and warmth. A site for an inn and a vineyard. Lifelong dreams.

As scientists are sometimes wont, André assumed his academic expertise would easily translate into practical skills. A mistake compounded by the arcane intricacies of winemaking. Happily his sons were quick learners and hard workers. The professor, sadly, would not live to celebrate it, but there would ultimately be a Provençal wine proudly flourishing the Velleda name. A rubicund, fruity rosé: *Velleda de Coirón.*

The Velleda Winery continues to produce a respectable white and an excellent rosé to this day. They abandoned their red wine ambitions in 1956, something about the acidity of the soil in this specific region.

Sadly, the myriad onsets of age, health and journey were overtaking the Professor. Their pilgrimage to the south had taken a serious toll. Macular degeneration and dementia were seriously enfeebling his sight and his mind. As a result, Prof. Velleda committed a botanical contra variance. He mistook the coarse, amber clumps of Guinea grass prevalent throughout the region, for a nearly indestructible Latin-American grass: *Coirón* (*Festuca* spp. and *Stipa* spp., *aka* Antarctic Beech Grass *Nothofagus Antarctica*)

Coirón grass is exclusively indigenous to the arid steppes of Chilean Patagonia and Argentina. Thusly he christened his fledgling village with the utterly malapropos name: *Coirón*.

Professor Velleda lived to see his vines planted in the spring of 1721. A source of great joy. He also saw their home completed, a fourth grandchild, and the arrival of Coirón's first business. A roadside blacksmith & livery: *Écurie de Coirón*.

He passed away in September of 1722. Congenital heart failure, following a long happy life devoted to science and family. His daughter and granddaughters wept bitterly at his graveside. No man's life is utterly without merit when a lady's tears grace his passing.

His inn, *Les Herbes Intrépides*, welcomed its first guests in May of 1723 and the tiny byroad began its nonchalant evolution to tiny village.

In March of 1902, Coirón was re-ordained Coirón-*sur-Mer*, presumably to attract the new wave of foreign investment in the south-central coast. Coirón's new name rendered Doctor Velleda's botanical erratum still unrectified, and even more deeply ingrained.

To this day, senior Coirónaise refer to Guinea Grass as *les herbes de Coirón* [the grass of *Coirón*] as they repose in the warm sun taking in the verdant countryside, with its pervasive clumps of rugged Guinea grass.

Prelude: Kontz

LATE EVENING.

The jarring ring of a phone shattered the tranquil darkness.

Merde! [Damn!]

It had been almost two years since Officer Émile Kontz had thusly attained with his wife, Michelle. Sweet, petite, and oh so patient.

Jean, his friend and pharmacist, had presented him a box.

"Émile you will be amazed at these little blue pills. They are a miracle."

And they were. And now the damned phone.

"*Émile*." she whined.

"I'm so sorry *cherie*. [darling] Truly sorry. But it is the police phone and I must answer."

I could kill Mayor Drôme and his fancy phone system.

His brother-in-law, the former Mayor had not been nearly so zealous regarding police matters. In fact he took little, if any interest, and actually coddled Kontz to the point he was quite literally autonomous. And this was a man that sorely needed supervision.

"Allo?" gruffly.

"Police?" British accent.

"Yes."

"Do you speak English?"

"Yes."

"My name is Howard Carpenter."

"Yes?"

"There has been a horrible attack at my home. My wife I think. Vivian."

"You do not know?"

"Officer would you please come."

"The woman. Is she ah …"

"Dead? Yes. No. I don't know! Will you *please* come?"

"*Immediatement* Monsieur [immediately]. And I will contact the *Service d'Aide Médicale Urgente* [Rescue Squad]. Your name again please, your address and your …"

~~~~

It was a cool night. Dark. No moon. No stars. The Gendarme's wizened little blue Peugeot struggled up the road into the hills. The locals called this area Beverly Hills. A response to the preponderance of swank villas dominating the area. Not the friendliest of appellations, but not lacking in a bit of gentle humor either.

Christ, if these rich bastards lived just one kilometer further north, this wouldn't even be my jurisdiction. Probably some rich bitch got drunk on Dom Pérignon and her little dog bit her. Now her idiot husband wants me to hold her hand.

As he neared the area, there were no streetlights, only narrow, winding roads coiling through the mists. Murky silhouettes of towering hedges shone against the dark sky. He worried he might have trouble finding the address, then he saw the glow atop the next hill. A luminous palace suspended high in the black night.

When he arrived, all interior and exterior lights were ablaze, the main gate was open. Even the pool and fountain lights were on, but not a soul in evidence. The huge main entrance stood agape. He walked through the grand door. Intricately worked wrought iron, gilded, over a huge sheet of high-tensile glass.

Looks like bloody Versailles mused Kontz.

Inside the cavernous foyer he found a lone man in an expensive pin-stripe suit. He was seated on a velour loveseat. His mobile phone had dropped to the highly polished black marble floor, forgotten, alongside his brief case and overnight bag. His legs were spread, elbows on knees, face in hands, fingers buried in his dark hair.

"Monsieur Carpenter?"

The man started and looked up sharply. A dissonant fusion of anguish, loathing and rage conflicted his features.

"The sitting room. Down that hall." He gestured dismissively. "On the right."

His head fell to his hands again, mutely ignoring the Officer.

Kontz tread gingerly down the long passage, footsteps echoing despite his best efforts at discretion. Kontz was far from a cultured, tasteful man, but he wondered at the lavish art and antiques.

Must've cost a fortune. But it's so ... so gaudy ... so overdone ... it makes me a little woozy. Like those middle-eastern pastries so saturated with sugar and honey they make your teeth ache.

He reached the sitting room. Not too different from the hall. Same décor compounded by enormous oil paintings and long cascading drapes, like something from a funeral home. The room itself was immense.

These ceilings must be more than six meters. His fascination with the life styles of these rich bastards was insatiable.

He saw nothing out of order though. Nothing wrong whatsoever.

What the hell?

~~~~

He stealthfully entered the room. Suddenly he was alert. As police go, he was excessively average, or far less. But *something* was wrong here. Even his vapidity could sense it.

The room was brightly lit, quiet, as overdone as the gallery; and something was disturbing about it. Something not right. Something fearsome.

Then he smelled it. A foul dampness that wrinkled his nose and squinched his eyes.

What is that odor?

A sour, coppery, cloying, and darkly intimate effluvium strongly emanated from somewhere in this large intimidating room.

He followed his nose.

After a few moments, he noticed a spattering of crimson teardrops speckling the marble on the backside of a long sofa.

He moved around the sofa and froze, saying only two words: *Mon Dieu* [My God].

He then retched, violently and uncontrollably, on a carpet worth a great deal more than he would earn in five years.

Markets, Mistresses, Ministers & Moonshine

INITIALLY COIRÓN-SUR-MER was little more than a widening in the old byroad between Ste. Maxime and Marseilles. The village has not grown appreciably in the intervening three hundred years.

One Café: *Chez André.*

One Hôtel-Restaurant: *Les Herbes Intrépides* (Expanded around Monsieur Velleda's original inn, conserving its curious name.)

Coirón boasts a tiny *Mairie* [Town Hall], which also houses a one-man *Gendarmerie* [Police Station]. Next door, a part-time *Bureau de Poste* (Hours: 0830-1230 Monday through Saturday).

Beyond that, the town's *Épicerie* [Grocery], an excellent *Boulangerie-Pâtisserie* [bakery] and the ubiquitous *Office de Tourism*, with attached boutique, featuring the few local wines and regional chestnut products.

Sharing the shelves with Coirónaise wine, a few sun-bleached postcards and *Pâte de Châtaigne* [Chestnut Pâté], remain a few venerable Kodachrome glossy copies of the Guide Touristique et Histoire de Coirón [Tourist and Historic Guide to Coirón], the village's sole guidebook, carefully researched, photographed, and lovingly penned by a former Mayor, Monsieur Michel Ferron in 1972. A Deuxième Édition [Second Edition] was published in 1983 upon the discovery of seven faded tintypes depicting the old mill as it stood a century ago. An English edition was commissioned in 1983 as well. However, the designated translator, Madame Jeanette

Gerard (secretary to Mayor Ferron), succumbed to red wine prior to its completion. An *affection hépatique* [cirrhosis of the liver].

There is a Tabac/Newsstand/Bar: *Le Cheval Blanc* [The White Horse]

Le Cheval Blanc is Coirón's nominal nerve center. Newspapers, magazines, lottery tickets, stationary, sports TV, gossip, breakfast, lunch, candy, politics, cigarettes, coffee, a glass of wine. *Pastis* in summer. *Vin Chaud* [warm wine (as opposed to Germanic Mulled Wine)] in winter. *Une Bière* anytime. The necessities.

Rising above Place Velleda is Coirón's cathedral: *Nôtre Dame des Collines* [Our Lady of the Hills]

Construction of the cathedral began in 1781, completed to coincide with the dawn of the 19th century. In celebration of the occasion, Bishop Grimaldi of Nice presented the parish with a tiny, very old bit of ossified wood, resting on a cushion of red velvet, secured under an ornate gold and glass dome. This was purported to be a piece of the actual Holy Crucifix brought back from the Crusades in 1278. Held by the Order of the Knights Templar, not far to the northeast of Coirón, until their gory extirpation at the hands of Philip IV and Pope Clement V, in 1307 (The original Friday the 13th). The holy relic remains on display to this day in the cathedral's intimate Sacristy.

Nôtre Dame des Collines now dominates Coirón's shady town square, *Place Velleda*. Coirón shares its Priest (Père [Father] Francis Gilbert) with Le Rayol on alternating Sundays.

The Mairie, along with the town's commerce line the square's western side, affirming Place Velleda as the nucleus of this miniature metropolis. Parking is provided a few steps off the square, adjacent to shops. Hopefully this ensures Place Velleda will never be invaded by the automobile.

~~~~

The Coirónaise are justifiably proud of this lovely square.

Huge mottled sycamores with enormous leaves dapple gaily umbrella'd café tables sprinkled across ancient cobblestones, splashed with fitfully shifting sun and shade. Something of Renoir lives this kaleidoscopic interplay of color, texture, light and form.

Ever-present villagers fractiously compete on the pétanque pitch [boules], while others follow the matches from classic French wood and iron benches affixed to the cobble in neat rows paralleling the pitch. Tidy postage-sized plots adorned with ornamental boxwoods, enclosed by wrought iron, surround the square, as a mossy fountain plashes unobtrusively mid-square.

The eastern boundary of the square is defined by an ancient market pavilion. *Le Marché d'Hyères*. Vegetables, fruit, meat, fish and general produce on Wednesday and Saturday mornings. Flowers on Fridays. Antiques the first Sunday of each month. In autumn it hosts the Velleda Wine & Chestnut Festival. Come December, Coirón's *Marché de Noël* [Christmas Market]

Each spring, the *Marché d'Hyères* is the focal center of the Mayor's annual *Fête des Fleurs Coirónaise* [flower festival]. Flowers outpour from every interstice. Music echoes through its rafters. Dancers swirl beneath its eaves, while wine and Coirónaise specialty foods flow liberally from its stalls.

In earlier times it housed the town's *lavoir* [communal clothes washing trough] at its southern extremity, diverting water from the Maure. Village women congregated here to gossip and wash their clothing in the clear running waters. These days the long stone trough serves only as a planter, gaily overflowing with flowers in lieu of water.

Comte Albert d'Hyères, Gouverneur Régional [Count Albert of Hyères, Regional Governor from 1727 to 1735] granted Coirón authority to hold a market in June of 1729, much to the dismay of Le Rayol. Rumors abounded to the effect this had much to do with Professor Velleda's captivating eldest granddaughter. There was also guarded grumbling disputing the Comte's authority to grant such authority altogether. Commerce, sex and politics. Mankind's motley trio.

The market is nearly as ancient as *Les Herbes Intrépides*.

In appreciation of the Comte's magnanimity, the marketplace was artfully and painstakingly constructed. Massive oak beams, very dark, very old, nearly indestructible, intricately intertwined, sheltered beneath an immense multihued terra cotta roof. A stark, shady counterpoint to the riotous flowers festooning its massive flanks. The entire structure is supported by more than twenty ponderous oak columns. Open air. No walls, only columns sheltered by an enormous roof. A wizened and tarnished bronze plaque, bearing the likeness of the Comte, still glowers out from the gable above the north entrance.

Place Velleda reposes to the market's left, while the Maure flows quietly by on its right, reflecting huge willows and verdant, winding banks in its quiet waters. Not far beyond the market, the Maure divides into three branches.

The first branch is the natural mainstream of the Maure, flowing placidly onto the port.

The second is manmade. Roughly two hundred years ago a small canal was excavated and diverted to power the village mill. Primarily wheat. The Guide Touristique et Histoire de Coirón states the mill was pulled down at the end of the 19th century.

Pulled down is not entirely accurate.

Its *charred frame* was pulled down.

In 1892 the mill's owner, a Monsieur Evan Lebec, had a vision. He dreamt of developing mankind's first *EVP*. *Eau-de-Vie Pétillant* [sparkling-water-of-life].

Evan was fascinated by the discovery of CO_2 by the Flemish scientist, Jan Baptista van Helmont (1580–1644); and had gained a reasonable understanding of its effects and composition. Consequently he read with great interest of the more recent developments by Doctor John Pemberton and his business partner, Mr. Asa Candler. These gentlemen were respectively the inventor and founder of the modern-day colossus: *Coca Cola*.

Monsieur Lebec was promptly consumed by the idea of a liquor—uniquely Provençal—enlivened by the added sparkle and bite of CO_2.

Lebec was well aware the distillation process excluded natural carbonation based on fermentation. Therefore he turned to Pemberton's solution, eloquently describing it: *Champagne de Campagne de Liquor*. And he went so far as to furtively print labels for his forthcoming EVP. He planned to bottle his EVP in the same manner as Champagne; and as Coca Cola was dispensed solely through soda fountains at the time, in a certain sense (M. Dom Pérignon notwithstanding) his was the original innovation to bottle carbonated drinks. One of his labels appears in Coirón's guidebook today, under the cryptic notation: *Une expérience échouée* [a failed experiment].

Fittingly, he selected the local Mauresienne Chestnut for his proto-hooch. More than eight hundred kilos. He used his mill to produce a fine chestnut paste (which lent an interesting tang to his wheat-flour for days afterward). He was even able to capture over twelve liters of the chestnut oil. He vatted the resulting sludge with sugar, fruit-alcohol, nutmeg and water. He then stored his glop in the cool darkness of his mill, stirring it twice daily, thus inspiring fermentation's anaerobic, intoxicating bloom.

After eight weeks he carefully strained the mixture, and stored it in large bottles. He repeated the process until he had accumulated over six hundred liters. When he deemed he had sufficient *squeezin's*, he constructed a still in a corner opposite his vat. After several distillations, and multiple attempts, he produced a fairly respectable liquor, roughly 45% alcohol, nearly a transparent beige. Fiery, with a numbingly dry, nutty aftertaste. Monsieur Lebec distributed samples around Coirón, which were enthusiastically received with breathless, teary-eyed appreciation.

One balmy evening in March, all was in readiness.

Evan began the process of dissolving carbon dioxide into the solution, using the method he'd extrapolated from Dr. Pemberton's description. Unfortunately he was alone at the time and made no notes, so the Coirónaise never really understood what happened.

There was an explosion, followed by a conflagration. Only the rugged structural beams remained. According to local accounts, no trace of Evan was in evidence. They assumed he had died instantly, blown into the canal and carried out to sea.

Shortly thereafter Coirón's *Boulangerie-Pâtisserie* turned to Le Rayol for its flour, and the incident faded into obscurity. Lebec's lovingly crafted label was never to grace a bottle:

*Champagne-de-Campagne-
de-Liquor-de-Châtaigne-de-
Coirón*

◆

Evan Lebec - 1892

Regrettably, future tipplers would be deprived of the sapor, spume and sparkle of a novel new era in liquor.

Not to mention a catchy name [Champagne-of-the-Country-of-the-Liquor-of-the-Chestnut-of-Coirón].

~~~~

The third branch of the canal is manmade as well. Older even than the mill, a channel was painstakingly dredged diverting water to irrigate some of the early vineyards. Long abandoned now. The combined result however is an arresting network of gaily flowered canals crisscrossing the harbor quarter of the village.

Several years ago, Monsieur Larocque owner of *Café Chez André*, invested in a modest fleet of tiny two-man rowing skiffs. If his idea was to generate profits, he was to be disappointed. If his objective was to create a diversion for locals on lazy summer afternoons, he succeeded admirably.

Today the picturesque toy-boats ply the Maure and its miniature tributaries, available, untended and free-of-charge, for anyone's pleasure. *La Venise Sous les Maures* [Venice beneath the Moors] is the Office of Tourism's favored tag line for Coirón. A faithful analogy and one they use extensively.

Prelude: Alain

IT'S GOOD TO be home. *It's good to be back in Paris. It's good to be back on the job and away from that silly beast foolishness.*

It had been a long, complex journey for Chief Inspector Alain Mohsen. Many facets of this investigation had gone unreported. Were all the facts known, some would describe his endeavors as the questionable declension of an otherwise distinguished career. Others might characterize his lonely odyssey as the triumphant ascendancy of compassion over hidebound police procedures.

His education in English included some Shakespeare. One of his favored quotes came from Hamlet. Ophelia's father, Polonius, whom he thought an odd source for such wisdom. It never failed to move him however:

> *This above all: to thine own self be true,*
> *And it must follow, as the night the day,*
> *Thou cans't not be false to any man.*

He'd certainly been true to himself.

As to *cans'ting be false to any man,* well, he'd loved the quote for years. But recently he began to appreciate the galloping illogic of the statement. Often dissimulation directly serves self-interest. Dogmatic adherence to strict, unvarnished truth does not necessarily follow. *Non sequitur.*

He did know this though. For what little remained of his career, he would be a better cop.

Perhaps even a better man.

The violets in the mountains have broken the rocks.
Tennessee Williams

WHAT COIRÓN LACKS in size, it more than compensates in beauty.

In season the village is quite literally awash with flowers. Reds, blues, yellows, purples and whites, radiant in the sun. Blooms cascade from every planter, window and balcony. Even streetlights. They frame the town square, the market; they line the streets and the banks of the Maure, as well as the ancient canals. They cover the railings of the arched, stone bridge spanning the Maure. The restaurant, the café and bar are gloriously festooned with flowers within and without. The Mairie is extravagantly flowered, featuring *en face* [in front] a huge clock fashioned of hundreds of flowing plants. Even the traffic circle linking Coirón to the D559 erupts with the colors of hundreds of flowers worked into an intricate mosaic. A studious citizen of Coirón calculated there were nearly three hundred plants for every resident during the season.

~~~~

The French have an admirable tradition, awarding exceptionally 'flowered' villages with the honorific: *Ville Fleurie* (scoring ranges from one to four *fleurs*)

Coirón has been thusly honored for years, and consistently awarded four flowers [✿ ✿ ✿ ✿ *La Quatrième Fleur*]. This is France's highest rating, short of the coveted *Trophée Fleur d'Or* [Golden Flower Trophy]; and an official plaque proudly proclaims their lofty rating at the entry of the village.

Monsieur le Maire Emile Drôme, Coirón's girthy and flamboyant Mayor, is also its leading Restaurateur and Hôtelier (owner/operator of *Les Herbes Intrépides*). His passion however is the flowers. He labors long to achieve Coirón's recognition. With the first sunny stirrings of spring, he devotes exhaustive energies and not a little of the town's modest budget to extravagantly flowering the entire village. Drôme is the scourge of the town's two overworked handymen/gardeners, and relentlessly badgers citizens who fail to *fleurify* their premises with sufficient artistry and enthusiasm. The 31st of May each spring, when all is in readiness, Mayor Drôme sponsors their annual fête celebrating the flowering (*Fête des Fleurs Coirónaise*). The wine flows as smoothly as the Maure. Thusly are Mayor Drôme's zealous transgressions forgiven and forgotten until the following spring.

Prelude: Charley

"WE'RE HOME AGAIN love ..."

He sat alone in the damp coolness of his work shed. It was very late. A bare light bulb suspended by an electric wire cast a harsh yellow glare on the setting. He'd inadvertently hit the light with his head upon entering, so sharp angular shadows danced crazily about the room.

He was carefully, lovingly, cleaning a strange object, securely positioned on his workbench. The object was reminiscent of both a walking stick and an umbrella. In fact it was neither. He was delicately polishing the head/handle of the thing. A shiny brass Griffith. A creature of myth and magic, vengeance and death.

After every 'usage' he returning to his shed and carefully upended his treasure into a small pail of alcohol for ten minutes. Then he meticulously, lovingly, cleaned and examined every seam and every grove, missing nothing. When he was finished, the Griffith was always scrupulously faultless. Nothing remained save pristine brass.

Next: A liberal application and a brisk burnishing with brass polish.

Finally: He meticulously sharpened it—careful not to mar any of the beautiful surfaces.

Then his real pleasure: He mounted a jeweler's glass and inspected his handiwork, centimeter-by-centimeter. He marveled at the precise beauty of its workmanship. The razor sharpness of beak and claw. The glow of the metal in the radiant light. Charley had lovingly named it *Piquant Assessing* [Little Assassin]. His affectionate nickname was Pequeño; and it never failed to fill him with joy and excitement. He'd commissioned it from a master artisan in Málaga, who'd charged a small fortune—worth every cent.

Reluctantly he wrapped it in a large rectangle of purple velvet, then a plastic sheath.

He strode across the room opening a false air conduit, inserting the umbrella/walking stick and reclosing the shaft.

He said to himself; "There she is, safe and secure. She'll be fine now, until the next time …"

Stranger than the Strange Land

HE DIDN'T KNOW where he was born. When he was born. Who his parents were. Why he was born, or why he still lived. In fact, he didn't know one damned thing.

Not entirely true.

There were two things he did know.

One. He hated the world. The entire world, and every soul who dwelt upon it. Himself included. If there were a God, he hated him too. Were *he* God, the world itself would vanish in a cataclysm of fire and venom.

A singular thing hate. A hungry, fathomless thing. It infests anyone, anytime, for often frivolous reasons—sometimes with supreme justification. It befouls its host regardless of sex, age, economics, or suitability. It revels in reciprocity. Hate and its host feed upon one another. But hate feasts to the fullest. It makes endless demands. It gnaws. An incessant presence, in constant need of attention and excitation. It thrives on fantasy. It drains the mind and the body. Most of all, it demands satisfaction. Retribution, revenge and retaliation. All the stuff best served cold.

Two. He had no recourse. No entrée into the region of reprisal. He couldn't kill the whole world. He certainly couldn't murder God. He lacked the power to kill a single person, including himself.

This allowed him few options. Live or die. If he chose to die, he didn't know how. He was as yet beatifically unaware of death's elegant, resigned assent. So he must live, and he must wait. Live and wait. And prepare. Prepare for the towering unknown.

He knew his forename, although he'd long discarded it. And with all the ensuing years—mercifully removed from the wretchedness—he had totally forgotten his surname, which was an arbitrary assignment in any event since he was a foundling orphan.

During the horrors of his early years it was irrelevant what they called him; and call him they did.

"Come here boy. Don't be shy."

"Let us see you lad."

"Get undressed ... slowly ... and then come here to me."

"You're such a lovely lad."

"No. That's not quite right son. Give me your hand. I'll show you how. Ah! That's better ...""

All this, and he but a child.

There is no resolve stronger than the iron determination imprinted on the blossoming awareness of the innocent. No matter what might happen in the future. What he became. What he might do when he was no longer young and unprepared. For now, he was young. He was corrupted. His innocence ravaged. And he hated. He *burned*.

Flower-Chide

TO COIRÓN'S NORTHWEST lies one of the loveliest towns in France. Bormes les Mimosas. Securely perched in the high country. Commanding views of the Massif. Charming shops, restaurants, hotels and cafés. In February the town literally explodes in golden-yellow blooms. The world famous Mimosa. First harbinger of spring's rebirth. The stuff of perfume and romance and winter's wane. Even the sunny south of France celebrates spring's coming, though winter sometimes fails to call.

Bormes also proudly holds the *Quatrième Fleur* award. With Coirón, they are the only two towns of the region to be so honored. Bormes is larger, more beautiful, and far more prosperous than Coirón. The darling of the Massif. The joy of tourists and flower lovers alike.

Bormes les Mimosas is also the bane of Mayor Drôme's existence. At times his jealousy is such his jaws literally ache. Consequently, each year he works ever more furiously at beautifying Coirón and surpassing his secret arch-rival, racing towards the 31st of May, the fête, and the commencement of inspections. Although their four flowers rate them as equal, the local journals make much of the unsurpassed beauty of Bormes, and it was for their recognition he hungered.

On the 1st of June for the last six years, Mayor Drôme surreptitiously dons blue workman's overalls, a well-worn New York Yankees baseball cap, dark glasses, and mounts an aging motor scooter. Thus incognitoed, he begins his secret pilgrimage to Bormes.

Each 1st of June, he ends his journey depressed, beaten, consoling himself with far too much wine in Bormes' central café, *La Belle Vue*.

Far better qualified than any local scrivener, Mayor Drôme was painfully aware which town would again win their highest praise. He was only too aware of the value such recognition could bring to his hotel and to his village. After brooding over this reality, he braves the long, dark, wine-wobbly, ignominious ride down the hills, back to Coirón, not to return until the following spring.

This particular 1st of June fell on a Monday. At 11:30 Mayor Drôme furtively navigated his ancient Vespa from the cellar of the Mairie, lurching through the town square, out to the D559, spewing oily exhaust into the clear morning air.

Lounging in Place Velleda, dawdling purposefully over their coffee, were three men. Claude Larocque—*Café Chez André*, Philippe Demers—*Le Cheval Blanc*, and Henri Tondreau—*Office de Tourism*. As the Mayor's Vespa labored past, each looked at the other with knowing smiles.

"Emile's late this year."

Philippe grinned more broadly. "He drank a flock of wine last night."

Claude asked, "Shall we call Mayor Vacheron? Let him know Emile's going to be late? He loves to wait on the steps of St. Trophyme to watch him ride into town."

Henri shook his head. "Pah! Don't bother. Vacheron retires next month. He sits on those steps *every* day until lunch. He inspects the flowers and counts the tourists. But I think mostly he watches the girls."

~~~~

Coirón's population amounts to approximately 650 souls in winter. The summer population exceeds 1100. Year round inhabitants live mostly in town, although the village is surrounded by assorted farms and vineries.

Across the D559, grand Villas adorn the hills. They range from huge archetypical provençal stone mas [farmhouse], to neo-classical châteaux, to glittering ultra-modern confections of purest white provençal limestone, glass, and stainless steel.

Whatever the style, elegant gardens, tennis courts, extravagant pools and huge Jacuzzis are *de rigueur* for the Coirónaise gentry of summer. Some even boast a stable, or a modest lake.

The villagers of Coirón exhibit striking similarities.

Stoic and independent. Droll and good-natured. Proud of their town. Disdainful of the glitzy towns to the east. Generally tolerant of the wealthy villa owners ensconced high above Coirón, or 'Beverly Hills' as they wryly refer to it. Content with their lot, almost to the point of complacency. Sadly, it is only a matter of time until this charming, hidden gem is discovered and overwhelmed by the *fleshpotters*.

In fact it's already been discovered by something.

Something nameless and foul.

For the present though, Coirón typifies idyllic Provençal life.

In their bars and restaurants they incessantly discuss the latest developments.

Except their fear.

Fear the villagers avoid discussing, as though they harbored some guilty secret.

Fear that prowls the tiny village, torturing the hushed astral nights with deadly avarice.

Dark Odyssey

HE WAS A fine looking boy, almost beautiful in fact. Tall for his age. Strong and slim. Thick blond hair curling snugly to his head. Rendered in stone, he would incarnate a Greek godchild, or a budding Olympian.

Sadly, his looks were marred by his brooding countenance. The hatred in his eyes was chilling. The set of his jaw implacable. Unadoptable by normal folk, he reconciled himself to growing up in the cold, sterile institution consigned him at birth, retrieved from a filthy cellar in south London, one freezing morning in February. His was a stark sanctuary, instilling him with dark animus and deep resentment.

Unexpectedly, he was fostered-out from this dreary asylum less than a year later. A couple already keeping four other foster children, ostensibly to earn public-trust subsidies and aid luckless youngsters. 'Mum' was allegedly a 'charwoman' [cleaning lady]. 'Dad', a full time drunk, and mum's *enforcer*.

This was before the GLA (Greater London Authority), in the days when the GLC (Greater London Council) held sway over such matters. Therefore fosterage was relatively easy and unquestioned. The pay automatic and follow-up spotty at best. There were very occasional surprise visits and home inspections, however. So his foster-parents ensured their wards were never at home during the day. Nor were they in school much of the time either. Instead, mother would bring one or more with her when she went *a-charring*. Those who didn't accompany mum would attend school, or undertake some furtive mission for 'Dad.' Mum determined the day's duty roster based on the day's client itinerary. Sadly, his natural allure excited the appetites and opened the purses of mum's clients. So the poor boy always loomed large on her list.

Mum's name was Ellen. A large garish blonde woman. Heavily made up. Ossified in powders and florid waxes. Cunning, voracious eyes of the raptor. Pendulous breasts and a pearish bottom. Dressed luridly, more to entice than to clothe—deluding herself she remained, or ever was a sex object. She had a hard, brassy reptilian look the boy found repellent and not just a little frightening. In truth, Ellen had never worked as a charwoman. She had been a 'working girl' for years however. Now she was 'retired'. She'd discovered the impressive fees one could earn through the 'letting out' of particularly attractive children to those of such tastes. Assuming of course they had funds enough to sustain their repulsive vice; and Ellen's clients wallowed in riches. The challenge lay in locating just the right clients. In such respect, her previous career proved an invaluable network to bolster her fleshy traffic.

Ellen would supply them children once a week, in exchange for exorbitant fees. Never more often. Such tactic served to pique their appetites and buoy the yield per child-flesh. Both she and her clients were nicely protected under the guise that Ellen was one of their cleaning ladies compelled to bring her children to look after as she worked. Ellen would turn over the child to the man, or the woman, or men, or women, or both, and then pass a comfortable two hours indulging herself in their scotch, their TV and their larder, as they indulged themselves in the hapless boy. Ellen had no idea what transpired during these sessions, nor did she care. However, she sometimes heard sounds emanating from the bedrooms that were disturbing, even to a lady of Ellen's raw sensitivities.

Ellen rigorously drilled into the children a bashful smile was the irremissibly, permanent visage. Should they weep, cry out, or resist in any way, their 'Dad' would beat them senseless.

Every word was unerringly true.

The unfortunate boy, being of such youth and beauty, spent much of his early life locked away in vulgar, gilded cages. Enduring creatures of riches rather than wealth. Hunger rather than taste. Gluttony rather than contentment. Forced to submit to abasements so intimate, degrading, painful, excessive and humiliating, he would quite literally entomb them from his memory.

After three unspeakable years and uncountable beatings from 'Dad', he could endure no more. How to escape? A subject of much rumination for the astute boy. Dissimulation was not his strong point, and the consequences of detection were unthinkable. Out-and-out escape seemed impossible. They were never alone, locked in and constantly watched. No. He must foster trust, which he would then reward with revenge. Towards that end he began to cheerily do chores around the flat. Make beds, pick up clothes, dispose of the incessant garbage and liquor bottles, or help out in the kitchen. This paid off well. He was swiftly becoming trusted and useful.

One drunken Wednesday night round the dinner table, he made clear his feelings. He'd had enough. It was time to deliver.

Dad got an ice pick in the thigh, deep into the bone with all the force he could muster. Mum received a butcher knife in her corpulent abdomen. Neither mum, nor dad had the time, or presence of mind, or the sobriety to react.

He had adequate time to leisurely pack his few belongings, steal whatever money he could find, wrap up some food, and bid his 'family' an icy farewell. His pseudo-siblings begged him to take them, until he whirled on them in a rage. A single glance palliated their pleas.

"Run you Wankers! [Contemptible idiots] You'll never have a better chance. *They* can't stop you. Once we've all gotten away they'll be out of business and in big trouble. But don't follow me. You hear? Bugger off!"

He made it as far as Wallingford before he attracted the attention of the police. He immediately concocted a new name. A name he'd seen on a London billboard. He informed the police he'd emigrated from South Africa with his parents, who had simply vanished, along with his papers, from their hotel somewhere in London a week ago. He had been wandering about alone since, begging, living out of dustbins, as he looked for his parents.

The police were understandably dubious and easily confirmed his tale was a fabrication. However, the boy would not budge. He stoically maintained his new name and his story throughout hours of patient questioning.

Thankfully he had journeyed far enough to evade GLC jurisdiction; and his foster parents were naturally reticent to report the child's absence. They needed time to sober up, heal, and formulate lies they hopefully would never be called upon to recount.

Inevitably he was assigned to a local children's refuge, smaller, kinder, cleaner and more principled. His life was still dreary, institutionalized and numbingly lonely. But it was also clean, the food was edible, and it was generally benign.

He never wondered after the fate of his 'siblings.' This was clearly a subject of little or no interest to the newly freed child-sex-slave.

Ultimately he was fostered out again.

For the first time in his short life, luck was with him.

The boy was entrusted to the stewardship of Susan and Frank MacAfee, lifelong natives of Wallingford in their upper thirties. He was a successful architect, she a skilled paralegal. These were decent, responsible people, and as was quickly evident, excellent parents. They owned a modern home surrounded by a large garden, with direct access to the verdant banks of the Thames. Suddenly he found himself amidst a large community of happy, well-adjusted children his age. A wonder he'd never experienced.

Then something exceptional occurred. Something phenomenal. For this young man it was nearly a miracle. A new persona arose within him, a boy for the very first time in his life. He was veritably developing into a well adjusted young human male, actually able to feel amity for others and even himself.

Within six months he began to timidly engender friends.

Within fourteen months he was working at his age level in school.

Within twenty-four months he discovered he loved his foster parents and they he.

Frank and Susan adopted him that same year and his nightmarish flashbacks of London began to fade.

Within thirty-six months his former life in London paled to a faint dark shadow, fading like footprints in sun-warmed snow.

The quality of mercy may not be strained, but it takes its own sweet time.

~~~~

The boy was remarkably bright and his parents were able to provide him an excellent education. Being both industrious and intelligent, he took full advantage of his newfound opportunities, ultimately earning him a PhD in Marine Biology. A life that once seemed destined to end only in despair and depravity became one of pride and quality, scholarship and accomplishment.

Occasionally the gods are gracious, if of but brief acquittal.

Domaine des Collines

COIRÓN'S HILLSIDE VILLAS (Beverly Hills) are generally closed half the year, opening in the off-season only for holidays and the occasional house party. A very few are occupied year-round. Those who prefer the Côte's fine-spun transitions from late Indian summers, to genial winters to, burgeoning springs, untroubled by the summer people. These are gentle people who simply live, or work in their own insular milieu.

One such villa is the *Domaine des Collines* [Domaine of the Hills]. Much loved year-round home to the Woods. David and Kitty.

The Domaine des Collines stands atop the western heights of the Maure valley, facing south to the river, towards the village, and out to the sea. Situated on eight hectares (19+ acres), surrounded by gardens, vineyards and woodland. The quintessence of Provençal living.

The Woods never aspired to wine production, but wine had been grown on the grounds for decades, hence the appellation: *domaine.*

Literally interpreted, domaine translates as a field or property. Ultimately the term came into popular use designating an estate, with vineyards, producing wine.

They negotiated with one of the local growers, Monsieur Giscard Lubeck, to work the vines on their behalf, along with some light gardening and occasional maintenance. Anyone who has lived in France is well aware that 'occasional maintenance' swiftly escalates into a full-time occupation.

The only fully equipped wine producer in the immediate area is the Velleda Winery. As Velleda's production utilizes all the winery's capacity, the Woods were compelled to engage the Coopératif de Vin [Wine Cooperative] in Le Rayol to processes their grapes. At season's end they divide the harvest with Giscard. The Domaine des Collines produces an anemic red, and an acetic white. Both are indifferently rated as Vin de Pays, so the Woods are pleased to allocate the lion's share of the yield to Monsieur Lubeck, the coarse wine sloshing about in large, cubical, opaque plastic containers. David imagined Lubeck's share found its way to local stores in large, squatty, low-cost four liter bottles under the ignominious appellation: Vin de Table Coirónaise.

The Domaine was constructed in the 19th century as a large symmetrical, rambling affair, reminiscent of the classical French manor homes prevalent for centuries around Paris and throughout the Loire valley. In the South of France it was considered a stately singularity at the time. Masterfully dressed limestone, textured, smoothly beveled, and precisely margined.

An imposing one-and-a-half story edifice, with a rounded copper roof, aged to a dignified greenish-bronze, dotted with twenty-five elegant, oval dormer windows. The building features some twenty-five arched, white, multi-paned French doors, evenly spaced, surrounding the entire villa, bathing it in sunshine at all hours of the day. A dormer window is positioned above each of the French doors, neatly extending from the proud copper roof. Architecturally, the manor is a sort of hybrid. Something between Versailles and Windsor.

David loved the open, liberating feel of walking directly out to the garden from anywhere in the villa. Equally, he loved the garden. No grass. Only small white buff, river-smoothed pebbles surrounding the villa, covering the winding paths between enormous boxwood, connecting the entire property. They lent a nicely groomed *châteauish* look to the property; and there was a satisfying crunch when he trod upon it, regardless how gingerly. An enjoyment much akin to his dubious life-long habit of crunching ice, much to the irritation of Kitty. The best part: There was no grass to cut, trim, rake, feed, weed, plant, nor any of the tedious demands of *festuca herba*.

The villa's interior is uniform in style, color, and material, throughout.

Checkerboard floors were laid with enduring black granite squares, alternating with white travertine. The variance in their respective renitence over time produced a subtly alternating—convex-black-concave-white undulation of the ancient floors. Kitty had often observed such floors in historic buildings, and, despite interminably teetering furniture and the occasional awkward stumble, she loved their wizened charm.

All rooms in the villa revolve around a hexagonal central axis. A sort of glass-roofed, utility atrium, ringed with six chimneys at rooftop level. In the 1800's, all water flowed and all chimneys passed through this curtilage. The glass roof had yet to be added. The kitchen's large ovens extended into this utility as well. Later the same century, coal heating was installed. Later still, the design conveniently facilitated the easy installation of modern appliances, hot water and central heating.

The massive fireplaces function to this day. Not so for the coal heating, which was immediately removed by the Woods. A coal chute had been excavated under the villa allowing for delivery and subsequent storage of anthracite as it was fed to the furnace, also beneath the villa. As a consequence there now remained a 'secret tunnel' of sorts under the villa, providing private access to the central atrium, which the Woods sealed off from any access. This was presumably a matter of security, and as a barrier against the various creepies in the tunnel. David found the tunnel all rather romantic. Kitty found it dark, dusty and foreboding, bringing to mind creatures dwelling in darkness, scritching through the night. Insects, rodents, reptiles and unspeakables. As a consequence David was ostensibly the sole explorer of this coal-dust underworld.

Due to the Domaine's unique style and sunny ambience, furnishings required careful selection. Interior furnishings and decorations had to be starkly minimal. Large austere rooms with high vaulted ceilings do not lend themselves to lavish furnishings and over-ornamentation. Ten pieces in a room are easy. Three or four are difficult. David's sole decorating suggestion was a well-worn suit of armor from the local *Antiquaire* [antique dealer], instantly overruled by Kitty. Nonetheless, after endless hours in showrooms and antique markets, the Domaine des Collines was finally furnished, consistent with Kitty's exacting standards, and David's great relief.

The Woods installed eight imposing chandeliers, identical throughout. Glittering, shapely and new. The latest electricity/plumbing, state-of-the-art bathrooms, and kitchen. Everything modern, bright and open. Night and day.

Primarily for David, satellite English television was installed. And for Kitty, high-speed communications.

The finishing touch: The expansive Madame Hélène Moreau.

Hélène cohabits with their vintner-gardener Giscard, although she is loath to admit the relationship. Nonetheless, it is convenient for her to accompany Giscard to the Domaine as their *femme de ménage* [housekeeper]. Outspoken and assertive, she lovingly cleans and maintains the place as though her own. She also speaks excellent English, affording Kitty a source of local gossip and a useful intermediary with local artisans. Giscard speaks passable English, but neither his interest nor his vocabulary extend to household matters.

~~~~

Their back garden looks to the northwest, affording the Woods a towering panorama of the Massif, its hills and forests. The garden ends abruptly in a limestone cliff line, some eight meters high [24 feet]. This is the eastern boundary of a rugged gorge dotted with sizable stones, cactus and dense scrub oak. This tiny valley descends down to the Maure River, subject to its own flash floods on occasion. On the western side of the gully, the Domain's vines initiate their tidy rows. So narrow is the gorge at this point, it is connected to the Domain by a small, venerable stone bridge. The land-scape architect who laid out the grounds and defined the pool made opti-mal use of this dramatic little ripple in the Earth's dermis. The pool's cliff side margin ended in what is locally known as a negative edge, or infinity pool. Without an opposing side, the pool seems to extend endlessly into the Massif and on to the sea. In actuality, the water simply cascades into a lower trough for filtering and recycling. Nonetheless, it represents a costly refine-ment.

Kitty and David pass many pleasant hours taking in this view, lazing in the sun around the pool, savoring the fine coastal rosés, accompanied by tangy Coirónaise cheeses and crisp crusty breads dipped in olive oil, with pungent local fruits. Apples, cherries, pears, peaches, apricots, melons and grapes. Such interludes have often been known to begin on sunny afternoons, ending only as the sun rises the next morning. Crimson setting sun, moon, stars and golden rising sun.

Their broad front drive describes a graceful oval, centered on the villa's main entrance. It then meanders through the forest for three kilometers before encountering any further evidence of humanity. After which it descends to the valley following the river, passing a water tower, more villas, a switching station, and various other public appurtenances as it nears Coirón. All in all, about a ten minute drive to the D559 roundabout at the edge of town. Two more minutes through the circle to *centre ville* [town's center]. One more minute to the port. During rush hour in Coirón, add two minutes. On market days, add three.

If you're interested in shopping, turn left at the circle and it's ten minutes to a large Intermarché between Coirón and St. Tropez. A little further on there is an excellent Land Rover garage, which prompted David to immediately order a Range Rover, diesel, with every conceivable option. Kitty continued to favor her little Mercedes sports car.

Nearby there is also a bricobois [hardware], pharmacy, the Centre Médical du Var [The Var Medical Center] and various other conveniences. All in all, a near perfect setting: An impeccable 19th century Domaine, modernized to their exact specification, surrounded by the breathtaking topography of the Massif. Secluded, yet only minutes from a charming 18th century village, with the convenient trappings of the 21st century close-by.

The Woods snugly hidden away in the forest.

~~~~

As they lived in 'Beverly Hills', on a large estate, their neighbors assumed them to be 'Coirónaise Gentry' and therefore accepted into their society. An unfortunate assumption.

Rather quickly, David Woods concluded their neighbors fell into two categories.

The first category hailed from reasonably successful and interesting backgrounds, which finally brought them to this pleasant valley, as with themselves. Doctors, academics, writers, even a celebrity or two. They sought privacy in a provincial setting, and little else. David referred to them as the *Gray Cells*. Kitty assumed this was David's allusion to Agatha Christie's Hercule Poirot, as in 'little gray cells.'

The second category consisted of unrepentantly rich, rapacious accumulators of prestigious possessions, in prestigious locales. A penchant for parties and a knack for offending the locals, tolerated primarily due to their lavish expenditure. David referred to them as the *Green Cells*. What a Green Cell represented to David, she had no idea.

Failure to differentiate *Grays* from *Greens* could result in greatly feared *Green Invitations*. Evenings filled with endless, forced, airheaded banter, artlessly witty and clumsily sophisticated. The brittle tinkle of ice blended with mindless laughter. Such idiocy would go on for hours, transforming erstwhile enchanting nights into a vapid moonlit gas, choking and blinding them. When the interminable agony finally ended, all parties would proclaim it a marvelous evening. David would invariably realize to his dismay he was not yet drunk enough to purge the endless night from his memory. So, Kitty close behind, he hurried home and his liquid counteragents.

The Woods quickly learned to look for signs. Normally a quick review of possessions such as cars, yachts, clothing and jewelry was enough. As their skills developed though, they could perceive the difference in but a moment's conversation.

David had little or no interest in socializing whatsoever. Grays *or* Greens. He simply preferred to be alone. Kitty however enjoyed people and social interaction, so she inevitably gravitated to the *Grays*.

~~~~

Ultimately David realized something deeply disturbing.

The victims of the gruesome murders were *Greens*. Exclusively. Women. To Kitty's great revulsion, David began referring to these unfortunate female *Greens* as *les Amorces Vertes du Monstre* [Green Monster-Bait].

Again and Always

DAVID IS BRITISH. Kitty American. Both had lived and worked multi-nationally for many years. Both had owned and managed successful businesses. Both had inhabited the arcane world of advanced language syllogistics, quite successfully. Pragmatic functional applications of Artificial Intelligence, Heuristics, Chaos Theory, Random Matrices, Emergence, Information Theory and the like. Thanks to an assignment in France, David had also mastered high-speed telecommunications and wireless data transport.

Corporations can be lamentably credulous however; and both David and Kitty were ultimately drawn into frustrating years of trendy, formulaic projects. Projects lacking originality, creativity, or sometimes even a discernable objective. Eager engineers increasingly seemed to be turning away from pragmatic R&D, favoring instead cosmetic rendition and slick consumerism. Quite often nothing was achieved. Huge amounts of time and money were squandered without the least introspection; and much of the money found its way to their pockets. All the same, they sensed their lives trickling away into a sea of perpetual meetings, monotony and frivolous politics, with few if any accomplishments of redeeming value.

Both finally had enough. Both finally sold out for surprisingly comfortable sums. Financial independence. The burdens of business suddenly behind them. What a world!

Unknown to either, they'd sold out to the same French firm, a firm that happened to be beefing up its client list with their checkbook. The legal work was completed in France, so when the time came to finalize their respective sales, they first met at the offices of their now common *Notaire* [notary]. Both were coincidentally completing their individual *Vente de Fond* [sale of business], on the same sunny morning in Paris.

They first met in the officious waiting room over tepid coffee, they chatted politely and superficially, but soon discovered they had much in common. In fact they might have lived the same lives in many respects. Of greatest moment however, they both had something to celebrate. So they celebrated.

Together.

David, a tall, hearty, good-looking fellow with an engaging dry humor. Kitty, slender, very attractive and charming, with a compelling intelligence. Their lives until this promising day had been largely solitary, as a function of their work and travel, so they were naturally drawn to each other. The same word occurred to each as they explored their budding amity. They had an *AFFINITY* for each other.

Over a festive lunch stretching into breakfast, they found they both had nearly unlimited time and more than adequate funds with which to indulge themselves in the finest life can offer. The finest Europe can offer. So they did.

Together.

They launched themselves into an opulent entrada, exploring countries they had hitherto looked upon only as workplaces. They never dreamt they could enjoy travel, or another's company quite so much.

They had *fun.*

And a pleasing surprise, their time of growing was far from over.

So they grew. Together.

They found romance.

Soon they fell in love. Together.

Propitiously.

At a comfortable, loose-fitting time in their lives.

~~~~

Six months later they were married in La Celle St. Cloud, just outside Paris. Giggling witnesses were kindly provided by the offices of the Mayor. David and Kitty sat together before the *tricolore* [tri-color] sash of the Deputy Mayor, regaling officiously from his huge antique desk, as the sun poured through high windows. Consistent with French law, the ceremony was conducted exclusively in French. Therefore, David translated for Kitty, gently coaching her on appropriate responses. For years afterward he teased her about what exactly she'd agreed to.

This occurred only after extensive preparation. Foreigners who wish to get married in France face a long, complex and sometimes costly process. David and Kitty had staunchly persevered. Among other trials, the French demand a current physical, conducted by a French physician.

Accordingly, the two duly found themselves confronting a Dr. Robert du Bois at his cabinets in Porte d'Orléans. Unfortunately the doctor spoke only French and had apparently had his sense of humor surgically removed upon graduation from Medical School. So, as he was droning on about the various aspects of their examination, the doctor explained among other things, he would be testing them for venereal disease.

David glanced at Kitty and then the doctor. In French "Bon! J'ai été inquiété de elle." [Good! I've been worried about her.]

The doctor removed his glasses, methodically cleaning them and staring blankly at Kitty for several moments. She smiled back charmingly, enduring his scrutiny in total ignorance of David's inane witticism. David was greatly amused.

As they strolled away from the doctor's office, David laughingly recounted his joke, anticipating a delightful reaction. None was forthcoming.

In fact there was very nearly no wedding.

Ultimately, they celebrated their wedding lunch amongst the gaiety, bustle and opulence of the grandest of the grand pavillons [pavilion] in the Bois de Bologne: Le Pré Catelan. Impeccable service. Waiters in spotless black tie. Wonderful food, exquisitely presented.

They celebrated their wedding dinner with a crispy *baguette* [bread], a nutty French gruyère [cheese] and a bottle of Beaujolais—quiet and alone in a suite at the Hôtel George V. Holding one another. Looking out on

Avenue George V. Looking out even further, far beyond the limits of Paris, to the undiscovered joys and sorrows lying in wait for them somewhere out there, latent and implacable.

~~~~

They honeymooned all over Europe. Wherever caught their fancy, for months.

After a time they finally grew weary of even the finest hotels, and restaurants. Trains and planes and ships can take you too far at times.

Neither was really comfortable in the role of *bon vivant* and their recent lifestyle had begun to wear somewhat. So their thoughts turned to residence. A home. Somewhere. So they continued to roam, but now there was method to their wandering. The methodical search of Italy, France, Spain and Corsica, for home. They were seeking *the* place where Monsieur and Madame Woods would fashion their new life.

David was insistent on sun, warm weather and close proximity to water. Not to mention modern conveniences, and most important, access to English satellite television. He needed to see the ocean and he loved sailing. He was also militantly addicted to TV.

Kitty sought charm, privacy, beauty, a home with beauty and character, with reasonable access to other humans and the diverse necessities of modern life.

Neither was more than mildly interested in returning home, either to the UK or the US. They had both been expatriates far too long. They no longer understood their own countrymen and the many changes wrought in their absence. Expatriate prisoners in nomad purgatory. Always missing homeland. But upon returning, finding it alien and unfulfilling.

On those occasions when Kitty did return to the US, she missed home more bitterly than ever. It just wasn't there anymore. They'd not destroyed it. They'd annihilated it far more thoroughly. They'd *adulterated* it.

So, away. Again. Only to miss home. Again. A home which no longer existed. Again. Strangers in their own strange lands. Endless. No escape. No home. Again and always.

Thomas Wolfe wrote 'You can never go home again.' He was right.

James Baldwin lived and died in St. Paul de Vence, above the Riviera. From St. Paul's idyllic hilltop perspective he observed 'Once you find yourself in another civilization, you're forced to examine your own.' He was right too.

The fact is, when you've truly forsaken your native land, you are forever homeless, somehow lonely and never, never fulfilled.

They began their domiciliary quest by scouring newspapers, computers, estate agents, magazines and friends. Nothing. Somehow they needed to investigate personally. Onsite. Feel the area as well as the property in question. Perhaps this was a natural product of habitual travel. Or perhaps something else.

Either way: *L'une ou l'autre manière ... frappez la rue Jacques ... encore.* [One way or the other ... hit the road Jack ... again.]

Late one steamy July morning they were fleeing St. Tropez, pursuing visions of Spanish Cataluña. On impulse, they decided to cruise the coast roads as opposed to the frenetic sterility of the motorway. After a hot, bumper-to-bumper forty-five minutes, they escaped to the countryside. In an additional twenty minutes, they gratefully found refuge and a fine lunch at a curious little auberge named *Les Herbes Intrépide,* in a village with the unusual Spanish-sounding name of Coirón. The food was classic Provençale, and they loved it. The tiny town was beautiful and serene and welcoming, and they loved that too. After lunch, as they strolled the town, their interest grew. Later they invested some time and a few glasses of wine at the local bar and struck up an acquaintance with the flamboyant owner, a Monsieur Claude Larocque, who seemed to know everything about the town. They quizzed him about the people, the area and real estate, and it paid off. They checked into the *Les Herbes Intrépide* for the night, and in the company of Monsieur Larocque, visited the Domaine des Collines the next morning guided by a Monsieur Olivier, the local realtor. Sold.

After the exhaustive formalities of closing, they contracted for some fairly extensive renovations, given ironclad promises all would be easily completed within six months. Nearly a year later they were ready to move in, with at least enough of the work complete to permit habitation, if not total comfort and the absence of dust and noise. An object lesson in French on-time performance. Sympathetic neighbors told them things could have been worse. They could have bought a home in Italy. As it ended though, they'd finally found *the* place. They'd also found the time. A time for happiness, and the intimacy which grows from the gradual, gentle acquittal of barriers. Intimacies that betray vulnerabilities and the dulcet indignities of flesh and spirit. A warm, questing time of outreach and revelation and mutual desire. Thus they grew closer and closer. As the famous local Mimosa, love blossomed at the Domaine des Collines.

Given their financial sovereignty and maturity, the Woods were spared the trivial and often demeaning struggles of the fledgling married. They fell instead into a halcyon cadence, comfortable with themselves and each other. And they laughed. Together. All the time. Kitty believed the optimum age for marriage (children notwithstanding) should be past forty—when the itchy wantonness for the next adventure grows tedious; and the attainment of self was finally underway—now she was sure of it. Kitty celebrated her thirty-eighth birthday the day they moved into the Domaine des Collines.

Kitty

KATHERINE (KITTY) DAY-WOODS. Not the dazzling, cover-girl beauty of adolescent fantasy. But striking, and engagingly attractive. Rich auburn hair tumbled down a graceful neck, onto shoulders men best preferred bare. A provocative figure. Long legs tapering to slim, well-shaped ankles. Her face enjoyed a near perfect symmetry, with lively features emphasizing her gnarly character and her keen, ready wit. Astute green eyes which missed nothing, kindled to embers in moonlight and blazing in the sun. Full lips. Tiny, finely etched laugh lines framing her mouth and eyes. A handsome, often sun-freckled nose. Mischievous dimples completed her striking features. The overall effect was of slim, desirable, feminine luster.

~~~~

Later in their marriage, Kitty was mystified, and not a little hurt, when she realized David despised her name. Not *her* name precisely. She didn't believe there was anything personal about it. Rather it was the name: Kitty.

Her name seemed to almost physically distress him and she had no idea why. With time, it became clear he was oblivious of his aversion, and unable, or possibly unwilling to explain it. All her life people reacted most favorably to her name, especially boys. She suspected they found it friendly and approachable, perhaps even a flirtatious promise of promiscuity. Yet, as she pondered it, she finally recalled David's unconscious shudder the day they were first introduced in Paris. Now, years later, this was to be the catalyst of their first real dispute.

She'd been vaguely aware for months David had consistently avoided calling her by any name at all and she'd finally had enough. No more tip-toeing around the mute, metaphorical elephant meandering ponderously from boudoir to back garden. So one morning over breakfast she con-fronted him as he was occupied with newspaper and breakfast.

"David?"

"Yes m'dear?"

"Why don't you use my name?"

He looked up. Confused. "Pardon?"

"My name David. Why don't you use it?"

"I don't use your name?"

"That's right David. You don't use my name. You never use my name. You've been talking around it for years. *Why*?"

"Kitty?"

She was growing frustrated.

"Yes David. Kitty. My name."

Realizing he was confronted with a question of some import, David neatly folded his paper and thoughtfully sipped his coffee.

"Never really thought about it. But looking at it objectively ... well ... yes, I suppose you're right. I'm sorry. But ... Kitty ... *Kitty*." He squinted into the distance with a frown. "Did you ever see any old American B-westerns? Kitty ah, sounds like a saloon girl in an old 1950's film. Green taffeta, enormous busts, tinny piano in the background, hard drinking, mesh stockings, made-up like a Kabuki dancer, dicey past, but a heart of gold, and ..."

"Alright, alright. I get it. You think I sound like some cowboy whore."

"Not *you* dear. Your *name*. And not a cowboy. And certainly not a whore so much as perhaps a ..."

"*David* ..." He could hear the threat in her voice.

"Fine." He slowly nodded his head affably, seeking a diplomatic escape from a situation he had neither summoned, nor foreseen. "We need a name. Something we both like. Something that suits you." He grinned up at her, eyes brightly expectant. "This should be fun, especially for you. It is not every day one can select a new name. Let me think for a minute."

Kitty stared back dryly as though to say *Get on with it David.*

This was not what she'd had in mind at all. When she set out this morning, she simply wanted to know why David disliked her name. Now she was caught up in some sort of nutty re-naming workshop.

I hope this isn't going be followed by some half-assed christening.

He cocked his head, squinting at her, tapping his fingers "... Katherine. Kitty Day-Woods ..." Then with a gracefully extended fore-finger, he signaled success. He'd found a name.

He peered at her smiling broadly and proudly. "How about Katie?" Presumably short for Katherine. To David's British ear, an affectionate, light hearted abridgement.

For Kitty, an American westerner, it was a source of great annoyance.

"Katie? *Katie?* Sounds like gingham and rocking chairs. Old and countrified. Cowboys and buckboards and dusty wooden porches ..."

"Okay. I understand. You don't care for Katie. I happen to like the name. I think it's charming and feminine. Ever hear of Katherine Hepburn? They called her Katie and ..."

Kitty interrupted "They called her Kate." She saw David's eyebrows raised in hopeful anticipation of a solution. "... and *no.* Kate is also a nonstarter."

"Yes. I believe you're right. They're both good names, but they don't suit you."

David continued in mock despair. "Well, if you don't care for it ... Mm. Let's see ..." He sat back, legs crossed, head down, hands on neck, working out a kink. Then he looked up eyebrow arched. "Katherine?"

Kitty shook her head *no.*

"Cat?"

She stared at him coldly.

"Kit?" Before she could react he reversed himself. "No. No good."

She continued to stare at him coldly.

"Cathy?"

She tilted her head with an indecisive grimace. "Not too bad."

"I like it too. But it doesn't really suit you either."

Kitty was growing frustrated and beginning to feel damned silly.

How the hell did I let him suck me into this idiotic discussion?

"Susan?"

"*Susan?* No."

"Sue?"

"No."

"Suzy?"

"*Hell* no."

"*Candy?*"

Now she was growing angry. "This is not a goddamned guessing game David; and I'm growing tired of it. And if you try Rumpelstiltskin next, I swear I'll ..."

"Okay ... okay ... calm down old girl." He raised both hands placating. "Give me a minute ..."

After a brief pause, his eyes lit up.

Regrettably, David now chose a truly irritatingly sobriquet. "How about Ranny?"

Eyes blazing, she bristled indignantly. "Did you say *Randy?*" [oversexed, lustful]

He laughed. "No dear. No." He frowned thoughtfully, with a half-smile. "Although I rather like that too. No. I said Ranny. *Ranny.* R-A-N-N-Y. RAN as in run and NY as in New York." He gestured triumphantly. "Yes! Definitely. Ranny. I like it! Ranny! Ranny it is. I'm glad we had this discussion dear. We must keep things out in the open. We mustn't keep things bottled up, or brood about them. Pass the butter" he smiled "please, *Ranny.*"

Clearly satisfied with the name and with himself, Kitty thought she could almost hear him smugly humming to himself, sub-vocally as he buttered his toast.

She methodically contemplated her hands, folded neatly in her lap, head down.

Why in the name of God did I open this squabble? I believe he's actually serious about this idiotic name. This is getting humiliating. Infuriating. I should have never brought it up. What was I thinking? I should've known better. My name is Kitty and he can goddamn well use it. No. Wait. I'm not going to reopen this damned thing. He'll forget it all anyway.

But her curiosity was aroused.

What the hell was he thinking? What led him to this bizarre name?

Taking a deep breath, she stared at him, speaking softly, measuredly, as she tried to remain calm. "May I ask where you got the name *Ranny* from?"

David frowned down at his toast. An ebon flicker of gravity raced across his features. "Mm. Not sure really Ranny." Then his mood lightened again. "Really-Ranny. *Ranny-Really*." His smile complacent, pleased with his witty nickname, chuckling lightly and irritatingly. "How did I come by it? Mm Katherine. Cathe-*rine*. Ran? Ranny? No. I'm not at all clear about the connection. But I like it. And after all, how important is the etymology of an eponym we elect to affectionately innovate in loving reference to one another?" He paused to catch his breath. "And certainly it is the responsibility of the *namer* to bestow the most appropriate name to the *namee*. Isn't it?" He smiled pleasantly, an eminently reasonable tone to his voice.

She was beginning to feel slightly surreal.

Omigod, from bad to worse. This would be funny if it weren't so damned stupid. Has he gone nuts? Where in the world did he come up with Ranny? Never heard it in my life.

Sounds like a medical condition. An unpleasant one.

Such a bright man at times. Such an idiot at others.

She closed her eyes, silently took a breath and calmed herself.

Breakfast was over, as was their discussion.

Both had ended abruptly and unsatisfactorily.

This is not worth fighting over. I'll just let it drop for now.

He'll forget about it and we'll look at it again sometime.

When he can discuss it more sensibly …

~~~~

He didn't forget though. The name stuck. And its power to annoy grew.

It seemed permanently fixed in David's mind.

And it presented one of the few sources of real discord between them. Little to do however, except stoically endure the fatuous nickname. At home she learned to live with it. After a time she hardly noticed it.

When they were out though, or with friends, his thoughtless use of the irksome diminutive never failed to abrade and embarrass her. Particularly in the company of Europeans, the name made her feel callow, artless and rough. She could practically hear their thoughts: *Ranny ... odd name ... as if Kitty wasn't queer enough ... must be an American thing.*

Try as she might though—whines, sulks, screams, threats, curses, notwithstanding—she could not dislodge the abhorrent moniker from his mind. All she got in return were blank stares and vapid smiles. It was so atypical of David. Usually he was sensitive to her feelings. He normally demonstrated reasonable social acuity, as well. So what was his problem? She found herself grinding her teeth and muttering imprecations about David's heritage.

Kitty

RANNY (NÉE KATHERINE, nicknamed Kitty) was born in Castle Rock, Colorado.

Katherine Susan Day.

Mother: Elizabeth Thompson Day.

Father: Glenn Harrison Day.

Her parents called her Kitty from the instant the pediatric nurse delivered her into Elizabeth's arms.

When she was four they moved to Steamboat Springs, finally attending university in Boulder. The rugged beauty of Colorado gifted her with a superb body, self-reliance and an independent spirit. By the time she was sixteen, she could ride, shoot, climb, ski, hike for hours, and camp in any type of weather, with or without benefit of tent. A happy loner exploring the high and low lands of one of Earth's grandest panorama.

Despite her good looks and brightness, Kitty affixed herself at the periphery of her young society. She'd had a few, short-lived boyfriends. No girlfriends. And happily passed her time with her father and Tom helping around his ranch and exploring. Tom was Glenn's lifelong friend and ranch hand.

Her mother died while they lived in Castle Rock. Cervical cancer. Pervasive, implacable, and atypically swift. On the day she died, a sadness clouded Glenn's eyes which never passed. Kitty always suspected their move to Steamboat Springs was motivated less by ranching than her father's wish to escape the memory.

After high school, the University of Colorado at Boulder was a jarring change. She was surrounded by far more humanity than she cared for and far less nature. Still, she enjoyed the lifestyle and the open, freewheeling campus. She also discovered she rather really enjoyed boys, and zestfully made up for lost time. She took her undergraduate degree in Mathematics, with honors. Two years later she was awarded a Double Masters Degree in Mathematical Sciences and Information Theory.

She was recruited so quickly after graduation, her head literally swam. One of the big consulting firms in Chicago. Willows & Byrne (W&B). After an emotional farewell to father, ranch and Colorado, she was off to the big windy city.

Being a Colorado girl, born and bred, she hated it. Instantly. Every bit of it.

A stifling apartment. Icy in winter. Steamy in summer. Noisy all the time. Crowds, crime and crabbiness. Prices that greedily evaporated her seemingly generous salary. She did enjoy the food, the music, and the resilient spirit of the people. But after a life in Colorado these proved poor compensation.

Two years of by-the-numbers development. Militantly compliant with whatever vacuous, analytical nostrum was currently trendy, or profitable. Endless meetings and bureaucratic project over-management. Form instead of function. Platitudes versus analysis. Reports in lieu of results. At the end of the day she was always depressed. She had accomplished nothing and she had developed nothing. She concluded consulting firms were as bad as, if not worse than law firms. At least law firms produced a discernable result, if not always a judicious one.

When she was ready to flee to the fresh air and blue skies of Colorado, she was offered a two-year assignment in Paris. Paris! Suddenly consulting didn't look so bad.

Unlike Chicago, Paris was everything she had hoped, and more. The crowds were exciting. The ambience was exotic, romantic and glamorous, with an exotic, underlying sapor of mystery and danger. The museums, the architecture and parks. The restaurants, bars and *les boîtes de nuit* [nightclubs]. She was in love.

After a time she discovered the wonderful freedom of living amongst strangers in a foreign culture. Always the outsider. L'étranger [The Stranger]. Never really certain what was expected, or even acceptable. Not knowing what was right, she could do no wrong. The barriers of language and culture always kept her at arm's length. Exactly where she was most comfortable. She quickly developed an abiding affection for France.

Unhappily her work was not a great improvement over Chicago. In fact it was worse in many ways. She was assigned a major project for the Kuwait Development Authority, on the Avenue Grand Armée. Boss lady of her own group. A reasonably large design and development team. Good salary. Office overlooking the Avenue. Company apartment and car. A challenging project for which she was superbly qualified. It should have been the assignment of a lifetime.

The project lasted four years. During which time, she never worked with, or even met a Kuwaiti. Apparently they would only communicate with the W&B Country Director. Certainly not with a mere Project Manager, and most certainly not a woman. Even her French colleagues seemed reticent to work for, or with a woman. Good old-style male supremacy. This she knew well. This she could handle.

Kitty bit down. Hard. She aggressively assumed the role of ironclad bitch and kicked the project into high gear. God help anyone who got in her way. Soon she was legend in W&B, who promptly and astutely exploited her. Showcasing her project and her success throughout W&B with prospective clients and throughout industry conferences. She had developed both a skillfully pre-canned presentation and a formidable reputation worldwide.

Better, she was still based in Paris. Her base in name only. In fact, Kitty found herself travelling the world. Speaking and working in cities she'd never dreamt of visiting.

Her title was elevated to Project Director a few years into the Paris posting. Her duties unchanged, nor responsibilities. In fact, she had no actual project at all, and began to see herself as a sort of trained animal. The W&B-Kitty-Day-Dog-and-Pony-Show trotted out whenever W&B wished to laud their enlightened image. Then back to the wings. Clearly W&B had no serious, long-term intentions for Kitty, or she for they.

Later in the year a Swiss Pharmaceuticals giant awarded W&B an enormous contract. The primary objective of the system was to produce an extremely advanced AI Diagnostics System. Employing techniques as diverse as heuristics, emergence and fuzzy logic, it was hoped the new system could consider all aspects of the patients physiognomy, identify maladies, and extrapolate a prognosis. It would draw from a worldwide database of the latest medications and treatments. It would also include, Prognosis Formulation, Convalescence Tracking, Process Control, Inventory Management, Job Management, Logistics Tracking, Pharmacist's & Doctor's Query-base, Order Control, Customer Management, Central Patient Records and a great deal more. Millions were involved, and should early results be forthcoming, the potential for years of profitable contracts was a pronounced opportunity.

W&B named her Executive Project Director.

~~~~

"*Executive* Project Director?" She was soundlessly drumming her fingers on a conference table in Boston, facing W&B's VP Personnel—Bill Pearson, and the EVP European Operations—Angelo Falcón. They were led by a slick young MBA she immediately found insufferable.

"That's exact." The young man continued. "You are to be congratulated Ms. Day. This will certainly be one of our most important, high visibility projects this decade." Somewhere in those beady eyes she perceived unease and confusion. She knew what he was thinking.

Why wasn't she literally quivering with joy?

"You will have overall responsibility for the project, liaising with top management here in Boston, Swiss user management, and the onsite team."

"I see. Will I have direct control over specification and development?"

"No. Design & Build will fall to Mr. Thomas Withers and his team."

"And Mr. Withers reports to me?"

"No. He reports to Mr. White, Executive VP Products & Services in Chicago, with dotted line to you."

"Dotted line. I see. Who *does* report to me?"

"You are free to develop your own staff, consistent with your requirements. You will be provided a generous budget."

She sat back *"Executive* Project Director. So I *liaise* the shit out of this project, with no authority, and I'm screwed if it fails."

The young MBA flushed. "Now *really* Ms. Day ..."

Angelo Falcón leaned into the table. An amused smile smarmying his tanned, even features. "Ms. Day your remark is not altogether inappropriate. Your assessment may have some degree of validity. At the same time, we are offering you an opportunity to make your career ..."

"... or break it." She chimed in cheerily.

Ignoring her interruption, he continued. "Take it or not Ms. Day. If not, I assume you intend to walk. Clear?"

Kitty thought for some moments. And came to a conclusion.

I'm not prepared to kiss off W&B ... yet.

"Unequivocal Mr. Falcón. Thank you. I appreciate straight talk. May I ask where I will be assigned?"

"I understand you will continue to be based in Paris. Is that right Bill?"

"Right. We'll have to locate suitable offices of course. You will retain your apartment and automobile. Jim Wilson, our VP personnel, will be in touch to work out the details and your salary."

"Fine. Any other questions Ms Day?"

"Naturally I'm pleased to remain in Paris." She frowned delicately. "But, this is a Swiss project. Why *Paris?*"

Pearson glanced at Falcón, clearly re-fielding the ball to him. Falcón nodded acknowledgement. "Ah, the Kuwaitis have an interest in this project now, financially and technically. In part this is a direct byproduct of your own work with them. You're to be congratulated." Unsmiling.

"I see." Actually she *saw* nothing. She'd literally had nothing to do with the Kuwaitis.

"Any other questions?" He sounded impatient and bored.

"No sir. Thank you." She flashed her most ingratiating smile. "I look forward to an exciting project."

"Thank you, Ms. Day. I believe we've covered everything." His dismissive tone unconcealed.

She found herself back on Cambridge Street looking for a restaurant.
The bastards could have offered lunch anyhow.
She sighed.
SOS. Same-Old-Shit. Little choice but to get with the program though.

This time would be different however. This time she would immediately began vetting potential employees for her own company. Her days of answering to insipid androcrats were at an end.

~~~~

Her first act as Executive Director was to name the project, with no authority to do so whatsoever.

Strangely, this was her first priority. Not unilaterally though. At least not to outward appearances. Kitty was far too astute for such a rash action. Instead, she invested in a long, boring, expensive lunch with the Swiss Project Leader, who agreed readily enough, after their second bottle of wine, to Kitty's carefully contrived acronym:

IM-HOTEP

Im-hotep The Egyptian:
(He who comes in peace.) Astounding genius 4,600 years in the past. Visionary. Doctor. Architect. High Priest. Scribe and Vizier to the Pharonic King Djoser. Designer of the first pyramid, the most colossal monument in human history to date. Elevated to the Egyptian demi-god of medicine, his immortality assured.

IM-HOTEP the Acronym:
Interactive **M**anagement—**H**elvetian **O**nline **T**elecommunication **E**lectronic **P**harmaceuticals

She was acutely aware she would endure a good deal of ribbing over the acronym's clumsy pomposity. Not to mention its complexity and length. Which was okay. She had method and an agenda. And she'd used the magic word: Helvetia.

Helvetia: The luke-warm, committee borne, compromise name for Switzerland. *Confoederatio Helvetica* [Helvetic Confederation]. As though a seasoning of ancient Latin and central European tribes (Helvetians, 500 B.C.–450 A.D.) would lend strength and credibility to their cognomen.

In truth, the literal composition of the acronym was irrelevant. Any dynamic-sounding techno-babble was fine. As long as it contained the magic word: Helvetia.

For Kitty it was a minor victory.

After worldwide industry press releases, advertising, receptions, elaborate launch parties, press kits and giveaways, she now prevailed as the keystone patriarch of the IM-HOTEP Project. She had bestowed a project name to attract attention, a rallying point for W&B, and the Swiss.

Made a nifty project logo as well:

The Egyptian Ankh: Iconic symbol of life.

More importantly, the lion's share of both the Swiss and W&B would now studiously avoid her. A consequence she had astutely anticipated. Kitty had now proven herself to be deceitful, self-serving and devious. Normally useful traits in her business. But she'd annoyed the big guys in Chicago, Boston, Paris, and even Geneva. Ms. Day, despite her celebrated prominence, had achieved the status of a mid-level pariah. And she couldn't be more pleased. She now had ample room to maneuver and act.

Pariah: From Indian Tamil *paraiyar* [drummer]. Its contemporary usage is 'outcast'. How apropos.

The heady freedom of the untouchable.

Best of all, it aggravated the hell out of Tom Withers and his little MBA dip-shit in Boston. She was certain Angelo Falcón was amused when confronted with her opening coup. Although he was conspicuously absent during the various inaugural festivities.

Within months they had prototyped and even codified a fairly solid foundation, during which Kitty had discreetly infiltrated the functional team.

Her competency was irresistible.

Accordingly she now possessed a working understanding of the systems and the team looked to her for guidance in most critical respects.

Four months later, she hung out her own shingle. A modern office building on Todley Street in London, and another on Boulevard St. Michel in Paris.

Sooner or later, bullshit walks. Angelo had permitted her two choices: Take the job or walk. She did both.

~~~~

She named her company DAYnet-Advanced-Systems Ltd. DASL. Catchy name. Her own company. Something she had never aspired to, yet suddenly a source of great pride. Six W&B staffers followed her. Four of them women.

After two intermittently hungry years, with four substantial contracts behind them, they had become a prosperous, going concern, with twenty-five employees, a progressively excellent reputation, adequate cash flow and a reasonably solid financial base.

Kitty Susan Day had travelled light-years since her tearful farewell in Steamboat Springs eleven years earlier.

~~~~

The time would come when she would weary of DASL, but only after a few years. DASL had pirated an impressive client list from W&B, one of them being W&B itself. Significant elements of the IM-HOTEP Project insisted on her expertise; and she took pains to support it well. Kitty supported IM-

HOTEP personally. And soon they were cultivating their own customer base.

Inevitably though, DASL fell into the same stylish bog as W&B: flavor-of the-month management systems, peddling safety-in-numbers applications, using smoke-and-mirrors. Snake-oil development tools with innocuous names like workflow, event triggering, reach-ability analysis, embedded design, process engineering … anything to avoid honest, workmanlike production of source logic.

By the time Kitty finally had enough, DASL was worth far more money than she'd ever dreamt possible.

Sometimes bullshit doesn't just walk. Sometimes it pays off nicely.

David

STANFORD (STAN) WORTHINGTON Woods. David's father. British. Born to William Worthington and Margaret Smithson Woods in the tranquil rural village of Broadwindsor, Dorset. All male members of the Woods shared the same middle name.

William managed a local clinic. His mother kept house and doted on Stanford. Margaret was a witty, intelligent woman and Stanford never knew a woman with brighter eyes. She was pretty, petite and totally devoted to William.

William was a robust, active man. Close cropped, blue-black hair and piercing brown eyes, highlighted by a ruddy, square-jawed face. His son Stanford (Stan) had been fascinated nearly all his life by the pervasive fossils in the surrounding countryside.

~~~~

At age seven, Stan discovered a small stone as he was rolling in the garden with his dog. A convoluted disc of dark, hard stone. Fascinated by the strange swirl and ribbing of the thing, he took it into the house and carefully cleaned it. He was delighted with the beauty and symmetry that emerged, proudly showing it to his parents. His father, a well-educated man, entranced him with the stone's description. He explained to Stan the small stone had actually been a living creature, millions of years ago. An Ammonite. Devonian precursor to the contemporary Chambered Nautilus.

He delighted Stan with the process called fossilization. Though there are literally billions of fossils salted throughout Earth's geologic *Mille-feuille*, they are respectively unbelievably rare. Less than one creature in a million effectuates fossilization. The gradual, almost mystical replacement over eons, of bone and shell and teeth and scales, leeched from the mineralogical matrix enshrouding the creature.

They researched Stan's fossil in the Encyclopedia Britannica. His father showed him drawings that revealed the living animal had tentacles, like a squid. This amazed his son even more.

"Where are his arms, dad? Why aren't they on the fossil?"

"Tentacles Stanford, not arms. They're gone because only the hard parts of the animal survive, like the shell. The soft tissues, like the tentacles and organs are eaten up by bacteria and other creatures long before they can be fossilized." He thought for a moment, lighting his pipe. Billowing smoke he conjectured, more to himself than his son "I suppose soft tissue might be fossilized if it were covered by a matrix which doesn't permit oxygen, thereby proscribing bacterial decomposition as well."

Stan didn't understand. He stared at the fossil. "What if I was a fossil dad?"

His mother corrected. "What if you *were* a fossil, Stanford ..."

William flashed Margaret a good-natured, dismissive scowl and continued. "Why you'd be a skeleton son. Just bones."

"What about my eyes?"

"Gone."

"Would I have teeth?"

"Sure."

"Fingernails?"

"Possibly."

"What about my hair?"

"That's a very good question Stanley. I'm not quite sure."

Sensing Stan's interest, William returned to the book and continued to regale his son with more *Ammonitia.*

Ammonoidea are mollusks, closely related to contemporary colloids, such as octopus, squid and cuttlefish. Their shell could grow to well over six feet in diameter. They swam the seas of Earth four hundred million years before man walked the land, commencing in the Devonian Period. And there were billions of them. Inhabiting every sea on Earth. He pointed out the beautiful, delicate suture lines delineating the growth chambers of the creature as it progressively grew in stature, modulating its buoyancy. Pliny the Elder in 79 AD christened them *Ammonite*, as their graceful swirls resembled the ram-like horns imperiously carried by the Egyptian god Amon, the foremost god of ancient Egypt.

Stan was utterly captivated. Neither he nor his father realized it, but their quiet deliberation was defining the pivotal tangent of Stan's life, and that of his own future son.

When Stan was eighteen, he painstakingly fixed the fossil in his father's vice, drilled a small hole in the center and suspended it from a silver chain. He wore it constantly, night and day for years. He relinquished it only as an adoring memento to his beloved friend. Elisabeth.

She wore it for the rest of her life.

~~~~

While his friends played sports, ogled girls and practiced boyish mischief, Stan would race his bicycle the few kilometers down to Lyme Bay on the English Channel. One of the finest Jurassic sites in England.

Hanging perilously from landslides, chalk and clay cliffs, washes, creek beds and road-cuts, he would search out fossils endemic to the coast. Ammonites, other nautiloids and cephalopods, all sorts of gastropods, and assorted shark's teeth in the chalky seaside cliffs. As he matured, Stan upgraded his bike to a wizened Land Rover, considerably older than he, and his range dramatically increased. The entire Channel coastline, from Dungeness to Land's End was now his dig.

One sunny morning in Torbey, he made an exceptional find. The fearsome serrated tooth of a large Triassic carnivore, not sufficiently articulated to precisely categorize, but enough to inspire his paleontological passion.

From that day he realized an all-consuming interest in the large predators of the Mesozoic. Rare, particularly in the UK. Difficult to find and excavate, but a source of unending fascination for the burgeoning young paleontologist.

The manifold mysteries of these rapacious predators fired the imagination and captivated the intellect of the small boy still dwelling in Stan's mind. The mating and parenting aspects of such creatures would comprise the basis of Stan's Doctoral Dissertation, and the cornerstone of his promising career.

Stan attended the University of Plymouth where he proved himself a brilliant student. Happily, the University sits in the heart of the fossil beds. He was awarded his PhD in Vertebrate Paleontology. And he fell hopelessly in love with his wife-to-be. Elisabeth.

He could not conceive of a finer life.

~~~~

The young couple settled in Plymouth.

Stan taught paleontology at his *alma mater*. He fathered a daughter (June Elizabeth Woods), then a son (David Worthington Woods), and hunted fossils. Incessantly. Elizabeth totally succumbed to Stanford's passion for paleontology, becoming his life-partner in every way.

When son David celebrated his fifth birthday, he was given his very own fossil hammer, and was soon drawn in as deeply as his mother.

David's older sister, June, entering adolescence, would have none of it.

She even coined an airily derisive verbification: *Fossilizing* ... which she lamented as boring, dirty, cold drudgery never yielding anything but 'filthy old rocks.'

So, three-quarters of the Woods family would devote nearly every weekend to fossil hunting. Ranging the countryside, weather permitting. During inclemency they would labor away in Stan's work shed. Painstakingly wresting finds from stubborn matrices. Classifying, digging, hammering, chiseling, dusting, extracting, chipping, drilling, scraping, often up to their elbows in rubber gauntlets and chemical baths. Loving every bit of it.

June was happily occupied with her own pursuits, aloof and disinterested. In fact she was gratified by the freedom and privacy their obsession allowed her.

When alone, David would devote hours sorting through Stan's hundreds of specimen drawers, lining the entirety of their home. By the time he was eleven, David was totally enchanted by the wondrous life of an earlier Earth and had acquired a formidable expertise for his tender years. Stan was hugely pleased he was raising a burgeoning young paleontologist.

~~~~

When David was in range of twelve, his father arrived home early one Friday evening. Very excited.

"What is it dear?"

"Look at this Liz. One of my PostDocs found this on the Isle of Wight last weekend. He'd love to work it himself, but he's leaving this weekend for a three-year posting in Patagonia."

He extended a bone fragment. Liz could sense his eagerness.

"What is it?"

"We've classified it as the proximal phalanx of the third digital of a Tyrannosauroid Theropod left phalanges."

"A what?"

"*Eotyrannus lengi!* (Eotyrannus lengi: A large Cretaceous carnivore. Remote and savage ancestor to Tyrannosaurus Rex. Indigenous to the nearby Isle of Wight. Extremely rare.) A bone from the third digit of its left claw."

The front door slammed signaling David's arrival home, thrilled by what he'd just overheard.

"Eotyrannus! Really Dad?"

Grinning warmly "Really Davie."

Stan turned to Elizabeth. "Let's get packed! We'll leave tonight and start the dig first thing tomorrow morning. I've got a detailed map of the site and there's a small inn close by. Can June look after herself? We should pack some food, and water too. I wonder if ..."

"Calm down Stan." She smiled. "One thing at a time. David, you get packed and dress warm. Wear your boots and don't forget your gloves, your hardhat and your goggles. I'll make a picnic lunch. Then I'll pack our things." She glanced at Stan. "Why don't you book the inn and look after our gear. I'll tell June to invite friends for a sleepover. She's quite the young lady now and should be trusted home alone I suppose."

The three departed two hours later. Car packed. Inn booked. Excited. Together. Perhaps the happiest moment of their lives.

~~~~

The next morning dawned crystal and cold. Their breath an alabaster vapor in the clear air. The site was near the village of Chale, nearby the channel, on the rugged southern tip of the island.

The Isle of Wight is a craggy windblown island, six miles off the coast of England, awash in the turbulent and frigid waters of the English Channel. It is surrounded by occasional stratified slate outcroppings, alternating with massive chalk cliffs formed of plankton, accreted when the island-to-be slumbered beneath the warm, clear seas of the Cretaceous. Eighty million years ago, in the midst of Earth's juvenile advance.

After two hours walking and searching, they discovered the first marker tied around a scraggly, wind-blown pine perched atop a rocky promontory, cascading down to a tiny rocky inlet on the channel. They spotted the second marker two-thirds of the way down, just above a modest ledge. The regular gouges of their predecessor's crampons were still visible tracking down and up the cliff-side.

They rested at the cliff's edge sipping and warming their hands from a thermos of hot tea, appraising the site. Stan's anticipation and excitement was palpable in the bright morning light, voraciously eager to begin. The only way down was by rope. There was a narrow trail leading up the beach, barely clearing the rocky access to the inlet. But from the inlet there was no access up to the second marker.

"We'll have to rappel down. Think you can make it down Davie?"

"Sure dad. I climb our tree-house all the time."

"Not scared?"

David grimaced. "*No* dad."

"You can wait up here if you like?"

"*No* dad. I can do it."

"Liz?"

"If we're careful it should be fine. He's getting to be a big boy now."

"Okay. Davie, you go first. I'm going to tie this rope around your waist. You can't fall, but hold tight on the rope, and slowly back down until you reach the ledge. Watch your footing. Keep your eyes down and always concentrate on the next step. Don't look at a thing except your feet and the next step. I'll lower you slowly and tell you when you've reached the ledge. When you're safe on the ledge, I want you to carefully untie yourself. I'll pull up the rope, and then I'll lower the tools to you. Then I'll lower your mother."

"How are you getting down dad?"

"I'll tie off up here and rappel down and we'll reverse the procedure going back up. I'll climb up, and then help you and your mum up. Got it?"

"Sure."

"Okay. Let's go. Don't be afraid, but be *very* careful. Put on your hard-hat, and your gloves, and your goggles."

Minutes later David was happily settled on the ledge, tools secured at his side. He examined the jagged, white, stone-like protrusion jutting from the irregular strata of rock and clay, seeking clues to the monster that might be secreted in the shale just inches before him.

Dirt and pebbles began to rain down from above, bouncing off his hard-hat and goggles signaling his mother's descent. David broke off his inspection, head raised, arms extended, ready to assist. He heard his mother and father exchanging terse comments as she slowly worked her way down. David shook dirt from his face and sputtered it from his lips.

Suddenly his mother was falling. After a short, surprised ejaculation, she was eerily silent as she fell, save a pitiful, almost childlike "uh!" as she collided with the cascading cliff-front two meters above David. She literally flew by, as David stared helplessly in horror. Arms still comically extended. His father high above simply moaned "Oh God."

Then the rope wrenched to a jarring, deadly tautness, dragging Stan down as well. Neither did he scream, nor cry out. David could hear air being forcefully expelled from his lungs, punctuating his terrifying plummet.

It was over in seconds with two abrupt, staccato, smacking splashes.

David was weeping with horror and terror and shock. He looked down at his parents some six meters below, struggling to focus tear-drenched eyes.

"Mum? Dad?"

"Mum! Dad!"

Oh God!

I must do something. I must do something. I must get down there. How? Oh God. Are they dead? Oh God. Oh God!

They were both prostrate. Face up, in the shallow water. His Father half atop his Mother's legs. Hard hats and goggles knocked violently from their heads. She was absolutely still and totally quiet, blood trickling from her left ear. His Father barely moved. After a time he began fitfully casting a bloody arm about. His left leg was folded under him at a grotesquely unnatural angle. Worst of all, David saw the spiked point of a jagged rock surrealistically tenting his shirt to a sharp point above his abdomen as it emerged from his midsection.

Oh God. Dad's been stuck. Like a sword. Only it's a rock. My God! What about his back? Oh God. I've got to get down …

He got down.

In little more than a second.

His teary vision caused him to stumble from the ledge as he attempted to rise. He now lay unconscious on his Mother's chest. His Mother had suffered extensive internal damage when she'd hit the rocky bottom. The impact of assorted tools and a seventy-pound boy on her upper torso from a height of six meters was the final assault to her tortured body. Her heart nearly exploded, triggering a massive cerebral hemorrhage. Elisabeth's solitary passing was now ordained, briefly stayed by hypotension. No grieving sentinel to stand her deathwatch, her passing would barter David's survival.

David regained consciousness four hours later, awaking in the throes of hell itself.

Pouring rain. Mossy, slate-black precipices enshrouding him—towering all round—jagged, wet and freezing. An icy wind howled down the huge caliginous shaft spewing its freezing breath out to sea. David's body wailed in an agony of paralyzing cold and pain. It was ominously overcast. The little remaining light was fading fast. Roiling black clouds racing across the window of the chasm far above him.

His Mother's face was chalk white, stiff and dreadfully still. His Father's covered in darkening, dried blood, eyes black and swollen, nose grotesquely misshapen, lips comically huge. He must've been thrashing terribly in shock and agony. Now the blood was slowly dissipating, fading in the rain, and haloing blackly about him in the shallow saltwater. He was mercifully unconscious and hardly breathing—minutes from death.

The tide was coming in and the inlet was beginning to fill. The tides here can be massive, freezing and deadly—a function of wind, moon and prevailing currents.

David mewed and groaned and wept for a time. His grief and terror beyond reason. Finally, mercifully, he drifted into unconsciousness yet again.

Thirty minutes later, a slowly dawning cognizance of sounds. Wind. Distant thunder. Crashing surf. The caustic squawking of seagulls. And a strange, metallic, clacking sound.

Haltingly his awareness returned. His vision cleared. And a waking nightmare engulfed him like a sulfurous vapor materializing from the pits of hell itself.

Six enormous King Crab. Flattened ovoid bodies. Spiky, armored and pale with the repellent spidery aspect of the arthropod, lurching about on long, banded pink and beige legs.

The redolence of seaborne blood had seduced them from the depths. They were … feeding … as were three ravenous seagulls … all of them greedily clicking and scraping and cawing and fluttering and jealously brawling over the choice bits. Feathers and claws, chitinous arms and bits of flesh flying in a frenzy of gluttony. Offal, innards, soft tissues, bowels, and the like. Fast, easy pickings. Tasty. Rich in fat and proteins. Succulent fare for the hungry scavenger on the go. They devoured his family in front of his horrified eyes, with as much regard as the vulture for its putrefied carrion.

His parent's eyes were rendered grisly crimson pits. Then beaks and pincers gorged on their viscera. He discovered he'd been violated himself. Several bloody punctures seeped from his arms and stomach and God knows where else.

The ghoulish specter quite literally drove him to madness. Beaks dripping in blood and gore. Mindless, invertebrate mandibles, mechanically chewing the dead and dying flesh of his mother and father, beneath eye-stalks so cold and lifeless they belied a life form no human could grasp.

Aliens do exist. They share this planet with us. Sometimes they feast upon us.

Though near paralyzed with numbness and grievously injured, David struggled woodenly to his feet, powerless in the throes of shock, horror and panic. The misery of simple movement was nearly overwhelming, but his eyes could endure no more of this monstrous tableau. Terror seized him beyond reason. He *must* escape this ghastly pit. Floundering through the freezing water towards the inlet's only egress, he painfully groped his way round the huge rock walls. Falling and bleeding, futilely beseeching a dispassionate God and cadaverous parents for sanctuary, warmth and mercy and release.

Only the numbing rain and cruel wind responded with icy indifference. Weeping uncontrollably, blinded by driving rain and tears, his world dissolving. Ebbing out to the freezing sea.

When he finally reached the beach he ran and ran and ran.

~~~~

In the icy gray dawn they found him unconscious far down the beach. David was nearly dead, frozen and severely frostbitten. He'd run as far as he could before he collapsed into a numb, exhausted oblivion. This saved his life. He'd mercifully succumbed near the local inn where he was discovered.

His parents were both dead for hours now. If not already dead, the icy tides should have delivered the *coup de grace*. As was later discovered, the tide had not dislodged their bodies, sparing the need for a search.

In his rash eagerness, David's father had fumbled the rope, having foolishly tied it to himself, the opposite end to Elizabeth, failing to secure the rope to a tree or bolder. In two tragic rookie mistakes Stan's zeal had fatally clouded his concentration and blinded his judgment.

Impact trauma, scavengers, salt water, and mutilation had rendered them horrific to identify, an onerous task that befell David's Aunt Carol.

David was unconscious for three weeks. Hospitalized for five months. Physical therapy went on much longer. Ultimately his only apparent permanent affliction was the loss of the third digit of his left foot, to frostbite and three puckered scars on his abdomen. The scars would fade with time. The toe would never return.

He remembered nothing and he was told only there had been 'an accident.'

He evidenced no interest and no emotion upon receiving the news, and never requested further detail.

He and his sister were sent to live with Aunt Carol in London.

Home and belongings were sold at auction.

Stanford's extensive fossil collection was donated to the University.

Elizabeth's ammonite and its silver chain were entrusted to Aunt Carol.

David would adamantly, near violently, refuse to eat crab for the rest of his life. He would refuse even to sit at the same table if crabs were consumed.

When seagulls aviated the skies, friends, family and even strangers were awed by the sight of David's eyes. Forever following them. A piercing, haunted, unswerving vigil. A vision adrift in malevolent paramnesia and melancholy.

The ancient Eotyrannus lengi still slumbered, undisturbed in its desolate cliff-line above the icy, turbulent channel.

David would not touch a fossil hammer again for decades.

~~~~

Carol Woods did an admirable job of raising her wards. She forged them into a loving family and made as happy a home as could be hoped. The two children grew into sound, well-adjusted adulthood, although perhaps June more than David. Carol worked hard to see they were decent, healthy, well mannered, superbly educated, well protected and well turned out, despite her limited means.

She'd worked as an accountant at a local car dealership for over thirty years as she raised David and June. She never married. She maintained a loving home, set an excellent table, and finally retired, much loved by family and friends.

June grew into a beautiful woman.

She married young and quite well.

One bright Saturday afternoon in London, June was having drinks with friends at the stylish Bar & Café, atop Harvey Nichols. Before the second round, she found she'd locked eyes with a charming man at the next table. Within two minutes he'd insinuated himself at her table. Within two hours they were having dinner. Within two days they were totally smitten with one another. Within two months they were married in Monaco, hopelessly happy and in love.

She was divorced two months before David took his Masters Degree.

She'd married Albert Morrison Granshell, the elegant and wealthy son of Lord Burnside (Bernie) Granshell. Twenty thousand acres, surrounding an enormous extrusion plant, huge estates, and a vast fortune. Old pockets. Deep pockets. Tried and true pockets.

Albert truly loved June. Sadly he also loved rare cognacs and thoroughbred horses. Most of all though, he loved the ladies—rarity and breeding not amongst his primary criteria respective to the ladies.

June gathered her shattered hopes with her broken heart and presented them to Lord Granshell, in the company of their respective councils. Soon Albert's considerable legacy was materially diminished and June was fixed for life. No courts. No scandal. No histrionics. No questions. No muss, no fuss.

Albert returned to his horses, his cognac and his ladies.

June took a fashionable London townhome in Kensington and concentrated on travel, men, shopping, lunch, fashion, art, puppies and parties.

Aunt Carol visited often. June even constructed private quarters for her, annexed onto her own Kensington residence.

All in all, she was gloriously happy, as was Albert. Only poor Lord Granshell seemed the worse for the experience.

~~~~

David graduated the University of London with honors in mathematics and numbers theory MSc/MA [U.K. Masters Degree]. His achievements were sufficiently impressive to allow him an exchange scholarship with MIT, concentrating on Information Science. He distinguished himself and after roughly twelve months, produced his Doctor's Dissertation:

Emergent Construct Projections of Non-Invariant Population Behavior

Not a bestseller, although it was published, and even found mention in various journals.

Possibly as a result, David was offered a junior partnership with a well-known consulting firm in London. He immediately accepted, in the mistaken belief he would devote the lion's share of his energies to research and development.

Eagerly anticipating a distinguished career of analytical creativity and achievement, he attended his first Executive Committee Meeting (or EXCOM as it was lovingly referred to) in the second tier, only to find it consisted of an amalgam of unimaginative, self-serving, political Neanderthals, having zero appreciation for the business they were engaged in; and even less for any other consideration than profits, if even that. Clearly he would not fit in.

One evening after a tedious workday, David found himself at a nearby bar dourly sharing the day's events with a large whiskey and soda, when a colleague appeared at his table, interrupting his thoughts.

"Hi David. How go things?"

"Oh, pretty much the same I guess."

"Jesus David, try to curb your enthusiasm."

Bob's sarcasm suddenly engaged his attention.

"What do you mean?"

"Well it sounds like you're bloody fed up."

It was as though a light bulb lit above his head.

"Son of a bitch! I've been sodding about, up to my knees in bullshit so long I've gotten used to it. I didn't even notice. Thank-you Bob. Thanks very much. Drinks on me!"

Within six months he'd formed his own company. ADL. Six months later they were profitable, providing cutting-edged software and services at rates bordering on exorbitant.

Trouble was, no one David recruited had his skills in presenting the capabilities of ADL (Advanced Design and Logistics). Therefore, he found himself relegated to executive level marketing, on the road constantly. This was compounded by the inevitable decline in the creativity of ADL. It was far easier to capitalize on the inventory of existing tools designed and essentially developed by David. Within four years it had become a tiresome routine. So he sold out.

~~~~

Following an abbreviated, but amazingly prosperous career, David found himself retired. Wealthy. Free to do as he pleased surprisingly early in his life. He was deeply in love with a lovely woman, living in a Domaine dreams are made of, in the fairytale village of Coirón, in the glamorous South of France.

Providential Provençal life.

Life was good. The brooding darkness long behind him. Forgotten. Buried and so far abaft, neither he nor his wife were aware such specter ever existed.

There was a problem though. Specters persist. They don't die passively. They want killing. And they can be formidable in the killing.

Human memory is not articulated into discrete removable modules. When information is suppressed, it isn't simply unplugged. It resides within a network of memories and knowledge and feelings, opinions, beliefs, mores and much more. It resides within, enjoins, and constitutes the wonder of sentience itself.

The mosaic defining a life cannot be abridged without consequence. Rip a memory from its matrix, particularly a momentous one, and a precarious gap dangles menacingly in the mind. The circumambient labyrinth is profoundly imperiled. A fuse is lit.

Sometimes a wondrous long fuse.

Quotidian Rhythm

DAVID AND RANNY were highly accomplished *Ausländer* [out-landers]. Seasoned strangers. Strangers in endlessly strange lands. These were the roles they'd chosen all their lives and were comfortable with.

When installed in their new home—their nest fully feathered—they found they unexpectedly enjoyed the process of familiarization, learning about their surroundings and meeting their neighbors and coefficients of the Domaine.

Ranny became fast friends with Hélène Moreau, their housekeeper. They worked the house. They gossiped. Hélène briefed Ranny on the town and the locals. Together they methodically enlisted a roster of merchants, plumbers, carpenters, handymen, masons, electricians and cleaners. All the diverse suppliers of skills needed to support an extensive complex estate. Never having owned property, Ranny was grateful for Hélène's expertise and Hélène was proud to assume such a commanding role in the manage-ment of the Domaine.

As for David, he developed a growing familiarity with hardware and garden stores, garages and local bars and cafés. Most notably the 'old boys' constantly in attendance at the Cheval Blanc.

They even began to understand the Provençal mind, through knotty experience (Author's note: These are true stories.):

~~~~

David discovered a truly excellent roadside pizza stand/trailer with the unlikely name of *Pam-Pam-Pizza*.

Every evening the owner/operator/chef, Monsieur Fabriano, would raise the awning, fire up the oven, mix and knead the dough, grate cheese, spice the tomato paste, chop and slice the toppings, and finally activate a gay little neon light at the side of the roadway.

Pam-Pam-Pizza is open for business.

Despite the fly-by-night look of the place, Monsieur Fabriano made incredible pizza. Slightly oily, spicy, copious *sauce tomate*, two cheeses, crisp paper-thin crust, piled high with taste and originality.

The Woods were smitten. Often they grew hungry just thinking about it.

They kept Monsieur Fabriano's business-card-cum-menu in a strategic kitchen drawer, which they used at least twice a week. Normally Wednesday and Sunday evenings.

Late one warm Wednesday afternoon David withdrew the card, dialed the phone, and prepared to make their usual order (salami with extra cheese, onions, artichokes, mushrooms and chorizo). No answer. Second try. No answer.

I know he's open on Wednesdays. What the hell, I'll just drive down there.

Ten minutes later David arrived chez *Pam-Pam* to discover Monsieur Fabriano in the process of cleaning up and closing down.

"You are closing Monsieur Fabriano?"

"Yes. I had a huge rush earlier, a large group of students, and now I'm out of dough. So I must close. Désolé [sorry] Monsieur Woods. You have our card? *Non?*"

"Yes."

"Well Monsieur, you should have called before coming here."

"I did call. You didn't answer."

"Of course I didn't answer. I'm out of dough."

David smiled warmly, bid Monsieur Fabriano a pleasant evening and returned to his car. On the inglorious drive home, he speculated on a lesson learned, and dinner *sans pizza*. [without pizza]

~~~~

Roughly a month later, Ranny's close friend, Janet, was visiting them for the first time. The weather was dreary in London and gorgeous in Coirón, so one bright Saturday morning she simply showed up at their door. Most welcome nonetheless.

The Woods took mail home delivery of the International Herald Tribune, but Janet militantly preferred the Daily Mail, available at the Cheval Blanc in the village. Accordingly, each mid-morning she borrowed Ranny's Mercedes and drove into town. She took a café au lait and a croissant (as well as a discreet cognac) at Chez André. Then she would stroll to the Cheval Blanc to buy her paper and a sweet for later. All in all, a comfortable routine affording her diversion and pleasure. And the Daily Mail.

Possibly the Cheval Blanc's proprietor, Jacques, resented her breakfasting elsewhere? His sharp eyes missed nothing within the confines of Place Velleda. Perhaps he was feeling mischievous? Maybe it was an honest mistake? Whatever. One morning Janet returned to the Domaine and discovered to her indignant dismay, Jacques had sold her *yesterday's* paper. She loved her Daily Mail. In fact, she needed her Daily Mail. The critical term being *Daily*. Not *yester*-Daily. On returning to the Domaine she passionately outpoured her frustration and outrage. Janet was Ranny's best friend and she spoke little French. Therefore David agreed to accompany her for a retaliatory assault on Monsieur Jacques. To the Cheval Blanc. To set things right. To get *today's* Daily Mail.

"Monsieur David. *Mon ami* [my friend]. Madame should have requested *today's* paper."

"*What?*" David bristled.

Sensing David might find that tack unpalatable, he tried another.

"How do I know she didn't buy this paper yesterday? This is not a lending library after all. I cannot afford to sell a paper one day and then just buy it back the next. That would be ..."

Rejecting any reward to Jacques by purchasing another paper, David simply smiled, turned smartly about and left the Cheval Blanc, without further comment, or today's Daily Mail.

Over sunny cognacs at a shady table on the Place (his first, her second), David tried to mollify Janet.

"We'll just go to the *tabac* [café/newsstand/tobacconist] on the St. Tropez road and buy today's paper. Five minutes out of our way. I think we'll want another cognac anyway. In fact, I'm sure of it."

"But David, I thought he was your friend. How can he treat you in such a way?"

"He *is* my friend Janet. You have to understand how they think …"

~~~~

A long, lazy Sunday. Neither Ranny nor David had the energy to consider cooking. Yet it was late lunchtime, growing later and hungrier every minute. As it was offseason, they knew it was too late to call upon the local restaurants in Coirón, but perhaps the nearby village of Gassin held promise. Anyhow, it was a nice day for a drive.

Accordingly they entered the village some twenty minutes later, parked and embarked on a walking tour-cum-culinary-exploration. As the clock neared two-thirty they came upon a pleasing little provincial restaurant named *La Fleur Ravi*.

Upon entering they noted three tables were occupied and six were now empty. A nicely appointed lady greeted them. When they requested a table for two, she stated she would have to check with the chef.

After a few moments the lady returned smiling, stating they could be served, with the exception of certain dishes, which she would enumerate when she delivered the menu.

They were seated at the rear of the restaurant. Nice view of the village on one side and an interesting view into the kitchen on the other.

Madame brought menus, a carafe of cool wine, and a careful explanation of those items the chef was willing to prepare at this hour.

They ordered accordingly.

As the lady bustled about the tables, preparing bills and collecting money, serving coffees and deserts, the Woods noticed with greatly amused appreciation that the lady was also 'the chef.'

~~~~

About this time they met Dr. Adam MacAfee (or Doc Adams à la *Gunsmoke* fame, as Ranny soon nicknamed him, much to David's confusion).

Janet was brightly attractive, fun-loving and far from a shrinking violet. As she was running her Daily Mail circuit between *Chez André* and the *Cheval Blanc*, in the midst of savoring her single-mid-morning cognac, she struck up an acquaintance with a lively group of Brits at the next table. Forty-five minutes later she'd finished her third single-mid-morning-cognac and found she'd been invited to a party. When they learned she was staying with the 'Woods in the Forest.' they exclaimed "The Yank and the Brit!" Apparently the group had been looking forward to meeting the elusive Woods, who were now invited as well. Janet readily accepted the invitation on behalf of all.

Later at the Domaine, after a fair amount of cajoling David warily agreed to 'a quick drop-by and *one-and-only-one-drink*.' He petulantly professed, "I'm sick of Greenies and I've even had enough of Grays."

Ranny quietly explained the terms to a puzzled but amused Janet.

She grinned. "*Greens and Grays*. I like it."

Later that afternoon, after a little hunting around, they found the house. The Woods were pleasantly surprised to discover an area previously unknown to them in this tiny village. They decided this must have been the site of the old vineries that had benefitted from the ancient canal. Parking was impossible, so they found themselves walking up a narrow street admiring a very fashionable villa. Silver-gray barn-wood and flagstone with huge modern windows, crowned by a rakish roofline opening onto a small sandy beach at the rear.

The front door was propped open, clearly by intent. They could hear the boisterous sounds of a party at the rear of the house. As it was clear no one would be greeting them, they simply entered. Inside they found slate flooring, limestone walls and dizzying suspended walkways railed by ship's canvass and cabling. Minimalist furnishings, accented by enormous abstract seascapes.

"Not bad." David gestured to his dates, impressed in spite of himself.

They nodded in agreement.

It turned out these specific Brits were neither Greens nor Grays. Instead they lived in a small British enclave close to the sea, west of town.

They were a blithe, good-natured crew. Quick to smile and laugh. Honest. Unassuming. Crisp. Sailors all.

David was instantly enamored.

Half an hour later, Ranny strolled out to the terrace, remains of a drink in hand, shading her eyes from the setting sun. David was just shaking hands with a strapping, wind-ruddy man, en-route to a refill. Clearly a fellow sailor.

As the man walked away Ranny approached.

"What happened to the *one-and-only-one-quick-drink*?"

"I like these people. How's your Herodotus?"

"Herodotus?"

He quoted. "*Neither Green nor Gray are they …*"

She affectionately huffed. "Cute pun David. But, as I'm sure you are aware, it was *not* Herodotus, and the quote goes: *Neither Greek, nor Graaiai were they …*"

He smiled at her fondly, tanned and golden in the waning sun. "Never marry an intelligent …"

"You're both wrong. And you both know it. And there really is no such quote. And if there were, it would be Aeschylus. And I believe I *would* marry an intelligent woman." Squinching a friendly smile at David "Clearly you have. Hi. My name is Adam MacAfee." He extended his hand.

MacAfee had been propped between the wall and the railing, out of their line of sight.

"David Woods."

"Ranny Woods."

MacAfee shook both hands. "Ah! The Gringo and the Limy."

David corrected "The Gringo and the Brit."

Ranny corrected "The Yank and the Limy."

"Glad to meet all four of you. You're from Beverly Hills I think."

"We don't much care for the term. But you're essentially correct. And you are from?"

"This is my home."

"So this is your party."

"Yes. But I'm not sure the term *party* really applies. We have a small handicapper regatta Wednesdays and Sundays, and the loser hosts the booze the next day."

Adam's smile flushed under a nut-dark tan, eyes accented by whitish squint lines against sun and wind. A huge shock of sun-frosted hair, brown, beige, blonde and near white. Nearly transparent blue eyes. Even features. A strong nose and chin, and a captivating smile. The ladies nearly swooned when they met him. He was dressed in a dark blue, long sleeved, silk shirt, un-tucked, high turned up collar, half buttoned, sleeves rolled up. A rugged Rolex on his left wrist. White, pleated shorts. Deck-shoes. No socks. Far and away too stylish and good looking for David's taste. David had visions of film actors, producers, gigolos, decadent rich playboys, and all manner of unfitting people.

Ranny's thoughts however, ran in a *totally* different direction.

David appraised Adam with affable interest. "What do you do Mr. MacAfee?"

Half embarrassed "Actually it's Dr. MacAfee. I'm a marine biologist cum vet these days."

"So you are a Doctor-Doctor?"

"Well yes. That is the German phraseology."

"And you Dave? What do you do?"

"Well, I'm half retired and ..."

"Young for retirement. I must say I'm jealous."

"Well, I keep busy. I'm getting into local ..."

"Interesting. What about you ... Ranny is it?"

"Yes. Ranny. That's another story. I suppose I'm semi-retired as well. Although I still do some consulting."

David and Ranny were unaware, but Adam was imperceptibly fidgeting. He was conflicted between openly staring at Ranny, attempting to ignore her altogether, or somehow surreptitiously observing her, schoolboy style. Either way, he couldn't seem to keep his eyes from her. A deer transfixed by headlights. Blinded, yet unable to look away.

A crooked moue pursed his lips. The expression in his darting eyes was unreadable. At first glace it might appear as though he'd never seen a woman before. A sort of wonder and fascination. There was something deeper though, something truly unplumbed. If Ranny felt the fervor of his scrutiny, she didn't show it. Happily, Adam's skills allowed him to quickly gloss over his difficulties, as he roused himself to a response.

"Mm. What sort of consulting … Ranny?"

"Essentially advanced AI systems. I'd explain, but I need another drink."

Adam jumped to his feet "I'd be pleased to accommodate. What are you drinking?"

"Gin-Tonic please."

"No problem."

As Adam moved to fetch the drink, David asked, "So you're a sailor?"

He paused "Yes. But apparently not a terribly good one, since I'm buying the drinks this evening."

"What do you sail?"

"A 36' Dufour. She's called *Probo Mare*."

"Nice boat."

"I like her. She's a very strong, forgiving boat and I need forgiveness. You should come along one day."

"I'd like that. *Probo Mare?*"

"Translates to 'Sea Trials' from the Latin."

"Good name. You're British?"

"You bet Dave. East end of London. Born and bred."

"Lived here long?"

"A year or so."

"And before that?"

"All over the UK, and the world for that matter. My work involves some fairly arcane locations at times."

"Married?"

"Nope. But hope springs eternal."

"Found anyone yet?"

Adam grinned. "Always looking Dave. Which is half the fun." His eyes ran back to Ranny. "I'll get you that G&T now."

David followed his retreat. "Don't like being called *Dave*, but he's a nice fellow. Impressive too."

"Yes. So he is. So why did you cross examine the poor man?"

"Cross examine? I thought he was interesting. I meant no harm."

"The poor man couldn't even escape to get me a drink."

"Ah ... I think I'll get another one too."

~~~~

Thus began a lively friendship.

Adam worked from his home most of the time, and David had time on his hands so soon the two fell into a routine. Adam moored his boat at Port Grimaud and they sailed out Tuesday mornings. After sailing they would have a few drinks at local bars, followed by a late lunch with Ranny at the Domaine. Both Ranny and Hélène were excellent cooks. Ranny: French and American food, mostly fiery southwestern fare. Hélène: Classical Provençal. Cuisines they were all greatly fond of. So lunch was usually an excellent, all-afternoon-into-evening-cocktails-affair as the three grew into fast friends.

Soon, Tuesday sailing progressing to dinner and drinks, three, sometimes four nights a week. All three looked forward to these times. Quiet, easy and friendly. Lots of laughter, with good food and drink, as they basked in the warmth of their company. They had grown sufficiently comfortable together they no longer felt compelled to constantly chatter. David studied his fossils. Ranny would work on her computer, or nap by the pool. Adam would often pour over medical journals, or sailing magazines.

As the days and weeks drifted into months, David and Ranny and Adam fell into the easy cadence of life on the coast.

Tasks previously requiring minutes might now occupy the better part of a morning, or even a day. Lunch was an event. Dinner was a pleasant afterthought, under moon and stars.

Life was a pleasant, waking dream.

Dreams end.

Escape Claws

BEFORE DAVID SOLD his business, he maintained offices in London. Travelling nine months out of twelve, dividing his efforts between conferences, clients and prospects. As is often the case with such work, when he finally returned to his office, he was damned if he knew what to do. He simply did not have an office routine, nor did he have routine duties. Between his Sales & Marketing group, support staff, R&D techs, accountants, lawyers and secretary, the business literally ran itself. There was really no work for him in London. So after short intervals of filing reports, expenses, coffee, project reviews, re-familiarizing with colleagues, gossiping and re-briefing with his secretary and signature formalities, he would retreat to his office. Lost. Alone. Staring out the window, wondering what in hell he was supposed to be doing. Invariably the same inspiration always came to him: Lunch!

He would enlist a couple of favored colleagues and set off for the afternoon. So much for the office, until preparations for the next trip.

~~~~

When they were fully installed in the Domaine, and life assumed a serene routine, it occurred to him he was facing a similar dilemma. Exponentially. The rest of his life. What was he to do? His life could not be a permanent lunch.

Find another job? He had no need of money. Why? Doing what? Become an artist, a sculptor, a writer, poet, philosopher? Maybe. Given time. He was still young. He had ambition, if for now only the ambition to have ambition.

But for now. *Right now.* What?

Ranny had friends and diverse interests. She even maintained her links with the IM-HOTEP Project. She was allowed near unrestricted access to the system; and provided fairly regular consulting at an hourly rate that took David's breath away.

But what of David?

One evening around the pool, Ranny was reviewing the upcoming *visiting-relations-season,* blithely enumerating the list of relatives who would soon be houseguests at the Domaine, thoughtfully edited to exclude a host of friends who would also be calling. David grew increasingly morose.

"What about your father?"

"My father?"

"Yes. You know I've never met him. I've hardly even spoken with him on the phone."

"You know he'll never leave Colorado. If you want to meet him, it'll have to be on his terms, and his turf."

"Mm."

David's was a curiously contradictory nature. He liked people. People liked him. Men and women alike.

People interested him. He was constantly dazzled by the genius and courage of uncountable, and too often obscure, fellow humans. Toilers in mankind's ceaseless quest for attainment.

His profession had demanded of him superb communications and social skills, which he mastered with great ease—such ability being inherent to his nature. He'd formed affectionate and abiding relationships all his life. He was not a victim of social anxiety, or debilitating shyness. He simply preferred to be alone, keeping his own company. Ranny was a part of him now. It followed she was vital to 'keeping his own company' as well. For such a man, a cavalcade of houseguests was anathema.

The first of the 'visitors of summer' was to be his sister, June. He sincerely loved her. He had always admired her wit, beauty and intelligence.

Yet she disturbed him with her seeming flighty ways and flamboyance. He suspected he was actually a little jealous of her confident insouciance.

Invariably he would be utterly charmed with her for the first day or so. Then she began to summon memories of their youth. Then they would both seek refuge for some reason. He never understood why this occurred. One day he hoped he would.

Next, his Aunt Carol was visiting. He loved her as well. He never tired of her crusty, pragmatic approach to life. Yet she also seemed to awaken something disturbing in him. It upset him. Which upset her. Then he would grow restless and uneasy around her. As with June, he suddenly needed escape.

Lastly, Ranny's Aunt Debra from Colorado. A colorful and lively spirit of the American Southwest. A true mountain-child. He liked and admired her, but she was so alien to his mindset he could barely communicate with her. She'd been a teacher all her life, beginning her career as one of the very last of the real-honest-to-God *Schoolmarms*; three-R-ing grades one through six, from a single room schoolhouse in a tiny mining town nestled far into the high foothills of the Rockies. Long retired now, she happily passed her days just outside Steamboat Springs with friends and her brother Glenn, Ranny's father.

During earlier visits by Ranny's friends, David would simply resort to jogging. He would sometimes actually jog. Normally though, he simply absented himself for hours at a time. David and the old boys at the *Café Chez André* became fast friends. The run back up the hill to the Domain, after a few hours chez André, was exponentially more difficult than the morning's run down. In any event, it assured a credibly sober, sweaty arrival.

All in all, pretty dreary prospects for the next four months. Neither his liver, nor his lungs could withstand constant retreats to the bar. Clearly another solution was called for.

What did he need? He needed escape. How does one escape? One goes somewhere else. How? Without offending? Under what guise?

David gave the problem a good deal of thought. What can you do to leave one's own home and guests with impunity? Any time you want. For any destination. For any length of time. With total credibility. Without bruised feelings.

Suddenly it came to him. A true *eureka* moment. He almost laughed aloud. So simple. So believable. Logical. Interesting. Productive. Consistent with his nature. Nothing could be better suited.

Paleontology!

Fossil hunting in a given bed sometimes enjoyed a very short half-life. Perhaps the land was accessible only on a given date. Maybe construction would destroy the site. Often geologic and climactic conditions exposed and then quickly obliterated a potential site. Therefore, he might have to leave home at a moment's notice. Perfect!

Fossil hunting! I loved it as a kid. I was good at it. I probably had a future in Paleontology. Wonder why I let it go? The solution is brilliant! Combined with sailing, my problem is solved.

He could go out for days. *Incommunicado.* Or as much as one could, considering the technology of these times. 'Loss of Signal' would become his catch-all, catch-phrase. Best of all, these were journeys he could repeat *ad infinitum*. Over and over. Re-visiting and re-working the same site. Or new ones. Wherever and whenever he wished. Always a reason to return to a dig. Ranny could invite whom-ever-the-hell she wished. For as long as she liked. He had discovered an *escape route*. Wonderful freedom.

~~~~

He tactfully introduced Ranny to his newfound passion over breakfast the next morning.

"Paleontology?"

"Yes. Paleontology. From the Greek *palaios* meaning ancient, conjuncted with *ology*, as in the study of."

"Uh huh. And what exactly does *that* mean?"

"Well Ranny, it largely implies searching for fossils."

"Fossils?"

"Yes. Fossils. From the Latin meaning to *dig up*. Creatures that died tens or hundreds of millions of years ago whose remains were gradually replaced by their mineralogical matrices."

"Um yeah. I know what they are. So you want to practice *Paleontology* and *dig up fossils*?"

"Yes."

She cocked her head with the slightest of frowns, trying to understand. "Why?"

David chuckled. A light huff through his nose.

"I enjoy paleontology very much. My father was a Paleontologist."

"I didn't know that. And there are fossils around here?"

"There are fossils pretty much all over the Earth dear, if you know where and how to look."

"Well," she shrugged airily with a lighthearted smile. "Enjoy yourself." The smallest trace of skepticism tinted her voice.

He'd done it! He'd pulled it off. But he must be careful to convince Ranny of his sincerity. God help him if she found this was but an evasion. He set to work immediately. Starting with memories of his father's methods, he began to research sites around the Massif, tools, reference books, universities, suppliers, museums and organizations … all the requisite trappings of a serious paleontologist. He began to realize how much he really missed paleontology. What had he done with his life? Suddenly he was excited. He was a youth again, eager to recover an important aspect of his life he had somehow contrived to misplace. He considered returning to University and undertaking intensive study. Yet his French, however fluent, wasn't up to University-level science. The nearest English-speaking University was in Paris, so he opted instead for an online curriculum with Iowa State University's College of Physical Sciences.

He identified four sites, all sufficiently remote. Rich hunting. Close to interesting villages, hotels, restaurants, stores and fossil beds. Four of a kind. A winning hand. His Fab-Four.

Next he began ordering books, specialty topographical maps, tools, clothes, woodland accoutrements. Always by mail, ensuring Ranny would observe their arrivals, fleshing out this declaration of his newfound, old love.

He was truly engrossed with this new pursuit. But he wanted no doubts, or suspicions about his sincerity lingering in Ranny's mind. Should she even remotely suspect this was a ploy to escape houseguests, her reprisal would be fearsome indeed.

Then he began calling local organizations. Inquiring after membership, qualifications, activities, sites, services, anything of interest. Always gratified by callbacks. Always strengthening his professed interests and devotion to Paleontology. He wasn't conning Ranny. He didn't have to. He was conning himself. He really was falling in love again, with all the passion of his long forgotten childhood.

Every night he poured over books and maps and his computer. He would soon be very well versed on the sites, strata and specimen of southern France.

Then, in advance of their first houseguest: his first trip. A proto-hunt. Two nights. The city of Digne les Bains in the area known as Haute Provence. There is even a regional GeoPark there, charged with preservation of Provence's prehistory. Not one of his Fab-Four, but a region rich with fossiliferous rock deposits. His Land Rover was perfectly suited to the task. Lots of room for his gear. Comfortable. And more than a match for the local terrain. He had excellent maps. He knew the rules. And he knew how to look. He was gratified, and in some way moved, how quickly it all came back. How little he had really forgotten, and how his early skills remained extant. There was a puzzling bittersweet melancholy about it though. Hazy, confusing and strange, somehow lost in enigmatic memories of sadness and pain.

Upon his arrival at Digne les Bains, on impulse, he stopped at a fresh road-cut just north of the town and began to search through the rubble. Within minutes he spotted a small bivalve. A fossilized Gryphea, with the disturbing pseudonym 'The Devil's Toenail'. An ancient mussel. Not terribly rare, but very old—on the order of 500 million years. This one was quite small. A juvenile, but well formed and nicely replaced. Common and fairly uninteresting. David was greatly pleased however. Gratified to find he retained the acuity to discern form and order amongst chaotic strata of sand, dirt and stone. Stone that looks like bone, and bone that looks like stone. Order, form and beauty from chaos. At home, after he carefully cleaned it, he kept the small fossil in his pocket. A talisman of sorts. He suddenly remembered his father's first find. The wonder of his youth: The Ammonite Necklace.

I wonder whatever became of it?

David passed the days prospecting for fossils, and the nights in a comfortable hotel, good food, good bed, and a friendly bar. Not bad at all. Yet he missed Ranny. They had hardly been apart a day since they met. At the same time, he enjoyed the independence. The temporary illusion of freedom.

He thought about his parents. The first time in over twenty years. Consequently he felt a certain guilt at having invested so little regard in them. He knew he'd loved them. Missed them profoundly. So why had he simply forgotten them? He really didn't know how they died. He'd never even asked. He'd never visited their graves. Good grief. He didn't even know where they were buried.

He happened to be sitting alone in the bar when these specters chose to visit him. Just as awareness might have been in the throes of awakening, a man entered the bar with whom he'd shared a drink the previous evening. His phantoms fled as quickly as they had appeared. Incorporeal casualties of scotch, ice, peanuts and trivial bar-chatter.

He called Ranny later. Generally boring her with his various finds.

"… The *Devil's Toenail*? What the hell is that? It sounds repulsive."

"No dear, It's just a nomen nudem for …"

"Okay. I'll bite. What's a no-men-noodle?"

David laughed good-naturedly. "Not 'no-men-noodle,' *Nomen nudem*. Naa-min-neu-dim. A Latin term designating an unofficial classification. A sort of an alias. Consider it the common usage name. In this case it nicknames a bi-valvic fossil called a Gryphaeidae. A very common fossil, but my first find in years."

Ranny could hear he was clearly balancing phone between chin and shoulder, his attention divided between his specimens and her, which she found mildly annoying.

"I see. Well, I'm glad you're enjoying."

"By the way, when is June coming?"

"Why?"

"Why what?"

"Why are you suddenly interested in June's visit? You've been totally unconcerned until now."

"Oh, I … well … let's see … yes … I was just thinking about my parents. Thought maybe June and I might talk a bit about those days. We never have, strangely enough."

"Well, she'll be here in about a week."

"Good. So how're things at home …"

David returned home the next day. Tired, happy and confident he would make many such expeditions. Almost immediately he was back on his computer searching for specimen trays, containers and display cases.

He'd found what he'd been in need of for years and hadn't known it.

He wasn't master of his fate. No one is. But he was becoming master of his time.

~~~~

June arrived a week later. Gorgeous, stylish and bubbly. She literally lit up the Domaine. Ranny and June scurried about the place, sharing its wonders, discussing changes and gossiping about the neighbors—the Grays and the Greens. June thought the 'wine-gardener-guy' was funny, and his girlfriend 'very French'. She loved the place and Coirón. But she was surprised and strangely, a little uneasy to learn David was 'fossilizing' again (a term Ranny was immediately taken with). When Ranny quizzed her about this, she was suddenly reticent; and though casual about it, would discuss it no further. The first time Ranny used the term with David, he stopped in his tracks, looked at her quizzically, and made no comment. Then or thereafter.

The next morning over breakfast David broached the topic of their parents.

"Do you ever think about Mum and Dad, June?"

June was concentrating on her eggs. "Mm?"

"Our folks. I really don't know how they died. Do you? I haven't visited their grave, or the old home. Have you?"

"Oh, I haven't been south of London since we went to live with Aunt Carol. That was a long time ago David."

David was taken aback when June then cheerily rose from the table, wolfing her toast and gulping her remaining tea. She turned to Ranny, glibly disregarding David utterly.

"What say we go into St. Tropez? Some shopping and lunch?" She winked with a conspiratorial smile. "Maybe we'll pick up a couple of sailors too."

Ranny laughed good-naturedly. June had unexpectedly put her on the spot. "Uh, sure. Just give me a minute."

Soon David sat alone at table picking at his breakfast.

Well. That was cold as hell. What's her problem? Doesn't she want to talk about her own goddamned parents with her own goddamned brother?

At that moment, he'd found what he wanted, though unknown to him. He could now resolutely acquit himself. Reacting to June's puzzling and detached reaction, he seceded from the remnants of his beleaguered family. He would ask but once. This he had done. Now it was ended.

He would never admit it to himself, but she had granted him his fondest wish. He now had leave to absent himself. A leave which he could easily rationalize as not of his doing. Yet somewhere deep in his mind, perhaps he was honest with himself. Perhaps he wondered how he would have reacted had she been forthcoming. Showed interest. Shared. Opened up. He knew he would have found some fault nonetheless. Some excuse, any excuse, to recede further into solitude, into the detached isolation of his own contrivance.

Ranny and June drove away within fifteen minutes, and David resolved to avoid any serious subjects with June in the future. An hour later, he penned a note to the effect he was off to a town called *Vallon Pont-d'Arc*, and would return 'in a few days.'

Ranny and June returned home in the late afternoon, their bubbly mood somewhat muted when they found David's note.

Thus did a barrier slowly begin to rise between David and June. Perhaps between David and Ranny as well. This same scenario played out pretty much *verbatim* with David's Aunt Carol.

Barriers springing up all round. Bastions of loneliness appearing like mushrooms, spun of uncertain, negligent love, and *a priori* alienation. Ranny was more than just a bit miffed that she was swiftly becoming the primary connection with David's family, as David *de facto* deferred more and more communications to her. Ranny was also gradually becoming aware of a yawning gap in David's past. She was convinced he was keeping nothing from her. It seemed more probable there was something he was unaware of. Forgotten? An incident when he was too young to remember? Something physical? An emotional trauma? Repression? Whatever it was, she suspected it related to his parents. This was all she knew. She also knew she was intrigued. And she would somehow learn about this mysterious lacuna.

Meanwhile, David was becoming a seasoned fossil hunter. He'd formed friendships with fellow rock and fossil hounds and various organizations. He linked with fossil dealers and attended a few Mineral & Fossil Shows. He now passed his time genuinely absorbed in the pursuit of fossils. Sitting in his office for hours, researching, categorizing and mounting his finds.

In fact, it was swiftly monopolizing his time, to the exclusion of all else, including Ranny.

Quo Vadis Prius?
From Whither Goest Thou?

IN FAIRNESS TO June, her reticence with David was understandable. She really hadn't much to share about their youth. She remembered very little and cared to remember even less. Yet, unbeknownst to all save Aunt Carol, she was only following instructions. Unaware of other factors, Ranny suspected she might feel some guilt at her studied isolation during those years. Perhaps she felt things might have been different had she taken more interest. Possibly this was even remotely true in part.

Aunt Carol's visit was to play out quite differently.

The subtle breach growing between David and his family worked quite the opposite between Ranny and Carol. David observed their growing friendship and intimacy as they ran errands, cooked, relaxed around the pool, and talked. And talk they did. Nearly incessantly. At first their sessions were limited to gossip and swapping anecdotes of their pasts and their families. They discussed the area, the French, the murders, and the Domaine. Ranny regaled Carol with colorful tales of the locals.

Then their discussions took on a different quality. Their tone developed into something more serious. Sometimes intense. Furtive glances and drifts of his name led him to suspect many of their private talks related to him. He could hear the quiet murmur of their voices late into the night, sharing a bottle of wine in front of the fire as he worked in his office. Listening to the hushed interplay of their voices. Watching the flickering reflection of their fire on his wall.

Listening to them, David discovered something surprising. Their quiet voices awakened an odd feeling in him, and not a good one. There was a fundamental melancholy dwelling within. A despondency so obscure and impenetrable, he might never make out its dark nature. Even thinking about it was depressing. So he sought escape.

He sighed, reaching into his lower drawer, radiating resignation.

Nothing a few fingers of Scotch can't clear up.

~~~~

Carol and June knew David had been with his parents when they died. This was a revelation for Ranny. Carol also confided they had been fossil hunting and David had been seriously hurt. Nearly died. He was in hospital for many painful months, and then in agonizing physical therapy. Then, as with David, the topic was never mentioned again. This was all June knew. And all she cared to know. A curtain was drawn when Aunt Carol took brother and sister away to London.

~~~~

Whilst David was away on a dig, Carol recognized the opportunity to open up, and was suddenly exponentially forthcoming.

It was as though she had been waiting for years to share with someone and now she'd found Ranny.

Ranny and Carol were talking in the kitchen after a light lunch.

"It's a hideous story Ranny. I've never been able to talk about this with anyone close. Only doctors and friends with a clinical interest in my problem."

"You have a problem?"

She studied Ranny thoughtfully. "I believe *we* have a problem."

She paused, as though a thought had just occurred. She studied Ranny closely for a few moments. Her eyes took on a penetrating, hawk-like aspect. Ranny began to grow uncomfortable under her scrutiny.

"Ranny ... *Ranny.* How did you come by such an interesting name?"

"Long story. My real name is Kitty."

"*Kitty!*" Her tone suddenly incredulous.

"Actually it's Katherine. But that's yet another story. David couldn't tolerate the name Kitty for some reason, so somehow he came up with Ranny."

Carol shook her head. "It fits."

"Hmm?"

Disregarding Ranny's puzzlement for the moment, Carol continued.

"I learned about most of this from the doctors and the rescue service. David and I have never exchanged a word about that day."

"What the hell are you talking about?"

Pausing again she looked around. "May I have a cup of tea dear?"

Ranny rose and began brewing a pot of tea.

Carol continued. "According to June, Stan came home one night all excited about a fossil discovered by one of his students."

"Stan?"

"David's father. Stanley."

"Oh. Right."

Carol continued. "The find was so important to him they rushed out that same night. The next thing June knew, her parents were dead and David was in hospital. The rest I learned from the doctors and recovery workers in Chale."

"Chale?"

"The village of Chale, on the Isle of Wight. I went down there as soon as I learned of the accident. I arrived on the second day. In fact, I was called upon to identify the bodies."

"Was it bad Carol?"

"Ranny, I've never faced such horror in my life. As near as they could determine, they fell from a cliff of some twenty meters above the sea. They fell into a rocky inlet right on the Channel. David's mother, Elizabeth, died within a few hours or so. She was a lovely, gentle woman. It must have been terrible for her.

"Stan died from shock, exposure and a massive wound to his spine and midsection.

"It was a miracle David survived.

"He was pummeled by falling rocks and tools. Concussed, broken arm and wrist. Extensive cuts and blood loss. His bruising was so profound he nearly lost an arm. He was nearly frozen to death. Internal injuries. Frost-bite covered his extremities and he lost a toe. He was brutally traumatized. Some of the local wildlife scavenged the bodies of his parents rather exten-sively; and the police were convinced David must have witnessed it. The damned beasties even chewed on him a bit." Carol dropped her head. "Good God Ranny, I think he saw *everything*. Hellofa damned thing for a kid to see."

"How old was he at the time?"

"Let's see. I would guess ten or eleven."

"Jesus."

"Yes. Exactly. Well, when David was well enough to leave hospital, we closed up things in Plymouth and moved to my home in London. He underwent a good deal of physical therapy with a specialist clinic in Kensington. David remembered nothing of the entire nightmare, nor was he the least bit interested. The doctors said David's reaction to the incident was not totally abnormal. But they did feel it was not an altogether healthy reaction either. They said if his memories and emotions didn't eventually surface, it could be a source of real concern."

"And they've never surfaced?"

"Not as far as I know. But they were adamant I not question David about the affair. They were quite firm. If I wished to pursue it, I should bring in professional help. I shouldn't even discuss it or bring it up in any context. June was given the same injunction, in the strongest terms by the doctors. I told her we were never to mention it to David unless he brought it up first, and then not without professional help. He never did. That was more than twenty years ago."

"What effect do you suppose this has had on David?"

Carol tilted her head and thought long about the question, eyes down-cast, hands nervously working in her lap.

"David is a wonderful man. He's as kind and intelligent as anyone I've ever known. He's funny too, in a quirky way, and I believe he's a funda-mentally happy person. Even happier now you're part of his life. But somewhere in that big hominoid brain of his lurks a terrible malady, howling for attention over decades."

"I had no idea ..."

"I know. That's my fault. I never could bring myself to bring in a professional. The timing never seemed right; and David was maturing into such a happy, intelligent man. I should have told you about all this much sooner. In my own defense, this is the first real time we've had together. But we know each other now. Had I brought this to you earlier, you'd have probably thought me a crazy old woman. We needed the time. I hope you see that. I've grown very fond of you Ranny. I hope you can forgive me."

"Carol. There's nothing to forgive. I realize you couldn't just pull something like this out of your hat until we knew each other better. But I still think you're a crazy old broad."

Carol smiled appreciatively. She took Ranny's hand in hers. Both clumsily affectionate.

"Wait here for a moment dear. I have some things for you."

"Sure." This was becoming something of an ordeal. *What now?*

Carol left the room, returning shortly. She handed Ranny a lacy handkerchief wrapped into a ball.

"What is this?"

"Open it."

Inside were two objects. A silver necklace threaded through a hole in a small, curly rock. The second object was less obvious. A short length of stone-like bone.

Ranny looked up at Carol questioningly.

Carol smiled nostalgically and picked up the necklace. "This is a fossil Stanley found. His first. When he was seven. He was very proud of it. They call it an ammonite I think. Stan and Liz treasured it. He wore it for years and then gave it to her during his university years. They took it from Elizabeth's body. I've been holding it in trust for David. I think you're its guardian now."

She handed it to Ranny.

Ranny held it up, examining it closely.

"It's rather lovely actually. Thank you." She raised the bone-like stone. "And this?"

"It's the thing that got them killed dear. The fossil Stan was so god-damned jazzed up about."

"I see. What is it anyway?"

Hesitantly, her eyes sharp and steady, never leaving Ranny's eyes, Carol reached into a pocket and withdrew a neatly folded piece of paper. "I had some friends from the Natural History Museum research this for me." She extended the paper to Ranny. "Here's what they came up with. They also reported this is the third left digit of the creature's left hand, or paw, or claw, or whatever. This document describes the animal, or more properly, the dinosaur I suppose."

Carol sat back in her chair keenly studying Ranny as she unfolded the document and read.

Eotyrannus

Eotyrannus lengi ('dawn tyrant'). Genus, Tyrannosauroid Theropod dinosaur, found in the Cretaceous Wessex Formation, most notably on the Isle of Wight, UK.
A six meter Theropod demonstrating tyronnosauroid characteristics.
Apex and primary predator of the Iguanodon.
Distinguished by serrated premaxillary teeth, long forelimbs with three fingered functionally grasping hands.
Eotyrannus is also referred to by the *nomen nudem* <u>Kittysaurus</u>.

Ranny stared at the paper in stunned silence.

"Ranny?"

She raised her head, blinked a few times and began to speak, nearly a whisper.

"My God. Eo-ty-*rannus* … Ranny? *Kitty*-saurus … Kitty?"

"I think so dear. As they explained it to me, that's just the sort of con-nection a damaged mind might construct."

"Damaged mind? What are you talking about Carol?"

"Bear with me dear. There's more."

"Okay …"

"The rescue team reported David probably fled the accident site in terror. That he ran and ran, until he dropped."

"Ran, or Ranny again."

"Right."

"Do you suppose he felt guilt about running from the site? Some sort of burden he carries? He might have been able to save his parents?"

"Most certainly."

"Could he have saved them?"

"No. Absolutely not. But I believe he harbors a great deal of guilt over the incident nonetheless."

"Does June know about this?"

"I very much doubt it."

Ranny studied the paper intently. As though she could learn something more if she just looked harder.

"How about David? Does he remember anything?"

"Consciously? No. Certainly not. Unconsciously? I wouldn't know. But I think, yes. Are you familiar with the term Dissociative Identity Disorder?"

"No. What is it? It sounds bad."

"It is dear. And some of the people I've consulted believe David's been suffering from an acute iteration of this disorder, since the day his parents were killed on the Isle of Wight." She withdrew another piece of paper from a pocket.

Ranny studied Carol appraisingly. "You're really loaded for bear today Carol."

She smiled shallowly, without humor. "If I understand your metaphor, you're right. I felt I should be prepared for this. I felt *you* should be prepared for this. I've watched this disease metastasize in David for years. I love him as my own son, and I worry so much for him. You're a wonderful influence on him. I've never seen him happier, or more open. Maybe you can find your way through all this. I hope so. I'm an old woman. You must take charge now." She handed the paper to Ranny. "This is a partial list of DID symptoms."

"DID?"

"Dissociative Identity Disorder dear."

"Oh, right." She unfolded the paper.

DID Symptoms

Multiple mannerisms, Unexplainable headaches, Distortion or loss of subjective time, Comorbidity, Depersonalization, Derealization, Severe memory loss, Depression, Flashbacks of abuse/trauma, Unexplainable phobias, Sudden anger, Lack of intimacy and personal connections, Frequent panic/anxiety attacks, Auditory hallucinations of the personalities inside their mind, Schizoid condition that may manifest in multiple personalities.

DID Causes

This disorder is theoretically linked with the interaction of overwhelming stress, traumatic antecedents, insufficient childhood nurturing, and an innate ability to dissociate memories or experiences from consciousness. A high percentage of patients report child abuse. People diagnosed with DID often report that they have experienced severe physical and sexual abuse, especially during their childhood. Several psychiatric rating scales of DID sufferers suggested that DID is strongly related to childhood trauma rather than to an underlying electrophysiological dysfunction.

Background

By the late 19th century there was a general acceptance that emotionally traumatic experiences could cause long-term disorders which may manifest with a variety of symptoms, the most striking of such being multiple personalities cohabiting the same mind, with the concomitant complexities and dangers that may present.

"I don't understand much of this. But I do understand this indicates a serious condition, and David may have serious problems. It even sounds as though he might have *multiple personalities*?"

"If the term is accurate, that's my understanding as well. Likewise I believe it states multiple personalities are not *always* a symptom of DID. Like you, there is much on this small bit of paper I do not understand." Confessed Carol.

"Could he be dangerous?"

"In what respect?"

Ranny felt the coldness of fear and misgivings stirring with. "Dangerous Carol. Could he do harm to himself, or others?"

Carol looked at Ranny incredulously. "Why in hell do you suppose I'm giving you these things?"

"Yes. Of course." She flushed. "Where did you get this document Carol?"

"From my cousin Fredrick."

"And he is?"

"An MD. You would call him a GP."

"Not a specialist?"

"No."

"And he knows David?"

"Passingly. He does know his background, to the extent you do now."

"I see." Her voice waivered. "What shall I do?"

"I haven't one damned clue dear … I'm sorry."

Something in her voice alerted Ranny.

"There's something else isn't there?"

"No. Not really."

"Don't bullshit me Carol."

"I try not to engage in bullshit, as you call it."

"Goddamnit Carol …"

"Okay. It's just that … well … have you …"

"Have I *what*?"

It burst from her. "Have you thought about the murders?"

"The *murders*?"

"What you call the Beverly Hills murders."

"Carol, I do not understand."

Carol said nothing. She looked drained, and suddenly fragile.

"Carol?"

She looked tired and old as she sipped her tea, eyes closed. "I remember a book, or a film, or a play, or some such. I'm not sure. I only recall an incident in the story: A lifelong friend of the principal character was hopelessly trapped and about to burn alive. The man was screaming in terror not to let him burn, over and over. The man didn't hesitate. He picked up a tool and crushed his friend's skull on the spot."

"It's a film. I've seen it. About aviation I think. What's your point?"

"Well. Sometimes we're *forced* into terrible decisions. Inhuman tasks are demanded of us. If we're decent humans we have no choice but to act. Sometimes horrific responsibilities become our burdens as decent beings. Inaction can be inhuman." She looked hard to Ranny. No longer the fragile aunt.

"What are you saying Carol?"

"*Don't let David burn.*" Her bright eyes bored unyieldingly into Ranny's.

Ranny said nothing for long moments.

"Carol, I'm going to take a drive."

"Drive carefully dear. I care about you. I care about you both."

~~~~

Carol's visit came to a quiet end. Subdued, but not without affection and understanding growing with Ranny. David returned before her departure, which eased things for everyone.

At odd moments David would catch Ranny looking his way in thoughtful contemplation.

If he found this troubling, he never mentioned it.

Nor was he aware when he called her *Ranny* she shivered inwardly.

A few days later Carol had returned to London and they were finally alone.

Western Sunset

THE SHRILL RINGING of the phone shocked her into wakefulness. David, asleep in his own room, slept on.

Who in hell's calling at this hour?

Ranny roused herself in the darkness, groping for clock and phone and lamp ... fumbling all three, as the phone shrilly jangled on and on. Finally she juggled the phone to her ear.

She answered brusquely and a little sharply. "Hello?"

"Kitty?"

Kitty? Who calls me Kitty anymore?

"Uh, yes it is. Who is calling please?"

"Kitty, this is Aunt Debra. I'm sorry to call at such an hour. But I have terrible news dear."

"What is it Aunt Deb?"

"It's your father Kit."

"*Yes?*" She griped the phone so tightly her hand shook. The tone in her aunt's voice was unmistakable. This was the unthinkable call every daughter and son dread during the sleepless night-watch that mercifully fades with dawn's ascent.

"He passed away last night Kitty. Doc Simmons says his heart probably gave out. Tom found Glenn this morning when he brought in the winterfeed. He died alone, but we don't believe he suffered Kit. Tom said he just looked like he was sleeping. Peaceful."

"Oh God!" Ranny could say no more.

"We're not sure what you want to do now Kit. Glenn's memorial service is scheduled for Wednesday, but the coroner's ..."

"Aunt Deb, I'll call you back in a hour or so. Just now I can't ..."

"I understand dear. I'm at the ranch and I'll be here all day. I'll do anything I can to help dear. Call me when you're up to it."

She rolled into her pillow sobbing. Grief and guilt and a sudden aching void churning within her.

"Your father?" David stood, a dark backlit silhouette in her doorway.

She responded with a muffled "Yes."

He walked to the bed and sat. "I'm so sorry." He sat besides her, gently smoothing her hair. After several quiet minutes he asked softly "What shall we do?"

Ranny visibly stiffened, willing herself to suppress her emotions. She sat up and appraised the situation. Things needed doing. She would grieve when there was time enough for pain.

"First I've got to get to Colorado. I'll fly into Denver and rent a car. When I know my arrival info I'll call Aunt Debra and go over the arrangements. We'll probably ..."

"Ranny, I'm happy to go with you."

He was instantly shamed by a selfishly unworthy thought: *Dinosaur Monument is only a hundred or so miles from Steamboat Springs. Hundreds of huge Jurassic specimens beautifully preserved in their native ...*

"No David. No. I don't want to hurt your feelings. Believe me. But I need to do this alone. You never knew my father, or the ranch, or Colorado, or any of those people, because of my neglect ... of you ... of my father ... and even myself. And it's too late now." She paused and swallowed. "So I'll manage this myself ..." She peered at David imploringly "... if that's alright?"

"Certainly. I understand. I'll look after things here. Right now I'll get on the computer and start making travel arrangements."

~~~~

An hour or so later, David was quietly listening to Ranny's end of their phone call.

"Aunt Deb?"

"Hi."

"I'm better now and I'll be there soon. I'm flying into Denver and I'll take a car from there. I should arrive tomorrow evening around six, or seven. Will you be at the ranch?"

"Good."

"No. Please don't bother to cook. I'll grab something on the way. You said the services were scheduled for Wednesday?"

"What?"

"Why in the world would the coroner want to delay my father's burial?"

"*Suicide!*"

"Oh God Aunt Deb, it can't be true."

"They found a *note?*"

Pause.

"Why wouldn't he call me? I've asked him to visit us a thousand times. I'd have paid all expen ..."

"Yeah. I know. He wouldn't leave Colorado and he'd never accept money from me. I don't blame him. I guess he never got over mom. Then there was that damned dog and ..."

Long pause.

"*Me?* Oh Jesus Aunt Deb, let's talk about this when I get there."

"Yes. I will. See you tomorrow. I love you too."

David looked concerned. "What is it Ranny?"

"The coroner seems to suspect dad killed himself. He was apparently quite depressed."

"Do you know why?"

"Deb says his health was failing. He never really got past mom's death. He lost a dog he really loved a few weeks ago. And she says he was un-happy about *me.*"

"*You?* Why?"

"He felt abandoned. I never visited, or called, or wrote and rarely even emailed. Just the occasional invitation to see us here at the Domaine. Which he never took seriously, knowing that he never left Colorado. You heard he left a note."

"What did it say?"

"FUCK IT."

"That's all it said?"

"That's all. I think it was a message with me in mind."

"You and your father weren't estranged in any way, were you?"

"No. Just the opposite. But I got so involved in Chicago and Paris and London and finally here, I simply ignored him. I was thoughtless and self-centered. And it killed him."

"Ranny, you don't know that. Your father was a grown man with his own life. You're taking on a lot of guilt without the facts. Guilt serves little purpose when things can't be changed. Guilt can hurt beyond belief though, and do great harm. I know. You mustn't let this happen to you. Please. Believe me."

She peered at him as though he were speaking Chinese.

"I better get packed. I suppose we leave for Nice early tomorrow?"

"We need to be on the road by 0630."

~~~~

She'd forgotten how breathtaking Colorado's topography could be. Geologically adolescent mountains, graphic against infinite blue skies so sharp and angular they look like a child's rendering. Horizons breathtaking with colossal ivory thunderheads towering miles into the blue. The long, flat east-western build-up to the apex of the Rockies themselves.

Despite her mood, she thrilled at the long approach into Denver International, and the heady drive up to Steamboat Springs. She found her way to the ranch, as though she'd never left.

This would have been such fun, so easy and so … if I'd just come before.

Tom and Aunt Debra were waiting for her at the ranch. She hugged both fondly, not sure whether there was a certain hesitation in their manner. Perhaps it was simply a function of her guilty imaginings, or maybe it expressed their very real disappointment with her.

Disregarding Ranny's objection, Debra had laid out dinner. Biscuits, iced-tea, steaming chicken-noodle casserole with carrots and fresh green peas, followed by chocolate cake. It felt so much like home she nearly wept.

After dinner Tom found a bottle of wine and they reviewed arrangements, tacitly avoiding any discussion of Glenn's death, or its possible catalysts.

The Coroner had thoughtfully withdrawn his insistence on an autopsy. Not because he was convinced of death by natural causes. He simply didn't see what purpose it would serve, nor did the Medical Examiner, nor the Sheriff's Office. Glenn was well known and respected throughout the county.

Memorial Services were to be held at the First Presbyterian Church of Steamboat Springs, eleven o'clock, Wednesday morning, followed by a wake at the ranch house, a buffet as per Glenn's explicit instructions. Glenn had repeatedly said over the years that he didn't give a damn if people attended his service, but he damned sure wanted to buy them a last drink.

Bourbon—Pinto Beans—Bacon—Biscuits

Tin coffee cups, tin plates and spoons. No knives, or forks. Napkins were an afterthought, thanks to Aunt Debra.

'Catering' was fondly provided by a local restaurant (Sally's Diner), of Glenn's long acquaintance, locally renowned for their beans in chili sauce. Tom had already laid in two cases of I. W. Harper, so all was in readiness.

Beans, bourbon, biscuits and bacon? Oh Dad, what were you thinking? Were you just getting lonelier and more and more colorful, isolated on this godforsaken ranch? Or were you slowly going crazy?

Glenn was to be cremated at ten o'clock. His ashes were to be spread on the ranch after the wake. Tom witnessed the cremation alone, bearing the ashes back to the ranch. Neither Debra, nor Ranny wished to attend. Debra adamantly refused to attend such ritual. Ranny on the other hand, was sickened and haunted by an ironically related admonition. A grievous burden imparted by David's Aunt Carol: *Don't let David burn.*

Well Dad, I guess I let you burn. I'll live with that the rest of my life. But, I don't believe I'll let David burn as well. God help me, I've learned my lesson. I hope you can forgive me.

An ominous resolution crystallized in her mind.

Mr. Howard Glover (Glenn's attorney) would conduct the reading of the will at three o'clock on Wednesday.

The Memorial Service was held at eleven sharp.

Roughly thirty people attended. Aside from Debra and Tom, Ranny literally knew no one.

A young Minister solemnly conducted the service.

"It was Glenn's wish that only these words, his own, be read at his service."

> *We shouldn't take death so damned seriously.*
> *All the fear and grieving ...*
> *We should take life seriously.*
> *Death looks after itself.*

"We pray his soul is blessed with peace and grace in his divine rest."

Ranny winced inwardly. *Not sure dad would have approved of that ending.*

Mercifully delivered from a harangue of longwinded eulogies, the mourners gratefully retreated to the ranch and its beans and bourbon. All shared a common, though unspoken indebtedness to a crusty southwestern rancher who never suffered bullshit—alive or dead.

Ranny knew no one at the wake either. A good deal more people attended the wake than the memorial service. Glenn had more friends than she realized. What little conversation she engaged in was stilted, impersonal and forced. She was always awkward with expressions of sympathy and discreetly tried to avoid them.

After a time she gave up conversation altogether. Taking a tin cup of bourbon she retreated to an alcove seat, preferring to listen to reminiscences of her father, and simply observe. Soon she found herself absorbed by the discourse.

Some guests were openly puzzled by the buffet, mawkishly pecking at their beans and timidly sampling their I. W. Harper with wry perplexity. She had to give them credit though. They were clearly good sports and loyal friends, determined to attend Glenn's last supper and raise a glass (or tin cup) in his honor.

Others ate with gusto. Tall rangy men. Men with wrinkles within their sunburned wrinkles. Men who'd dressed up for this event with their best pressed Levi's, spit-shined boots and pearl buttons on their Saturday-night-out-dancin' shirts. These men were not snow-bunnies.

They apparently approved of lunch, and had it down to a routine. A generous spoonful of beans stuffed into gaunt left cheeks and a bite of biscuit, chew a few times, then tear off a shred of bacon, long slow chews for a while longer, down some bourbon (holding the fiery liquid outside the teeth in a sort of tight-lipped fluid pout), chew some more, slowly blending the bourbon with beans and pork, then swallow. They made it look delicious. She was getting hungry just watching. Warm memories with her father began to awaken, long ago with dad and men like these. Although, as they swallowed she drolly noted a near imperceptible twitch of their heads, subtle squints, and slight tearing of eyes. She suspected it had been some time since these men had regularly partaken of such fiery fare.

I was wrong about the menu. Wrong about a lot of thing I guess. I've forgotten how we lived and the things we loved in those days ... maybe Daddy wasn't so crazy after all.

Not surprisingly, as she listened she discovered her father had dimensions she'd never imagined. Friends, interests, skills, humor. A life she knew nothing of. More guilty coals to an already conscience-stricken Newcastle.

When the guests had departed, Howard Glover read the will. Aside from a beloved horse for Tom and some keepsakes for Aunt Debra, Ranny was the sole beneficiary. When all was completed she took Howard aside, instructing him to distribute all properties jointly and equally—chattel, liquid and real—between Tom and Aunt Debra. She signed a statement to that effect in front of Howard. Howard was further instructed to wait until Friday, at the very earliest before enacting her wishes.

When she was old enough to become aware of such things, she'd sensed a diffident affection between the two. And although it was growing late in life for both, perhaps it wasn't too late for them to find happiness and companionship. Ranny was happy to do her share. More importantly, it was they, not she, who were there for Glenn during his lonely final years.

Later that afternoon she spread her father's ashes in the barren hills above the ranch house. Alone. Cradling Glenn's urn in her left arm, casting ashes to the lee wind with her right, as though she were some bygone farmer sowing the seeds of a new generation. Perhaps she was. The blinding rays of the setting sun, the frigid early evening wind, the ashy dust, or her grief. Something misted her eyes. She wasn't sure which.

When the ashes were sown Ranny placed the urn under a small pine at the edge of the forest. Truly an empty vessel now.

She would sign all papers and settle legal costs and taxes from France.

And that was all.

That night she slept alone in the ranch house listening to the creak of the timbers in the cold wind, and the whine of that same wind through the soaring pines. She thought she heard the wuthering howl of coyotes high in the foothills, a sound which had always made her feel lonely and morose. She wondered why she hadn't called David. She wondered why she'd never visited her father. She wondered that her life had so suddenly gone awry. She wondered how she'd lost her way from the bright happy days of her girlhood, when her father had always been there for her, and she for him.

She arose early the next morning, drove to Denver, turned in her car, and boarded an aircraft. On the return flight she avoided looking out on Colorado altogether. Ranny would furtively grieve the rest of her life. A day would not pass without thoughts of Glenn. As she prepared a favorite dish of his. When she saw a horse, heard a certain joke, or watched something in the news she knew would aggravate him. She would smile fondly and she would grieve after him in her own fashion.

Suspicion's Dawn

FOLLOWING THEIR CUSTOMARY Tuesday sail, Adam suggested they stop for a drink at the bar of the hotel Villa Belrose, in Gassin. It was in 'line of tack' home, and David was always a sucker for a lush bar overlooking the sea. Cool comfort, service, sea, sun, olives & nuts, and a tall icy Gin and Tonic. He readily accepted.

As they strode across the opulent lobby towards the bar, David noted an interesting aberration in the elegant stone flooring. A dark, sleek, aft-finned, torpedo shape. He leaned down and quickly determined he was looking at a small, but excellent specimen of Coleoidea, ancestor to the Amonite, the Chambered Nautilus and the squid. Some grew into giants, the apex predators of the seas four hundred million years ago. This specimen was roughly seven centimeters. A beautiful cross-section of the fossil polished into the native stone.

Without another thought, David was on hands and knees, glasses mounted, studying his find.

"Look Adam. A Coleoidea. Devonian. A beauty."

Adam looked down on David dubiously, self-conscious of the stares his crawling friend was attracting. Before he could comment, David was all over the lobby.

"Here's another. And another. And ... look at this Adam ... I'm not familiar with this specie. Here, take a look."

Adam patiently walked over and bent down, inspecting David's find.

"Dave. My friend. That *sir* is a scuffmark from a rubber-soled shoe. Probably a Gucci Loafer, circa the third millennia AD. The *Doeskinus-Piedipus* Period I believe."

David frowned, clearly nonplussed, looking up at Adam.

Adam laughed. "You really are your father's son Davey. Let's get a drink."

They chortled about the incident over drinks, careful to return to the Domaine in good time for lunch. Neither wished to face the wrath of either Ranny or Hélène after hours in the kitchen.

The day passed agreeably. A pleasant occupation the three always looked forward to with anticipation. They shared lunch by the pool, lingering over wine and sunshine. Later in the afternoon David excused himself to make arrangements for a dig planned for Thursday in Vallon-Pont-d'Arc. He was on the phone with Marcel for nearly twenty minutes, after which he made himself a tall Gin & Tonic.

Walking out to rejoin them poolside, he paused at the French door. Ranny and Adam were sitting together on the edge of the pool, dangling legs in the water, shoulder-to-shoulder, knee-to-knee. To David's eyes they were conversing in an intensely intimate manner. Heads close, demeanor suggestively familiar, voices beyond hearing. Adam seemed to be somehow consoling Ran.

Is she upset about something? What's the problem here? What in hell's going on?

A nauseating wave of suspicion washed over him. He was not jealous by nature and found the emotion belittling and unworthy. Unworthy to all three. It shamed him. An insult to Ranny and a breach of faith with Adam. All the same, what was this all about? A whispering campaign like June and Aunt Carol? But this was Adam. *Yes.* Adam. Good-looking, lady-killer Adam.

He returned to his office and threw himself into his chair, nursing his G&T. He needed to settle down and think.

Unbidden, a quote from Shakespeare reverberated through his mind:

O, beware, my lord, of jealousy;
'Tis the green-eyed monster which doth mock
The meat it feeds on.

The irony was not wasted on him: *Othello the Moor* and David's own *jalousie* [jealousy] inhabiting the *Maures* [Moors]

He drained half his drink and took a huge, deep breath followed by a long, calming sigh.

Okay. Okay. This is silly. I'm going back to the pool, finish my drink and enjoy the rest of the afternoon with my two favorite people.

Now relaxed, even smiling, he rose from his chair. Then it hit him. Almost a physical blow, driving him back into his chair ...

One Goddamned minute! What was it Adam said in the lobby of Villa Belrose? 'You really are your father's son Davey.'

The words pounding through his mind.

I never said a goddamned thing about my father to Adam. Not one goddamned thing. Nothing. Nothing about my father. Nothing about fossil hunting with him. Nothing about anything. Nothing!

... But I bet I know who did ...

The remainder of an erstwhile pleasant day ended with an awkward, bewildering chill. Ranny and Adam mutely wondered what bleak brume had so abruptly beset David.

The SEED of Our Undoing

ONE WEEK LATER, Ranny entered David's office coffee in hand, a look of resolve commanding her features.

"David, we need to talk."

"What's up?" He swiveled and leaned back in his chair, fingers laced behind his neck, an uneasy frown astraddle his forehead.

"I'm very pleased with your Paleontology. You know that."

"Yes ... *but* ...?"

"But there are still many chores around here and I think we should work together. Each pulling their own weight. There are bills to pay, groceries to buy, posts to mail, taxes, garden and house supplies, cars to be serviced, registrations at the Mairie, all sorts of crap. And I've been doing it all for months and I don't think that's right. What do you think?"

David relaxed. He leant back even further, studying the ceiling. Shakespeare had been lurking in his mind since the preceding week.

She's looking to make some kind of sea change around here. I wonder why? Certainly not because she wants help with chores. She wants ... what?

He leant back even further, a faraway look in his eyes, reciting:

> *Full fathom five thy father lies.*
> *Of his bones are coral made;*
> *Those are pearls that were his eyes:*
> *Nothing of that doth fade,*
> *But doth suffer a sea-change into something rich and strange ...*

Ranny was suddenly deathly pale. Her voice was razor sharp and shrill.

"*David!* How could you? My God! What in the world are you saying David? Why? *Why* would you mock my father's death? What are you thinking?" Her voice rose to a screech. "This can't be you talking David. *It's not.*" Visions of Aunt Carol and DID thundered through her mind.

Shocked. David slammed forward in his chair. "Ranny. For God's sake I wasn't ridiculing your father. I was quoting Shakespeare. A sort of a sea sonnet from *The Tempest.* It speaks of a *sea change*. I was simply pointing out you want to *change* things around here. A sea-change."

Taken aback, Ranny simply stared at David.

"Oh David. I'm so sorry. I guess I'm still upset about dad. I'm really sorry." She leant forward and grasped David's hands across David's desk.

After a few breaths "Don't give it a another thought dear. You can make it up to me over drinks. Poolside. After the help's gone home." He smiled wolfishly and could tell Ranny already felt better. Oddly, he sensed relief as well. "Meanwhile, give me minute to consider this *sea change* you are proposing." He leaned back again.

After a few moments he leaned forward again. Placing both hands on the desk, looking up and favoring her with a warm, ingratiating smile.

"We'll call it Sharrandqualday."

"What? *Sharon crawl day*? What the hell does that mean?"

"No. Shar-rand-qual-day. Sharrandqualday." He spelled it out. "S-h-a-r-r-a-n-d-q-u-a-l-d-a-y." Then he defined it. "Share Errands Equally Day."

David was surpassingly fond of forming silly composite words, which produced abstruse meanings, or sometimes no meaning at all.

"It's what they term a *portmanteau* word."

"A *what* word?"

"A *portmanteau* word. From the French. Literally 'carries the cloak'. In English it's a conjunction of words implying something, not necessarily in the nature of their components. Irritating term, isn't it?"

She mumbled under her breath "Something's damned sure irritating around here." Sometimes David's mind moved so swiftly even she had difficulty following him. But she could be quick as well. She sipped her coffee and squinted in mock thoughtfulness. "Let's see … If we're obliged to assign some half-baked label to this, what's wrong with SEED?"

"SEED?"

"Share Errands Equally Day. An acronym." She tilted her head. An angelic smile. Gently decisive. Eyes dreamy with mock equanimity, she persuasively nodded her head as she spoke, right index finger tapping her nose and a sage look in her eyes. "A *niiiice* acronym."

Eyebrows elevated, head cocked, he smiled. "Not bad. Not bad at all. Problem is, it wants to say SEED Day. Which repeats *day*."

"Mm. I suppose we could call it SEE Day, but I see you've thought this out carefully. I think I'll avoid that trap. So …" She turned to David. "Stupid term. Smart Idea. I buy it. How 'bout every Wednesday? The midweek hump. It shouldn't get in the way of your fossilizing. And you still have Tuesdays to sail with Adam."

David thought for a moment and then agreed. "Done. Wednesdays it is. We'll do the posting, the banking, the shopping and whatever else wants doing. We can do a nice lunch too. Sharrandqualday Wednesdays." He flashed her a charming smile.

It really should be Sharrandqual-Wednesdays. But I'm damned if I'm going to let him suck me into that.

David warmed to the idea. "There's lots more of course. If you write out the bills, I'll do some gardening and look after the dust bins."

Ranny beamed. "Yes. That's fine. I'll *pay* the bills. You do some *yard work*, and *take out the garbage*."

David good-naturedly ignored her corrective Americanization. American-speak versus British-speak had been, and would always be a source of entertaining bicker between them.

"We're agreed then dear?"

"Yup."

"See how reasonable and responsible I can be?"

She'd kissed him on the nose and was already walking away.

"We all act responsibly given our penchants David. It's our priorities which reveal our nature."

David made no response. He didn't understand her statement and he wasn't sure he wanted to.

~~~~

Next day.

"Morning! Beautiful day out there. Did you see the deer? The little buggers must have been out there all ... My God!" He was looking down on the breakfast table in wonder and delight.

"Kippers, fried eggs and a Bloomer! [Bread] And *tea* instead of coffee."

"With kippers, never drink coffee, and milk in the cup before the tea is poured." she recited.

He seated himself at the table. "Well remembered."

"We must respect your rules."

"Agreed. Rules are rules. But I don't make 'em up dear. I just follow 'em." He built a generous bite on his fork and tasted.

"Mm, excellent kippers. Masterfully Jugged [poached]. They hold together perfectly. Moist and savory. Wherever did you find all this wonderment?"

"The Bloomer I baked myself."

"... and excellent it is! The kippers?"

"I was at the English shop in Port Grimaud with Jeanette and they'd just gotten them in. They were literally putting them on the shelf as I was taking them off. Actually they're German. Tinned Smoked Kippered Herring. *Appel* brand I think."

"One of the best. This is really good of you. I know you don't care for kippers."

"I can't even stand cooking them. But I bought you eight tins. So eat up." She seated herself at the table. "I do like the bread though, but I like it toasted."

She appraised his rough clothes and boots over her teacup. "So, where are you off to today?"

"Going to try a new dig up north. It's supposed to have some outstanding cephalopods. Dad wouldn't have cared much for it. He loved the big carnivores. Glory stuff. And it burned a lot of daylight. They're just too rare in this part of the world. But I find these little guys have a genuine beauty. They ..."

"You hunted fossils with your father?"

He gave her a puzzled look. *I know damned well Aunt Carol told her we hunted together. I also know damned well she's discussed this with Adam ... and who knows what else? What's the game?*

"Aah ... sure ... I guess. Yes. All the time. With my mother as well. June didn't care for it." He cut into another kipper. "I suspect we passed up many excellent sites in those days because dad was so fixated on the big predators. All the same, we managed to find some excellent specimens without really ..."

"So you did a *lot* of fossil hunting with them?"

He looked at her blankly for a moment.

"Yes, I suppose so. As I remember, nothing gave us more ..."

"... got a question David ..."

"What's that Ran?"

Ran. He called me Ran! Better than Ranny anyhow. Best not to mention it. Maybe he'll keep it. Maybe there's hope ...

"When did your parents pass away?"

"Oh. I was pretty young at the time. That's all I remember."

"How old were you?"

He thought for a moment. "I'm not really sure. I was in school though."

"How did they die?" She mentally held her breath.

David thoughtfully picked at his breakfast. Ranny was pleasantly surprised at his relaxed manner.

He leant back in his chair, tea in hand, frowning. "Not sure. I think it was an accident of some sort. I really don't know. I wanted to discuss it with June when she visited, but she wasn't the least bit interested. Struck me as pretty cold on her part." He extended his right arm in a taunt stretch and yawned. "But that was all a long time ago. Perhaps she remembers as little as I."

"But you seem to have such vivid memories of your parents. Your mother's cooking. Your father and paleontology. Hunting for fossils. You've even spoken about ..."

"Why the sudden interest? Been discussing this with June and Carol have we?"

"Oh, passingly. Among other things, I suppose."

David laid out his napkin neatly. "Got to run, Ran." He ghosted a smile at his inadvertent paronym. *Run-Ran.* It both pleased and troubled him somehow. Smile and frown coursing his features in a fluttering relay. "I'm meeting Marcel in less than three hours under the stone arch. I've just got time to make it."

"Marcel? Stone arch?"

"Marcel Briançon. Damned fine rock hound and fossil-hunter. I'm sure I've mentioned him."

"I suppose so. But I don't think I focused on his name. I should write that down. If I can't reach your mobile ..." She retrieved a pen and paper from her bric-a-brac drawer and sat down. "That's Marcel Bran ..."

"Marcel Briançon. B-r-i-a-n-ç-o-n. *Brie-an-khan.*" He retrieved a scrap of paper from his wallet, held it at arm's length, and squinted out the phone number. "Ah, 04 75 88 ... Oh wait, he told me he had his land-line replaced ... something about changing to a new wide-band service." He discarded the paper.

"And that number is ...?"

"I don't have it yet. Anyhow. He owns a Rock and Fossil shop in Vallon-Pont-d'Arc. The stone arch crosses the river near there. It's rather famous actually. Thanks for a great breakfast. See you Monday night. Gotta run ..."

He jumped to his feet, leaned down and kissed Ranny on the forehead, and was out the door. She could hear the door slam on his Range Rover as he revved and spun down the drive, a good deal faster than his normal, methodical pace.

She stood to clear the table, unconsciously shaking her head, concern clouding her features. The breakfast that so pleased him was only half eaten.

Well. That didn't go very well. I suppose I pushed too hard. I've got to go slow. I think Carol's right. David does have a problem.

DID. For Chrissake. It could stand for David Is Demented.

Shadow Fade

IT WAS SHARRANDQUALDAY. Wednesday.

Ranny was seated in their foyer, legs crossed, her foot vibrating like a ribbon in the wind. She was sightlessly flipping the pages of a magazine as though she wanted to rip it to shreds. She had been waiting for David to join her on their weekly junket for nearly fifteen minutes. She was dressed and set to leave. Mail, deposit slips, shopping list, prescriptions, all in hand. Everything in readiness. Even her car was out front, top down and warmed up. David's Range Rover was in for servicing, so they would make do with Ranny's Merc.

Sharrandqualday ... stupid name.

He was late, as always.

And he was slow, as always.

And he couldn't tear himself away from his damned fossils, as always.

Until now, it had been a lovely winter morning, sun breaking over the east side of the valley, washing the quiet morning tableau with warm saffron light.

I was actually looking forward to this ... idiotic me.

Her brooding was suddenly interrupted by a deafening clap of thunder. She rushed to the door as it echoed down the valley. The sky was now a dark charcoal gray, roiling with wind and storm clouds. It was raining, as it rains only in the foothills of the Massif. Worse, her top was down.

Goddamnit!

She ran out of the villa unprotected by either raincoat or umbrella.

As she finished raising the top, the rain suddenly relented. Even a tentative ray of golden sun peaked out for a moment. Just then, David stepped out jauntily. Dry. Decked out stylishly in foul weather gear. Whistling. She could kill him.

Then some paleontological idiot like him would find his fossilized bones in these hills a million years from now and wonder at the huge gash in his skull.

He opened his door and stepped in smiling "Happy Sharrandqualday Ranny ..." His greeting and his smile faded as he looked around the rain-soaked interior with a bewildered frown. "Quelle mess!" [What a mess!]

Ranny's only response "Get in!"

She was shivering. Her hair hung in long sodden strings. Water dripped from nose and chin. Her clothes clung wetly to her body. David rather enjoyed that aspect of her misery. Though wisely, he abjured from commenting on any facet of her appearance.

Her car was little better. Only two minutes with the top down and the inside was soaked. Carpeting squished underfoot. The leather seats were a misery to sit upon. The windows were fogged and running with water. The steering wheel and gear shift cold and slippery in her hands.

She set the air on high, put the car in gear, revved it a few times and threw out the clutch. Gravel sprayed for two meters in their wake, effectively belying her mood.

She looked about and grumbled "You know, when the damned Tourist Office is not telling us we're goddamned *Venice under the Massif,* they're bragging we have three-hundred days of *sunshine.*"

David smiled genially "I suppose both statements are reasonably accurate."

"Yes, I suppose so. But don't forget, that's still *sixty-five days of rain.* That's one hellofa lot of rain, and a hellofa lot of days. Especially if they fall in a row."

"Well it is January after all. The rainy season. Best to get it over with. Don't you agree?"

"You're damned irritating this morning. You know that?"

It began to rain again. In earnest.

"Mm. The Post Box is coming up on your right. Going to pull over?"

The Post Box was affixed to the wizened stonewall of a charming old bus stop which provided a convenient roadside area to pull over and post mail.

"I *suppose* so ..." She threw the wheel to the right, then left, hit the brakes and came to a skidding fishtail just in front of the box.

"Skillfully done. And what the hell, my trousers were already damp anyhow."

Ranny only glared at him.

David realized he was going to have to find her an excellent lunch if the day was to be salvaged.

Envelopes secured under his jacket, he sprang from the car and jumped the two steps to the large yellow mailbox, inserting the mail in a single smooth movement. He was turning back to the car when something incongruous caught his eye. Atop the box, in the pouring rain, was a neat package roughly the size of a video case, but twice the thickness. It was wrapped in shiny brown paper with a plastic envelope impressed on the paper. The rain had already saturated the envelope and blurred the addresses to illegibility. The paper itself still bore a logo, *Kodak Express,* despite extensive stains. It was clear the interior of the box was soaked as well. Disregarding the cold rain running down his neck, he decided to do the right thing. He inserted the small package into the mail slot.

No good. It's too thick. That explains why some stupid son-of-a-bitch left it out here in the first place. Silly bastard. Damn! Okay. What the hell, I'll take it with me and drop it at the Post Office.

He jumped back in the car. As expected, Kitty was annoyed at his dalliance.

As they drove away "What were you doing out there?"

"Some dumb bastard left this on the Post Box." He brandished the package. "He couldn't fit it through the slot, so I guess he just left it. Probably wasn't raining then. I think it's a film mailer."

"Film mailer?"

"Yes. A pre-addressed, prepaid package for mailing film prints or slides, or even digital format these days."

"They still use those things?"

"They're still in limited use. Yes. Technology has not totally obsoleted them altogether quite yet, particularly the old Kodachromes. I think this package was destined for Switzerland. They still have a facility in Lausanne I believe."

"You're remarkably well informed."

"If you recall, my company provided visual site surveys as part of our service in the old days, just as digital photography was conquering the world."

"Right."

With a playful grin he added "… not to mention the address printed on this box, albeit faded somewhat, is Kodak S.A., Case Postale, CH1001, Lausanne, Switzerland."

She smirked wryly. "Uh hmm. I see. Can you tell who mailed it?"

"Nope. The rain washed away the return address. I imagine the Post Office won't accept it now." For some reason his mind drifted to Northern France, and then even further. Other places and events obscured by time. He absently murmured "Shadow fade." Then softer still "Charle …"

"What did you say David? Shadow fade? Charlie?"

He stared blankly out the window, at the rain, saying nothing.

"David?"

"Ah." He roused himself from his reverie and brightened. "Shadow fade, or rain fade. The terms are interchangeable. It's a term we use in wireless communications. Radio frequency, microwave and whatnot. It refers to the attenuation of a signal through absorption by atmospheric conditions. Rain, snow, hail. That sort of thing. The signal fades, reemerging when the condition has passed. The way the rain faded the address on this package. It reminded me of the term. *Shadow fade.*"

"I see. And what does someone named Charlie have to do with it?"

"Um, not Charlie actually. I was referring to—let's see—uh, Charleville-Mézières in the Champagne-Ardenne region of Northern France. We did some topographical wireless studies there for France Telecom."

Ranny peered at him skeptically for a moment. "You never told me about that. Anyhow, what are we going to do with the damned thing now?"

"Well, I suppose we'll have to open it and hopefully find an address. Then the next time we're at the Post Office we'll take it in and sort it out."

"The *royal* we … I suppose?"

David slipped the package into the glove box, ignoring her sarcasm. "Umm. So where shall we go for lunch?"

~~~~

Their chores took them out to the D98 and the village of Môle, so they decided on one of their favorite restaurants, *Les Murennes*. A lovely old Provençal inn, secluded at the crossroad of the D98 and the Route des Guiols, two kilometers east of Môle.

The dish that brought them back again and again: *Sanglier à la Provençale* [Wild Boar]. Sanglier was not normally a favored dish of David. But Murennes' Sanglier is very special. The Woods knew of only one restaurant which equaled the *Les Murennes'* Sanglier. A small inland village to the east, *La Garde-Freinet*. The village harbored a tiny restaurant with the unlikely name, *My Way*. They serve essentially the same dish, more often with lamb however. Debilitatingly delicious. Sunny Sunday afternoons chez *My Way* easily justified the beautiful hour's drive through the Massif. David always posted a wistful eye at restaurants throughout the region for this dish. Fond memories of the Ardenne.

Les Murennes simmered their boar for hours in cider and white wine. Delicately spiced with herbs de Provence. A sweet hint of curry, with carrots and stewed potatoes and just enough olive oil to make the sauce rich and lustrous. Its flavor deepened with savory olives and sweet yellow peppers. The perfect dish.

The boar, generous, hearty and meaty. A haunch on the bone. Fall-apart tender.

A rich relish of caramelized onion on the side, to lend sweetness and tang. The edgy, nutty bread they serve was made for the sauce.

Ranny was taught that scouring the plate with bread expressed appreciation for the meal. Western style. David's Aunt Carol taught him it was coarse and ill-mannered. Something of the Welsh coal mines. At Les Murennes however, diners always clean their plates thusly. David was no exception.

Flavors that excite the pallet, enhanced by aromas that flare the nostrils, practically a drug.

Factor in a cool Provençal rosé, followed by a light, sweet Baba au Rhum. It never gets better.

The weather cleared. All thoughts of rain faded. All previous irritations were forgotten.

Outstanding food always had a wonderful effect on Ranny's mood.

After the meal they hugged, shook hands and congratulated their hosts on yet another amazing meal.

They then completed their chores and passed an unexpectedly pleasant afternoon.

They returned to the Domaine bathed in the amber, fading sun.

Stalking the Greenies

Evil is obvious only in retrospect

Gloria Steinem

CONSIDERING THEIR CONSIDERABLE lunch, they skipped dinner altogether, and wined before the fire. Snug in thick robes, warm, alone and happy, David poured the wine. A deep fruity red Gigondas Grenache. They raised their glasses. The wine, imbued by firelight, twinkled and danced, a nebulous glowing crimson.

David smiled, looking Ranny in the eyes as he whispered "Tchin-tchin."

A friendly chime as they tipped their glasses.

Ranny frowned "What does that really mean anyhow? Is there a translation?"

"To what?"

"Chin-Chin."

"No. The expressions is Tchin-tchin. T-C-H-I-N. Not C-H-I-N. I know it's subtle to the ear. The tip of the tongue lightly touches the pallet just behind the teeth. The idiom is interpreted as *le bruit de deux verres de contact.*"

"Meaning?"

"The sound of two glasses tipping."

"Mm. Still reminds me of the Big Bad Wolf."

"Big bad wolf?" David laughed. "What are you talking about?"

"You know. The Three Little Pigs—not by the hair of my chinny-chin-chin?"

"Oh. Right."

The hair of my chinny-chin-chin? What the hell? Pigs? Wolves? Must be an American thing.

Somehow Ranny's allusion to the wolf subtly altered their mood. They both felt the troubling sense something was changing. Something had transpired that day. Unrealized as yet. But something. Between them. Their world. The Domaine. Even the tiny village of Coirón. Nothing dramatic. Not a calamitous event. More like the silent movement of the lock vents in a canal. Initially no more than a subtle surge in the flow of the water. Soon overwhelmed by a massive cataract.

They made love on Ranny's new Ardabil Carpet in the firelight. Fortunately David had no clue of its value and Ranny never gave it a thought. They made love, thoughtfully, maturely, even languidly. Their days of sweaty rutting had waned. The galloping, grunting, pounding, self-centered race to the climax had faded in favor of thoughtfully pleasuring each other. David loved nothing so much as Ranny's magical sigh of attainment.

Afterward they lay in the glow of the fire and spoke of each other and their lives together as he stroked her back.

She peered at the fire pensively. Rolling over, she gently embraced David's face with her hands. Searching his eyes. Stroking his hair.

"Sometimes I feel I love you so much David, it frightens me."

"I love you Ran. More than you know. But there's no need to be frightened. We're impregnable, you and I."

"Nothing's impregnable David. Nothing. Look at Coirón."

"Coirón?"

She sighed and chuckled lovingly. "You really do live in your own world. You know more about Les Maures millions of years ago than you do the last few months."

He frowned "Meaning?"

"The *murders* David. You've forgotten?"

"Oh right. No, I've not forgotten. The Beverly Hill Beast. Sickening. Wretched. But it's far too nice tonight to talk about such things ..."

"The last six months have been very difficult for Coirón, David. Our neighbors are suffering and some are dying horribly. We should be concerned. We should fear for ourselves as well."

David absently balanced his jaw on his wrist, fingers languidly facing forward, elbow resting on the carpet, peering blasély into the fire. "I suppose you're right." He grimaced wryly, his eyes fixed sightlessly. "And I suppose we should ..." He pursed his lips grudgingly. "... be concerned, that is." Then his mind seemed to engage, eyes suddenly animated, glowing ominously in the firelight. He smiled without humor. "Think about it Ran. A ravenous monster converting Greenies into something finally of use. *Le Fabricant de la Viande Verte.*"

"Good grief David. This is real life you know. These aren't fossils we're discussing. They're real people, real blood, pain and terror. Real death David."

He's not at all nervous about so many murders so nearby. Not even about me. Why?

"What does that mean David?"

David appeared not to be listening, but her query roused him. Chin still idling on his wrist, he smoothly rounded on her. A reptilian movement. An easy mechanical glide. A smooth, faultless swivel. Something of the viper, or the Cobra.

"What does *what* mean?"

"What you said. In French. What does it mean?"

He swiveled away. His presence now very *un-David* ...

Eyes glittering. "The Maker of Green Meat."

She inwardly gasped at the insinuation in his detached, indifferent voice.

A slithering wraith within.

Magistralis

THE NEXT MORNING a booming Mistral exploded out of the Rhone Delta. Southerly as always, from the Rhone Valley to the Gulf of Lion, whipping the sea into a furious white squall. Exceptionally, a brawny high-pressure system in eastern Spain had the unusual effect of diverting the winds from their normal fixed pattern, slightly eastward. In fact, the perfect angle to roar down the Maure Valley directly into Coirón. The ever-narrowing valley produced a vortex accelerating its power immensely—a rare anomaly for the tiny village.

Aside from brief encounters in upper Provence, the Woods had yet to experience a real, unremitting Mistral. Their quiet little valley had always protected them. This one endured for ten days. Relentlessly, twenty-four hours a day. They awakened that morning to the alarming sound of cyclonic winds gusting up to a staggering ninety kilometers per hour. Leaves, papers and assorted detritus flew wildly about the garden. Chairs and tables were blown over. The pool was whipped into a roiling fury. The skies were brilliantly blue, cloudless and blinding. The air was so clear it seemed they could see all the way to Corsica. There was no escaping the wind though. Indoors, outdoors, in the car, walking. It was incessant, constant, onerous and exhausting.

They'd heard stories about the Mistral and its power to drive men mad. Murders, rapes, fights, suicides and lives devastated. They were always skeptical of such stories, now swiftly becoming believers. Even the local wildlife seemed to seclude themselves in their various dens seeking shelter from this terrible wind.

On the third day, falling trees knocked out their power and telephone. It was nearly three days before EDF was able to repair their regional transformer and two days longer before telephone and data links were restored.

Unfazed, Ranny contentedly read her books by daylight, firelight, or candlelight. She cooked with gas, emptying fridge and freezer, listening to a small battery powered radio. With a little jury-rigging their oil heater provided a semblance of hot water. Despite the storm, the endless blue skies and starry nights were a joy. All in all, Ranny was untroubled, except for the ceaseless wailing of the wind.

David's reaction was vastly different. Without his computer, his television, videos and electricity, he was well and truly lost. He refused to expose himself to the storm. He couldn't, or wouldn't go into town. In any event most of the town was closed and without power as well. The pool was out of the question. He didn't want to leave Ranny alone. Consequently fossilizing was not an option either, even were he willing to face the Mistral. He couldn't work in the garden. He even grew weary of studying his fossils. The Domaine des Collines was suddenly his prison.

Inevitably, boredom and the incessant wind took their toll. The long latent melancholy within him rose darkly to the surface. He needed escape. Badly. And he found it.

Scotch.

He sat in his office staring out at the maelstrom, sipping Scotch from his coffee cup. Despite Ranny's coaxing he wouldn't leave for meals, or any other reason, including sleep. He wasn't the least unpleasant about it. He was simply adamant.

By the end of the first day he had consumed more than a bottle. As he kept several bottles in his sideboard he was in no risk of running dry. He would drink until he dozed off in his chair. When he awoke he began anew. Ranny was deeply concerned for him; and even a little frightened. There was no reasoning with him, or budging him. She'd seen him drink in the past. Always a happy, jovial inebriate. The dark, brooding man in David's office was a shadowy, frightening stranger.

The third day, around three in the morning, the screaming began.

Ranny burst into David's office. A dim gray figure staggered about the room in the darkness, bottle in hand, lamentably bedraggled, staring at the floor transfixed, in abject horror, shrieking like a banshee from hell.

My God he's gone insane.

"David. David! *David!*"

She stepped up and slapped him. Hard. Three times before he stopped. Then he simply stared blankly, no recognition or ration discernible in his eyes.

Could he have the DT's after only two days of this, or alcohol poisoning? Should I take him to the hospital? Can I get him to the hospital?

"David what's wrong with you?"

He continued to stare.

"David. *David!*"

He looked at her unseeing. "Did you see them?"

"Did I see *what* David? See *what?*"

"Were you down there?" he sobbed. "Did you see them? Were you down there?"

He began to weep uncontrollably. She'd never seen such a display of grief in another human. She had to control herself not to weep as well.

"I've never seen anything so hid ... hideou ... so horrib ... so ..."

He fell on his face like a giant tree felled by the Mistral. Ranny could see blood gushing from his nose.

She dragged him to his room and wrestled him into his bed. She then bandaged his nose and cleaned him up. He slept for eighteen hours. When he awoke Ranny had removed his bandage. He rose, hungry, in good spirits, remembering nothing. Power had been restored. Ranny made his breakfast as David showered and shaved. They never spoke of it. Ever.

The Mistral was over and Ranny shivered from an icy foreboding.

Fade Alpha

TWO YEARS AFTER the Woods settled into the Domaine, the first
of the murders occurred. At the time it was thought to be an anomaly.
Nothing of this nature had ever happened in Coirón's long history. In fact,
it was not initially deemed a homicide. Instead, they considered some sort
of berserk animal was responsible. When the atrocities began to assume
epidemic proportion however, local thinking required some material adap-
tation. Yet all the killings occurred within the same, relatively small area.
Beverly Hills. Which consists essentially of woodlands. This continued to
lend some degree of credence to the idea a non-human might be the killer.

There is an impressive range of wildlife indigenous to the Massif.
Deer, wild boar, lynx, fox, wolves, rabbit, squirrels, hedgehogs, turtles and
assorted reptiles, wolverine, purportedly even gray panther on extraordinary
occasion.

The Woods loved the croak of tiny, jade-green tree-frogs in early
evenings, the braying of fox at night, and the charming parade of wild boar
as they single-filed across their garden in the morning. Adults in the lead,
piglets following, snouts and tails arrow-straight, as they return to their lair,
after a night of wreaking havoc upon their garden. Periodically they would
find a boar swimming circles in their pool. Surprisingly, boars are exceedingly strong swimmers. Legend has it they even swim from the mainland to
Corsica. One hundred and twenty-eight nautical miles. Seemingly impossible. However, on several, documented occasions, fishermen and sailors
have encountered boars, swimming kilometers out at sea. Their heading:

Corsica. Only with great difficulty are they redirected, or captured and brought back to the mainland. Whatever the season, or the weather, there were always boars about the Domaine. Often they grow quite large. A full-grown male can weigh more than 90 kilos (200 pounds).

Their gardener, Giscard, had on several occasions suggested they put down poison to control the beasts. The Woods wouldn't hear of it. They loved the boars. Poisoning them was probably against the law and most probably would have no significant effect. So, the boars came as they pleased, and they stayed. Safe. Happy. Well fed. And their garden was constantly under repair, much to Giscard's frustration.

There was even talk of the European Brown Bear, which was never accorded much credulity. Therefore, there were really no creatures considered truly dangerous to man, much less capable of such a gruesome kill. Throat ferociously ripped out, massively efficient, savage and brutal.

The Woods were snug in bed now, staring into the darkness, trying to make sense of it all.

David smirked. "The old boys at the café are clucking about the *loup-garou.*"

"The what?"

"Werewolf. Ever heard of the La Bête du Gévaudan?"

"The what?"

"The Beast of Gevaudan?"

"No. Never."

"It's the most infamous case of purported lycanthropy in the history of France—probably the world, Hollywood notwithstanding. From 1764 to 1767, reported attacks ranged from 129 to 210. Deaths between 99 and 113. Many were partly consumed. Sexual assault was claimed. The vast majority of victims were women and children. Although some claim the creature was female. Throats torn out, dismemberment and so on. The King of France, Louis XV, even got involved. It was a real-life-mystery-horror and was never solved to anyone's satisfaction."

"Good grief David, how do you know so much about this?"

"I looked it up after the boys at the Cheval Blanc carried on so much." He continued. "Witnesses claimed the Beast was wolf-like, exhibiting behavior more human than animal. A well documented, factual case.

Something terrible did transpire. This much is proven and confirmed. Beast, human, or whatever, it was an amazing anthology of savagery and a documented, historical fact."

There was one disquieting fact favoring the loup-garou exponents: The town of Gevaudan is not far from Coirón. It lies to the northeast, midway between St. Paul de Vence and Draguignan.

Naturally such talk served only to exacerbate Coirón's unease. Particularly with the second incident. And then the next. And the next. And on and on. Coirón was clearly suffering from a deadly, serial virus. Holding David, Ranny peered into the darkness. "Jesus, this is scary stuff. Yet in a bizarre way it's almost fun. Like Halloween, or those old 1950's horror films, only real people are actually dying. How did you learn so much?"

"As I said, the old boys in town. Then I looked it up."

"You certainly don't hold any credence with all this werewolf foolishness, do you?"

"Don't be silly. Nor do I think some poor animal is responsible. There's someone murderous out there, stalking the Greenies. A stealth killer."

Ranny was suddenly cold. She wrapped herself in her blanket, and in David. They reviewed what they knew of the killings. Ranny did most of the talking. All the victims were females. All the murders (as the police now considered them) took place in 'Beverly Hills'. Pretentious estates. Horrific violence. Slaughter of the *Greenies* as David referred to them.

All save one occurred indoors. All the victims were murdered when the women were home alone. The killer passed all security systems, entering the premises without a trace, irrespective of lights, CCTV, alarms, dogs, or motion sensors. There was literally no record of the attack. These were ostensibly premeditated murders, but without discernable motive. The ease with which the killer passed all alarm systems seems more a function of almost preternatural skill, than craft. This was certainly not an animal. No thievery. No sexual violation. No commonality beyond primitive brute force. Throats simply ripped out. Fast and efficient, mindless and appallingly violent. Murders that smacked more of the abattoir than preternatural deranged assassins. Investigators expressed the feeling the crimes were somehow not targeted so much to inflict suffering or fear, or even death on the victim. They suspected they were contrived to kindle fear at the crime's periphery. Beverly Hills. Scare hell out of the rich, pretentious locals. There was no evidence for their feelings. None whatsoever. Nonetheless, the authorities were growing generally unanimous in their suspicion the killer's target was Beverly Hills itself. Also unsettling was the dearth of clues. No fingerprints, or bits of clothing, or semen, or DNA, or footprints, or blood, or flesh, or hair, or skin, beyond those of the victim. There was a massive claw wound. Nothing more. All the victims were women of roughly the same type. They shared common elements such as economic and marital status. Age groups and background were generally similar. Although unconfirmed, it was rumored the victims shared a reputation for promiscuity as well. This complicated things considerably. Each victim may have engendered any number of potential murderers. Arithmetically the odds of identifying a common paramour from the number of possible lovers (known and unknown) by the number of libidinous victims yielded a population of truly formidable proportion.

Although the murders appeared to be confined to Beverly Hills, the towns-people were understandably frightened. They were also highly upset about the effects on the local economy. The murders were splashed in the Paris papers and across France, Italy, Spain and the UK. Property values were suffering. Villa rentals were nonexistent. Tourism, what there was of it before the murders, was forecast to be depressed. Most painful of all, many villa owners were expected to stay away this year unless the killer was found quickly. Mayor Drôme was literally tearing his hair out, wondering what perverse god would visit such horror on Coirón. Especially when Bormes les Mimosas was so conveniently located, just up the D559. Of the many dire prognostications, only one failed to materialize. Tourism, predicted to be depressed, actually increased. Morbid curiosity proved to be an enticing allure to day-trippers and fun-seekers, thus those businesses catering to tourism prospered. In fact many capitalized on it, with lurid photos of werewolves and all manner of strange creatures purported to lurk about the region. Local, regional and national police were cooperating on the problem. Rumor had it Chief Inspector Alain Mohsen from Paris was en-route, if not already on site.

Chez André and Le Cheval Blanc buzzed with talk of the murders. Various nicknames had been coined. *La Bête de Coirón* [The Beast of Coirón]. *Le Monstre des Maures* [The Monster of the Moors]. *Le Meurtrier Mauresienne* [The Murderer of the Maures]. *Le Loup-Garou de Velleda* [Velleda's Werewolf]. *La Mort Rouge* [The Red Death]. And so on …

Fade Beta

RANNY WAS AT breakfast table surrounded by coffee, newspaper and correspondence. She was presently working the mail.

That's the problem with mail when you're virtually retired. It's goddamned boring. Bills, ads, taxes, the garage and … damn! … my inspection's due. What a pain in the …

"Mornin' Ran. Howyadoin'?" His best mock American accent.

"Just going through the blasted mail. Breakfast?"

"Sure."

She began making breakfast. "So this being Thursday I assume you're off fossilizing? Point des Arcs?"

"*Vallon*-Pont-d'Arc." he corrected. "And yes, I am meeting Marcel in a few hours."

"Mm."

"Problem?"

"No. Not really. My damned car needs inspection."

"Well that can certainly wait a few days."

"No. I think I'll get it done today. Maybe I'll go into Port Grimaud and meet Jeanette for lunch. Perhaps I'll even get you some more kippers while I'm there."

"Sounds like a plan."

They finished breakfast. David grabbed his gear, kissing Ranny on his way out. "See you tomorrow afternoon. Maybe we'll go out to dinner?"

"Sure."

"*Les Herbes Intrépides?*"

"Fine. I'll make the booking."

"Good. I'll call you tonight."

~~~~

An hour later Ranny was ten kilometers down the D559, pulling into an inspection station. The officious inspector grudgingly agreed to take her car without an appointment, although she noticed, mildly irritated, no other cars were in evidence.

"Your Carte Gris s'il vous plait Madame?" [Gray Card please Madame?]

"Ah yes. Just a moment." She returned to her car to fetch her registration. As she stretched across her seat opening the glovebox, a small rectangular package dropped to the floorboard.

"What the …" Staring at it in confusion, she realized this was the box David had rescued from the Post Box in the rain. They'd totally forgotten it.

Damn! Now I'll have to go to the post office. What was he thinking?

Happily there was a Bureau de Post just two kilometers from the inspection point. And so—when her car was officially sanctioned by the *République Française*—she continued on to the Post.

"Désolé [sorry] Madame. But there is no proper address with which I may accept this object for delivery, either to the *expéditeur* [sender] or the *destinaire* [addressee]. All we have is a commercial logo on the exterior of the package. As Switzerland is considered international mail, we have certain rules Madame."

This is getting stupid. I think I'll just throw the damned thing away. No that's wrong. Damnit David, the crap you get me in to. Okay. Okay, I'll get whatever this is developed. Then maybe we can figure what to do with it. But I really, really don't know why the hell I'm doing this.

Among its many other services, Le Cheval Blanc developed film. Ranny had returned to Coirón in far improved spirits after a long lunch with her friend Jeanette, so she magnanimously opted to drop the packet off for development.

"Mais oui Madame Woods, I can have this developed for you. But this is a Kodachrome boîte [box]. We must mail away for prints and it could be expensive."

"Jacques I really don't give a ... ah, that's fine Jacques, just order the prints."

"Très bien." He handed her a slip of paper. "Your reçu [receipt] Madame. Your prints will be ready in one or two weeks."

~~~~

It was actually three weeks before the prints were picked up and paid for. And it was David who completed the transaction while having drinks with the 'old boys' at the Cheval Blanc.

"Monsieur Woods, your prints have been ready for a week."

"Prints?"

"Yes. Your wife brought them in. Would you care to collect them?"

"Sure. How much do I owe you?"

As he entered his home, David was enveloped by a dizzying aroma. An intoxicating fog, redolent with burgundy wine, *bouquet garni*, garlic and sautéed onions, fortified with the hearty aroma of seared beef. Yankee pot roast! He knew there would be roasted potatoes, carrots simmered in the sauce and fresh baby green peas swimming in butter. Some of the finest of American cuisine.

... and there I was swilling beer at the Cheval Blanc. I ought to be ...

"Is that pot roast I smell, Ran?"

He arrived to a welcoming kiss and a warm hug. He looked at her quizzically pleased.

"I decided I liked you today. And I wanted to show Hélène Americans know how to simmer a chuck roast."

Chuck Roast? Roast Chuck? Who or what is Chuck? Must be another American thing.

"Do we have time for a drink?"

"Lots of time."

"G&T's by the pool?"

"I'll be out in ten minutes."

"Good. I'll make the drinks. Oh by the way, I picked up your photos from Aunt Carol's visit. They're on the coffee table."

Ran frowned down at the simmering meat. "I took no pictures while Carol was here."

"Okay. June or Aunt Debra."

"Neither of them either. What are you talking about?"

"Jacques at the Le Cheval Blanc said you dropped them off a while ago."

"Oh Christ. It's those stupid ... how much were they anyway?"

David was in the adjoining bar making drinks.

"Say again?"

"The photos. How much?"

"I'm not really sure actually. I paid for everything at the same time."

"Everything?"

"What?"

"You paid for what?"

"Oh. Drinks, batteries, a lottery ticket and ..."

"Never mind dear."

"What?"

"I'll be right out dear."

David was well into his first tall Gin and Tonic, sparkling golden in the setting sun. He'd been staring down at a small fossil he spotted in the gravel, when he realized it must have dropped from his pocket.

Pretty little thing. Oh, it's the cephalopod I found in ...

"David."

The harsh, determined tone of her voice commanded his immediate attention. He briskly leant forward, heedlessly dropping the fossil again.

He hadn't noticed her approach. She was now standing above him, a radiant backlit profile in the setting sun's glare. Insofar as he could make out, she had an odd expression on her face.

"What?"

"Look at these." She threw a stack of photographs on the wrought-iron table, next to his drink.

Frowning at Ranny, he picked up the photos. As he shuffled through the prints he made a running commentary. "Pictures of the Domaine, of you. Looks to have been taken from the outside ... some at night. The lights are on ... from various windows ... over a period of time. Here's one taken from the interior atrium. These are pretty good. Where'd they come from?"

Ran was staring at him hard. She was trembling. "Those are the prints from the package you rescued from atop the Post Box in the rain."

David clearly did not remember. "Post Box in the rain?"

"*Damnit* David. *Sharrandqual-Wednesday!*"

Understanding dawned.

David was stunned. "Shadow fade ..." he murmured. They were both silent for some minutes. She threw down her drink in two long pulls and David was nearly as fast with the remainder of his. He rose wordlessly, taking the two empty glasses for refills.

When he returned, he hoarsely forced out a single word. "Police."

"What?"

He cleared his throat. "We must call the police. *Now.*"

"What are you saying David?"

"I'm saying you may be in danger. Whoever took those photos could be dangerous."

"You think this is the work of some Peeping-Tom?"

His voice became distinct and calm. "No Ran. I'm worried this could be *The Beast.*"

"Oh God David, you're serious?"

"Yes. But I'm far from sure dear. I'm only speculating." He heaved a noiseless sigh. "Let's just sit down. Relax. Enjoy our drinks and rationally analyze this. Okay?"

"Okay." She moved to the chair opposite David's, her mood already brightening. "So where do we start?" As with Sherlock Holmes, she clearly felt the thrill of a 'game afoot.'

"Well, let's first try to understand how those goddamned photos landed on the Post Box in the rain."

"Fine. Any ideas?"

"Not a damned one. But I'll make it up as I go along. Whoever it was may have been terribly pressed for time ... getting panicky ... tried to mail the package ... but the police (or someone) was getting nearer and it wouldn't fit in the Post Box ... he couldn't be caught with the package ... but didn't want to lose it ... so left it on the box hoping to either return, or the postman would pick it up and mail it for him."

"Right David. But you're missing a few points."

"Such as?"

"Such as, after taking the pictures, he committed them to the development media discs, assuming he didn't record directly to the discs, then he methodically put them in the wrapper, addressed everything, and applied postage? See what I mean? Your assumption of panic is spurious. It just doesn't hold up. And why would anyone be panicky about carrying an innocuous little brown box? He may have been totally calm, a nice day, and just left the damned thing for the postman."

"Nicely reasoned Ran. So we know ... nothing."

"Exact. Except for one thing."

"Yes?"

"Its seems clear to me he is insane."

"Twisted certainly. But we cannot be sure he's insane. Neither do we know *it's* a '*he*'."

"Agreed. But if we're considering The Beast of Coirón, do you think a woman is physically capable of such horrendous attacks?"

"I've known a few in my time ..."

"Be serious David."

"I am being serious. And I'm calling the police."

Fade Gamma

THE POLICE IN Coirón had been long notified. Officer Kontz had filed a cursory report more than three weeks ago, which he handled with indifferent interest and the most indifferent follow-up. David saw little else he could do, so soon the bizarre shadow-fade-photo incident faded into lethargic obscurity.

~~~~

David answered the phone in his office.

"Allo?" [Hello?]

"David mon ami ..." [my friend] Marcel sounded excited.

"Yes. Marcel?"

"I must tell you about a most excellent opportunity here on the river Ibie."

"Yes?"

"We have just passed a rare period beginning with flooding rains and severe droughts. The result is fluvial forces have stripped the Ibie's bend and reach banks of topsoil and debris. Now the river has lowered sufficiently to cleanly expose some extremely rich Cretaceous deposits. The fossil hunting should be formidable until the river rises again. I want to hunt it myself, but my wife insists we visit her mother. She is quite ill apparently. But this is such a unique circumstance which will not last long ..."

"Understood Marcel. I'll drop by your shop when I get to Pont-d'Arc. If you're not there, I'll go on alone. Merci Marcel. Et j'espère, à bientôt." [And I hope to see you soon.]

Weather conditions would inevitably change and the window of opportunity would close. Rains were already meandering to the south. Understandably, David was driven to take advantage of these unique conditions.

Ranny reassured David she could take care of herself. After all it had been weeks since the photos were found. There were guns and rifles in the Domain and she was an expert in their use. In fact she was far more skilled than David. She would be fine. They couldn't be prisoners of fear indefinitely. They couldn't cloister themselves in the Domaine.

They decided David should go.

David notified Adam.

Adam assured David he would keep an eye on things from time to time.

Despite his disquiet, David decided to go to Pont-d'Arc. To search out creatures 140 million years past, while his loved-one lived in harm's way, in the jarring reality of the present.

David was vaguely aware how potentially irresponsible he was acting. Yet he seemed incapable of controlling his actions, or Ran's, or Adam's. Some element was in play, which seemed to render them impotent to rouse themselves to take control over events.

David was master of his time, but not his fate, nor his emotions, nor his marriage. And an alien mist was stealthfully accreting between David and Ranny. The murky specter of Adam. They seldom laughed any more. Or made love. Shared intimacies. Or trusted.

~~~~

Although she would stridently reject such assertion, in truth Ranny was greatly conflicted about David's trip as well. She secretly feared to be alone. Yet she very much wanted time to herself. She was relieved to be rid of David. Yet she was hurt he would desert her when danger could be lurking nearby.

She was frustrated at her fear. She was more than capable of defending herself, more so than David. Yet she wanted his love and protection.

Adam would undoubtedly come calling. He was a beloved fixture now. He would bring security. And she was unconsciously aroused at the prospect. Yet she wanted Adam to stay away.

And so it went. Uncertainties. Desires, fantasies, temptations and trepidations.

~~~~

Blond, pretty, young. An outsized angora sweater hung loosely about her, provocatively revealing enthralling breasts whenever she leant down—which she did often, and well. She was literally dripping with jewelry, down to a heavy gold chain masquerading as a belt, allegedly holding up skin-tight, black leather pants, culminating in bright red stiletto heels. Were not her clothes clearly expensive she could be mistaken for *une femme de joie.* [working girl] She was nestled close to a tanned, good looking man who had been seated alone at the bar talking quietly with Paul Bell until she'd affixed herself.

He was looking her in the eye, smiling, speaking intimately, despite Paul's waggling ears and his fruitless efforts to appear otherwise occupied.

"So … your name is Erica. You're an American. You've just renovated a huge villa in the hills, and your husband is ferrying your new yacht in from the UK."

She giggled childishly, running her hand down his thigh. "You got everything right! You're so *clever.* What's your name?"

He smiled. "Charley. That's C-H-A-R-L-E-Y."

"Nice name. What do you do Charley?"

"Oh, I come and go."

Her eyelids fluttered flirtatiously. "I like your accent. I like it a lot. British?"

"Born and bred, Erica."

"Do you have a car Charley?"

"In fact I'm without car tonight."

"I have one."

"How nice for you."

"It's red."

"Better still."

"A Lam ... Lamber ... Lamborg ..."

"Lamborghini?"

"Right! Wanna go for a ride?" Her hand was firmly parked on his thigh now.

"Ah. But it's such fun here. Where would we go?"

She lowered her head, speaking in a low voice, almost a whisper. "My place."

"And what about your husband." He whispered back playfully.

"Aw, I told you, he's still on his damned boat. He won't get in for two more days. Besides you look like lots more fun. So, you wanna play? You'll be glad you did. Worth your while, if you know what I mean." She grinned suggestively.

He intently peered into her eyes. Then he straightened and smiled, a cynical, steely leer.

"How could I refuse?" He placed money on the bar. "Let's go play."

As he approached the bar's doorway, Charley smoothly reached down to the stand and plucked an umbrella-like walking-stick, holding it by its ornate brass handle, swinging it jauntily, clicking away on the pavement every other step.

Erica looked at his stick, head cocked questioningly. "An umbrella this time of year?"

He glanced at her smiling. "More of a walking-stick really. I'm afraid it's a bit of an affectation."

"Mm. I don't believe it suits you. You don't strike me as an affected man."

Maybe she's not such a dumb little tramp after-all. Perhaps she's simply drunk and bored and spoiled and rich.

As they found the car, she smartly threw him the keys. "Here. You drive. I want to get to know you better."

He hesitantly unlocked the car and cranked up the big engine with an impressively throaty rumble.

"You'll have to tell me how to get there."

She thought he seemed a little distant. Not as fun as in the bar. Well, she'd soon cheer him up.

"Do you know the D559?"

"Yes."

"Good. Go to the 559 and I'll tell you where to turn. Just before Coirón. Mm, I'll be a little busy." She giggled coquettishly. "But I'll come up for air once in a while."

Thankfully she relented until they were well out of town before she got 'a little busy.' The roads had turned misty and dark, and driving the powerful sports car was exacting. She unzipped him and busied herself exposing him, caressing him, and taking him between her lips, into her moist warmth.

Cheap little tramp. She's just like the others. She's nothing like ... nothing like ... nothing like who? Who? She's ... she's nothing like ... like ... Ranny! My God, Ranny. Ranny.

For a moment it was as if he had suddenly awakened from a nightmare. Only to fall asleep once again.

They were now on the D559. Dark. Deserted. Woody. The mist became more a fog as the warm sea air contested with cool land breezes from the Maures.

Erica eagerly applied her considerable skills for minutes with disappointingly little reaction. Erica straightened, pursing and languidly licking her lips. "Charley? You don't like this?"

Until now Erica's attentions had been no more than an irritation. Now his irritation was swiftly advancing into a raging hatred.

The horny little slut thinks she can do whatever she wants with my body. Wait till she sees what I can do to her body.

"Charley?" she whined.

"Ah, yeah. Sure. I like it a lot, it feels great, but it's difficult to drive at the same time." His voice took on a sly, threatening tone. "Probably dangerous as well."

"You queer or something? If you are, that's okay. Maybe we can get another guy, or whatever you like. But don't waste my time, or my money."

That's it!

He slammed on the brakes throwing her hard into the dashboard—
pulled to the side of the road—threw open his door—walked quickly to her
door, throwing it open as well—dragging her roughly out by her arm. When
she was clear of the car, he tossed her to the ground. He had contrived to
have his 'umbrella' in hand, which he leaned against his leg, regarding her
disdainfully, as he slowly zipped up his trousers.

"What the fuck do you think you're doing you faggoty bastard? Do
you know who my husband is?" She shook with anger, spitting her words
vehemently.

"Don't know. Don't care. Shut the fuck up bitch." He upended his
'umbrella' and held it by its pointed end. There was just enough light to
gleam on the large scythe-like handle, jeweled eyes glowing, talons glittering.
His aspect was that of a giant praying mantis, extending its claw for the kill.
Erica felt the icy prickle of fear rising in her belly, growing, freezing her
viscera and robbing her of breath.

She was instantly sober. Her mouth was suddenly dry. Her lips caught
on her teeth and speech was growing difficult. "Look Charley. I uh … I
don't know what the problem is. I like you." She paused to wet her lips and
attempt to swallow. "I don't know what went wrong. I'm sorry about what
I said. Let's just forget about it okay? I'll drive you anywhere you want to
go, and then I'll just go home. Not a word to anyone." Her voice childlike,
she mewed "Okay Charley? *Charley?*"

He advanced on her silently and relentlessly. A cowl-less Grim Reaper
drifting, floating through the cloying mist. He held the scythe in his right
hand, pointed to the ground, slightly to his rear. Ready for use. Preparing
for a careful aim and a deadly *coup de grace*. Erica was lost in the throes of
blind panic now. She wept and whimpered. Drool escaped her lips. "No
Charley. Don't do this. *Please.*" Her voice rose and quivered. Her eyes
implored, as tears streaked her cheeks. "Why? Why Charley? *Please Charley!*"

They always ask why he sardonically mused. *What they really mean is 'why
me.'*

Wiping her chin and licking her lips, trembling with fear, she desperately tried again. "Charley. I'm your friend. D-don't do this. I won't hurt
you. I won't tell anyone. You can trust me Charley. Look Charley, I run

from problems. Maybe like you. Not tonight Charley … Charley I'm not running now!"

Charley suddenly stopped. He seemed catatonic. Unmoving. Unspeaking.

"Charley?"

A cruel spark of hope kindled in Erica's mind, the icy, jeering torture of brief respite in the face of inevitable death. She feared to speak. She feared to remain silent. She feared to run. She feared to stay or move in the slightest. Or even breathe. So she *froze*, as a rabbit transfixed by the horror and death coiled in the mesmerizing icy eyes of the cobra.

Two statues, one recumbent, one standing. Both suspended, eerily quiet in the vaporous darkness. Each fixed in their own forlorn purgatory. For Erica it seemed to go on endlessly. Her fear slowly began to fade. As did her hope. She succumbed to numbing, overpowering resignation. Life or death. Either was preferable to this forever hell.

A truck roared by. It ruffled Charley's hair in its passing, and billowed his shirt. The unexpected gust roused Erica somewhat. Charley appeared to awaken as well. He cocked his head, looking down, reptilian and unseeing, upon Erica.

This man is insane. He's really going to kill me. What's holding him back? Oh God, this can't go on and on. Get it over with you bastard!

Finally his eyes focused on her. A glint of recognition.

"I'm dying Erica."

"What?" She whispered in disbelief. These were the last words she expected to hear.

"We pass through many dark places on our march towards death. This is the darkest. Right here. Now. This moment. Tonight. I'm sorry I forced you to share this with me. You are safe now Erica."

Fear—The Mother of Courage

HER HEART POUNDED with renewed hope.

"I died once before. Many years ago. I was just a child. Not an innocent or playful child. Not at all. I was *happy* to die. I faded into gentle arms and loving eyes. I was so happy to go …

"Tonight though, I am really frightened. Terribly. I know death is best now. The only solution really. But I don't know why I returned, or what monstrous force brought me forth again. But it did, against my will. I've been living in hell itself ever since. Now, I must die yet again. Mercy does not exist in this world. Not for me. Not for Charley. Oh God I'm scared."

Somewhere in her mind that still functioned, Erica was reminded of watching huge buildings and monuments crumble and fall through time-lapse photography. Charley was quite literally falling apart, in exactly the same way, right before her eyes.

He seemed to freeze again.

Erica was quietly weeping now.

She found her voice and her courage. "Are you really dying Charley?"

"Yes. Soon. Now. Charley is fading as we speak. He feels it and he is terrified of the darkness."

"Can I help you Charley? What can I do?"

"Nothing … no. Yes." He turned to her. "There is a thing …" He sounded dreamy, wistful. She could see the trails of tears tracing his cheeks and chin and neck.

"Yes?" Her voice was very soft almost inaudible.

"Erica was to die this night. She knows?"

"Yes Charley."

Why is he speaking to me in the third person?

"Erica is young and lovely and most important, alive. Erica would have us believe she is nothing but a superficial, rich, over-sexed brat. But Charley knows beneath all the make-up and slutty clothes, Erica is not like that at all. She may have fallen into degradation and baseness, but she will rise again ... and find grace."

She neither agreed, nor objected. Her fear had faded. She simply studied him as closely through the gloom. The damp grass was growing cold and disagreeable. Yet she took some comfort from the realization she could suddenly be aware of such detail. Hopefully it signaled her ordeal was nearing its end?

It began to rain softly.

"Erica's shabby charade must end. She must shed her corrupt facade. A dying man understands the tragedy of a squandered life. Charley understands that. Erica will live. Erica will save herself. And Erica will never again torment poor, sad Charleys."

It took her some moments to truly understand his words.

"Alright Charley." Her voice was clear now.

Through the dimness, she thought she could see the shadow of a smile.

"Don't let Charley down Erica. Charley *could* return again ..."

She found his remark a poor joke and an unworthy farewell. Still she remained deeply saddened for him.

"Good-bye Erica."

~~~~

Charley turned away, a fading specter into the dark and the mist. He cast the murderous scythe aside, whispering softly to it "*Adiós el Pequeño, le faltaré.*" [Es. Goodbye little one, I will miss you.]

Erica collapsed, prostrate on the soggy ground, shivering. She quavered and wept for long minutes. She was desperately aware she should flee. But somehow she couldn't find the strength, or presence of mind to act.

Finally she lurched unsteadily across the slippery grass to her car. She pushed the starter and was soon negotiating her way home, struggling to navigate through the murky night and her tears.

September Morn

A LARGE TRUCK rumbled by. Breathtakingly close. So close he was sprayed with the icy slurry of water and gravel spewed by its huge tires spawning a faux morning wind. He awoke with a start.

He was wet, stiff, freezing, dirty, and had no idea where he was. This was becoming a tedious theme in his life. A tiresome litany. Yet, this morning it did not trouble him as he looked about.

It's morning. How did I get here? Where is my car? Was there an accident?

He inspected himself for injuries. He was rumpled, wet and dirty. A shower and a shave would be great improvements. But there was no noticeable damage.

Did I get drunk last night? Must've been one hellofa blowout. Where am I? In the woods? No. Roadside. The D559 I think. Outside Coirón. Damn I'm hungry. I'd kill for a coffee and cognac. It must be about a fifteen minute walk to Le Cheval Blanc.

Then it dawned on him.

Oh, I see. It's happened again. I blacked out and I, I went somewhere else.

He ached. He was exhausted. Dehydrated and ravenous. Confused and disoriented. But he felt ... good. Better than he had in months. Younger, lighter, stronger and free. And he felt something else. Innocence. As innocent as a guileless child playing in the sun on the vernal morn of an incipient world. He smiled, eyes squinting into the giant, brilliant, rising sun.

With some wobbly effort, he stood. Once standing, he gingerly tested his stability and balance and found neither materially wanting. He carefully peered up and down the gleaming highway, wispy with mist, gleaming with dew in the golden morning sun. He reviewed his situation. No car. Nothing to indicate how he got here. Not a thing. Not a problem. Overcoming his stiffness, he checked his pockets for money. There was certainly enough for breakfast and a cognac. He turned towards the village, whistling softly, hands in pockets. Tired, hungry and happy.

A damp and rumpled Dickensian caricature striking out bravely and brightly in quest of breakfast.

~~~~

Friday morning dawned pristine and new.

Ranny felt an exciting flush of adventure. Danger. Mystery. The fleshy threshold portending the calamity of temptation. Such delightful risks. Such delightful rewards.

Sex. The succulent art. The obsession of humans. The source of joy and frenzied, needy anxiety. Our legacy from four hundred million years removed.

The compulsion to procreate—to immerse in the sensual pleasure of it—to struggle, sometimes until death to win such requite. The stuff of love and hatred and violence. Sadly, we seem unable to shed the priggish canons of our forebears and simply relish in the delight of it, uninhibited by jealousy, or guilt, possessiveness, hypocrisy, or social diminution.

All these things and more heated Ranny's blood as she pondered Adam's arrival. She knew her feelings would be adjudged unworthy and infidel, but she was simply unable to care. Such is the human obsession with love and desire. The need to need. The urge to urge. The love of love. Lusting after lust. Flesh craving flesh. Spirits testing the limits and seeking the precipice.

Of all this, she was dizzyingly, concupiscently aware. Her secret passion whispered of her lamentable control, as powerless as the tides over the moon, futilely struggling to master her thirsty exigency.

Lust. The itchy, beguiling haze which ebbs from toe to throat, inundating reason, restraint and faith. The enthralling narcotic, demanding many things and taking much, returning rutting pain and sublime pleasure, breathtaking and lush.

Adam fevered with the same virus.

He cherished the fantasy of finding an intimacy he'd never known, and thrilled at its promise.

Despite his personable good looks, wealth and flamboyancy, he was hardly able to relate to women beyond lighthearted flirtations. He was routinely approached by women, their intent unmistakable. Most were charming and quite attractive. But for some reason, their overtures aroused in him only barely concealed asperity. This was a troubling source of bemusement to the ladies, and to Adam himself.

He wondered if he favored men. He even ventured a brief dabble, and found his feelings were no different than his intense animus for women.

Something about sexual intimacy awoke a bristling resentment in him he could do nothing to suppress, whatever gender. Frustration and loneliness became his incessant companion.

He resigned himself to an ascetic life of abstinent isolation. Accordingly he'd passed much of his strange life in remote locations pursuing his career as a marine biologist. Pole to pole. Continent to continent.

When his parents were killed in a senseless traffic accident he was profoundly grief-stricken. Upon returning to Wallingford to look after their affairs, to his great surprise he found they had left him a considerable inheritance. After some soul-searching, he made a decision.

He returned to university.

Building upon his PhD in Marine Biology, he reemerged surprisingly fast as a veterinarian as well (MRCVS, PhD, DVM). Whereupon he launched himself into a new, two-pronged career, studying, and now caring for creatures in and around Earth's seas.

Within three years he had gained considerable expertise and an impressive reputation. He had published four papers and was sought out as guest lecturer at several universities. Soon though, to his chagrin, he found he was trapped in a web of resistance and resentment from his colleagues. His youth, good looks, prominence, wealth and education had become a source of an intense jealousy he had not foreseen.

Not a problem. The solution came to him immediately.

Adam's projects were funded by University grants and directly by two or three biotech corporations. Thanks to technology, none were concerned where he worked, allowing him unfettered mobility. So he moved to the south of France, purchased the home of his dreams, and the sailboat he had yearned for all his life. He would pursue his research and look after his marine creatures in relative luxury and sublime contentment, independent and alone. He might even take a stab at a textbook. With two doctorates and experience all over the world, he felt he was well qualified to face the future he had planned.

Despite his many colleagues, fellow sailors, regattas and cocktail parties, Adam's isolation was now nearly absolute.

Then came Ranny. The evening they met, she connected with something in him. Her intelligence, her acerbic wit, her crusty resilience and her beauty engaged his respect and his affection. He saw deeper as well. He saw her vulnerability. Deeper beneath the aplomb lurked a gentleness and basic goodness. Fundamental decency—the most intoxicating aphrodisiac.

Was he smitten? In love? Randy? He couldn't judge. Every fresh new feeling was a wonder. He only knew he cared for her, liked her, respected her and was excited at the prospect of seeing her, for the first time in his life. For now at least, the prospects of guilt and betrayal were a remote blindness in his mind.

~~~~

"Hello?"

"Adam?"

"Yes ... *Ranny*?" a coursing thrill, immediate and powerful.

"Yes. Have you heard there may have been another murder?"

"No. Where?"

"About five kilometers from here."

"Damn. When?"

"Last night."

"Same type?"

"I suppose so."

"Are you alright?"

"I've been better."

"Christ. When are these women going to learn they shouldn't be alone up there?"

"*I'm* alone up here Adam."

"Where's Dave?"

"Actually, that's why I'm calling. David's been fossilizing in Vallon-Pont-d'Arc the last few days."

"He's not back *yet*?"

"No. And his mobile phone is apparently out of range. I can't contact him."

"Have you tried his hotel?"

"Of course. He's not been there. But he carries camping gear. I wanted to try his friend Marcel, but I can't find his number in any of David's files. Do you have it by any chance?"

"No. I do know whom you mean though. But I haven't his number. Have you tried looking it up?"

"I was just getting ready to try, but I couldn't remember his full name."

"Oh that's easy. It's Marcel Briançon. That would be spelled B-R-I-A-N-C (cedilla)-O-N. Dave says he's got a fossil shop up there."

"Yes. I remember. Do you know the name of the shop?"

"In fact I do. David goes on and on about it. Says we must go there one day and see all the great stuff he's got."

"Yes?"

"Yes what Ranny?"

"Yes ... what's the name?"

"Oh, right. It's Marcel Briançon et Fils [& Sons]."

"Great. Thank you Adam."

"No problem. Say, how 'bout if I drop over for a drink later on? Maybe I could bring some Chinese? I think you could use some company."

"Aah. That would be very nice Adam. But not Chinese. I was thinking of making fried chicken. I need some comfort food."

"Real *suuuthern* fried chicken?" he drawled in a clumsy parody of an American southern accent.

"That's right Adam."

"Sounds wonderful. Can I bring something?"

"Only your thirst and your appetite."

"Great. What time?"

"Oh, say around five. Drinks poolside?"

"Sure. I'll bring my bathing trunks."

"Yeah Adam, and bring your swimming suit too."

Adam laughed lightly. He'd played this game before. "See you soon."

Fade Delta

VALLON-PONT-D'ARC IS A community in the Ardèche department of southwestern France. It is the regional hub of archeological and paleontological exploration. Cro-Magnon Man painted the walls of its caves thirty thousand years ago. Mollusks swam the shallow seas that blanketed these lands, two hundred million years before man's descent from the trees.

This small village, near comatose in winter, sees its population multiply nearly twelvefold in season. Its fame derives from Vallon's position at the summit of the Ardèche River's descent through the Ardèche Canyon (from *Pont d'Arc* to *Saint-Martin-d'Ardeche*).

Vallon-Pont-d'Arc is the site of one of the most dramatic natural marvels of France: Les gorges de l'Ardèche [the Ardèche gorge] and the world-famous Pont d'Arc [the Arc Bridge], a huge natural stone arch some 60 meters wide (180 feet) and 40 meters high (120 ft), carved out of native bedrock over eons by the Ardèche River.

South of the village, the river Ibie flows into the Ardèche, which forms the commune's southwestern border. It is here David finds the richest fossil deposits.

David stopped by Marcel's shop. Locked up tight. So he moved on to the site. Soon he was happily squishing through chilly, rushing waters nearly up to his waist, pulling feet from sucking mud, stumbling clumsily over slippery stones and boulders. Fortunately he'd had the foresight to bring his waders. For many months he'd worked the cliff-sides on either side of the river, which were normally nominal hunting. However, the uncommon cycle of hard rains, followed by hot, extended drought had repeated for several weeks. The result was a rich Pleistocene bounty. The reach banks had been eroded down to bedrock and shale ... and a wealth of cleanly exposed fossils, many excellently preserved. An entire riverbank, normally submerged, hard washed, now suddenly exposed. Millions of years of Earth's adolescence were suddenly vulnerable to his intimate probe. The river would assume normal levels soon; and the fossils would once again be inaccessible, awash beneath the cool waters of the Ibie.

After Marcel had alerted David of this unique opportunity he couldn't resist. Away from the uncertainties at home it was wonderful to find himself in the sunshine and fresh air, far from other humans, doing what he enjoyed most. He contentedly worked his way down the river, concentrating his efforts on the bend and reach banks. He was even whistling.

When the sun was high, he stopped for a sandwich and a drink, resting on a huge boulder midstream. Afterwards he relaxed on the warm stone, peering up into the cloudless sky, when he noticed an interesting protrusion approximately halfway up the opposite cliff-line. It appeared to be an interestingly shaped white stone extruding from the native slate, just above a ledge comprised of the same dark, weathered lamina.

Some sort of Theropod? I doubt it. The big stuff is very rare around here. All the same it could be a large Ammonite, or, judging from the height of the strata, perhaps something much younger, maybe the Cenozoic. Might be interesting. Probably it's nothing. All the same, there's something suggestive about it. What the hell, I'll take a look.

He sloshed across to the opposite bank and scrambled up. He removed his pack, his waders and most of his gear, dawning his boots, leaving him only a belt with hammer, chisel and brush. He commenced climbing the cliff. Climbing was difficult. Soil and sharp shale rocks in a loose, crumbly matrix. Two steps up. Half a step back. Tedious going. As the cliff grew more perpendicular it became all the more difficult. At about ten meters David realized this was a no-go. The ledge was now only two meters above him. But he had no idea how to bridge the gap. It hadn't looked quite this vertical from below. Plus he was growing hot and very tired. And he was growing a little nervous. He gave it up and began his descent, resolved to return one day to rappel down from above.

I think I should move to the left. More stones, less dirt. And it levels out more gradually at the … SHIT! …

Seconds later he found himself prostrate at the foot of the cliff atop a mercifully soft grassy hummock, covered in pebbles and dirt. He'd been out for a few seconds and he lay still for a time trying to determine if he was injured. His legs hurt, as did his left hand and his head ached, but none seemed serious. Generally he seemed in good condition, so he began to climb to his feet, only to find himself again prostrate on the grass, groaning in pain. A quick appraisal told him his left leg had been shredded by the spiky cliff-line, and his right leg was cocked beneath him now at a disturbingly unnatural angle. There was a sharp section of bone protruding from his trousers.

Agh! Christ! A goddamned compound fracture. Crap.

He forced himself to remain calm. He realized he was as angry as he was fearful. How *stupid*. He'd seen the cliff was unstable. Somehow he'd known it was not climbable. Why had he attempted something so foolish? And alone no less! He rolled over and gingerly rested his head on his right arm staring up at the sky. Taking inventory of his situation. It didn't look promising.

There's no one for miles. But Marcel knows where I am. When I'm missed they'll contact him and he'll find me. It could be two or three days though. Although, kayakers come through here all the time. It gets pretty cold here at night. I wonder what kind of beasties prowl around here in the dark? My phone's in my backpack and doesn't it work out here anyway. There's one sandwich left, another soda and matches, also in the backpack. Got a river full of fresh water. No med-kit, but some aspirin. No flares. No wood for a splint, or a crutch, or a fire. No nothing … wish I had a good book and a bottle of Scotch.

The Paris-Coirón Express

THE LITTLE MAN was exhausted. He'd just driven nine hours from the center of Paris to the center of Coirón, after an early and difficult morning studying a singularly grotesque murder of two prostitutes in the Bois de Boulogne.

He was short, compact and stood arrow-straight. A posture beaten into him during an arduous, six-year, ill-conceived, overly-romanticized, pissed-off-at-his-father enlistment as an officer in the Légion Étrangère. The French Foreign Legion. Yes. The Foreign Legion. Still one of the toughest military units pounding ground on the planet. Courageous, optionally anonymous, outrageous, dangerous and onerous. The stuff of legend and bravery and cowardice and pride and shame. The experience had a profound and hardening effect on the man. He learned to value life and the courage to protect it. The result was an exceptional police officer.

In younger years he'd been fit and well built, with the good looks, piercing hazel eyes, dark skin and raven hair indicative of the peoples generally referred to as either the Acadians [French: *Acadiens*], or Creole [French: *Créole*]. Of recent, his jet-black hair had bloomed salt and pepper, emphasized by a dignified graying at the temples. Reading glasses were no longer optional, and he trod the streets of Paris a good deal more slowly.

He was Chief Criminal Investigator Alain Mohsen of the DCPJ (*Direction Centrale de la Police Judiciaire*). The DCPJ is the national authority over the criminal divisions of the French National Police, formerly the *La Sûreté Nationale*. It is the primary authority over the actions of the two law enforcement agencies (the *Police Nationale* and the *Gendarmerie Nationale*) regarding any major criminal activity.

Mohsen was on temporary assignment to put an end to the horrific murders plaguing the western Côte for months, and not a bit happy about it. He had enough problems in Paris without this *loup-garou* foolishness. Why couldn't the officials in Nice, or Cannes, or St. Tropez, or Marseilles handle this? He'd been told he was thusly assigned because they seemed at a loss and he was generally regarded as indisputably 'the best.'

A little tired, a little shopworn, a little disillusioned, but in the past— and perhaps even now—the best. In fact, he really was the best in earlier days. Once acknowledged the finest officer in the Sûreté, now the DCPJ, and possibly all of France. His incisive style was now tempered with sensitivity, thoroughness, method … and fatigue.

He carried no gun, but remained a crack shot. He kept a 9mm Saur in his briefcase, with four reload clips, which he had never drawn in the line of duty. He'd never roughed up a suspect and seldom exchanged even cross words with them. In fact he took pains to maintain relaxed, respectful, easy relations with suspects and witnesses alike, finding the tactic the most rational and practical course to the truth.

He was happily married. Honest to a fault. Drank only wine, in moderation. Wouldn't dream of touching a drug or another woman. There was nothing unorthodox about the man whatsoever. No colorful, endearing quirks. A sort of diminutive Gregory Peck. Solid. Stolid. Smart. Steadfast. Beloved and respected by family, friends, subordinates, peers and superiors throughout a long career. He was thorough, intelligent, imaginative and dogged. He really knew his business. A world-class pro. What Americans would call a real 'no-bullshit cop.'

He was also a pragmatist. He assumed the Ministry had assigned him because they needed cover. Proof they were doing their job. They would therefore ostensibly gave their best begotten to this problem. If he failed, *he* would be their aging dupe. If he succeeded, *they* would be the sage and responsible guardians of France. A tediously shopworn scenario; and in fact he was wrong.

Meanwhile, all his cases in Paris would grow older and colder. Truly a lose-lose proposition from his perspective. Were he not sensitive about his age, he would have recognized the truth. He'd been assigned the case, not despite his age, or to cast him as scapegoat, but because of his age. His experienced, plodding, methodical pace. A patient, dogged persistence was called for where serial killers were concerned.

His wife, Katherine, petite, sparklingly pretty, graceful, with an under-stated sophistication. An art *les femmes Française* [French ladies] excelled at. Her devotion to Alain was total. They met in the southeastern town of Montelimar. She was an art student. He was a captivating young *Aspirant* [Officer Cadet] in *l'Académie de la Légion Étrangère* [Foreign Legionnaire Officer's Candidate School]. He looked like an emerging movie star, right off the set of *Beau Geste*. She was an impressionist's dream.

Despite years of difficult assignments, frequent separations and nox-ious postings, their love remained steadfast. She was six years his younger and pre-maturely gray—primarily attributable to years of worry over his dangerous work and ever-advancing despondency.

Too many years of trolling *les égouts et les ruelle sordides* [sewers and back alleys] of Paris had rendered him cynical, tired, aging, demoralized and sad-dened. In short, he suffered from what the Germans term *Weltschmerz* [world-pain or world-weariness]. Retirement beckoned—more so all the time.

Tonight he was exhausted and wanted only to know where he was to be lodged, as he wearily held himself erect against the cheap plywood counter under the garish lights of Coirón's depressingly tiny, squalid Gendarmerie, while the *rustre local* [local yokels] officiously welcomed, briefed and generally obsequioused him.

He had made the grave tactical error of agreeing to alert the Mayor when he passed Hyères, allowing them nearly an hour to finish dining, or drinking, or both, in time to prepare and assemble for his arrival. Accord-ingly, the dizzying fog of garlic, cigarettes and cheap red wine in the small space was overpowering.

"Gentlemen, I appreciate your most gracious welcome, but it is late and I wish to start early tomorrow morning. So if you would kindly direct me to my hotel I will …"

"Chief Investigator Mohsen." Mayor Drôme stepped forward. An atypically serious expression clouding his normally affable features. "May I ask a very few questions first? It will require but moments."

Sighing silently, reddened eyes blinking rapidly "Certainly Monsieur le Maire, please proceed."

"Thank you. First. How long will you be with us?"

"My instructions are to conduct this investigation, on site, until it is resolved."

"How long do you suppose?"

"It is difficult to say. I have reviewed the files transmitted to my office and I suspect these are quite obscure crimes, committed by a person or persons of intellect and complexity, driven by psychotic motives. These sorts of things are not resolved in a day."

"This could take weeks?"

"Yes."

"Even months?"

"As long as it takes."

"I understand. In deference to your rank Monsieur le Investigator, what is the extent of your authority?"

"I have total charge over this matter, with full authority to bring in any resource I deem necessary. This explains why I arrive unaccompanied from Paris."

"Can you give me some idea regarding the scope of the resource you might require?"

"Certainly. I confine my investigations to very small teams. Actually tiny. Normally myself and one or two other investigators at most. A larger team becomes as much a task of coordination, as investigation. It also generates a surprising amount of disinformation. I delegate the reception, filtering and validation of telephone leads, confessions, letters, walk-ins, and so forth. The vast majority of such material amounts to little more than distraction. That is not to say they can be ignored, or neglected. I imagine we will establish a call center in St. Tropez. I will work here in Coirón, initially with Officer Kontz." He acknowledged Kontz with a cordial nod.

"I am indeed pleased to hear these things. What will you need from us?"

"To begin with: Your staff, your records, total access to any citizen, the forensic labs in Marseilles, all available Gendarmes when needed from Coirón, Cavalaire, Le Rayol, Gassin and St. Tropez at my disposition, and a detailed cartography of the region outlining ownership and murder sites. Ideally your instructions will be issued in writing and I will be favored a copy. *S'il vous plait* [Please, or literally: If it pleases you.].”

The Mayor nodded meaningfully at Officer Kontz in tacit imprecation to look after this immediately.

"What of the press Inspector? These incidents are attracting a great deal of attention.”

Mohsen finally drooped against the counter, fatigue overtaking, turning slightly, staring at the bleak, utilitarian wall. Thinking.

Merde!

That issue hadn't occurred to him. Normally his Division HQ in Paris looked after such matters. The press seldom attempted to speak with him directly. If they did, he would simply refer them to the Division of Public Affairs. He would have no such a luxury here in this tiny, provincial backwater.

He sighed. "I would request you appoint someone in your administration to take charge of managing the press. He will act as my liaison shuttling questions and scheduling occasional press conferences, which I will conduct. I would appreciate if you or your designate were to attend as well.”

"Excellent. I will appoint Monsieur Henri Tondreau of our Office de Tourism. I will speak with him tomorrow. Perhaps the three of us ...” He stopped himself, gesturing deferentially to Officer Kontz. "Excuse me, the four of us, should meet for lunch tomorrow?”

"That would be fine Mayor Drôme. I'll call you in the morning. *Merci* [Thank you].”

"One last question. What may I personally do to assist Inspector?”

Now the politician raises his head.

"I would kindly request you contact and coordinate with the mayors of surrounding villages. Brief them of my presence, assignment and authority and enlist their cooperation.”

"I shall begin first thing tomorrow morning. Thank you Inspector."

"*Pas de tout* [Not at all]. Will someone kindly direct me to my hotel?"

Interlude

ADAM WAS SAVORING the day with intense pleasure.

Roistering sunshine.

Top down. Wind coursing through his hair.

The sailing had been breathtaking. Early morning. Not another boat on the water. Blinding, infinite, azure skies. The faint alabaster radiance of a ghostly morn-tide moon. Twenty-six knot winds from the east. Steady and strong. *Probo Mare* fell in love with that wind. She laid into her slot, and cut the water like a scythe, burying her bow in the rhythmic swells. When she wasn't burying her bow, she nosed high, or buried her aft gunnels. Rails under, salt spray in his face. All he needed was a reefed mainsail and a storm jib and he was pointing higher than he believed possible. He was single-handing the boat, and loving it. The boat had never been so quick to his touch, so yare. He'd never been as exhilarated, on or off the water.

All the while, Ranny lived in the wind, and the sun, and the whitecaps. She sang from the sheets and sails. He breathed her, sailed her and caressed her as *Probo Mare's* rudder cut the sea, her keel slipping through the clear water, the wheel trembling in his hands.

My God. Is this love?

After an immensely satisfying sail, he'd treated himself to a superb rosé amongst the flowers on the shady terrace of *Les Herbes Intrépides.*

And then she'd called.

He didn't know love. Or at least he'd never known love before. Perhaps now though … well … in any event, he felt like a giddy child … his newfound world glittered like morning dew at first dawn.

Adam passed the afternoon impatiently, willing himself not to go to Ranny until the agreed hour. Yet he could think of nothing else. It was maddening, intoxicating and joyous.

Finally it was half past four. Time to cast off for the Domaine. The sun was gold. The forest was a magic Sherwood green. The wind was wine. And Adam? Well, Adam was a child of enchantment.

When he arrived at the Domaine all was curiously quiet. No answer to his knock. No one in evidence. Although the doors were open and he breathed the lingering enticement of frying and simmering, but seemingly, nobody home. He rang the bell again. Still no answer.

Again. No answer.

He self-consciously padded into the villa. Sitting rooms, kitchen, bar, study, terrace, back garden. No one. He fumed, aggrieved.

Why are the best of times always and forever screwed up by something?

Then he thought he heard a sort of mewing sound, soft and feminine. He was instantly panic-stricken. The Beast? He followed the troubling sound through rooms and hallways and finally found himself at Ranny's bedroom door.

"Ranny?" He tapped at her door.

"Adam?" Her voice was soft and muted.

"Yes Ranny. It's Adam. May I come in?"

No sound. Nothing for a time, as Adam grew uneasy.

"Come in Adam."

She was seated at her computer, head down. She appeared exhausted. As Adam entered she looked up. Her eyes were red, and she looked very drawn, even fearful.

Adam stopped at her door. "What is it?"

"Oh Christ Adam, I don't know. I just don't know. David's been gone for days and I haven't heard a thing from him. His phone's out of network and he hasn't called. He's not been to his hotel. For God's sake he could be dead. And if he's not dead, I'll kill him myself."

"Did you contact Marcel?"

"I tried to goddamnit!"

Adam's voice was gentle and calming. "He wasn't *available?*"

"He doesn't fucking exist!"

"I don't understand Ranny."

"I used the phone, the computer and all the books. I called France Telecom. I even called the *Syndicat d'Initiative* [Chamber of Commerce] in Pont d'Arc. There is *no* Marcel Briançon or business named *Marcel Briançon et Fils* in Vallon Pont-d'Arc."

"Ranny. Help me here. I do not understand what you're saying."

"Okay." She inhaled deeply. "There is no listing, whatsoever, of a Marcel Briançon, or a *Marcel Briançon et Fils* in any telephone, or other listing in Vallon Pont-d'Arc. He simply does not exist. Understand?"

"Ranny. That is simply not possible. You know, your French is rather limited …"

"Check it yourself Adam. There is *no* Marcel Briançon."

"Think about it. Dave's been regaling us with tales of Marcel for months. If Marcel doesn't truly exist, Dave would have to be …" Adam stared stupidly at her.

"Insane. Exactly Adam. *Nuts*. Bat-shit. Goony. I've told you about his horrific suffering on the Isle of Wight. You know about DID. You know what he's been through. You know I'm right." She rested her forehead on her two hands on the desk.

Adam moved to the bed and the two simply sat in silence.

"Let's get ourselves a couple of stiff GT's, take a dip in the pool, cool off a bit and figure this out. What say?"

Attacking a problem head-on always improved her spirits. "Okay. Why not?"

She rose slowly, arching her neck and back. "Give me a minute to change. You can get into your trunks in the guest bath. I'll be out in a few minutes, and I expect a gin and tonic on deck that'll burn the hide off a goddamned rhino."

"Done."

They started with cold drinks on the edge of the pool. Resting. Cooling off. Getting their minds in order.

After a few brief laps they sat at the side of the pool, dripping, legs in water.

Ranny looked down, into the pool and realized she was seeing a left foot, missing a third toe. David!

"*Adam?* Good grief, for a moment I thought you were David."

"Why?"

"Why? You're missing a toe. Just like David. I never noticed."

Adam Laughed. "Oh that. An Oceanic Whitetip off Tarogi Reef, on Guam."

"Oceanic Whitetip?"

"A shark. Big fellow. About a twelve footer. I was doing post-doc work on reef decimation. Those big Japanese honeymoon hotels were tearing hell out of the island's aquatic life, not to mention the goddamn Brown Tree Snakes ... millions of 'em ... decimating the bird popula-tion ... and everything else for that matter ..." He seemed lost in visions of sharks and snakes and fading sea life. Then he roused himself, smiling self-consciously. "But the toe's far from everything ..."

He lifted his arm revealing ten inches of stitched scarring, then raised his foot, showing massive scars across the sole.

Ranny wondered at the wound. "I never noticed."

"Well, it's faded a good deal over the years."

Ranny blanched slightly. "I think you're lucky to be alive."

With a sardonic half-smile, Adam said, "I think you're right. It was months before I could face the water again."

"But this is unbelievable. It is beyond credible that both of you should lose the same toe, on the same foot. What are the odds?"

Adam reminisced. "Back in university days I had a professor who said there are no odds ... only evens."

"And what the hell does that mean?"

Adam smiled again "I really don't know. I never did. But I think he was referring to some sort of balance in the universe."

"Some sort of matter-antimatter cancellation?"

"No. That would probably yield odds. More of a Soto-Zen thing I think. Although the term is often misused and over used in my opinion."

Ranny shook her head dismissively. "I was discussing a couple of toes and now we're seeking some sort of damned quantum entanglement. It still seems too coincidental to be believed."

She wasn't sure what had just transpired. It was troubling and more than coincidence. Perhaps it was damned important. She'd have to think about this.

They were half-standing, half-floating now. Close. Nearly touching. Up to their necks in the clear water, undulating their hands for balance. Eyes earnestly studying one another. Ranny's hair was wet and thrown back, revealing a face enlivened by a whisper of sun freckling. Somehow the glare of the afternoon sun heightened her loveliness. Two nearly drained drinks stood at the margin of the pool, forgotten.

The cool water and the gin and Adam had done their work well. Ranny was calm and their exchange, while intense, was now more the stuff of analysis than anxiety.

After several minutes of explanation, Adam responded "Ranny I understand your fears. Dave *may* have gone missing and apparently he's delusional about this Briançon fellow. Now you tell me you two have grown apart. I'm truly sorry to hear this." He thought for a moment, noting how drained she looked. "When was the last time you ate something?"

"Not sure. A day or so. Why?"

"I'm concerned about you. And frankly, I have the distinct feeling there's more to this. I think something else troubles you. Am I right?"

Ranny stared at him for long moments. Then she submerged herself and simply held herself and her breath under the water so long Adam didn't know whether to be impressed or frightened. Suddenly she burst from the water, her head thrown back at a rakish angle. Adam watched her emergence, her face and graceful neck, her ascent from the water propelling her sufficiently to expose her shapely torso nearly to the waist. Adam suddenly thirsted for the remainder of his drink.

She sleeted water from her face, wrung it from her hair and squeezed it from her eyes. When she'd regained her breath, she looked up at Adam and hissed. "You're right."

"Care to tell me about it?"

"Let's finish our drinks."

They turned and swam to the side of the pool. When they'd drained their glasses, they stood in the water, arms crossed over the soft gurgle of the poolside drain, shoulders touching, as were their legs. From this perspective they could see far down the valley, which they wordlessly contemplated.

After a time Adam spoke. "Ranny?"

"I'm not sure you want to hear this Adam." Her speech was suddenly slightly slurred.

"I do."

"You won't like it. It's terrible. Horrifying."

"Bloody hell. What is it?"

"It's probably not even true."

"*Ranny* ..."

"Okay. I'll ... I'll uh just lay it out." She ran her fingers through her hair as Adam observed her jaw muscles contract She seemed suddenly tired again. "I compared David's trips with the uh ... the dates of the murders as best I could. Of course he's taken far more trips than there have been murders and the dates were difficult to recon ... reconstruct."

"Yes?"

"But they ... ah ... seem to coincide."

With that she broke down. Fatigue, worry, the sun, the gin, fear. They combined to militate against her and they won. She collapsed.

She was nearly under water before Adam could seize her. He lifted her into his arms and gently placed her poolside. She wasn't really unconscious, but she didn't appear fully cognizant either. Eyes closed, tossing her head and hands, mumbling occasionally; and after a time, finally still. Adam believed she must be profoundly overwrought.

My God, she's exhausted.

He felt like weeping. For her. For David. For himself. Instead, he climbed out of the pool. He stood before Ranny and gently lifted her. Other than an occasional, soft unintelligible murmur, she evidenced no awareness of his actions. He carefully carried her into the house, down the hall, into her bedroom. She was still dripping wet, so he rejected her bed in favor of a settee next to her dressing table. He found a towel in her bath and returned to the settee. He drew the straps of her swimming suit lightly down from her shoulders and gently worked the damp suit from her body, revealing her breasts, over her hips, down her legs. Then he dried her. Tenderly and slowly.

Suddenly it was difficult to swallow. His breathing came faster. He thrilled at her body He knew he should feel guilt, but his intent was totally innocent, so he allowed himself to revel in the experience. As he soundlessly carried her to her bed, he drank in her body. Sun, wind and air to a drowning man.

Oh my.

Stirrings he'd yearned to feel his entire life.

So lovely. So fine and innocent. Perhaps I … perhaps I do love her.

He coursed with the strident temptation of simply being close to her.

He placed her on the bed. Lit a fire. Closed the shutters. Hung her suit to dry. Put away the towel. As he ensured she was covered properly, he realized he was simply looking for excuses to remain.

He closed her door quietly and wandered into the bar.

He made himself another drink. His suit was dry now, so he threw himself on an easy chair and began the process of making sense out of it all. A task he dreaded. A task he feared. A useless task, as he already suspected the truth.

David must be my best friend. My only friend in fact. As long as I can remember, I never had a friend. I wonder why that is? I wonder why I've always been alone? Why women, even men, have always been … impossible?

So now I finally have a friend. David. As fine a fellow as I've ever known. And now I'm in love with his wife. And I don't find her … impossible. And I suspect David of being a monstrous serial killer and myself of being a potential adulterer.

His mind wandered mechanically: *Adultery from the French avoutrie, to corrupt, to corrupt the marriage bed and the burdens it conveyed.*

He lit a fire, made himself another drink and resumed the easy chair.

This is all wrong. I swear it. There's something I'm missing. Something important. Maybe the key to this whole mess. It feels like a horse pill lodged in my throat. I can't choke it down. I can't throw it up. I can't breathe with it. I can't live with it. I can't endure it, whatever the hell it is. Damn, I wish I could remember. I think it's important. I can almost make it out. Hell, I can almost taste it. A rancid, sick, bitter thing. In the past? Yes. I think it … has … to do with … and then he was fast asleep.

He was as susceptible as Ranny to sun and gin and anxiety and fatigue.

Fade Zeta

HE'D BEEN HERE for longer than he cared to think about. The weather was a joy. The food was excellent. He loved the funny little hotel and its restaurant. He liked the people. Much more *gentil* [nice] than the crusty *Parisiennes*. The town was very much to his liking as well. A classical French *village de la moyen age* [village of the middle ages]. A beautiful square, even a tiny network of canals. They called it *La Venise Sous les Maures* [Venice beneath the Moors], and they weren't far wrong. It was almost a vacation, except he was here alone, to resolve a chain of puzzling murders. Quickly. So far there was nothing to report and Paris was growing anxious. As the preponderance victims were British, or American, pressure on Paris from those two countries compounded the strain. He on the other hand was growing lonely and weary of it all.

Chief Inspector Alain Mohsen sat in the steamy little office of the Gendarmerie, smelling of stale coffee, cigarettes long consumed, and the oddly dusty-sweet aroma of cheap, aging paper. The scent of bureaucracy. He was thumbing through the dog-eared reports surrounding the *Beast of Coirón* (God, how he hated that term). He could only describe them as indifferent, bland and of marginal utility at best. Clearly Officer Kontz had little enthusiasm for detecting, or any sort of work as far as he could determine.

Alain had been to all the murder sites, made extensive, repetitive interviews, much to the frustration (and often embarrassment) of victim's friends and family.

The repetitive routine of re-interviewing grew numbingly tedious: 'Désole monsieur/Madame. Je sais bien que vous avez raconté cette histoire plusieurs fois. Mais je fais une dernière fois d'appel à votre patience et votre aide.' [I'm very sorry. I know very well that you've told this story many times already. But I ask your patience and help one last time.]

How many times had he said these words?

The Call Center in St. Tropez had fielded a few dozen calls, a few crank letters, and two crackpots who walked in and simply confessed. All dead ends, information of negative value at best. Time and resource squandered as women were murdered. He often daydreamed of laws and resources permitting indictment and prosecution of evanescent fools insinuating themselves into criminal investigations simply for the thrill. Alain believed they should suffer the penalty as accessories to the crime, of which they confessed. Of course though, that was exactly what those morons wanted.

Staunchly returning to his current duties, Alain turned his attention to the files at hand.

Throughout the files there was only one minor variation: A single object was stolen from the murder site of a Mrs. Angela Zaparelli. A fairly simple yellow gold band. What is termed a baguette in France. Two parallel bands separated by a precisely worked trough. Made by BVLGARI, 18kt yellow gold, it was of excellent quality, though not excessively expense by Zaparelli standards. BVLGARI designated it model B.ZERO1 1-band ring AN852260 (as indicated by Mr. Zaparelli's insurance records). Why would the killer take a relatively simple ring amongst the extravagant watch and jewelry worn by Mrs. Zaparelli? Not to mention the preposterous amount of cash she carried. Mr. Zaparelli stated the ring was merely a sentimental bauble. The only distinguishing aspect of the ring, differentiating it from other BVLGARI B.ZER01's, were the initials AZ engraved inside the ring. Alain finally shrugged it off as an impulse theft, or had simply been lost by Madame Zaparelli. In either case, of little interest.

Back to the files …

These people simply don't know how to keep records. He's ve been busy looking busy. I'll give him that. But there's nothing here I can use. Nothing that brings traction to this investigation.

He closed the file and stood to restore it to the dusty archive they termed their Dossier en Attente [Case Pending]. As he extended his arm, an interior folder fell out. Then another. Clearly they had been wedged in the rear pocket of the jacket. He retrieved the files from the floor.

What is this? Folders within a folder? Quelle sorte d'une manière de garder des dossiers. [What a way to keep records.]

Opening the first file, he discovered a watch report detailing a telephone call, a subsequent on-site interview and some twelve photographs. A married couple in 'Beverly Hills' had discovered a package containing interior photos of their own home, taken from outside, mainly at night. A most disquieting discovery. Alain was immediately intrigued.

Officer Kontz had clearly accorded the matter perfunctory interest at best. Kontz was apparently certain the perpetrator was the product of a mistake, a prank, or some idiot *voyeur* [Peeping-Tom]. Alain could easily envision Kontz filling out his report while sitting in the Cheval Blanc, sipping wine, ogling the breathtaking legs of Sophie, the café's part-time hostess and star attraction.

Well, at least he'd had the brains to file it with the murders. Mon Dieu! [My God!] *Perhaps a break … finally.*

He raised the huge antique telephone receiver to his ear and pushed a button on the set.

"Françoise, will you please connect me with a Monsieur … David Woods. He lives in Beverly Hills. Merci."

Two minutes pass.

"Hello?"

Alain's mind worked on automatic. *A woman's voice. Clearly English speaking. Sounded youngish and American. A pretty voice. Clear and melodic. Probably an attractive woman as well.* He felt he could nearly see her.

"Madame Woods?"

"Yes."

"Bonjour."

"Bonjour. Who is on the line please?"

Hmm. Businesslike.

"This is Chief Inspector Mohsen. I am with the police and I've been assigned from Paris to investigate the recent killings in this area."

"I see. What can I do for you Inspector Mohsen?"

"May I speak with Monsieur Woods?"

Alain listened to a hushed delay for a moment.

"I'm sorry, he's out of town just now. May I help you?"

"Oui Madame, bien sûr [certainly]. Merci. I have been reviewing your report regarding photographs taken on your Domaine some weeks ago. Are you familiar with this report?"

"Why yes I am."

Do I hear relief in her voice? I think she doesn't want me speak with her husband for some reason.

"I have some additional questions if you don't mind. May I drop by and discuss this with you?"

"Certainly. When would you care to come?"

"Ah. Actually now would be quite convenient."

"Fine. I'll be here all morning."

"Merci Madame. A bientôt. [See you soon.]"

~~~~

Before leaving, he glanced at the second file. Just a single sheet of paper. A memorandum from an Officer Thommes of the St. Tropez Police. He scanned the short document and barked *"Merde!"*

His imprecation was sufficiently loud and harsh as to startle Françoise at reception.

"Chief Inspector? Is everything alright?"

"Fine Françoise. Désolé." [Sorry].

The report outlined an interview at an up-market club in St. Tropez named *Cubana.* Trendy, chic, expensive, lots of pick-up action, some drugs, but no serious problems. The inquiry was conducted by an Officer Thommes, in connection with the murders in Coirón. As several victims were known to habituate the club, Thommes was wisely seeking some connection. The bar staff had little to contribute, but a short interview with one of the barmen, a fellow named Paul Bell, suggested he may have seen some of these ladies with the same man. A man he called 'Charley.' Such was the essence of the report. And the idiot Officer Kontz simply filed it. Probably because it came from the St. Tropez Police. A source of great envy for the bumbling Gendarme. Again however, somehow he'd demonstrated the sense to at least place the file in the murder dossier.

Despite his irritation with Kontz, his mood was brightening considerably. *Finally progress. Two leads in the space of half an hour! Of course I would have had these immediately were it not for that idiot. Il est bete comme ses pieds.* [He is as stupid as his feet.] *He would be facing disciplinary action if he worked for me, which would not be for long.*

Alain always prepared for interviews as much as possible. This was one of his great strengths and one of the secrets of his success. In this case he stopped at the Cheval Blanc for a coffee and an informal discussion with Philippe Demers, the proprietor. Philippe was an invaluable source of knowledge regarding nearly anyone in the Maure Valley, and he was always most pleased to share. Fifteen minutes later Alain was in his car, equipped with surprisingly detailed background information on the Woods.

When he arrived he took a discrete walkabout around the Domaine, ending his circumnavigation at the main entrance to the villa. The door was opened by a very substantial lady. Drying her hands on a kitchen towel, blue apron, frumpy housedress, pendulous breasts, auburn dyed hair, lipstick loosely tracking her lips … all balanced atop legs reminiscent of ancient oak trees, terminating with two well-worn, unlaced sneakers. Alain was certain he wasn't confronting Madame Woods.

"Oui Monsieur?"

"I am Chief Inspector Mohsen. Madame Woods s'il vous plait."

"Oui Monsieur. Entrez s'il vous plait." Alain entered the foyer as the woman went to fetch Ranny.

What a beautiful place. I am ashamed to admit I would never have credited Americans with such taste.

A lithe and lovely woman entered the room, walked purposefully to Alain and shook hands in a very forthright manner.

"Chief Inspector Mohsen?"

"Yes. Madame Woods? Wife of Monsieur David Woods?" He presented her his card.

"Yes and yes." She smiled. "Please have a seat. I'm having some rosé. Would you care to join me?" Her manner was open, welcoming and friendly.

Alain was immediately put at ease, with a tiny cautionary light flashing somewhere in the recesses of his mind.

He glanced theatrically at his watch. "Certainly. Thank you." He was on duty. But it was nearly lunchtime and accepting a glass of wine would probably lull her into a relaxed mood. Unlike many Police officials, Alain felt interviews were best conducted in a spirit of trust and openness. Truculent officiousness was reserved for hard-core criminals, and then only sparingly. With ladies such as Madame Woods he simply let them play the game out.

She left the room to fetch the wine. He seated himself, still looking about.

I certainly see where the good taste comes from. She is quite lovely.

Soon she returned carrying two glasses and an ice bucket containing a chilled bottle of Bandol. He approved. When the wine was poured she looked at the Chief Inspector inquiringly.

"Santé."

"Santé Madame." With a slight nod, he took a long sip. "Mm. A most excellent rosé." He held his glass towards the windows. "Like drinking sunlight."

"I agree. I believe they make the best rosé in the world here; and I believe rosé is a lamentably underrated wine. People who don't know the wine can be such snobs. And now these disturbing reports out of the European Union indicating there is continued pressure to approve of rosés simply blended from indifferent reds and whites. They want to reduce the cost, the skill, the quality and the reputation. I believe it is an attempt to buttress the price of the already expensive reds and whites. I hope it never happens. Next we'll discover Austrians mixing antifreeze into the stuff."

Alain smiled politely and raised his glass in accord.

She either likes to talk, or does not wish to talk about the photographs for some reason.

"Madame Woods I have been reviewing your report and the photos taken outside your residence, and I have some questions. If I may?"

"Certainly. Frankly I was somewhat disappointed at the reaction of your Officer Kontz to our report."

"He is not, as you say, *my* Officer Kontz. I am on assignment here from Paris. I apologize nonetheless if we seemed inattentive. I assure you, you have *my* attention now."

"Thank you."

"Everyone seemed to think this was the work of some sort of, as you say, Peeping-Tom."

"Yes."

"Well Madame ... how shall I put this? All the photos show you fully clad, in various rooms of your lovely home. No, ah, boudoir settings, if you gather my meaning."

"I understand."

"Do you shutter your bedroom windows at night?"

"As you can see, we are surrounded by woodlands and have no neighbors for about three kilometers. So no, we normally leave our windows unshuttered."

"Then a relatively unskilled Peeping-Tom would be able to take such pictures?"

She thought for a minute. "I suspect you've toured the outside of this building?"

"In fact, I have. Yes."

"What is your opinion?"

This is an intelligent woman.

"I believe at night, it would be facile to acquire some rather ... revealing photographs. Much more ... provocative ... than those in this file."

"You know better than I Inspector. I suppose I must count myself as fortunate. May I pour you some more wine?"

She is careful with her words.

"Thank you Madame."

"Your next question?"

"These *are* all the photographs. Are they not Madame?"

"They certainly are Inspector. I have a receipt for them if you would care to inspect it?"

She is well prepared.

"Perhaps we may request the receipt as our investigation proceeds. I would ask you not to discard it for the present."

"Certainly."

"Monsieur Woods. Was he at home during these periods?"

"How would I know? Why do you ask?"

"I understand your husband travels quite extensively pursuing his avocation, as a paleontologist?"

A whisper of a frown raced across her forehead.

He knows David is a paleontologist?

She softly acquiesced "Yes."

"Since the date and time of each photograph is recorded on the reverse side of each print, it should be easy to determine if your husband was in residence at the time the picture was taken. I understand this is inherent to the process."

"Oh. I hadn't noticed."

Hmm.

He opened his briefcase, withdrew the photos and extended them for her inspection. "You see Madame? Right there."

"Oh yes."

"And there is another interesting aspect to these photographs ..."

"Yes?"

"Monsieur Woods appears in none of the pictures. Only you."

"Really? I guess I didn't focus on that."

She is not being honest with me. I am sure of it. She knew he was not in the photos. I can see it in the flicker of her eyes.

"Would you happen to know your husband's schedule in recent months?"

"No. I don't keep a diary, and as far as I know he does not log his trips."

"Dommage."

"Pardon?"

"Oh. Excuse please. I lapse into French. I meant it is a shame we have no such log."

"Why? When were the photographs taken?"

"Why they were taken over of a period of weeks."

Ranny visibly paled. "I uh thought it was just one session ... I guess."

She holds her hands together in her lap as she lies to me.

"Madame, aside from the dates, regard the photos. You wear different clothes. Some are at night, others very early morning. You are in rooms all over the Domaine. Surely you observed this?"

"Look Inspector, when I saw my pictures, which were simply laying atop a mailbox in the pouring rain, taken by person or persons unknown, I was so upset I didn't care to inspect for fashion, setting, or quality of lighting."

She is quick this one. But she said 'my' pictures.

"I certainly understand Madame Woods." his tone calm and conciliatory.

He selected a specific picture. "I note all these pictures were taken outside the villa, through these marvelous windows." He gestured at one of the French doors.

"We noticed as well."

He extended the photo he had selected. "Except this one. When I toured the villa I saw no such window."

Ranny took the photo from his hand. "Oh yes. We have an interior atrium where all utilities are located. This was taken from within the atrium through an interior window, looking into the kitchen."

"May I see this window please?"

They walked to the kitchen allowing Alain to inspect the window carefully.

"How does one gain access to this atrium?"

"There is a tunnel under the building which opens directly into the atrium. I believe it was excavated more than a hundred years ago to accommodate coal heating."

"How interesting. A secret passage. Very romantic."

"I don't believe you'd find it very romantic if you saw it."

"In fact I would like to see it. Our *peeper* apparently knew of its existence and how to gain access. Is this tunnel commonly known?"

"No, I don't suppose it is."

Licking her lips.

"Mm. I assume you and your husband have studied this passage after these pictures were discovered?"

Ranny bristled slightly. "Frankly inspector we had expected the *police* to investigate."

"And Officer Kontz did not do so?"

"No. He evidenced no interest whatsoever."

"Désolé Madame. I intend to correct our short-comings immediately. Can you direct me to the entrance of this secret tunnel?"

"Certainly. Do you need a flashlight?"

"Non merci Madame." He opened his briefcase and withdrew a flashlight, a small digital camera, and an evidence bag.

He followed her around the building to a pair of small wooden doors, worn heart shaped ventilators carved into each, obscured by bushes, descending down six weathered stone steps below ground level.

He pushed through the bushes and descended the stairs.

"This door has no lock."

"No. It's never been locked as far as I know. I believe there used to be a chain and padlock running through the two hearts. It only goes to the atrium, and we removed the interior atrium door when we renovated, so there is no real access to the villa itself."

"I see." Opening the doors he stood back to allow Ranny entrance.

"Uh, no Inspector. You go ahead. There's too many krispy-kritters down there for me."

He cocked his head, frowning. "Krispy-kritters?"

Ranny smiled. "Sorry. I mean varmits, vermin, rats and bugs, snakes and God knows what."

Alain smiled as well. "I understand. Shall I rejoin you in the villa? I will not be long."

"Certainly."

Fifteen minutes later the Inspector rejoined Ranny in the sitting room, returning his various paraphernalia to his briefcase. "May I borrow a washroom Madame? I cleaned my shoes most carefully, but my hands ..."

"It's the door just off the foyer."

"Thank you."

When he returned. "More wine inspector?"

"Just a half please."

She's pouring the wine with two hands now.

"Did you find anything of interest?"

"One thing. It is very dark and dusty in there. Much coal dust. Stones and broken glass. Nails and bits of wood. Water. Traps and rat poison. Difficult walking. I would even say hazardous. Yet I discovered footprints ascending the ramp into the atrium."

"Footprints?"

"*Bare* footprints. Fairly recent. In the coal dust, on the ramp, missing the third toe on the left foot. Unfortunately smeared, so we cannot use them for prints. Although footprints are normally of little value, unless we have access to birth records." He quickly glanced at her eyes, searching for any reaction. Her face seemed frozen, enigmatic and unreadable. Her eyes betrayed nothing. She simply stared out the window into the distance.

A strange reaction. What is she thinking about?

"A very singular place to visit barefooted. N'est-ce pas? [Is it not so?] Numerous 'krispy-kritters', as you say?"

Ranny's attention seemed suddenly engaged. She frowned quizzically. "How do you know they are *recent* prints Inspector?"

"Very little dust has accumulated. This could easily place the prints during the same period as your photographs."

Lost in thought for a moment, she finally responded. "I see."

"Did you take a photograph of this footprint?"

"Indeed. Why do you ask?"

"Oh, I was just thinking that the print won't last long down there."

"You are quite right. Regarding the pictures themselves. Unfortunately, the mailing box was discarded by the photo-lab, as you know. But we found two sets of latent prints on the interior case. The print technicians, they wear cotton gloves, so we suspect they are those of you and your husband. But we need to verify this. Do you mind if I take your prints now? It will require but a moment."

"Please go ahead. It sounds fun."

Alain raised his eyebrows in response to her comment. *Fun?*

He began to set up. As he worked he casually rambled. "Latent prints. An interesting word latent." He took her left hand. "The same in English and French. From the Latin *lat□ ns*. To lie hidden. Let's see ... something which awaits, lies in waiting, a power or a danger, or an illness standing ready to spring at the right time." Gently guiding her fingers through the ink to the pad, he glanced up at Ranny closely studying her reaction.

She studied him in return. "You're an interesting man Inspector."

"It is an interesting life Madame. Ah, there we are. May I have your right hand now please …"

When they were finished and Ranny had cleaned her hands "I must say Inspector, your work is exceptionally thorough. Quite the opposite from the initial police inquiry. Is there possibly more to all this than I am aware?"

"No. Not really. It is remotely possible this may have some connection with the recent murders, but I doubt it."

"The *Beast* murders?"

He tilted his head gently, raising his right eyebrow. "I am aware of no others in this area Madame."

"Right." She breathed in relief. "So, can I do anything else for you?"

"I wonder if you have a photograph of your husband I might borrow? I will return it."

"You need a photograph of my husband?"

"… only until I have the opportunity to meet and interview him. I will return it."

She studied him dubiously. "Well, I have a passport photo?"

"That would be fine."

She retrieved a faded black-and-white photo-booth print from David's study and presented it to him.

"Thank you. This will do nicely. One last question s'il vous plait Madame."

"Yes?"

"When do you expect your husband to return home?"

"I'm not sure. When he's working in the field it is often difficult to project when a dig will be completed."

There's a quaver in her voice. Ever so slight, but it's there.

"So you have spoken to him?"

"In fact, his mobile phone is currently out of range. Why? What do you need of him?"

She begins to sound defensive.

"Aside from his fingerprints, it's normal for us to gather as much information from witnesses as possible. Perhaps he noticed something you overlooked or were not privy to. Will you ask him to contact me at the Gendarmerie in Coirón when he returns?"

"Certainly."

He rose. "Thank you Madame, for your time, your charming company, and your excellent wine."

"You are welcome Inspector. I enjoyed it as well. Good-by."

Ranny followed his car with her eyes until it disappeared into the forest.

Mohsen curved out their drive and began the descent to the coast.

I like that woman. I don't trust her. But I like her.

His next destination: Lunch.

Afterwards: Cubana in St. Tropez.

As he drove, he pondered the last hour.

A formidable woman. I think she is troubled, or in trouble, or both. I now have more questions than when I came. She was nervous the moment I spoke to her on the phone. Why call the police if they didn't want us to investigate the pictures? Someone is innocent and the other not? Did something change after the initial report? Whose footprints were those? They appeared to upset her. Why? She was lying about being unaware of the dates, or being the only one in the photos. I'm sure of it. She is much too intelligent not to have observed these things. Is she protecting her husband? Herself? Someone else? Despite her offer of the receipt, are these truly all the pictures? And yet, I find her essentially straightforward. An interesting mix of contradictions.

I think she wants watching. A pleasant prospect that.

He chuckled to himself. *I think I need some lunch.*

Fade Eta

WHEN THE INSPECTOR finally departed, Ranny collapsed on the sofa and poured herself the last of the wine. She downed it in one throw and inspected her right hand. Barely visible, but it trembled.

I hope to God the Inspector didn't notice. At first I thought he wanted to question me about the shooting last night. Perhaps they found they body? At least he didn't want that. But now I have that damned footprint to worry about.

When she was calmer, she laid back and let her mind replay the events of the previous night ... with Adam ... a vivid, bittersweet memory.

~~~~

She had awakened from a deep sleep, totally befuddled. Initially she assumed it was morning. But as she peered out her window she realized the sun was pouring in from the west, soon to set. Overcoming her disorientation, she realized it was only later that same afternoon.

The last thing she could remember was sitting at the pool with Adam in the ... Adam! Where was he? How did she get to her bedroom? Feeling herself, she realized she was naked. She was both alarmed and suddenly aroused. She knew quite well she didn't bring herself into her bedroom, undress herself and tuck herself into bed. That left only Adam.

She sat up, wrapping her sheet around herself and called out. "Adam?"

No response.

"Adam?"

"Adam, are you there?"

The door opened gently. Adam looked in without actually entering the room. A pleasant smile and soft voice "Hi."

"What happened Adam?"

"Well, I believe hunger, fatigue, worry, gin and the sun ganged up on you. You lost." He smiled sympathetically.

"... and you carried me here and uh, got me into bed?"

"And left immediately thereafter."

"Yes but ..."

"I *am* a doctor Ranny."

"You're a *vet* Adam. And yes, I'm sure you've seen your share of naked Norwegian Elkhounds!"

He laughed and she laughed as well.

She relaxed and patted the bed. "Come in Adam. Sit down and talk to me."

He sat at the foot of her bed.

She contemplated him affectionately. "How are you Adam? What have you been doing?"

"I'm just fine. As soon as my suit was dry, I relaxed on your easy chair and immediately fell asleep myself. Guess the sun got to me too. How are *you*?"

"Better." She ran her tongue about her mouth. "I feel much better. Although I'm embarrassed to admit I'd kill for another Gin & Tonic."

Adam rose. "I'll be right back."

He returned with two drinks.

"Ah! Better. Thank you." She drained nearly half her glass.

"Easy there. We don't want you passing out again."

"Oh really? Take a look at *your* glass."

"Hmm. I guess we were both thirsty. I feel better too. Now."

"Now?"

"Well, I was a little worried you might be upset ... undressing you and all."

"Don't be silly Adam. Not you. Never you."

Adam searched her eyes intently. "This has been a very hard time for you I think."

She said nothing. She simply pressed her lips together with a near imperceptible quiver of her chin. He took her hand.

"Ranny, I've never loved a woman, or any other human. But Ranny, I love you."

"I love you Adam."

"No. You don't understand. Not simply as a friend. I believe I'm deeply in love with you."

She stroked his face. "I do understand Adam. And I feel the same." She smiled wistfully. "Hellofa note isn't it?"

Ranny saw the thrill in his eyes. A look somehow akin to pain. She'd seen men look the same as she caressed them. But she'd never seen a man respond this way to her words. She found it wonderfully moving.

"And what of David?"

She frowned. "Yes. And what of David? The truth is I love him as deeply as you Adam. We've grown apart lately. But that will pass. I fear there may be ah, deeper problems though. And it frightens me. I'm so thankful to have you here."

"You'll never imagine how thankful I am to *be* here."

She took his face in both hands and drew him to her. She began to kiss him, tenderly. He responded passionately, even eagerly, but clumsily. As would an inexperienced youth bumbling with excitement into his first kiss. She found it puzzling, yet endearing.

A questioning thought flashed through her mind, unbidden.

The charming, handsome Dr. Adam MacAfee? Beloved by women? Wealthy rake about town? The quintessential lady-killer?

She found something in the term somehow disturbing, and so put the matter from her mind. Instead she surrendered herself to the searing longings blossoming deep within her.

Adam stood and almost lurched to the side of her bed, his newfound arousal excitingly self-evident. He simply stood there, looking down at her. Ranny allowed her bed-sheet to tumble down and was rewarded with a sharp intake of his breath and a muted sob.

Still he simply stood, drinking her in.

She was charmed at his reticence. Touched and growing more and more aroused, she leant forward and tenderly drew his swimming suit down until it fell about his ankles.

My what a beautiful body. Sculpted. Tanned. Tough with muscle. Supple with flesh.

Still he simply stood. Ranny thought she even detected a minute shivering.

He needs ...

She touched him, cupping him gently in her hand, squeezing, softly pulling and stroking.

His reaction was huge, immediate and wildly uncontrolled. He groaned in a frenzy of delight and relief. A hot surge, sensuously dewy. Her legs instinctively began to spread, her toes pointing and her thighs rigid with urgency.

Adam was trembling violently now. "Omigod, I'm sorr ... I didn't mean to ... I couldn't stop ..."

Ranny smiled up at him whispering "Shhhhh ... it's okay ... it's better than okay ... I loved it. I love *you* Adam."

"Lay down now ... lay back ... let me."

~~~~

Later she held him for a time, arms haloing his head. Then she moved beside him, taking his arm and enclosing herself. For minutes, no words were spoken. She tucked her legs under herself, brushed her hair back and looked up at him. Tear-tracks coursed down his cheeks.

My God he's been weeping. What goes on here? He weeps after sex and seems to be an absolute novice. A man with his magnetism, and I thought, experience? Is there something I don't understand?

"Adam? Adam? Are you all right? What's wrong dear? What's troubling you? Please tell me Adam."

"I'm fine Ran. I'm better than fine. That was ... the best thing in my life. I'm so grateful. More than you could ever know."

She sighed a tiny chuckle. "You're most welcome Adam. But what's troubling you?"

"Nothing. It's just that ... well ... no one has ever done that for me before."

"So this was your first ..."

"Um. Yeah. I guess it was."

"I don't understand Adam. You're such a charming, attractive man. Women are crazy about you. I've seen it. So why ..."

"Oh they like me alright. They like me just fine. Some are even ..."

"So why Adam?"

His voice took on an almost childlike quality. "Oh, there's this guy. I'd forgotten about him. But I'm beginning to remember. Someday I'll put it all together and then ..."

Totally engaged in their talk, they were heedless of a magnificent sunset, painting the bedroom wall in a vivid spectrum of red and gold and amethyst.

"What guy?"

Ranny was growing concerned. There seemed to be much roiling in his mind, just below the surface.

"What?"

"You said there was *this guy*, Adam."

"Ah, yeah."

"Adam. You're not making much sense. What is this all about?"

Adam was lost in thought for several minutes, as Ranny grew increasingly intrigued.

Finally. "I uh, my younger years were extremely difficult I think. Most of it is very obscure, but some things are slowing coming back to me. I believe you have a great deal to do with that. There are things I don't really want to remember, but somehow ... somehow it's important. I don't know. Anyhow, back then there was this guy. A bad guy. Or maybe just a sad guy. And angry. Very angry. I thought he was gone. But I think he's the reason I've never ... until now."

"You mean this man somehow interferes with your relationships?"

"Yes. I believe he does."

"How?"

"Well, I've never actually seen him. He just seems to track me somehow and then he interferes. Exactly how he does this, I don't know."

"This is all pretty weird Adam. This guy seems a pretty dark character." She frowned thoughtfully. "Why doesn't he come between you and me then?"

"I'm not sure. Perhaps my love prevails over his chicanery."

She gave him an encouraging hug.

"Let's eat some cold chicken Adam. We're both tired and hungry."

~~~~

Thick warm robes, a summer salad, crusty bread, cold chicken and chilled wine. They were feeling wonderfully better. Touching. Regarding each other affectionately. Even laughing. They were growing closer, more trusting. More intimate.

Two enormous issues lie between them. David and whomever this *guy* was. Throughout her solitary life the first man she loved was David. She thought he would truly be the first and the last. Her existence until David had been far from cloistered, but she'd never committed to any man. Now she realized it was actually possible to truly love more than one man. Deeply, sincerely and without guilt.

David needed her help and love and understanding. He was Ranny's husband and she loved him. Both Ranny and Adam knew he was deeply troubled. Both wanted him to find his way.

Adam needed her as well and this 'other guy' was a vastly different issue. Neither understood who, or even what he was. Ranny sensed he might represent a real threat.

They must talk through these things. But not tonight. Tonight was a time for …

"What was that?"

There was a clearly audible crunch in the gravel outside the dining room. Someone was out there. Someone dangerous.

"Damn!"

Ranny jumped to her feet and raced to the gun cabinet. She selected a Browning 625, over-and-under shotgun. With practiced ease, she broke it and confirmed its load of 16 gauge shot. She slowly unfastened a French door, firmly gripping its handle, taking great care to noiselessly open it. She gingerly stepping out and wryly noted her precautions were immediately frustrated by the stony crunch of gravel underfoot.

What the hell ... She shrugged inwardly in wry resignation ... *it makes no difference. He can see me anyhow.*

The evening had darkened. The moon was down. No stars to be seen yet—only Venus ascending to the northwest. This was the dusky transition to night the French refer to as *entre chien et loup* [between dog and wolf], when twilight despondently lingers and the ensuing dimness renders it impossible to distinguish between a dog and a wolf—thus the danger, cloaked in shadowy ambiguity, is impenetrable.

The air was cool and fresh. She could see the mist of her breath ghosting in the dimness. There was a soft wind and a humid, reticence of ozone. A storm was approaching from the east. Random flashes of mute lightning flickered the far horizon testifying to its approach.

She summoned her courage and called out as strongly as she could.

"Who is there? Qui est là?"

She listened to her voice in the darkness.

Goddamnit, my voice is quavering. Take a deep breath. Let it out slow and sound like you're a bitch, madder than hell, and ready to kill.

She waited for a response. Only a lonely whispering wind answered.

"I have a gun. J'ai un fusil."

That was stupid. The son of a bitch can see I have a gun.

She heard only the hushed stirring of air. Like a snake undulating across desert sands at midnight.

"Answer or I will shoot. Répondez ou je vais tirer."

One part of her mind marveled at her sudden command of French. Another part realized she was truly terrified.

Then she heard the steps on the gravel. Almost aimlessly rambling. Recklessly, as though her menace was totally irrelevant.

"Stop! Arrête!"

The glare from the villa rendered it impossible to see into the darkness, and still the steps continued. Slow. Relentless. They were coming towards her now, reminiscent of the spooky stories they used to share round the campfires in Colorado. But this was real, hideously real.

Her heart was beating ever faster. Fear was now thundering within her. She fought to remain calm. Her tongue was dust and she hungered just to swallow. She'd hunted in the wild and the darkness a thousand times in Colorado. She was an expert. Her father had taught her to subjugate her fear in such situations. She now struggled to engage her training.

"Use your fear Kit. Draw from it. Fear is your friend. It gives you strength and warns you of danger. Embrace your fear. Learn to love it. Just don't let it rule you. Do you understand dear?"

"Yes dad." as she must now.

She slowly rotated her head. Using her ears. Seeking auditory balance. Attempting to triangulate distance and direction—also as her father had taught her.

"Last warning! C'est votre avertissement final!"

Still the footsteps advanced on her. Relentless. Fearless. Mindless.

She squeezed the trigger.

First barrel. A deafening boom, the gun slamming into her shoulder, the acrid smell of cordite oddly comforting.

When her head cleared: nothing for nearly half a minute. Then the terrifying steps began again, slightly faster now, seemingly more random. The direction was unclear. Though Ranny was convinced they were targeting her.

This SOB must be insane. He must know I can kill him, yet he seems totally fearless. Okay. Take another breath. Listen and target the footsteps. Speed, direction and distance. Wedge the gun harder into your shoulder. Stand more firmly. Lean into it. Squeeze it off. Squeeze it off. Slowly, slowly …

BOOM! Second barrel. A roaring blast thundered down the valley.

She heard a grunt of pain and a sort of whining keen. This was followed by a rush of footsteps and a crush of breaking twigs and flattened bushes. Then the crashing sound of falling and the haunting keening sound again. Then a struggling thrash through the dense underbrush in the gully, meters below.

Afterwards: Total silence.

She was trembling uncontrollably now. It was difficult to breathe and suddenly the gun in her hands seemed terribly heavy.

My God. I've just shot a man. Maybe killed him.

The gun slipped to the ground and she stumbled a few steps away before she retched. She supported herself, hands on knees for a time, eyes closed, head down, the bitter taste of bile burning her throat and churning her stomach. Tears were pouring down her face. A consequence of fear? Nausea? Remorse? She didn't know.

She took several more deep breaths to control her shaking and clear her head. Her heart pounded and she trembled on wobbly knees as her body labored to shed adrenalin. She shivered in the night air.

She realized Adam was standing beside her now, a powerful flashlight in hand. Things were eerily quiet. Slowly the chorus of frogs and crickets and night-birds returned, and the night began to assume a semblance of normalcy. Adam slowly played the light across the graveled darkness. Slowly, back and forth. A precisely etched, silver-oval of bas-relief, a stark spotlight on textured black velvet.

Ranny touched his arm, whispering. "What's that?"

"I can't tell. Let's see."

Ranny retrieved her gun and they lightly crunched across the yard until they reached a large dark spot on the gravel. Adam squatted down and examined it more closely. "Blood."

Ranny breathed in. "And that?" She pointed to a rounded object resting in the bloody pool.

Adam picked it up, smearing the blood with his fingers. "Looks to be some sort of fossil."

He handed it to Ranny, red and sticky.

She examined it closely in the harsh light. After a moment she started and nearly dropped it. "My God. The Devil's Toe-nail."

"*What?*"

Her voice had a flat funereal, resigned quality. "Never mind Adam. It just confirms a few things."

He was confused, but pushed on.

"Where do you suppose the body is?"

She took the light and moved it a few meters forward. "See those broken bushes? I think he jumped, or was blown over the cliff-line. We better take a look."

They apprehensively peered over the precipice. The powerful light shone into the steep gully, revealing nothing but a tangle of dark greenery imprinted with a trail of broken branches and matted underbrush. A few dark blurs of coagulating blood.

After a careful inspection, perched atop the cliff Ranny said, "I can tell where he's been, but I don't hear or see a thing. We should wait until morning and have another look."

Adam turned to her. "Should we call the Police?"

"I don't think that's necessary. Maybe tomorrow, if we find something. We may want to keep the Police out of this if we can. There may be nothing to find and we could face a barrage of awkward questions."

~~~~

A violent storm blew in that night. Ranny and Adam held each other through the wind and rain and thunder, as the lightning flashed through her bedroom. And they talked.

Ranny struggled to keep her guilty thoughts of David out of her mind, so she turned to Adam.

The bedroom was suddenly bright with a dazzling blaze of white lightning, soon followed by a window-rattling boom.

~~~~

The morning dawned bright and summery warm.

Like children studiously avoiding an unsavory task, they drank coffee, took an early swim to rouse themselves, and then hesitantly peered down the gully, observing everything. To their relief they found nothing. The bloody pool was long dissipated by the rain, so aside from a blood stained fossil, two spent shotgun shells and assorted broken branches, there was no evidence of the night's adventure.

Ranny insisted she would be fine. Hélène and Giscard would be coming soon. Consequently they broke off their investigation and Adam hurried home before they arrived. The strange incident would be known only to the two of them.

And whomever she'd shot.

Fade Theta

DAVID STRUGGLED FOR nearly twenty minutes to reach his backpack. He had to get to the river while he still possessed some mobility. It took thirty more long minutes to drag himself, his pack and his waders to the water's edge. His horizontal trek was agonizing. He suffered not simply from a compound fracture, but more than fifty percent of the skin on his right leg had been scoured away by the jagged cliff-line and his wrist was on fire. Infection was a looming menace, yet he knew he was incapable of washing in the river. He'd nearly passed out from pain two or three times during his clawing, dragging journey, which drove him to doze for a time when he'd finally reached the river.

When he'd rested and was breathing normally, he took inventory.

I've got all the water I'll ever need ... a foul weather jacket (I'll need that at night) ... rubber waders (can serve as a pillow, foot protection, maybe even a splint) ... gloves (good) ... sandwich (good) ... a candy bar! (nice surprise) ... mobile phone (damned thing doesn't work) ... aspirins (great, I'll take one now) ... matches (but no goddamned wood) and one more can of Coke.

He tore a sleeve from his jacket to stem the bleeding. He then slipped off his shoe and slipped on his right wader to protect the jagged protrusion. An exquisitely painful process requiring in excess of fifteen minutes, after which he moaned and rested for more than an hour.

All-in-all his spirits were good though. Despite the pain he would be fine for a time. He knew kayakers traverse this river constantly. He would be discovered soon, and before he knew it, he would be resting his leg in its new cast, enjoying a tall drink in the hotel bar, telling brave tales and figuring out some way to explain his stupidity to Ranny.

Then, it began.

A slow, dark, frigid rain. Dark gray skies without end blew in on an icy wind. It looked like a rain that would wear on for hours, or a day, or for days.

Damn! So much for the kayakers.

In the course of mere minutes his situation had become far more serious. Potentially deadly.

~~~~

Four days later the aspirins were gone, as were the sandwich and candy bar and soda. He lay huddled beneath the rain jacket and his backpack. His gloves were soaked, along with everything else. His leg throbbed incessantly day and night. He was suffering from exposure, lack of sleep and lack of food. An exquisitely painful infection was blossoming in his leg and he was prostrate with the cold. It finally became real to him he was in a life-threatening predicament. Fear was becoming an icy, immovable malignancy in his gut. He passed the time betting with himself where the greatest danger lay. Starvation? Exposure? Perhaps some animal would find him and dispatch him from his suffering? He put his money on exposure. Although barely detectable, a disturbing whiff of corruption emanated from his leg. Perhaps gangrene was a contender as well? He briefly considered attempting to wash his legs in the river, which he immediately rejected based on the swift rain-fostered currents and the icy cold of the water; not to mention his legs were now effectively paralyzed.

He discovered some yellow berries camouflaged within the leafy ground cover, and ravenously ate all he could find. They were unbearably tart, but they staved starvation somewhat. At the back of his mind he suspected he might be acting rashly. He vaguely recalled something about avoiding berries spurned by birds, but his memory seemed to have atrophied. Anyhow, there were no damned birds nearby. Else he would have tried to eat them instead.

~~~~

In the late afternoon it began.

Far downriver he sighted a huge shape under the water. A dark, long shadow, so large the water swelled high in its advance and drew low to its aft. As the monstrous creature moved downriver, massive waves sloshed over the banks, soaking the shoreline, as it undulated through the rain-murkied water.

That damned thing must be twenty meters long! What in hell's name is it? It looks like a … it can't be … but it looks like a … my God it looks like a plesiosaur! A Jurassic monster sixty-five million years extinct, in this little spit of a river?

When nearly upon him, it raised its sinuous neck as its snake-like head opened its yawing jaws relentlessly bearing down on him. Huge teeth, he estimated longer than 30 centimeters, growing nearer and larger. The monster emitted a high-pitched hissing. A sound he'd never heard the like of. As it drew nearer he choked on its breath. A fetid, rotted fish wind from hell. In a blind panic he desperately rolled away, as much as his beleaguered body could manage, awaiting the agony and horror of its enormous dagger teeth.

Moments later his trembling subsided and he raised himself to an elbow. Was he still alive? Apparently so. As he attempted to look about for the monster, he found he was no longer on his elbow. His elbow, in fact his entire arm had sunk into the pudding that had been firm ground only moments ago. Then his body began to sink as well. Soon he was immersed in a cloying heavy wetness. Finally his head disappeared into the muck leaving only one hand grasping and flexing. He felt the cold rain on his fingers and screamed without sound, or air, or light.

He opened his eyes.

He was on his back staring up at the gloomy drizzle which scant days ago had been an infinite blue sky. There were six people standing around him. Men and women. They looked vaguely familiar, although he couldn't seem to actually identify any one of them. Their skin was a repulsive fish-belly white, heavily blemished with pocks and mottled, angry red spots. They looked very grave, serious, even malevolent. Moments later they began kicking him. Hard, everywhere, unremittingly. He could feel bones cracking, organs rupturing and flesh bruising and splitting. The pain was awful, unbearable and cruel. All he could whimper was "Please ... please ... please ..."

~~~~

"It's okay Davey. They won't hurt you any more. You're safe."

His attackers had vanished, only to be replaced by a soothing, incorporeal voice.

"Who are you?"

"A friend. Drink Davey. I know you're terribly thirsty. You must drink."

He rolled back and laid his head down. It ached incredibly. And whoever, or whatever it was, was right. He was horribly thirsty. He opened his mouth wide looking up to the sky watching hypnotic, crystal spheres of water slowly float into his mouth. As the cool water filled his mouth he greedily gulped and gulped. A sublime relief.

He looked down, trying to locate his new friend, and immediately spotted a beautiful green eye gently regarding him. Then he saw its twin some three feet away. Then another, and another, and another; and endless more until his entire world consisted of these disembodied, bizarre green orbs.

After an hour or so, his head finally cleared, at least to the degree the hallucinations subsided; and he was alone again.

Jesus. What the hell was in those damned berries?

But his suffering was far from over.

~~~~

Then came the dreams.

Spectral nightmares, frightening and alien, yet disturbingly familiar somehow. Until he'd eaten the berries, his only escape had been sleep. He was terrified of sleep now, but succumbed to it constantly. He would struggle to keep awake and he would always lose.

And the dreams would come.

He was lying spread-eagle, shallow icy water swirling all about him. A small boy once again. Naked and freezing. A supine, water-borne crucifixion. He looked down. A small, sharp, gray pyramid was protruding grotesquely from his abdomen. His life ebbing away as crimson stained waters washed over him. He was pinned like a butterfly on a corkboard. No escape. No running away. He was waiting to die.

The cold and the pain were unbearable, his hands and feet an agony of alternating stabbing needle pain and icy numbness. But he felt oddly requited. It all seemed somehow ... fitting. Even strangely redemptive. Was he dying for his own sins? A hallowed self-savior? His own solely begotten?

High above him in the gloom, his sister June was looking down on him. Beautiful. A scornful Madonna savoring David's lonely, hellacious rapture. She shook her head in disgust, arms crossed, her hair blowing in the wind. She seemed bored, and annoyed and, frustrated he couldn't understand her. She raised her arms high above her, still looking down on him, an expectant look lighting her features. He couldn't move. And he was afraid to speak, or make any sound. Soon, in disgust, she ascended into the darkness and was gone.

He realized two others were now holding his hands. Right and left. He felt better knowing someone cared for him and his plight, and he was not alone. He instinctively knew they were his parents. He was encouraged and wonderfully comforted. Their presence brought him joy. He raised their hands to draw them nearer, to bask in their love. He smiled happily, bringing their hands together to sooth his freezing cheeks—to merge their warmth. But their hands weren't warm. They were ice. Horrified, he realized they were only hands, jointed to the remnants of their arms, worms and maggots, bone splinters, veins and bits of flesh dangling from their stumps.

His howling screams interminably echoed down the valley. He awoke, as always, choking and gasping for air. No more outcries. No tears, just the overwhelming, breathless, panic-stricken compulsion to escape the vision so vividly playing out in his mind.

As the hours wore on endlessly, the dreams came more often, with greater clarity. More powerful, more painful, drawing a dark curtain back just a little more with each terrifying recital. Gruesome details came clear, additional creatures joined the maggots in their hideous feast. Finally he saw it as it really transpired. Crabs and seagulls and blood and icy pain and death. A more agonizing catharsis was impossible to imagine. It tested his sanity to its limits.

It tested his will to live.

~~~~

The dreary cold-front finally meandered north and morning broke warm and clear. This probably saved his life. By noon he was reasonably warm and had finally taken water. The bizarre effects of the berries had worn off, and his fever had mercifully relented. He began to feel warmth for the first time in days. Then he caught the sickening necrotic whiff of his leg. Clearly he was still in great danger. But this sunny respite certainly improved his chances.

Around two in the afternoon, his head was clear. He had been thinking hard about his ordeal, the last days, and those horrific nightmares. After much introspection, he arrived at a remarkable conclusion.

My God. It's true. It's all true. The nightmares were real. It actually happened.

That's what happened to my parents. I was injured and they died horribly. And I ran away. I let them die.

He wept until exhaustion overtook his grief. Then he slept. Blessedly there were no dreams now. Despite the horrors they had inflicted on him, in their strange way they actually initiated his recovery.

When he awoke, he lay looking up at the sky, near catatonic.

~~~~

At five that afternoon.

"Monsieur? Monsieur? Êtes vous bien?" [Are you all right?]

David painfully rolled to his side, staring in disbelief at two kayaks being held in place by their helmeted owners along the riverbank. He said only one word.

"Jesus."

And he passed out.

Cubana

PAUL BELL. AMERICAN. Young. Fit. Masters Degree. Biologist. Good looking and carefree. He'd spent the last three years working illegally in the bars and restaurants from Marrakech to St. Moritz. The work was fun. The tips were great. Women of every description, just the type he fancied. And he was seeing the most glamorous parts of Europe. What begun as a summer junket had become a three-year-plus addiction. He couldn't think of any other lifestyle for his immediate future. Until he earned his PhD, he was making a good deal more money slinging drinks in trendy clubs across southern Europe.

St. Tropez however was proving to be the top of the heap. He'd never made such money, never had so many women, never had such fun. Movie stars, millionaires and moguls. Just now he was on break in the back room of Cubana gulping soda water.

"What a day I'm having out there. Do you know I've already sold two bottles of Cristal Champagne? And it's not even four o'clock! Imagine what tonight's going to do." He was calculating the tips in his mind and bragging to a cute blonde hostess.

A barman walked in to the small room. "Paul, there's a flic [cop] out there, wants to talk to you."

"Shit! I wonder what it's …"

"Don't worry about it. He's just looking for a guy who comes around here sometimes. Could be one of your regulars. If it is the man, he always sits at your position and you guys talk a good deal."

"Now how in hell would some damn cop know all that?" He looked at him with a sarcastic glare.

"Uh yeah. I guess … I told him. But he already knew your name."

"Don't worry about it. I've already talked to the cops once about this. If that's all he wants, no problem."

"Anyhow, you better get out there."

"What's his name?"

"Uh. Inspector … Mohsen. Easy to spot. He's wearing the only tie in the joint. At the corner table near the door, drinking coffee."

"Thanks."

Paul walked into the bar. Crowded. Lots of action. Throbbing music. He approached the table.

"Inspector Mohsen?"

"Yes. You are Monsieur Paul Bell?"

"Yes I am. What can I do for you?"

"Suppose we move to a table outside. It's deafening in here."

"Sure."

When they were seated "That's better. Monsieur Bell, I'm looking for a man, about 1.8 meters, maybe 80 kilos, salt and pepper hair with some graying, or sun bleaching. Tanned. Well dressed. He's reportedly a big hit with the ladies. Good looking and apparently a real charmer. He has been reported as frequenting this bar; and I understand you have a regular customer who may fit his description. Familiar?"

"Familiar? It should be. I gave his description to a local cop a few weeks ago. This guy comes in from time to time. What'd he do?"

Mohsen just stared at him blankly. "What can you tell me about this man?"

"Let's see … he comes in once a month or so, round eleven. Normally knocks back three or four Scotch/rocks, single malt, Glenfiddich. And then he leaves. Nice guy. Good tipper. Lots of women come on to him and sometimes he leaves with them. But he's got strange tastes in women."

"Strange? How so?"

"Well a lot of really gorgeous ladies approach him. But he seems to prefer the boozy, pushy ones. Most of them are past their prime."

"Do you know this man's name?"

"They call him Charley."

"Charlie." He scribbled in his notebook. "C-H-A-R-L-I-E?"

"Interesting you ask. Actually no. C-H-A-R-L-E-Y. In fact, as I recall he is very particular about the spelling for some reason. I remember him spelling it out for women from time to time."

"Ever hear anyone use a surname?"

"No."

"Does he ever pay by credit card?"

"Nope. Always cash."

"Have you ever heard anyone call him by another name?"

"No. Never."

"What about his nationality?"

"Well, judging from his accent, I'd say British."

"Mm. What else can you tell me about this man?"

"That's about all really. Or if it's useful, he always wears fancy, long-sleeve silk shirts. Cuffs up. Dark colors, high collar, no design. They look very expensive."

"That is all you can remember?"

"Yup. No! Well. For a while I thought he might be a gig."

"What is this *gig*?"

"Ah, a gigolo. That can be very profitable around here. There're a lot of very rich, horny bitches. I do it myself sometimes when it looks like fun and money. Sex, drugs and rock 'n roll as they say." He paused, frowning. "Maybe I shouldn't have said so much. Is gigolo-ism a crime in France?"

"In times past it was seriously regarded. Today? I think it is generally overlooked in most quarters. Certainly supplying drugs is looked upon darkly."

"So, would you do anything ... based on something I may have just said?"

"I have no interest in this gigolo or drug business. In fact Monsieur, this area is far from my jurisdiction. I have no such authority here. Even if I did, you are being most helpful. I would never take any such action."

"So you have no authority to question me about this Charley guy either?"

"Oh Monsieur. I assure you I have every authority. So we will continue please. Why did you believe this Charley was this *gig*?"

"Well, this one night, this ditsy 'ol broad came on to Charley. Big time. She was drunk as hell and it was clear she wanted Charley to fuck her stupid."

"What is this *dit-say-ole-brooad*?"

"Uh, sorry: An eccentric woman maybe a little past her prime. Often drunk. A little crazy. Often horny as hell. Okay?"

"And what led you to suspect Charley was this gig?"

"Well for one thing, his choice in women as I told you. The cougars he left with are normally the ones with the most money."

Cougars?

Paul's constant use of American idioms was growing tiresome. Alain asked for no clarification, as he believed he could intuit its meaning.

"Fine. Please continue."

"Anyhow it was clear Charley was not interested in this woman … until she said he had a 'frizzy' tan."

"Which is …"

"Well, I'm really not sure. I think she was talking about the wrinkles around his eyes. He is really tan, but the wrinkles around his eyes are white. Like from squinting into the sun for a long time. She said it made him look like a street person."

"Street person."

"You know. The sorts you find all over the world living rough, often peddling sex, or drugs, or whatever."

"I see."

"Well, that seemed to really piss off Charley. He turned on the woman and asked if she'd ever met a sailor before. What they looked like. What they did. What the sun did to them. If she even knew what the hell a seaman was. What the sea was like. Things like that. Then he threw some money on the bar, took her by the hand, and stomped out, nearly dragging her."

"Mm. Can you describe this *ditsy broad*?"

"Hmm. Let's see. Blond, huge tits, lipstick from ear to ear, nasty ear-rings and a butt-ugly summer dress. Green and yellow stripes with puffy sleeves."

Alain jumped forward, grabbing Paul's arm, a sudden urgency in his voice.

"*You said green and yellow stripes with puffy sleeves?*"

Paul was surprised and taken aback. "Yes."

"Were perhaps these nasty earrings large ivory hoops with a red disc in the center?"

"Why yes, I think they were."

The third victim! Vivian Carpenter!

"Why? What's going on with this ..."

"Fine Monsieur Bell." He extended David's photo. "Is this the man?"

"Uh, it could be. Hard to tell. This photo is badly faded, and it wasn't much to start with. Is this an old passport photo or something?"

"I believe it is."

Did Madame Woods purposely give me an extremely poor photo?

Alain withdrew a card from his pocket and wrote in a phone number.

"Here is my card. Please call me at once, at this number, if you see this man, or this *Charley* again, night or day. You are on duty here every night?"

"Sure."

"The St. Tropez Police will be contacting you to arrange some time with you." Noting Paul's troubled look, he continued quickly. "Not to worry Monsieur Bell. They will simply be asking you to review some photo-graphs. What you in the U.S. refer to as *mug shots*. They will also request you assist in developing a mock-up sketch of this man."

"I see. I know the drill. No problem." Paul's expression grew troubled again. "Will you be stationing someone here on site, at the bar?"

"That would be problem for you?"

"Well, it could be. Bars are never happy to have cops hanging about, and they might hold me responsible."

"Not to worry Monsieur. You are the sole qualified sentry I know of. After all, you are the person who can identify this Charley."

Paul smiled with relief.

Alain placed money on the table, stood, and shook hands with Paul.

"You have been most helpful. I will keep in touch."

When Alain returned to Coirón, Officer Kontz was not to be found. Assuming Kontz carried the duty phone, he resolved to fill out his report the next morning and call it a day.

A good day.

Basta

CHIEF INSPECTOR MOHSEN was nursing a glass of wine in the shade of an umbrella on Place Velleda. He was watching the pétanque players, seeing nothing, lost in thought. He'd had enough. He'd been working non-stop, seven days a week for more than two months, two more women had joined the gruesome roster of victims, and he was burned out.

This moronic Loup Garou investigation has peaked. The peeper photographs and the lead on this man Charley have gone nowhere and I'm out of ideas. I need a few days off, away from here, with my family in Paris. I'll return with a clear mind and a fresh start.

Minutes later he was on the phone with the Deputy Minister.

"Yes Minister. I believe I've been on site too long. I'm getting stale. I'll take a few days off. Go home. See my family. Then try to find a new angle of attack on this maddening case."

The Deputy Minister heartily agreed.

"I'll take three or four days; and I'll call you when I'm back in Coirón."

"Yes, I *will* get some rest. Thank you Minister. A bientôt."

Inspector Mohsen returned to the Gendarmerie. Still no Officer Kontz. He wrote a note to Kontz explaining his absence and he would find the latest updates to the case in the file. He instructed Françoise to give the note to Kontz and wished her a happy four days. He then stopped at Les Herbes Intrépides, packed a bag and was off. It was only four days, but he reveled in the holiday feeling of going home.

Officer Kontz was thrilled to have Mohsen out of his hair for a few days. He had his office back. It wasn't much, but it was all his again. More importantly, perhaps he could try those magic blue pills again?

Michelle would like that. Hell ... I would like that.

~~~~

The phone rang. Again. Unanswered, it would continue to ring incessantly.

He and Michelle groaned in unison.

"I am so sorry *ma cherie* [my dear]. It is the Gendarmerie. And I *did* leave early."

He lifted the hated device.

"Kontz."

"Hello. Is this the Gendarmerie de Coirón?"

"Yes."

"Is Inspector Mohsen there please?"

"Who is calling please?"

"My name is Paul Bell. I'm calling from a bar, the Cubana in St. Tropez."

"You are calling from a *bar.*"

"Yes."

"I see. Inspector Mohsen is not here and I do not expect him until late Sunday. What is it you wish?"

"He asked me to call him if Charley showed up here."

"Charley."

"Yes."

"Charley is presently in your bar."

"Yes."

"I will tell the Inspector when he returns."

"Okay. Thanks."

Kontz replaced the phone, forcing himself not to slam it down.

Idiot!

"Michelle ... don't move a pretty muscle my dear, I'm coming right back."

Hélas, trop tard. [Alas, too late.]

Medi-Vac-Back

FOUR DAYS LATER David was informed his ambulance had arrived for the long ride home. They had loaded him with antibiotics, splinted his leg, cleaned and bandaged his enormous scrape (thankfully Gangrene had only just embarked on its pustulent rout), although maggots had been utilized for two long days, much to David's revulsion, in conjunction with other procedures. All were a mystery to him.

They had first fed him intravenously, then a vegetable consommé, then soft foods, then an omelet, then he graduated to some sort of dead white, tasteless fish. They had also painstakingly treated him for exposure.

He was in remarkably good shape, save the extensive damage to his legs.

His Land Rover was still parked near the river. The least of his problems. This he would address later.

"How do you feel Monsieur Woods?"

"Great Doctor. Thanks to you. Ready to go home."

"You know Monsieur, you have been through a very difficult, life threatening ordeal."

"Yes?"

"You should not be too anxious to leave our Clinique and simply go home, as though nothing has happened. We should ensure there is no additional infection in your leg and confirm you are strong enough to travel."

"Nonsense. I feel fine. My leg hurts, which is only natural. But I can tell the pain is that of healing, not of septicity. Besides, I've been away from home for days now. My wife will be worrying. I must go home now."

"Septicity? Monsieur Woods you seem to be most well informed."

"Thank you."

"May I then also assume you are familiar with *clostridial myonecrosis?*"

"Mm ... no."

"Perhaps the *Clostridium perfringens* bacteria?"

"No doc." Mildly irritated. "What is your point?"

"My point is this. I refer to highly toxic, anaerobic bacteria that are the primary contaminants of gangrenous putrefaction. This process produces a gas which is often subcutaneous as a byproduct, essentially comprised of nitrogen ... hence the disagreeable odor you have no doubt noticed."

"I say again doc. What is your point?"

"You were suffering from the early stages of what we call wet gangrene, a life threatening condition. Are you aware we were compelled to place you in our hyperbaric chamber for a time? Residual toxins may still be active in your body. These could even now provoke the condition you refer to as septicity."[2]

David nodded his head patiently, despite his impatience.

"Further Monsieur Woods, you are well aware we were forced to employ maggot therapy to effect debridement of a significant amount of necrotic tissue. These are very serious issues."

"I understand Doctor. I will exercise due care. I assure you."

Arms crossed, lips pursed, the doctor peered at David skeptically. Finally he relented.

"Very well Monsieur. Our bureau has prepared your facture [bill], and we would kindly request you to sign *un dégagement* [a release] as well."

"That would be fine."

"I trust you *will* see your doctor when you return home?"

"Certainly."

"An ambulance is waiting. Shall we call your family? Alert them of your arrival?"

"Don't bother. I've not called my wife since I've been here. She would only worry needlessly. I won't trouble her now for the two or three hours until I arrive home. Let's go."

"I also have a prescription for your druggist."

"Don't you have a pharmacy here at the clinic?"

"Oui Monsieur."

"Please fill it here. No need for another trip to the pharmacy at home."

"As you wish Monsieur. If you will be patient a moment more, we will have your medication in the ambulance, and we will add it to your bill, which you will receive within days. We have already set aside our standard fees on your credit card. Your nurse will take you by our business office on the way to the ambulance, if that is alright?"

"Certainly."

"You have my best wishes Monsieur Woods. You are an exceptionally lucky man."

2 _This Will Kill You_. HP Newquist & Rich Maloof. St. Martin's Griffen. 2009. pp. 129-132.

Home-Gumming

THE AMBULANCE TRAVERSED the oval drive, coming to a smooth stop at the entrance of the Domaine des Collines. Two uniformed men stepped down from the cab and moved to the back. With practiced efficiency, they opened the large doors, smoothly slipped out a folding gurney with David aboard, automatically extending the wheels, placing the stretcher at the doorway. They rang the bell and waited.

Ranny open the door and was immediately shocked by the site of David trussed, stretchered, plastered and bandaged.

"David! My God, what's happened to you? Do you know how worried I've been? Where were you? Why didn't you call?"

David raised his head a little shakily. "May we come in please?"

"Oh God. Of course. Come …"

Ranny stood aside as the two men rolled David into the villa, looking about in fascination. One of the men turned to her questioningly.

"Follow me."

She had many questions and attempted to speak with the ambulance team. But they spoke no English and their French was spoken far too fast. Soon she escorted them out the door.

David was installed in his own bed, surrounded by the various accoutrements accompanying him in the ambulance. Windows opened, covers drawn, pillows fluffed.

"Ranny, I need a drink. A stiff one. It's been days."

"Are you sure that's a good idea? Medicines and all?"

"I'm on no medication, other than the occasional Paracetamol for pain." Then he mumbled in an inaudible voice. "And some mild antibiotics."

"Are you in much pain?"

"It comes and goes ... as does my deep, abiding thirst."

"Okay. What do you want?"

"G&T. A triple. One for you too, I think. You look pretty shaky."

Soon she was sitting beside David's bed, both looking better.

"Now. What the hell happened?"

"Well, I was hunting along the banks of the Ibie River where they had washed ..."

"Where is the Ibie River?"

"It's outside Vallon Pont-d'Arc, below its junction with the ..."

"Was *Marcel* with you?"

David paused imperceptibly. "No. I was hunting alone. I guess that wasn't too ..."

"Where was Marcel?"

David looked confused and slightly irritated. "If you'll allow me to complete the story Ranny, I'm sure all your questions will be answered."

"Fine. Go ahead."

She's a little crusty for the wife of a husband returned half dead from the wars. I guess she's really upset I didn't call. She looks tired and was probably half-crazy with worry.

He took a long pull on his drink, remembering where he'd left off.

"Anyhow, I spotted what may have been an interesting find about twelve meters up a cliff-line, and I decided to climb up. It was a rookie mistake, especially alone. I fell from about ten meters, broke my leg and tore hell out of the other leg sliding down. I lay out by the river for—for—I don't know how many days I lay out there. It began raining, cold, no food, I made the mistake of eating some strange berries, little yellow things ..."

I've seen those same berries, in these woods, right here in Coirón. I believe the plant is called Mandrake.

"... and I spent much of the time out of my head. But the most important part is ..."

"You told me Pont-d'Arc was hugely popular this time of year. Lots of campers, tourists, kayakers and such."

"Yes?"

"So why did it take so long for someone to find you?"

"As I told you. It began raining, so the river was deserted while ..."

It rained here only one night.

"These berries you claim you ate. Did you report this to the doctors?"

David's jaw tightened. *Claim I ate?* Then he forced himself to calm.

"Yes, but they didn't feel there was adequate ..."

"So they administered no tests for toxicity?"

"No. As I was trying to say ..."

"You are absolutely sure they were berries? There's some pretty weird mushrooms around here and you were out of your head by your own ..."

"Ranny, I know what I ate. And I am sure they were ..."

"I don't think you do David. There's all sorts of poisonous crap out there, berries, legumes, leaves, flowers, and you may have stuffed any damned thing down your neck."

"Goddamnit Ranny ..."

"Where are you injured David?"

He sighed silently, gathering his patience. Her attitude was a great surprise. All the same, patience and understanding were called for.

"As I said, my leg has a compound fracture."

He could have done the same falling over the embankment after I shot him.

"More than fifty percent of the skin on the other leg was scraped off and a touch of gangrene set in, which is under control now."

Number 16 shot would do that from about twenty meters, and easily covered up afterwards. Especially if he picked them out himself. Must have hurt like hell though. A stick, or a rock, or maybe he had a knife? He must have been going through a DID interlude. Otherwise I doubt he would have been capable of operating on himself and he would have most certainly known I would shoot, and shoot accurately.

This trumped up story is just the sort of thing he would come up with. For God's sake, it's nearly a retelling of his parent's deaths.

Maybe David discovered Adam and me together. Perhaps he himself is unaware of our relationship. But somewhere in that tragically tortured mind of his ... if he knows ... then he must hurt ... deeply ... and he may want ...

"Ranny?" She seemed miles away.

"Yes?"

"You want to hear this?"

"Yes. Continue."

"I was suffering from dehydration ..."

"Dehydration? On a river bank?"

"The current was a killer. The water was freezing. I had no mobility and I was either too weak, or too disoriented to drink. As I was saying, I was suffering from *dehydration*, hunger and exposure. I had no wood for a fire. I was out of my head most of the time. Dreams from hell itself. Hallucinations, even when I was awake. It apparently cleared my system in a couple of days. Perhaps that's why the doctors didn't test for toxicity. But the amazing part. Damned near a miracle. I remembered how my paren ..."

"Are you certain no gangrene persists?"

David sighed. "So say the Doctors."

He could have suffered from the same exposure trapped in the gully. And there really is no water down there. He could have made a fire, of course. But it would have drawn our attention. Without a fire we'd never have seen him. I wonder how he finally got out? I suppose he could have crawled through the gully, under our bridge and out to the road. Must've been agony though. Only a deranged mind would be capable of such a ...

"The weather finally cleared and a couple of kayakers found me. I was brought to the clinic and they finally brought me home by ambulance."

She pushed on. "Is that where the ambulance came from? Pont-d'Arc?"

"Yes. I suppose so. Why do you ask?"

"It looked like one of our local ambulances. I thought I saw Centre Médical du Var on the side."

"Could be. It's a round trip either way. Maybe the clinic called a local service from here."

"You didn't have to pay the ambulance?"

"I assume they just added it to my bill."

Oh David. David. It all adds up. You're telling me foolishness. I think you actually believe it yourself. It's getting clearer all the time. It is you. The Beast. Oh God. None of this ... none of it ... not one bit of it is your fault ... but it's you who will pay ... you have been paying for years. You probably had those photos in your jacket when we left that day. You waited at the post box long enough to get them wet. And you certainly knew a hellofa lot about Kodachrome.

Despite all her control, tears began trickling down her cheeks. She couldn't stop it. Soon she was sobbing uncontrollably. Everything seemed at an end. Everything collapsing about her. All she loved. All they had built. All she'd begun to hope for. Even her fantasies. Crumbling into lifeless, dusty illusions.

It would kill David to confront these horrific crimes. Crimes really not of his doing. His conscience would destroy him. The ordeal of a trial would be more than he could bear. He'd rather die. 'Don't let David burn.'

A fearsome solution crystalized in her mind. She stood. "David, I'm sorry, but I cannot face this. I love you, but this is more than I can handle. I'm calling St. Tropez right now to arrange for a nurse. She will stay here in the Domaine until you are better. I'll be here. I'll look after you as well. I just think we need some additional help and I need some time to think."

"Ranny, I'm sorry I didn't call, but it was …" She walked out. David heard her on the phone in the next room a few minutes later.

Well, I'm damned. What the hell was that about? Something's pushed her over the edge. That's the only explanation. I bet the nurse will look like a warthog. Wish I had another drink. Should've told her to bring the bottle, goddamnit.

Dumbfounded was the only adequate word for David's mental state. What had he done? Why was Ranny behaving this way? He didn't admit it, but she'd hurt him deeply. David wasn't one to hunger after sympathy, but he had suffered greatly. He'd nearly died. And he'd educed one of the great mysteries of his life.

But who you gonna tell? He thought bitterly.

"Ranny!" He hollered when he determined she was off the phone. "Would you kindly bring in a bottle of Scotch, a glass and a bucket of ice?"

She called back. "Now there's a great idea. How about lunch?"

"Fuck it."

A few minutes later she entered his room carrying a tray with ice, a glass, a bottle of Scotch, a ham and tomato sandwich, and an antique cowbell. The cowbell they normally used in the garden to call each other.

She set the tray on his bed, brought him his current book, his mobile phone, the TV remote and his computer.

"I'm going to be uh, working on the computer in my office. Use the bell if you need something. Your nurse will be here in an hour or so." In a patronizing childlike voice "Do we need to use the little boy's room?"

"No. Would you kindly hand me the remote please?"

"There we are. Anything else?"

"Nothing."

~~~~

Before her computer was up, before she was even seated at her desk, she had roughed out a plan.

First, she connected to, and engaged two specialty ISP sites. The first was in Frankfurt, which could mask her true locator in France. The second in the Canaries, which she would route through from Germany, to mask her shadow Frankfurt site, which in turn would complete the loop to the main processing and development center in Paris. She considered adding a third intermediary, and deemed it unnecessary. As she was an expert in the systems, her session would require but minutes.

After her work was done she would dismantle the entire access chain and delete her footprints, as much as possible, particularly her search argu-ments. Thankfully she had the authority to easily accomplish such tasks. Ideally no, or a near undetectable audit trail would remain; and remain obscure for months, or years, until its final purging.

She then connected with the IM-HOTEP central processing site in Zurich. Using her securities she set up a reasonably credible user ID.

Lastly she opened a session on the IM-HOTEP Pharmacist's & Doctor's Querybase.

She was ready to begin her search.

Fade Iota

"SO, OFFICER KONTZ, if I understand this message correctly, a 'man' called yesterday from a 'bar' in St. Tropez to alert me 'another man' was in the bar the previous evening. Is that essentially correct?"

"Yes Inspector. The man was either drunk or an idiot."

"Mais oui. Vous avez raison. Sans doute. Bien sure mon ami. [Of course. You are right. Without doubt my friend.] But I have a few questions. Okay?"

"Certainly Inspector."

"*Chief* Inspector."

Kontz's eyebrows jumped imperceptibly and he stood a little straighter.

"You noted this incident on a scrap of paper and placed it unobtrusively in the daily log."

"Yes."

"Exactly how do you suppose I would access this report without thoroughly combing through the log? As I did."

With the classical French inverted smile, delicate frown, head bob and shrug, palms up, Kontz expressed mock confusion as he vied for the time to invent some sort of defensible response.

"Why it … well it … it seemed trivial … I thought the man was drunk."

"The man who called, what was his name?"

"I was at home Chief Inspector. I had little time to …"

"What was the name of the bar?"

"Well, I had the same ..."

"Who was the man in the bar?"

"Chief Inspector, as I said ..."

"Who was the man in the bar?"

"Uh. I could have been Charles."

"What time was the call?"

"Sir, really I ..."

"What time was the call?"

"At approximately three-forty-five yesterday afternoon on the remote mobile. But I ..."

"I see. The office was unattended and you were home during duty hours. A woman may be dead now because of your negligence and incompetence. You are aware of this?"

"Sir, I resent your ..."

"Get out. Do not return to this office until the Mayor issues a formal order you be reinstated. Go look after traffic. Help old ladies across Place Velleda. Drink wine. Go fishing. Steal apples from the Épicerie. Anything. Just stay out of my way. And never, *never* answer the phone. Return your phone to Françoise immediately. Instruct her she is on twenty-four hour phone duty, with extra pay, until I get competent help from St. Tropez. She must alert me of *any* and *all* incoming calls *at once*.

"Go home now. Get your forwarding phone. Bring it here *now*, and turn it over to Françoise. You may keep your own police mobile. On my authority, you are on immediate administrative leave, until I, or the Mayor modifies your status. Clear?"

"Yes. But I ..."

"Do you have any fire arms in your possession?"

"No."

"Remerciez Dieu de petites faveurs. [Thank God for small favors.] Now get out."

Kontz stomped from the room, slamming the door behind, snarling to himself sub vocally. "*Fils de put! Enculez une mouche.*" [Son of a bitch! Go fuck a fly.]

"Françoise, please put me through to Mayor Drôme. When I have finished with the Mayor, I'd like you to come in. I have some extra duty for you. Just temporary I hope."

After a moment his phone rang. "Monsieur le Maire. Bonjour."

"Bonjour Chief Inspector. Your investigation goes well?"

"Yes, the investigation is making some progress. Thank you. But I have had some serious problems with Officer Kontz."

"Kontz? I'm not surprised. I inherited him from my predecessor. His brother-in-law I think. I imagine he is of little utility in a serious investigation."

"He is of little utility. Full stop. I do appreciate he was inherited by you. I do not appreciate he was assigned to me. I will explain more fully when there is more time. For now I would like to simply inform you I have placed Officer Kontz on administrative leave, which can be rescinded only by you, although he may pursue his duties *outside* this office. Traffic control and such."

"Things are that serious eh?"

"Yes. It is that serious. His negligence may have contributed to yet another murder ..."

"Mon Dieu!" [My God!]

"I cannot even trust him to answer the phone, or stand his post. But as I said, I will explain more fully when I am not so pressed for time. I do have a request."

"Yes Inspector?"

"Would you be so kind as to contact the Mayor of St. Tropez and request an Officer Thommes be temporarily assigned here in Coirón? Please billet him at Les Herbes Intrépides. I have also assigned temporary telephone duties to Françoise. She will no doubt be looking to you for overtime compensation."

"I fully support your action and I will call the Mayor immediately."

"Thank you for your help sir."

He was still so angry he was actually shaking.

I must calm down. We need action now. What next? Aaah ... I'll go to St. Tropez as fast as possible. It's ten-thirty. Cubana should be open for business.

He nearly ran to his car. For the first time in many months he placed the pursuit light atop the dashboard, activated the siren and drove on the jagged edge. En-route he phoned Cubana. "Is Mr. Paul Bell there please?"

"Just a moment."

"This is Paul Bell."

"Allo Monsieur Bell. This is Inspector Mohsen. I just received your message."

"You guys certainly take your time …"

"Yes, I am well aware this is a rather belated response. There was a problem at the Gendarmerie. I have taken care of it. Obviously, you are at the bar. I will be there within twenty minutes. You will please await me?"

"I'm on shift all day."

"Thank you Monsieur Bell."

~~~~

"So. Last night around eleven, Charley and a woman named Erica made a liaison. Correct?"

"Yes. I called it into your office the next day, but I got some idiot who didn't seem to give a damn."

"That has been remedied."

"I suppose I should have called it in earlier."

"It would have made little difference. What can you tell me about this woman Erica?"

"A first timer at the bar as far as I know. Anyhow, *I* never saw her before. I think someone must've recommended the place to her. She clearly knew the game before she walked in. Good looking. American. Upper twenties to early thirties. Auburn hair. Nicely built. Dresses provocatively, to say the least, but expensive. Lots of jewelry. Clearly very rich. Clearly loves to screw around. Not Charley's usual type."

Alain noted with approval that Paul had abandoned his use of American colloquialisms. He assumed this welcome absence of vernacular was for his benefit.

"She and her husband have just purchased a villa above Coirón. The husband is bringing their new yacht in from the UK. He's due to arrive the day after tomorrow, so she's making the most of her time alone."

Alain laughed aloud and clapped his hands once. "Felicitations Monsieur Bell! You would be a formidable policeman."

Paul flushed, clearly pleased. "Thanks to you, I was getting interested in the goings on around Charley."

"You still do not know his surname?"

"No. He's careful about using it I think. I don't suppose you might tell me now what he's up to? Does this have anything to do with all the murders?"

Again, the Inspector simply stared at him.

"Did Charley and this Erica leave together Monsieur Bell?"

"Yup. She and Charley and his usual walking umbrella."

"An umbrella? In this weather?"

"Every time he comes in. Sorry, I thought I told you about it. He leaves it by the door and takes it with him when he leaves. He's a stickler about it."

"Interesting. This is the first time you mention this object."

"It was the rainy season when he first started coming in, so it wasn't unusual. I suppose I got so used to it I don't really notice anymore. Although I don't remember him actually using the thing."

"I see. Why do you refer to this thing as a 'walking' umbrella?"

"Say again?"

"You called it a *walking* umbrella instead of simply referring to it as an umbrella. There is a reason for this?"

Paul frowned down at the table, lost in thought for a time.

"Yes. I suppose there is. I never thought about it much, but this thing has a large, ornate handle. Brass I think. More like a cane really. Made for walking more so than rain. Seemed a bit archaic and ornate to me."

"Ornate. How?"

"Let's see. It looks very expensive. Maybe an antique. Beautifully worked brass and hardwood. The handle is strange. A creature. I've seen it before in statues. A mythological creature I think. The head of a bird, clearly a bird-of-prey, like an eagle, but with ears I think, and the body like a lion. The handle was hooked. Evil looking thing. It was fashioned into a big hook combining the lion's talons and the bird's beak. Dangerous looking damned thing. Sharp. The end of the umbrella was also tipped in brass, with black silk enclosing it, as though it were an umbrella. But it didn't really look umbrella-like, if you know what I mean. In fact I never saw him open it up, even in the rain. But he always walked with it. Clicking and strutting along."

Alain vaguely saw a pattern emerging.

"Your powers of observation remain most formidable Monsieur Bell. My compliments."

"Thanks. But I can't count the number of times I've seen that ugly damned thing."

"What time did Charley and Erica leave?"

"A little after eleven-thirty."

"Mm-hmm. Do you know where they were going?"

"I believe I do. They whispered and laughed a lot, but I think I heard her suggest they go to her place."

"Do you have anything to add to this?"

"Um, yes. Wherever they were going, they went in her car."

"Why do you say that?"

"Charley said he had no car that night."

"I see. Any idea what sort of car she was driving?"

"I heard them talking about a new red Lamborghini."

"Excellent. Thank you Monsieur Bell. You have been most helpful. May I ask a personal question?"

"Uh, sure, I suppose so." Paul appeared a little uneasy.

"What is your educational background?"

"I have a Masters Degree in Biology and I plan to go back for my PhD. Problem is, I'm having too much damned fun over here."

Alain smiled. "Let me know if you ever decide you are interested in police work. Perhaps forensics?"

"Now there's something I never thought about. Forensic Biology? Mm."

Alain smiled musingly. "*Qui sait?*" [Who knows?]

~~~~

On returning to the tiny Gendarmerie, Alain was dazzled by the difference. The windows were open and the air was fresh, refreshingly free of cigarettes, no foul scent of garlic, stale coffee, or cheap wine. Most of the paper and paraphernalia were gone. The place had been cleaned. Even the furniture had been rearranged. A nice looking, crisply uniformed young officer sat at the front desk, the 'Beast' files spread before him, which he was intently studying. He looked up and stood when the Chief Inspector entered. He walked forward and shook hands.

~~~~

"Chief Inspector Mohsen, I am Officer Robert Thommes. I am most honored to meet you, and I thank you for requesting my assignment to this case."

"Glad to meet you officer. I read your report from Cubana, and I thought it well done. In fact I have just returned from the bar. You remember a young man who works there? An American. Paul Bell?"

"Yes. I interviewed him a few weeks ago."

"Right. Well he is proving most helpful. When I get everything written up, I'll give it to you for review. Meanwhile, what do you know about mythology?"

"Mythology?" Frowning. "Not much really. Roman? Sumerian? Egyptian, or what?"

"Mm. Not sure. I'm looking for a creature with the head of an eagle and the body of a lion."

"Oh, that's easy. The Griffin, or Gryphon. Greek."

"Excellent Officer. See what you can find about this creature."

"Certainly Inspector."

"I need a few other things as well."

"Yes?" Thommes retrieved a small notebook and pen from his uniform pocket.

"I need to know the name of any foreigners who have recently purchased or built a large villa in the hills above Coirón. The north side of the

D559, in the area the locals call 'Beverly Hills.' Unless she lied about it, the wife's name is Erica.

"Second, I need to know who has recently engaged a slip for a large yacht, most probably in St. Tropez, Ste. Maxime, or Port Grimaud. But anywhere around here able to accommodate a large yacht. I would guess twenty to thirty meters. Again, a foreigner, expected to arrive within twenty-four to forty-eight hours.

"Next, I need to know the registration of any red Lamborghini in this area."

"Sir, there's dozens of Lamborghini in this area and most of them are red."

"This one's new. It is registered to an American, or at least, a foreigner.

"Finally, Paul Bell has reviewed photographs of known offenders in PACA. I'd like the results. [PACA = Provence, Alps, Côte d'Azur]

"Got it?"

"Certainly Inspector. I'll get right on it."

"If Paul Bell calls, contact me immediately, no matter what, or where, or when. He may be alerting us to the presence of our murderer. He is called Charley. If you cannot contact me, handle it yourself. Do anything you deem necessary. Top priority. I will support whatever actions you take. Clear?"

"Understood Chief Inspector. There is one other thing. Just came in. It might interest you."

"Yes?"

"Last night the Gendarmerie in Cavalaire received a fairly garbled report by radio from an Italian trucker enroute to Marseille. He said he noticed something strange on the D559. He wasn't at all sure what exactly he saw. It was dark and foggy and he was probably speeding. But he thought he should report it. Although he left no contact details."

"Yes?"

"He said he saw a sports car by the side of the road, and a man stand-ing near it holding a tool, or a rod, or something. Said he was just standing there. Not moving."

"Yes?"

"And he thinks he saw a woman sitting in the grass close by, facing him, not moving either. Could have been a break-down, or anything else actually, but the driver thought it looked strange enough to report, especially considering the weather conditions at the time."

Alain sat down, lost in concentration, trying to reconstruct the scene in his mind. Make some sense out of it.

Officer Thommes was certainly thorough—almost maddeningly so—but smart and reliable. And at least he wasn't like that idiot Kontz, who would jot down some half-assed note and then lose it in the ... MERDE! ... Charley and Erica!

He jumped up and began pacing. "Robert, did this lorry driver give any indication where on the D559 he observed these people?"

Robert looked down at the FAX. "He reported it occurred roughly three kilometers east of the Coirón roundabout. The turn-off for Coirón would be the left on the circle and the 'Beverly Hills' turnoff to the right."

"I see. Left or right-hand side of the road?"

"He reported the right side."

"About what time?"

Officer Thommes looked down at the FAX. "The report was radioed in at twenty-three-forty-eight."

"Color of the car?"

"He never mentioned it."

"Do we have any identity information on the trucker."

"None sir."

Alain tried to keep the excitement from his voice. "I'll be out on the D559. I want to take a look around. Then I'll make a call on the Woods. You are familiar with them?"

"Yes. From the file."

"Any questions before I go?"

Robert frowned. "Ah. Will I be working with Officer Kontz on this assignment sir?"

Alain grinned broadly. "Not unless you enjoy helping old ladies find their way across Place Velleda."

Fade Kappa

WHEN SHE WAS absolutely convinced of David's guilt. When she'd arrived at the inescapable, inevitable conclusion. She locked away all emotion and transformed herself into an analytically dispassionate internist, coldly interrogating IM-HOTEP for the optimal therapeutic.

The answer: *Castor Beans* (*Ricinus communis*—Family *Euphorbiaceae*)

She briefly considered collecting local Mandrake berries. After all they were the berries he claimed to have eaten. But they left traces, and residue from the berries would not naturally remain in his system for so long after his return home.

Her search quickly yielded the exact result she'd hoped for. She was in and out of the system in less than ten minutes. In three more minutes she had deleted all evidence of her specious user ID—insofar as possible. Considering there were quite literally thousands of users worldwide logged on at any given moment, she was not overly concerned.

To further obfuscate her activities, she signed in, on her own network access, using her own password/sign-on. Then she executed a lengthy, complex regression-test-script. Ranny had developed this particular script weeks ago to access literally every hypermedia information provenance in the entire IM-HOTEP system. It executed for more than four hours, leaving her footprints conspicuous throughout. As a key element of her contracted consulting services such activity would go unquestioned. Her presence on the system would appear routine and fully authorized.

Ironically, she would be forced to invoice the project for her time in order to consummate her subterfuge.

~~~~

An idea occurred to her. She thought back to the day when this all seemed to start. A shadow faded, rain soaked package, and a strangeness that never passed. She returned to her computer and looked up France Telecom in Charleville-Mézières. Soon she was on the phone with their Contracts Manager, Monsieur ADOLPHE Depaul, who happily spoke perfect English.

"Good afternoon Monsieur Depaul, I am Katherine Day of DAYnet-Advanced-Systems Ltd. You may know us as DASL."

"Uh yes. I believe I've heard of your company, a few years ago I think. What can I do for you?"

"I was wondering if you still outsource topographical studies for your wireless communications."

"I've been here many years Ms. Day, and in all that time we never contracted any such studies. In fact wireless communications has never been one of our activities at this branch."

Ranny sat in silence for a time.

"I understand. Have you ever done any work with a company called ADL (Advanced Design and Logistics)?"

She could hear his key clicks interrogating his computer. "No. Never."

"Well, thank you very much for your time Monsieur Depaul."

She sat motionless, inducing her memory to clearly recall David's words the day they found the film package in the rain. Thankfully she enjoyed near total recall.

Her eyes were closed. Tiny lines forming at her temples.

He said 'Rain fade' and then he said … he said 'Charlie.' No. No he said 'Charle …' and then I interrupted him, and then he stumbled around and came up with Charleville and some cock-and-bull contract with France Telecom.

Okay. Two possibilities. One. Monsieur Depaul has it all wrong. Or two. David really did say Charley, realizing his slip he came up with a damned fast recovery. I think I know which.

More damning evidence in the case against David.

~~~~

Castor beans are quite common. They grow wild and in gardens all over the world. Attractive foliage, pretty flowers, deadly beans. They are available in any garden shop, yet they are recognized as one of the most lethal in the entire plant kingdom. An adult can die within forty-eight to one-hundred and twenty hours as a result of ingesting from six to twelve beans. Their taste is essentially neutral, though slightly bitter. The active ingredient is the *phytotoxin* known as *ricin*. Totally absorbed or evacuated, and undetectable after having completed its murderous odyssey through the victim's body.

If treated in time a full recovery can be expected. Treatment is quite simplistic. Assisted breathing. Intravenous fluids. Medications to treat seizure and low blood pressure. Flushing of the lower tract with activated charcoal. Very straightforward.

Untreated, death begins with a burning sensation in the mouth and throat, abdominal pains, purging and bloody diarrhea. Within days there is severe dehydration, a drop in blood pressure and a decrease in urine. Unless treated, death can be expected to occur shortly thereafter. A great many ailments manifest nearly identical symptoms, rendering diagnosis all the more difficult; and effectively masking evidence of a crime. The real complication, the true danger to the victim, is the extreme difficulty in diagnosing and identifying the toxin itself. Therein lies the killer. A phantom assassin, sliping in unnoticed. Departing without trace.

Perfect.

It was already well established David had consumed some sort of unknown plant during his ordeal. Berry, leaf, root, or legume? Who knew? David certainly wasn't a reliable witness. Better still David had advised his doctors of his vegetal contamination.

His death would necessitate some pain and discomfort. Not excessive, and without fear, or shame, or guilt. Without even the suspicion of impending death. Either way, its quiescent acquittal would far outweigh the horror of discovery. The realization he is a serial killer. That he is a monster. The horrific trial to follow. The punishment which would certainly ensue. In David's case this was without doubt tantamount to, and far worse than a death sentence.

She was determined to see it through. She would see him dead before she would see him in the dock.

I will not let David burn.

Having concluded there was no other solution, no delay could be permitted. Other lives were imperiled beyond David's. It was time to act. Despite all other distractions, her plan was now precisely mapped out in her methodical mind.

The next morning she tucked her hair under a floppy garden-hat and donned dark glasses with a loose fitting smock. She then drove to the town of Fayence, roughly an hour and a half from Coirón. Fayence is well known for its pottery. It also boasts an excellent garden marché. There she bought grass seed, fertilizer, some decorative stone, a packet of clover, and four packets of Castor Beans. All of which would find its way into a deep, muddy drainage pit east of Fréjus, save the Castor Beans. These specific beans were sold for the purpose of killing moles, which were prevalent throughout the area in autumn.

She believed such a purchase was best made far from the intended murder site, at a busy, crowded market, in cash, lost amongst many other purchases. She could hardly be remembered.

On her return journey she stopped at a supermarché and purchased chicken breasts, onions, garlic, chili powder, cumin, cayenne pepper, black beans, masa-de-maiz flour, stewed tomatoes, corn, green chilies, jalapeño peppers and cilantro.

Tonight she would surprise David with one of his favorite dishes:

Santa Fe Skillet Chicken Stew with Black Beans

… a spicy, pungent dish from the American Southwest.

She'd learned how to make it in Colorado and she'd prepared it for her father since she was old enough to reach the stove. David was nearly as fond of it as her father. This time she would prepare it a little differently and a little spicier. First she soaked the beans in lukewarm water for four hours and then started the stew. When the stew was nearly ready, she would divide it into two skillets. One for her, the other for David, with the added ingredient of fifteen crushed Castor Beans. She was quite sure the fiery concoction would mask the bitterness of the Castor. Given a slow simmer, the beans would break down into the stew to the point of obscurity. She would serve black beans on the side, but very little for David. He should consume all his stew.

~~~~

Nurse Bridgette Landon arrived promptly at four the preceding afternoon and was working in well. She spoke perfect English, as Ranny had requested. David liked her. She looked nothing like a warthog and was actually rather pretty in fact. Ranny liked her as well. She also provided Ranny with the latitude to execute her plans. Moreover, she would provide an excellent expert witness should the need arise. She had made a point of discussing David's illness and subsequent delirium, attributable to eating 'some sort of plant' along the river. This, at a time when he was already half out of his mind with pain, fatigue, exposure and infection. She carefully briefed the nurse in David's presence, ostensibly to alert her of a potential relapse. Naturally, David did not dispute Ranny's account in any respect. Nurse Landon was now 'primed'.

As Nurse Landon entered the kitchen, she was overpowered by a haze of pungent Southwestern cuisine. Exactly as Ranny planned.

"Mon Dieu! Quelle odeur. [What a smell.] What is it you are preparing Madame?"

"It's an American dish which is also part American Indian and part Mexican. Chicken Stew with Black Beans. A specialty where I grew up and a favorite of David's."

"Mais Madame [but Madame] are you certain Monsieur Woods should take such spicy food so soon?"

"I thought about that. But frankly Bridgette, I think it's far more important for David to start eating. For that, he needs some dishes he is really fond of; and he's always had an exceptional tolerance to spicy foods. He makes a Madras Chicken Curry that can burn the enamel off your teeth."

"I see."

"I made enough for three. I thought you might like to join us?"

"Uh. Non. Merci Madame. I brought my dinner this evening."

"Okay. Well, too bad." *I love the French.*

Things were proceeding perfectly. She was beginning to somewhat savor this intrigue.

Suddenly she quite literally froze. She had immersed herself so fully in the intricacies of her plot she'd actually forgotten it was exactly that. A deadly plot to murder a man. A man she truly loved. Her husband. Her lover and partner. A man she loved, respected and hitherto protected.

In some perverse manner she'd found herself almost enjoying her role of stealth killer. Relishing the game. Was she crazy? What malevolent infection was borne by this DID virus David carries in his mind? Is it somehow contagious? Was she becoming a demented necrotic beast as well? She was no killer, no murderer. Ranny was not religious, but she deeply believed in the sanctity of human life. Decency and virtue are not contingent upon pietism. In many ways they thrive in its absence. She could imagine no greater crime than the intentional taking of ...

NO!

I'm being weak. I'm trying to give in, to rationalize myself out of this. Is there a greater crime than murder? You're damned right there is. Allowing death and horror and suffering to go on and on ... through inaction. I'm not doing this for fun, or because I'm sick, or for greed, or freedom, or even to be with Adam. I'm doing this because I love David.

She silently chanted Aunt Carol's mantra over and over again, the words ringing through her mind, galvanizing her resolve.

Don't let David burn ... Don't let David burn ... Don't let David ...

I've got to be hard, dispense with maudlin platitudes, and bogus morality, and get it done.

She set her jaw. Leaning into the stove. Gathering strength.

Ranny made a show of loading a tray with two large bowls of her stew, silverware, napkins, wine glasses and a chilled bottle of Bandol. She carried it into David's room.

"What is this? Good heavens! Ranny's infamous *Colorado-Wildfire-Chicken-Foot-Stew* ... feared and respected throughout the American Southwest. What a nice surprise. How thoughtful. It smells wonderful ... and a little dangerous."

She thought abjectly and not a little morbidly. *It is.*

"I thought you needed to eat a good meal. After all, you were stranded on that damned river for days."

She put the tray down and favored David with a kiss and a warm smile.

"I know you like it hot, and this should really float your boat. But I think you should take your pills first." She rang the cowbell.

"Oui Madame?"

"Would you please give David his medications before we have dinner?"

"Oui Madame."

When all was complete. "Let's eat! Bon appétit."

"Mm … This is your best yet … It's got a tang to it … and you certainly didn't spare the cayenne or jalapeño. The wine is excellent and a chilled rosé cools things down nicely. Good grief, I'm sweating. Could be a long night, up and down with all this plaster. The chicken literally falls apart …" and so it went until David's bowl was empty.

After Ranny had cleared the dishes away, she joined David on his bed and the two watched a movie, his arm warmly enfolding her.

After a time Ranny looked up at David. "Getting tired dear?"

"Uh yeah, I'm suddenly very sleepy."

After Ranny and Nurse Landon prepared David for bed, Ranny leant down and kissed him. "It's good to have you safely at home again David. I love you so much."

"I love *you* Ranny. Goodnight."

As David drifted off, he smiled.

Ranny seems normal again.

Thank God.

It's good to be home.

Fade Lambda

"OFFICER THOMMES?"

"Yes Inspector."

"I need a forensics team as soon as possible, on the D559, exactly 2.9 kilometers east of the Coirón Roundabout. Contact the Mayor for assistance, if need be. You should be able to find a team from St. Tropez, Cannes, or Marseilles. I've placed a traffic cone roadside, at the exact location. I want them to take photos and castings of tire tracks and various footprints. I want them to check for blood, semen, hair, anything that might yield DNA samples, or any sort of clue. It rained last night, so this will be extremely difficult.

"The good news is I've determined the site extends no more than five meters in any direction from my cone.

"I have retrieved and bagged a sort of a walking stick at the site's perimeter. What with the rain, I imagine we can forget about finger-prints, or reliable DNA residuals. However, I believe this stick may be our murder weapon. It's perfectly structured for the killings. I also believe it is the same object described by Paul Bell. I'm puzzled the killer would simply abandon it beside the road. It looks quite expensive and he reportedly prized it greatly. There is no indication of a struggle. So why did he abandon it?"

"Perhaps he's finished killing."

Alain chuckled humorlessly "I wish." He mused for a moment. "We might be able to retrieve blood samples in the grooves of the metalwork. When I've finished with the stick, I'll make it available to forensics. Got it?"

"Yes sir. I'll get on it right away."

"Good. Keep me posted. I'm on my way to the Woods home now."

~~~~

There was no response to his knock. Yet he could hear a great deal of activity within. The door was slightly ajar, so Alain hesitantly pushed into the room.

He walked into literally a three-ring circus.

Hélène was rushing about with pans and pails and mops and towels and bedclothes. Ranny was engaged in a highly animated discussion on the phone, a variety of medicines spread before her. Giscard the gardener was hurriedly moving a table and various, unidentifiable furniture into a room down the long angular hallway. Meanwhile, the disturbing sound of violent retching emanated from the same room.

Clearly this was no time to come calling. He turned on his heels and moved noiselessly towards the door.

"Inspector Mohsen?" She sounded harried, brusque, but oddly not displeased to see him.

"Madame Woods, I am terribly sorry to disturb you at such a time. I will contact you later in the week. Please forgive my ..."

"It's alright Inspector. I know things look pretty hectic, but all is in hand now and I'm just waiting for Doctor Lefebvre to arrive, which will take some time apparently. Please come in. Have a seat. This morning's been a nightmare. But it's calming down now; and I'm going to have a glass of wine. Care to join?"

Again she makes overtures of trust and calm. Fine. I shall do the same.

"Just a small one. Thank you."

Ranny brought their wine, served Alain, seated herself and drank deeply. She then looked at the Inspector inquiringly.

"I am sorry to bother you yet again Madame. Especially today, which appears particularly difficult. I have a few additional questions. I promise they will take but a moment."

"Yes?"

"Forgive my asking. Is someone ill?"

"Yes. My husband."

"He has returned then?"

"By ambulance. Seriously injured. He suffers from a compound fracture, prolonged exposure, some sort of toxin he possibly ingested during his ordeal, and possibly the residuals of gagrene."

"Ordeal?"

"He fell from a cliff-line on the Ibie River, outside Vallon Pont-d'Arc. He lay there for several days until help arrived. He suffered terribly and still suffers from the effects. I believe he was close to death."

"I am sorry to learn this Madame. What is his prognosis?"

"I believe he should fully recover, except perhaps for the plant toxin he ingested. As a result of the toxin he was delirious for two or three days, and apparently he still suffers from its effects. Or maybe it's just the result of his hardships. I hope Doctor Lefebvre will be able to identify the problem."

"As do I Madame. You're certain some sort of plant toxin is involved here?"

"Not at all Inspector. I'm basing my plant theory on a statement made by David."

"Statement?"

"Yes. He said he ate some strange little yellow berries, or some such, and was out of his head for a day or two, or possibly longer. Considering his condition, he could have eaten anything, a mushroom or something else, or perhaps nothing. He may have imagined the whole thing. I really don't know. He was quite nauseous this morning." She grimaced wryly. "But that could be attributable to almost anything … including my cooking."

"Your cooking Madame?" Alain smiled.

"I made one of David's favorite dishes last night. A sort of welcome home dinner. But it's rather spicy. It might not have agreed with him. My stomach is not all exactly settled today either. It *was* pretty hot. I probably should have exercised better judgment, but I thought it important he eat something."

"I see. The famous American Tex-Mex."

"Something like that."

"Did anyone else consume this dish?"

"Just David and I."

"Do you have any remnants of this meal?"

"I'm afraid not. We ate it all, and I cleaned the dishes last night."

"I see. Well, I hope he feels better. May I ask a few short questions now?" Alain withdrew a small notebook from his coat.

"Certainly. Proceed."

"Your husband, David. Does he have a middle name?"

Her look of surprise was impossible to mask. "Why?"

"For our files. We try to be thorough."

She studied him thoughtfully, even skeptically, for a few moments.

"His middle name is Worthington."

"Quel nom formidable." [What an impressive name]

"Mm." She smiled cynically. "Surely Inspector, you didn't come all the way out here to ask me my husband's middle name?"

He ignored her question. "Tell me Madame. Is the name 'Charley' familiar to you? Ending in L-E-Y, instead of L-I-E?"

Ice water flooded her veins. Ranny stared at him intensely. *CHARLEY!*

I know that name ...

"Any way you spell it Inspector, I don't know any Charley."

She is lying. I swear it. She cannot look at me. Her eyes are dilating and she's fidgeting with her sweater.

"Was there a missing persons report filed on your husband?"

"No. He is often gone for days and out of mobile phone range as well."

"I see. Strange. I heard nothing of this incident in the news, nor in our bulletins. When was he found?"

"Around four days ago now. He wasn't found by the authorities. A couple of kayakers found him and took him to the hospital. I don't see how the police or any official agency would have become involved.

"David arrived home yesterday morning by ambulance. The news is well beyond my control. Frankly, I'm pleased the press has overlooked the incident."

"So a police report was not filed Madame Woods?"

"I wouldn't know Inspector. I doubt it. Perhaps that's why it didn't appear in the news. I should think this was *your* field of expertise. By the way, any progress with those photos Inspector?"

Now she becomes a little aggressive.

"Alas, not as yet. Be assured we are giving the matter every consideration. Do you know when your husband may be able to speak with me?"

"I really couldn't say. Not today. As I said, he is quite ill. It could be a few days before he's fit to talk."

"I wonder if I might discuss this with his doctor?"

"You certainly could if he had one. As I said, he came in by ambulance. Whoever his doctor is, he's in Vallon Pont-d'Arc. I've called Doctor Lefebvre in because he came highly recommended. But as yet, he knows nothing of David's case. We seldom have need of doctors, so we don't have what you might call a family doctor."

"I see. You *will* call me when he is able to speak with me?"

"Most certainly Inspector. Shall I ask Doctor Lefebvre to call you after he's seen David?"

Nice touch. She thinks things through.

"That would be fine Madame."

Ranny sat back, crossed her legs and sipped her wine. Then she inquired casually. "Who is this Charley person?"

Excellent. She wants to know how much I really know.

Mohsen decided to take her into his confidence. Not because he trusted her. Instead he wanted to gauge her reaction.

He leant forward in mock conspiracy. "You must understand Madame nothing is substantiated. This is therefore … unofficial conjecture … but this *Charley* was reported as being in the company of several of the victims immediately prior to their deaths. It is highly possible we have found our murderer. But until these things are verified, they may mean nothing, so please keep this confidential. All the same, we also have a very reliable witness, which changes the complexion of the entire case."

Luck was with Ranny. She happened to be sipping her wine when the Inspector shocked her with this revelation. She took another long slow sip now. This gave her the time to gather her wits, and more importantly, wet her mouth. She watched Mohsen observing her closely, boldly and openly.

Now she understood the game. It took all her resources to maintain a semblance of calm.

Ah! I have surprised the lady.

Ranny offhandedly took her wine glass in both hands and took another long, slow draught.

Damn that little Frenchman. He blindsided me. This is why he came.

Alain regarded her pleasantly. "One last question please."

"Yes?"

"Would you have the name of the ambulance service which brought your husband home? And the name of his hospital in Vallon Pont-d'Arc?"

"No."

"No?"

"No. I'm not sure why you wish such information, but I imagine my husband knows. I'll ask him when he's better."

Alain studied her quizzically.

"Would you care for some more wine Inspector?"

She is frightened. There must be some sort of connection.

"Most kind, but no thank you. I must go. I will be in touch Madame."

I'm sure you will.

Fade Mu

ALAIN PASSED AN exceedingly indifferent lunch at Le Cheval Blanc. He had unwisely ordered the *plat du jour* [dish of the day], as he foolishly did nearly every day, and invariably wondered what exact day they'd had in mind. He rejected the remainder of his lunch in favor of a coffee when Officer Thommes approached his table.

In response to Alain's inquiring scrutiny, Thommes brandished the mobile phone with a knowing smile.

"Any phone calls?"

"I'm afraid not sir."

"Have a seat Officer. Care for a coffee?"

"Thank you. I have the information you requested this morning. It's rather interesting and I thought I might find you here."

"Already? How did you manage so fast?"

"Well it was a slow day at the Call Center in St. Tropez, so I enlisted some of the boys to help out."

"Well done. So what have you got?"

Thommes flipped open his notebook. "First. The Griffin is a mythical Bronze Age creature with the head of an eagle, body of a lion, often ears, occasionally wings and either the claws of a lion, or talons. It was considered as a protector from evil and ..." He glanced up at Alain meaningfully. "... it was also considered a reaper of vengeance. Revenge."

"Interesting. A deranged avenger nicely coincides with the emerging profile of our killer. What else?"

"I spoke with the local Notaire. He reports they conducted a closing on a very large property up in the hills, twelve weeks ago."

"The buyer?"

"A Mr. Abjörn Martin."

"Intriguing name."

"It's Danish. It means something like *the bear*."

"I see. Wife?"

The young officer grinned with pride. "Mrs. Erica Martin."

"My God! You've got it. Address?"

Thommes handed Alain a neatly written slip of paper with an address and phone number.

"Next. The Gendarmerie in St. Tropez reported that Monsieur Bell could identify none of the photographs presented him."

"Disappointing."

"On the other hand, the Harbor Master in St. Tropez reports a large slip was also leased about a month ago."

"Abjörn Martin?"

"Yes sir. His boat is expected in this week. This is its maiden voyage. Nice boat. A thirty-six meter Sunseeker. British registration, Port of London, QR133-B, white hull, named *Soløi*."

Alain whistled softly. "As the Americans say, *Bingo!*"

"Yes sir." Thommes agreed smiling.

"What was the boat's name again?"

"*Soløi*. Pronounced *sole-hoi*. It's also Danish. Translates to *Island in the Sun*."

"Interesting. Martin is not a Danish name."

"I thought the same, so I checked it out. It seems he changed his name from Martinsen about ten years ago after there was some sort of trouble in Denmark. His wife is American. He is a UK resident. Not a citizen. This is confirmed by British Immigration."

"You've certainly done your homework Officer. Anything on the red Lamborghini?"

"Registered by a dealer in Cannes last month, to a Mrs. Erica Martin."

Alain sat back beaming with satisfaction. He drained his coffee and glanced pointedly at Officer Thommes. "So what else do you have?"

He laughed at Robert's bulging eyes and incredulous expression. "A small joke Officer. You've done an outstanding job." He stood. "Finish your coffee. I believe I will make a call on Mrs. Erica Martin. I would appreciate it if you would alert the Service d'Aide Médicale Urgente." [Rescue Squad]

"I'll dispatch them immediately if you wish."

"No. I can't justify dispatch. I just want to be sure they're on standby and know the address. I would imagine it needs twenty minutes to arrive. And I don't want to alert Mrs. Martin in advance."

"No?"

"No Officer. I prefer to appear unexpectedly. I want to catch her off guard. Realistically, it's been long enough since her encounter with Charley she'll either be alive and well, or long dead. Either way, I hope she's at home."

~~~~

Alain located the villa with little difficulty. It was an enormous complex, very modern, housed under the largest slate roof he had every seen. Its high walls were encircled by the muddy roads and assorted detritus of heavy construction. The main gate was open and beyond he found several trucks heavily laden with greenery and tall elegant palms. Roughly twelve men were scattered about the extensive grounds, busily landscaping, digging, planting and shaping. Alain threaded his way to the main entrance and parked. At the imposing front entrance he pulled a rather ostentatious looking chain mounted at the left side of the door. He was rewarded with the toll of a large bell.

Sounds like a bloody monastery.

Moments later the large, intricate black door slowly opened and Alain was facing a nice looking younger woman, late twenties or early thirties, faded blue jeans, sandals and what used to be called a peasant blouse. Her hair was wrapped in a red bandanna and there were smudges on her face as though she had been working in the garden.

"Bonjour, is Madame Martin at home please?"

"I am Erica Martin."

Alain concealed his surprise admirably. This creature was far from the Erica Martin Paul Bell had described. Far from the corrupt, hardened woman he imagined would be the lady of this house.

She looks familiar ... or she reminds me of someone. Ah! Madame Woods. Interesting.

"Pardon Madame, I am with the police." He proffered his badge. "Forgive my intrusion. I can see you are busy, but I need a few moments of your time. You may possibly be of assistance in an investigation we are currently conducting."

She studied him for some moments. Not in a hostile manner, more as though she couldn't quite grasp the meaning of his words. Then she delicately started, suddenly aware.

"I'm sorry." She spoke falteringly. "Of course. Please come in."

As he followed her to a large sitting room "Please forgive the mess. We're just moving in, and I have no idea where half this junk is supposed to go."

They seated themselves, facing each other on opposing loveseats.

"Not a problem Madame. I will make this very brief."

"That would be fine. What would you like to know?"

"Just a few questions. Were you in St. Tropez three nights ago?"

She looked up thoughtfully at the ornate ceiling. "Three nights ago ... yes. I went there for dinner."

"Do you remember the name of the restaurant?"

"Yes. The *Café de Paris*, on the port."

"And then you went home?"

"Yes."

"You went *directly* home?" Alain spoke very softly.

"Yes."

"Madame, we have information you stopped at *une boîte de nuit*."

"A what?"

"Yes Madame. A nightclub ... a bar ..."

"Oh I see. Ah yes, I believe I did stop off for a nightcap on my way home."

"A *night cap?*"

She smiled. "Sorry. Nightcap is American slang for a last drink."

Alain smiled as well. "I understand. A charming expression. I must remember it." He pursed his lips good-naturedly. "I teach you the French colloquial and you teach me the English colloquial."

"It's rather outdated these days. It was in more common use in the nineteen-twenties and thirties when ..."

"With this serial killer about, were you not nervous being out alone?"

"We've just come to this area. I wasn't really aware ..."

"Where did you stop for this nightcap?"

"Oh, I'm not sure I knew the name of the bar, it was ..."

"Could it be a club known as Cubana?"

She seemed to think about the question.

She stalls for time. She begins to grow nervous. She is surprised to be confronted by the Police. It started with dinner. Alone. Her husband at sea. A little too much wine. Then a mischievous flirtation with a handsome stranger. More drinks. Inhibitions and judgment washed away in a haze of alcohol. Then something happened. What? Whatever it was, she somehow survived.

"Yes. Cubana could be the name. A very lively place. I think our realtor recommended it."

"What is your realtor's name?"

"Ah let's see ..."

"A woman?"

"Yes. But offhand I can't remember her name ..."

"It is not important. What time did you arrive at Cubana?"

"Oh, I'd say around ten-thirty."

"Mm-hmm." Alain was looking down at a pad, pencil in hand, as though he were reviewing notes. "Did you speak with a man there? Nice looking, tanned, well dressed, blondish hair?"

"I spoke to a few people."

Now I catch her in the lies.

He looked up sharply. "Who?"

"I beg your pardon?"

"With whom did you speak exactly?"

"Well I'm not sure. I spoke to many ..."

And so it went. Alain was forced to wrest each answer from her. A slow, tedious process. He maintained an impartial, even diplomatic demeanor, his voice unvaryingly soft and almost soothing.

"Do you own a red Lamborghini Madame?"

"Yes. I just bought it a few ..."

"Were you driving it that night?"

"Yes. I have no other ..."

"Did you leave the bar with this man?"

"Look, I don't know what ..."

They were both growing weary of the game.

"Inspector, do I need to engage a lawyer?"

"You certainly have that right Madame. However, there are no charges contemplated against you at this time. I only seek to learn certain facts that you may have in your possession. Clear?"

"Yes. Yes it is, but I ..."

"And you drove away together in your red car?"

"Listen Inspector, I think perhaps ..."

"Madame we have witnesses who will testify they saw you leave the bar with this man and others who testify you stopped with him at the side of the D559 roadway, close to Coirón."

She blanched and began to nervously run her hands over the couch, as the questions went on and on. The mood had changed. The pace staccato now. Each question from a different direction. Precisely timed to interrupt her response before she could divert his attention with irrelevancies.

"What time did you leave the bar with this man?"

"I didn't say we did leave ..."

"You were seen on the D559 at 2345. I therefore assume you left the bar at around 2330. Is that correct?"

She said nothing. She was tiring now. And frightened. She simply stared at the Inspector imploringly.

"This man. His name was Charley?"

"Will you please listen to me ...?" Her voice was clearly wavering now.

"Did Charley assault you, or harm you in any way?"

"Why are you ...?"

"Madame, this is an important matter. Withholding information, or obstructing my investigation in any way is a serious offense. I suggest you consider your words with extreme care. Starting now. Do you understand Madame?"

She is going to break any time now.

"I believe your husband arrives on his yacht, the *Soløi*, in a day or so."

She paled dramatically, clearly shocked at the extent of his knowledge.

"Is that why you refuse to answer my questions? You fear your husband?"

No response.

"Your husband. I believe he is actually Danish, is he not? Is not his original family name *Martinsen*?"

She peered at him in astonishment.

"The northern people are not very, ah, warm are they? They don't show their emotions easily. Except perhaps anger I think."

She sat stone-faced as tears began to slowly trickle down her cheeks.

He waited a few seconds for the tension to build even more.

"Madame? Am I right? I suggest you respond honestly."

She broke.

Holding her head in her hands she sobbed. Fear, strain and surprise overwhelming her defenses. Alain allowed it to run its course in silence. He felt a certain sympathy for this woman. Yet he could not relent at this critical moment.

He'd expected to find the devastated remains of a coarse sexual predator. Instead he was confronted with an honest, clearly intelligent, young woman—very much alive.

"We did nothing. Absolutely nothing. You must believe me."

"Oh Madame, believe *me*, I am convinced you did nothing. Else you would not be alive and speaking to me now."

She dropped all pretense, bordering on defiant.

"I don't believe you sir. This man Charley is a fine person who has clearly suffered greatly. He is incapable of violence and most certainly not murder."

"I fail to see any basis for your statement. I sympathize with your feelings. Nonetheless, I would ask you to accompany me to the

Gendarmerie in Coirón where you may file a complaint against this man. Certainly we will make out a complete report."

He voice grew calm. Quiet. "I will not. I cannot."

"Madame?"

"I will file no complaint against this man. He has done me no harm and I will do him no harm."

"Because of your husband?"

She pulled away her bandanna and ran a tired hand through her hair. "Partly I suppose. Also because he didn't harm me in any way. In fact he did me a great service. And … I'm convinced he is dead now."

Alain started and leaned in to study her eyes more clearly, nearly whispering. "*Why do you say this?*"

"He told me he was dying and I believed him. His pain is ended now I think. As is mine. I believe he represents no danger to anyone. He was as a terrified small boy. Lost, afraid and innocent."

"Your pain has ended Madame?"

Erica simply stared at Alain, the most delicate of frowns astraddle her forehead.

Alain pressed on. "You state this man represents no danger to anyone. I submit you are in no position to make such a judgment."

"Inspector. I'm telling you what I *believe.*"

"I understand Madame. But surely you realize your *beliefs* cannot form the basis of an official conclusion."

"Inspector. I have told you everything I can, or will. In fact you seem to know far more about this matter than I. I suppose you could press this issue. It is certainly within your purview. If you wish to do so, you will learn nothing more; and you will most likely ruin two lives. And I fear you will bring all the formidable legal and political resources of my husband crashing down about you and Coirón."

"I do not respond well to threats Madame."

"Please believe me. I'm not threatening you. I'm not that stupid and I'm not that sort. I do know my husband though."

Alain skeptically pursed his lips with a stubborn one-eyed squint. "I believe there were some legal difficulties in Denmark. This does not typically lend itself to political influence Madame."

Suppressing her surprise, she countered, "Inspector, men like my husband collect enemies as other men collect stamps. It would be a serious mistake to underestimate his influence. But please disregard my statement. I regret bringing it up. In fact, I apologize. I would ask you believe me in only one thing. You know absolutely everything I know. I am not the least bit culpable of withholding any information. I can contribute nothing more. Nothing ..." Her voice trailed off wearily.

Inspector Mohsen sat in silence, pursing lips between thumb and forefinger. Making no movement. His inactivity was not tactically calculated now. He was simply lost in thought. Contemplating an action he had taken only once before in his long career.

This young lady does not appear duplicitous in the least. I am ... what is the expression? I am flabbergasted. This young lady has defeated me. And there is nothing I can really do about it. I believe her. I like her. Her statements are intelligent and ring true. For now, for this afternoon, I am the sole authority. I can either impose the inflexible dictates of police procedure, or I can dispense justice. There is no need to ruin her life.

After a time he stood. "Madame, I thank you for your time. I very much doubt I shall require anything further of you. If I do, I will contact you; and I will do so with absolute discretion. Au revoir Madame."

With the slightest nod of his head, he took her hand for a moment and then departed.

Her expression was unreadable. Two men, with neither of whom she had passed more than an hour, had left her life indelibly marked. Perhaps even saved.

~~~~

"A dead end? It yielded nothing, Chief Inspector?"

Alain sounded very tired. "She did meet Charley at the bar. But they did not go home together, which probably explains why she is still alive. She knows nothing more of Charley than Monsieur Bell described."

"That is certain?" Officer Thommes strived to suppress his skepticism from his voice.

"Yes. There is no doubt. Otherwise she would be dead now as I said. Often what looks to be a perfect solution amounts to little, or nothing. Disappointing but true. I have gone over this many times, and now I'm going to my hotel. I've had enough for today. Thanks for all your hard work Robert. Bon nuit [Good night]."

Alain walked slowly back to his room in the cool evening air. He briefly considered a Cognac at Le Cheval Blanc, but rejected the idea. He needed to think. Instead he settled at one of the many benches in Place Velleda.

I did the right thing. The only thing in fact. There was really no reason to hold her, or submit her to the ordeal and probably a divorce emanating from an investigation. She broke no law. She revealed as much as she knew. I'm convinced. What was it she said? 'His pain is ended now. As is mine.' I wonder what she meant? Doesn't sound like suicide. Maybe it's something as benign as a life change? Then again, maybe it's not.

Fade Nu

HÉLÈNE SCURRIED ABOUT the villa, cleaning, cooking and carrying. She frequently slowed to cast furtive glances at Ranny. It was barely mid-morning and her mistress had already consumed the better part of a bottle of rosé. She had *never* behaved such in the past. Never. Hélène found it most upsetting. Ranny sat by the pool, sipping wine, looking down the valley, absorbed in her thoughts.

Nurse Landon was occupied with David. He grew weaker and more pallid every day. Doctor Lefebvre's visit had yielded no apparent result. He clearly dismissed David's condition to 'some bug' he was exposed to in that 'horrid river valley' and prescribed only a mild antibiotic and bed rest.

Hélène snorted silently. *Doctors. Pah!*

Giscard was busy clearing brush in the gorge below the pool. The recent storm had wreaked its customary havoc. She could hear chopping and smelled burning brush and deadwood.

~~~~

Ranny brooded for hours over her actions.

It must be David. It has to be David. Look at the evidence. David's 'injury'—scraping the skin off his leg as he fell. My shotgun blast. He broke his leg when he fell into the gorge right here on the Domaine. His imaginary friend 'Marcel.' He dropped his fossil in the yard when I shot him. His footprint in the tunnel beneath the house. The reality of his DID. He was always absent during the murders and the photographs. Christ! He even accidently blurted out the name 'Charley.'

She sipped her wine and continued.

His bizarre attitude towards the greenies and the maker of green meat. He claims he 'realized' or 'remembered' something during his ordeal, but he won't say what now. And the photographs. He probably took them himself and planted them on the post box. After all, he found them and never appears in them. Why? Because he took the pictures himself. He's insane! Not one fact is conclusive, but the number of them is undeniable.

Ranny rehashed things in her mind, over and over. She couldn't seem to stop. She had dreadfully misjudged the intense the pain of watching David die, slowly, day by day. The horror of coldly standing by, allowing it to happen. Doing nothing. Torturing herself and David. If she didn't stop going over and over it, soon she would be blithering. And she knew it.

Hélène heard a shout from below, which sounded vaguely like Giscard. Drying her hands, she walked out to the pool area, peering into the gorge below.

Adrift in her own concerns, Ranny paid no notice.

Giscard appeared, climbing through the broken hedge, breathing heavily and sweating profusely. He was straining at a rope, pulling something heavy up the cliff, through the hedge and into the yard.

He turned to Hélène, smiling proudly. "Take a look at this."

With a last heave, the body of a large boar crashed onto the gravel.

"Quel désordre. Quelle odeur! How long has that thing been down there?"

Giscard shrugged. "Two, maybe three days."

Ranny came alive. She jumped to her feet and approached the dead boar.

"It died the night of the storm?"

"Possibly."

"How did it die?"

He knelt down next to the carcass. "See here? The front leg and chest?"

"Yes."

"That is a gunshot wound. A shotgun. Small gauge. It didn't kill immediately though. It probably took hours to die. Finally it bled to death I suppose. I would guess it staggered into the bushes after it was shot it from the forest. Have you heard shots lately?"

Ranny was staring at the boar in silence.

"Madame?"

"Oh, uh, no."

"Then it probably occurred the night of the storm."

Ranny looked suddenly defensive. Frowning "Why do you say that?"

"It is illegal to shoot boar this time of year Madame. So the locals often hunt during storms. Their gunshots are easily mistaken for thunder."

"Are you sure of this?"

Giscard looked puzzled. "Why no Madame, not at all. However the animal has been dead at least two days."

Hélène gesticulated towards the animal. "Giscard, get that thing out of here immediately. It smells terrible and God knows what diseases it may carry ... and with Monsieur David so ill ... get it away as fast as possible."

Giscard turned to Ranny. "Madame I can take the animal away now in my truck and drop it at the décharge d'ordures [dump]. I can retrieve Monsieur David's car at the same time if you like. I am familiar with the area and I can find it easily. Yves at the next estate will accompany me to Vallon Pont-d'Arc and drive my truck back."

Ranny could hardly concentrate on his words. "Sure Giscard. Fine."

"May I have the keys Madame?"

"Keys?"

"The keys to Monsieur David's car."

"Oh, yes. I have no idea where they are. No wait, he has a second set in his desk. I'll be right back."

She stopped and turned back, revealing the extent of her distraction. "Do you know how to find his car?"

"Ah. Mais oui [but yes, or of course] Madame. I know the general area around the Ibie where Monsieur David would park his car."

Ranny was not thinking straight.

Damn that wine!

The underpinning of resolve was crumbling. Still, she had no intention of giving the keys to Giscard, as she was certain David had not actually been to Vallon Pont-d'Arc.

I wonder where the damned car really is?

She would go through the motions of looking and then tell Giscard she was unable to find the keys. In fact, her plan was to retrieve the keys and discard them.

She wandered, surreally, into David's office and began sorting through the disorderly assortment in the center drawer of his desk. Aside from the usual paraphernalia, Hélène had placed several unopened letters addressed to David. Some letters were postmarked before his ordeal, others after his return home. She pushed them aside, locating David's extra keys at the bottom of the stack. As she gathered the keys, she noticed a business card, immediately recognizing the name:

Marcel Briançon et fils

Fossile – Pierre Précieuse –Roche & Minéral

35 bis rue de Rome

Salavas F-07150 Ardèche Rhône-Alpes

T. 04.75.88.23.00 F. 04.75.88.23.59

www.fossils@briancon.fr

It struck her like a physical blow. Salavas? She stared at the card in horror. Then panic-stricken, she frantically opened David's map and scanned the area of Vallon Pont-d'Arc. There it was. Salavas. Marcel Briançon was located in *Salavas*, *not* Vallon Pont-d'Arc. And he was *real*. According to the map the two towns were so close—Salavas on one side of the street, the other side Vallon Pont-d'Arc—it was impossible to tell where one town started and the other left off. *And neither could David.*

She put her head down on the desk and closed her eyes. Exhausted, frustrated, frightened and confused. After a few moments she opened her eyes, the middle drawer was still open and she noticed the return address on the first envelope: Clinique St. Therese, 5 Blvd de Jacques Valbon, F-07105 Vallon-Pont-d'Arc.

My God. He really was in the Clinique in Pont-d'Arc and he was in Pont-d'Arc the night of the shooting. As if the Goddamned boar wasn't enough.

She literally broke into a sweat. Her hands began to tremble. Everything was falling apart. Her careful, coldly logical conclusions were being rendered as absurdities. They ran through her panic stricken mind in a kaleidoscope of crushing realities. David *was* in Pont-d'Arc. Marcel *does* exist. A local ambulance *did* pick him up. He was *never* in the back garden that night and I didn't shoot him. I shot a boar. He was in the hospital in Pont-d'Arc. He actually fell off that cliff by the river Ibie. David *didn't* take those pictures. Then it hit her. The killer might not, perhaps could not be David. She knew nothing. Absolutely nothing. Her remorseful corrections wore on and on until she was exhausted.

She stood weakly and returned as calmly as she could into the kitchen. Gathering her purse she went to David's room.

"Nurse Landon, I'm going to personally look after David. You are free to go now." She retrieved money from her purse and gave it to the nurse. "This will pay you out through the end of the week. Thank you for your help."

"Madame, have I done something to dis ...?"

"Your work has been exemplary Miss Landon. Excellent in fact. I would highly recommend you anytime. I simply want to devote all my time to looking after David until he is completely recovered."

"Comme vous voulez Madame. [As you wish Madam.]"

She realized that Giscard might as well fetch David's car. Beyond the practical aspects, it would constitute additional circumstantial evidence of his innocence. Ranny casually strolled out to the pool, carefully assuming a lighthearted demeanor.

"Giscard, here are David's keys. Dump the carcass somewhere and pick up his car." She looked thoughtful. "Considering how the animal died, would this interest the authorities?"

With a genial grin, Giscard tapped his generous nose with his index finger. "I know where I can dispose of the boar with no questions."

Ranny smiled in return. "When you're finished, take the rest of the day off. Bring David's car in tomorrow." She turned to Hélène. "You too Hélène. We've all been working too hard around here. Take the rest of the day off. Go shopping. Go to the beach. Have some fun. You both need some time and David and I need some quiet. He's doing better now and we all need rest. So go." She smiled engagingly, with a shooing gesture, stoutly disregarding Hélène's intense scrutiny.

"Very well, as you wish Madame." Hélène frowned skeptically. "I was not aware Monsieur David was improving. Please let me know if you need anything. Anything at all."

Soon she was alone.

New Zealand to the Sea

JOSEPH TURNER. BRITISH passport. Thirty-five years old. Born in Eden Bay, New Zealand, a tiny village north of Christchurch, which he hoped never to see again. His father had been a struggling sheep rancher, poor all his life. Then his parents were killed in a road accident when he was eighteen. Joe sold everything sellable, determined to find his way out of this suffocating and demeaning poverty—the primary constituents of his hitherto bleak existence.

He immigrated to the UK when he was nineteen. He'd been struggling since to find a place within the British middle class. No higher education to speak of. But he had worked hard learning the paper business since coming to the UK. As with many impromptu careers, paper was the first job he'd happened upon in London.

Not paper as in newspapers or stationary, or massive rolls. Paper, as in greeting cards for kids, children's party-decorations and favors. What they refer to in the business as 'Kitty-Litter'—the sort of paraphernalia sold in party stores, toy stores and stationary shops all over the world.

He was an intelligent, painfully immature, good-looking fellow, suffering from deep feelings of inferiority common to his lineage. He benefitted from regular, dark features, a generous shock of salt-and-pepper hair and an athlete's body. In part, it was Joe's looks that helped him rise within his small cellulite world, all the way to VP European Sales for a producer called Paper-Favors Ltd. The company was small with a single owner/manager, but profitable. And it paid well. He was thrilled with the

VP title, particularly at his young age. A posting he had received one week earlier. It seemed he might have finally *arrived*. Perhaps he could now find a niche in the coveted British Middle Class?

"Congratulations Joe. I don't know a better man for the job. You've earned it. Aside from a raise in pay, title and a private office, I'm throwing in a bonus of two weeks off and a fully paid round-trip to Nice for you and that girlfriend of yours. You can use my apartment in Cannes." He withdrew a well-stuffed envelope from his coat. "Here are your tickets … rent-a-car … apartment keys … directions … security codes, and some walking-around money. You and Sue have a great time."

The days were rushing by almost as fast as his head was swimming. He and Sue had sunbathed and frolicked up and down the Côte d'Azur for five days. Sue had never been out of the UK and had trouble adjusting to a foreign country, not to mention the glitz of the Riviera and she was worried Joe was drinking far too much. She was certain he was spending too much money. Not her business really. They lived together in a rather ersatz manner, still maintaining their own expenses, living largely in her flat in London. He had a studio in the east end, which he visited irregularly.

Sue was also growing increasingly peeved at Joe's incessant eagerness to insinuate himself with the tawny beach-girls up and down the Riviera. His hungry eyes, practically salivating, were a constant source of irritation.

The previous afternoon they'd driven to St. Tropez, checking into a local hotel, clutching their single shared suitcase. Sue had wisely insisted they pack light—needing little clothing during the season. Joe insisted they devote their first night to bar hopping (or as he put it: a *pub crawl*); spending more than a fair amount of money at most of St. Tropez's more stylish bars and night spots. Le Papagayo, Les Caves du Roy, L'Esquinade, Cubana, L'Octave Café and more. Sue was astounded at the amount of alcohol and money they ran through before lurching back to their hotel with the rising sun.

The second night they reserved dinner on the famous Pampelonne Beach. A club/restaurant/bar named Chez Maria. Italian cuisine. Just opened at the extreme limit of the beach and already trendy and popular. Beautiful. Expensive. Très chic. Joe was already dazzled as he ogled the many incredible cars in the sandy car park. Upon entering the restaurant, he was speechless. Never had he seen such beautiful women, such style, clothes, jewelry and sophistication. Turned out only in shorts, a polo shirt and deck shoes, he felt coarsely inadequate, certain he was pathetic and conspicuous.

So he did the logical thing. Drown his humiliation. He got stinking drunk, and then some.

Sue was mortified. Joe was slopping food and drinks everywhere. He crudely muttered slurred obscenities to himself and Sue and anyone within hearing. Surrounding tables were anxiously staring at them in revulsion. At one of the nearer tables she watched a man, strikingly attractive and vaguely familiar, studying them as though they were a lab experiment. His urbane good looks and seeming recognition made the experience all the more embarrassing.

Mid-meal, Joe careened away from their table mumbling about the men's room. After fifteen minutes, Sue grew concerned, leaving the table to find him. She found him groping a young blonde in the dimly lit hallway connecting the dance floor to the washrooms.

Without a word she withdrew, called a cab and returned to their hotel in total disgust. She appropriated their one bag and packed her belongings. She then helped herself to the cash in the room safe. This would pay for the extravagant return taxi fare to Nice, another hotel room, and a new return ticket to London.

What the hell. The dumb, horny bastard would only blow the money on liquor and women. He bloody deserves it.

Joe, only dimly aware of Sue' departure, returned to table and continued to drink. He even made it through to the main course. Then he threw down a wad of bills and staggered out. Moments later he realized he had no idea where his car was, or his girlfriend. Hell, he couldn't even find the car park. He was hopelessly lost on a moonless night, on a foreign beach. Drunk. So he did the logical thing. Again. He simply kept staggering down the beach, farther and farther from the restaurant and his car and his girlfriend, and his life.

After a time he spotted a sort of seedy bar-club-shack, La Cabane à Sucre [Sugar Shack], casting a lurid yellow lumination down the beach, glimmering in a thousand waves on the black water. The wind was picking up out of the northeast. Faraway lightning flashed on the horizon. A storm was coming in. Fast. He might need cover. Another drink? Some sympathetic company? Maybe a cab? Girls? He smiled to himself.

Things are looking up.

Moments later this proved dreadfully true. He was indeed looking up, eyes unseeing, flat on his back, critically beaten by a man springing from the shadows. His watch, his money, his wallet, keys, shoes, clothing ... everything taken. The thief looked carefully about, dragging the naked body into the rising tide, placing something on his left hand, he then inflicted something truly bizarre. Quickly the killer deftly returned to the shadows.

The gathering storm climaxed, descending with breathtaking fury. One of the worst in years. It would flood local communities, do extensive damage to the clubs and restaurants along the coast, destroy several docks, sink five boats, and wash Joseph Turner far out into the raging sea.

~~~~

When Sue arrived London, she changed her locks and her phone number.

She disdainfully banished Joe's few belongings to the storeroom. She was sure Joe's boss would try to contact them, but he only had Joe's address/phone, not hers, and her phone had now been changed and unlisted.

The hotel in St. Tropez stored Joe's abandoned possessions for a time. Then they then disposed of them as well.

Joe's rental car was finally retrieved from the parking lot of the restaurant Chez Maria. Deemed nothing more than yet another irresponsible renter impulsively abandoning their car without giving the matter another thought. Common on the Riviera. The stuff of contracts and credit card companies and collection agencies.

Thus did all trace and memory of Joseph Turner fade out to sea.

$$R_x$$

AS SOON AS Giscard and Hélène had left for the day and she was alone, Ranny rushed to the phone.

"Adam?"

"Ranny?"

"Yes."

She could hear the sudden warmth in his voice. "Hi. It's good to hear your ..."

"Adam there's no time. David is dying. I need your help. And I need it *now*."

"Jesus Ranny. What is it?"

"There's no time Adam. I need your help *now*."

After a brief moment's hesitation "What can I do?"

"Got a pen?"

"Yes."

"Take this down. I need a week's supply of Carbamazepine. Twenty cc doses. A week's supply of Pyridostignime, also twenty cc's. Activated Charcoal. I also need a week's supply of saline solution. I need an oxygen apparatus. Drips and the usual equipment. I assume we can drip caffeine as well, or administer it orally. But I need this fast. Right now. I would like your help administering this too. Can you stay here for a few days? Together I pray we can save David. Will you do it Adam?"

Silence.

"*Goddamnit Adam*. Will you help me?"

"Of course I'll help Ran. Just let me think. Carbamazepine's a treatment for seizures. Pyridostignime, a low blood pressure medication. It constricts the blood vessels and elevates systolic pressure. Saline and caffeine reinforce the process. Ranny, what the hell's wrong with David? Why isn't his doctor treating him?"

"I can't permit a doctor to interfere in this."

"Do you know what you're talking about? Do you even know what you're *doing*?"

"Can you do it Adam? *Will* you do it?"

"I have these things in inventory, not for humans of course, but essentially the same. I am a *vet* you know. And *you*, you're categorically unqualified." He thought for a moment longer. He seemed to be musing to himself more than speaking to Ranny. "I imagine vitamin B6 and a nonaggressive antihistamine would be a good idea as ..."

"*Adam!*"

"I'll be right there Ranny."

Fade Xi

ALAIN'S FEET WERE propped on the desk as he leaned back in his chair, sipping coffee and thumbing through the daily police bulletins circulated from Gendarmerie to Gendarmerie up and down the coast. It was good to work the routine. Simply doing 'cop stuff' again.

As he read, he mused. *Wherever you go it's all pretty much the same. Assault in a bar in Marseilles, a man stabbed ... several car thefts ... break-in at a villa near Ste. Maxime, some valuable art stolen ... extensive damage from the storm, up and down the Côte d'Azur ... fire and rescue on overtime, as were many police units ... a John Doe washed ashore on the beach east of Hyères. Severely battered but cause of death declared to be drowning. 30-40 years, sandy hair, tanned, naked, no I.D., only a gold pinky-ring, high blood-alcohol and so forth ... a yacht reported stolen in Antibes ... a Russian prostitute raped in Cannes, blonde, 25, badly beaten ... drug-bust in Nice ... six kilos of cocaine.*

Six kilos. Not bad. That must have a street value of about ...

Officer Thommes interrupted his musings.

"I have the Forensics Report Chief Inspector."

"So fast?"

"They thought you would ask. They said the site was so corrupted it required very little time to cover it thoroughly and confirm residuals."

"So they found what?"

"It's really more a matter of what they didn't find sir."

"Say again?"

"They found nothing on the site."

"Interesting. That's the second aspect of this incident which doesn't coincide with the other crimes."

"Second aspect sir?"

He raised his thumb. "One. This incident did not occur at the victims home." Then he raised his index finger. "The victim survived."

"Does this disqualify the incident as one of Charley's murders?"

"Perhaps."

Suddenly Alain froze. A deep frown, then a half-smile formed on his face. Feet firmly on the floor now, he turned into his desk, elbows on desk, forehead in hands.

Now I understand. I've been an idiot! Why it didn't occur to me earlier? How stupid can I be? A question that's been bothering me all along: Why were there never any security records of the murderer? No CCTV, no alarms, no motion sensors ... nothing.

The answer was so simple, his grim half-smile grew into a rueful smirk.

Security systems didn't record Charley because the ladies neutralized all security systems themselves. Of course! They wanted no record of this, or any man in their homes. Naturally, they shut down all security systems before going man-hunting. Predictably that idiot Kontz failed to investigate this aspect.

This was an obvious and fairly trivial realization, bringing him no closer to a solution. He felt better nonetheless, taking comfort in the knowledge his killer had no preternatural talents ... only the circumspect precautions of libidinous women. The picture grew increasingly coherent.

He raised his head and turned to Officer Thommes "We need to move on with this investigation. I'm going to call on Mrs. Woods now. I should be back shortly. When I return, please have all the relevant forensics available for review. We're bogging down. Too many dead ends. I'm going to take a fresh look at this case." He paused, a new thought forming in his mind. Thinking back to the morning's bulletins.

"I want you to do something else too ..."

"Sir?"

"Consider the possibility Charley is dead."

Thommes cocked his head dubiously. "Dead?"

"Yes. And if Charley were dead, where do you suppose we might we find him?"

~~~~

Ranny heard Adam's car's skidding stop, well beyond the front entrance. Clearly, Adam was making provision for an ambulance should it prove necessary. Ranny rushed out to assist with the medical supplies.

"I have everything you asked for Ranny, as well as a few more things I thought would help. I'm ready to begin treatment ... as soon as you tell me what the hell goes on here."

Immediately, her manner was serious and resigned. "What do you want to know Adam?"

Out of breath, he regarded her incredulously. *"What do I want to know?"*

"Adam we have so little time."

"Okay." He took a deep breath. "Judging from these medications, I would surmise he has ingested something."

"Yes."

"A toxin?"

"Yes."

"Ranny this is not a guessing game. What toxin?"

"Castor Beans. Fifteen. Two days ago. Since that time he has been extremely nauseous. Blood in his stool, urine and vomit. He is growing increasingly weak. He is severely dehydrated. He cannot now eat or drink. I estimate he will die within hours if untreated."

Adam shook his head. "Fifteen *Castor* Beans? Deadly. How in hell did he ingest *fifteen* Castor Beans?"

She peered at Adam woodenly. "I fed them to him. In a spicy dish so he couldn't taste them."

Adam was literally speechless. As he gathered his wits, he realized there was no time to pursue her incredible statement. His voice was resigned. "Let's get to work. Where is he?"

"His bedroom."

"Right. I'll get started. I want you to make tea, weak with light sugar, no milk ... *or Castor Beans.*"

She blanched and whirled round with a feral look in her eyes. Adam raised a palm in mock surrender.

"Sorry. I don't know why I said that." He then assumed a businesslike demeanor. "Let the tea cool to tepidity. While the tea cools I want you to prepare ice packs and keep them coming. Go buy ice if you haven't enough on hand."

"Can you save him Adam?"

"I don't know yet. You will know everything as soon as I do."

She had just given Adam a large pitcher of sweet lukewarm tea and an ice pack, when she heard a second car arrive at the front entrance. The massive doorknocker echoed ominously through the Domaine.

Damn! Who the hell is this now?

She opened the door and found herself even more frustrated. "Good afternoon Chief Inspector." *Oh God. Think fast!* "What can I do for you?"

"May I come in please?"

"No. Ah, that is, the flooring was treated with a sealant earlier and it is still drying. I wonder if you wouldn't mind going round to the pool and we can talk there?"

"Certainly Madame."

"Can I bring you something to drink?"

"No thank you."

"Okay, I'll meet you poolside."

As he crunched through the gravel, he mused *I wonder why Mme Woods can walk on her newly treated floors and I cannot?*

~~~~

She found Adam busily adjusting David's drip. "How is he?"

"Alive. And I think I can keep him alive. Two hours later though, and ..."

"I know."

"When are you going to explain this to me?"

"Tonight I hope. When David has stabilized."

"I'll look forward to it."

"Adam, there is a police inspector here."

"Why? Is it related to ... *this?*"

"No. Not directly. It's complicated and we're both very busy. We'll talk about it later. He's waiting for me by the pool. And for now, I'd like you to remain out of sight."

"Why?"

"Adam please just stay out of sight."

"Okay. No problem, so long as he stays out of this room."

"He won't even come inside the villa. I'll be only a few minutes I hope. Do you need anything before I go outside?"

"No. Just keep this door closed and keep him out of here."

Ranny stopped and poured herself a glass of wine on her way to the pool. Partly to present the Inspector with a blithe façade. Partly because she really needed a drink.

When this is over, if it's ever over, I've got to quit drinking for a while.

She realized she was reciting the classic mantra of drinkers around the world.

"Sorry to keep you waiting inspector. What with the floor work and David, it's been a difficult day. I had to send everyone home to avoid more of a mess."

"I am very sorry I didn't call before dropping by, but I was driving through the neighbor …"

"Nonsense Inspector. You're always welcome here. What can I do for you today?"

"How is your husband Madame?"

"Suppose you call me Ranny Inspector. Your formality is a bit intimidating."

As intended Madame.

"Ranny. Interesting name."

More interesting than you could possibly know Inspector.

When she failed to respond "Very well *Ranny.* You will please call me Alain?"

"With pleasure."

"So how is your husband's illness, Ranny?"

"It seems to have bottomed out. He was getting progressively worse and weaker every day. He couldn't eat or drink. He was losing weight and getting seriously dehydrated. Now it looks like he's beginning to stabilize."

"Sounds dangerous."

"I think it was."

"He is alone?"

"We had a nurse for a time, but as he's recovering we let her go. He is sleeping now. I'll check on him in a bit."

"What is the nature of his ailment?"

"I don't think they actually know. Dr. Lefebvre believes he caught some sort of bug. David claims he ate a plant—berries or whatever—from which he suffered hallucinations. I suspect he may have been already out of his head. He could have eaten nearly anything, or nothing at all."

"Actually it sounds like a toxin."

"A toxin. You mean a poison? Or a poisonous plant?"

"Correct. There are many more such plants than you may be aware in this area. It can be quite a problem at certain times of the year. Particularly with children ..."

"... or delirious adults."

"Yes. So what sort of treatment is he receiving?"

"Dr. Lefebvre put him on antibiotics."

"So the doctor does not believe a toxin is involved?"

"Apparently not. I personally believe David is improving based on his body's own defenses. He's a very fit man."

"They are monitoring his condition closely?"

"Umm."

"This is an odd time to treat your floors. Is it not? Ranny?"

Damn, this man is good at catching me off guard.

Her eyes focused exclusively on the Inspector's forehead, ideally rendering her expression unreadable, and breaking his concentration. A trick she'd learned during consulting days, from a girlfriend who had not yet treated her Amblyopia (Lazy Eye Syndrome). This she shrewdly exploited to her advantage by disorienting her client, or superior, or adversary. Ranny did the same. Playing for time, trying to spoil his rhythm, to break his concentration. It worked. She won the critical moments to formulate a credible response.

"This work has been scheduled for many weeks. It is difficult to reschedule and would have entailed a very long delay."

"I see. Who did the work for you?"

Damn he's quick.

"I really don't know. The work was ordered by Hélène. They'd already come and gone by the time I finished my morning routine with David."

"Hélène?"

"Our housekeeper."

"I see. And work continues?"

"I'm not sure I understand your question."

"The car parked in front of your Villa. A BMW cabriolet. [convertible] It is not yours I think."

"Oh. There's probably a workman finishing up around here some-where. So what can I do for you today?"

She emphasizes the word 'today' ever so slightly. I think she grows uneasy with my interest.

"Let me be very direct, if I may."

"Yes?" Fear began to weave its icy fingers into her bowels.

"During our previous interviews I believe I may have conveyed the impression I was somehow suspicious of David, with regard to the 'Beast Murders' and I believe you may have been somewhat defensive in response."

"Defensive?"

"Yes. Perhaps, less than forthcoming with certain information. You may even have reacted as such unconsciously."

"Look Inspector, if you …"

"Please Ranny. Do not exert yourself in denial. It is irrelevant none-theless. My point is very simple. Your husband is no longer a suspect. I am convinced he had nothing to do with these affairs."

"I'm pleased to learn this Alain." Her fear collapsed like water in a suddenly dry fountain.

Why in the name of God didn't he tell me this three days ago?

"So now, I have a direct question: Have you withheld anything from me?"

"For example?"

"For example, do you know anything about this Charley person?"

She looked him directly in the eye, relaxed and candid. "No."

I swear she is lying.

"Very well." Alain peered down the valley for a moment. "On the occasion of our last meeting, I revealed certain facts about this case. Specifically regarding the man named Charley."

"I recall very clearly Inspector. I appreciated your confidence."

"Thank you. I thought I might now share the rest of the story with you. You may have some thoughts that could be useful. Perhaps you know something of which you are unaware? It will take very little time. If you would care?"

"In fact, I'm quite interested. May I get you something before we start?"

Alain relented nostalgically. "With pleasure."

She quickly returned with a bottle of rosé and a bowl of cherries and olives.

She smiled.

Alain smiled and they tipped glasses without comment.

Then without preamble "Charley's last victim survived." He stared hard at her looking for any reaction.

She quickly rallied in response. "So Charley finally screwed up."

"No." His stare held, unflinching. "He released her."

Do I see surprise in her eyes? Something else? Confusion? Relief?

"He even threw his weapon away."

"Weapon?"

"The infamous brass claw. The razor-billed Griffin that ripped the throat and slashed the life from his victims."

She looked away. Sickened by his words. With a shaking hand, she sipped at her wine, eyes closed.

"Then he told her he was dying."

Surprise again. She didn't see that coming.

"Tell me about this woman Alain."

"Very much like you actually. Pretty. Young. American. Wealthy. Intelligent. Sensitive. Quite a nice young person. Well outside the profile of Charley's standard victim."

"Then perhaps it wasn't Charley at all?"

"Oh it was most certainly Charley, Ranny. Believe me."

Ranny sipped her wine.

Alain continued. "A man was found drowned on the coast east of Hyères this morning. The storm may have killed him. His blood-alcohol count was quite high. It could have been suicide, murder, or an accident. Who knows? Aside from a minor ornament, there were no identifying marks or personal items whatsoever. However he does fit Charley's description quite closely. I think perhaps it is Charley. I think he was telling the truth about dying. It makes sense. The tides along this coast could have easily carried him to the rocky point east of Hyères where he was found. Yes. I'm reasonably sure the dead man is Charley."

She was studying her wine, toying with a cherry, absorbed in her own thoughts, ostensibly disinterested in his discourse. Then he leaned in, taking in her every expression, his voice low, commanding and almost harsh. "But you don't believe this man is Charley." Then his voice took on a gentler tone. "Do you Ranny?"

She looked at him blankly.

"How is it you know this dead man is not Charley? Ranny?"

"You're taking some surprising leaps in logic Alain. That's not at all like you. How is it that you know that I know this dead man is not Charley?"

"Would you care to accompany me down the coast? To identify his body?"

"No, I don't believe I would. For two reasons Alain. First, I cannot leave David. Second, I can neither identify Charley, nor this body … whether or not he is this Charley person."

I think she knows the body can't be Charley. Else, she would be disturbed, and I would see. Just look at her. Chin on hand, toying with a cherry. She looks positively bored. I suspect the body is Charley. But I must be sure.

"You are very sure you have no knowledge of this body. Why is that Ranny?"

She favored him with a mute, quizzical look. "I imagine the morgues of the world hold millions of bodies. Why should one, or any of them for that matter, be familiar to me?"

"And were I to insist you accompany me?"

She smiled fondly at him. "Oh, that wouldn't be at all like you Alain. More wine?"

They sat in silence. Not an awkward or stilted silence. They were comfortable with each other now—congenial, contemplative friends of sorts. Theirs was a tacit, common silence. Their shared understanding that she knew that he knew that she might know something. And she wasn't telling.

"No thank you Ranny. I must go." He stood. "Thank you for your time."

"Not at all Alain. You're always welcome here. I hope to see you again. I look forward to our little talks."

"We shall Ranny. A bientôt."

~~~~

Before Alain could finish crunching back to his car, Ranny had returned to David and Adam.

"How is he?"

"Improving appreciably, believe it or not. And remarkably fast. His blood pressure is increasing. His temperature is approaching normal. He no longer requires oxygen. He drank some tea and he's sleeping now. A strong fellow, our Davey. The crisis has passed. I decided not to rinse and purge his lower tract. I believe the time has passed for charcoal treatments. The toxin has passed through his body. I believe he'll be fine soon. But we'll need to stay by him for the next twenty-four hours. He could develop some sort of complication during this period. I'm particularly concerned about a seizure, or perhaps some serious cramping. I have medications for either condition. I suggest one of us look in every half hour or so." Ranny visibly eased. Her relief was palpable. Her fears assuaged, only her guilt would remain.

"Thank you Adam. More than you know."

"I believe I know. And I know I need a drink."

~~~~

Ranny left Adam to the bar as she looked after David. Then she found her way to the drawing room and sat in the dim coolness reflecting on their destinies.

David. Good strong David. No longer a murderer. Never was. Never could be. Blessed luck had saved her from becoming a murderess.

All three of them appear to have threaded the eye of their needles. It all seemed so clear now, so smoothly resolved. It was almost too easy.

She leant back in the silence and solitude, and surrendered to something she seldom acquitted. She wept with relief.

Enormous burdens suddenly lifted.

Fade Omicron

"HELLO?"

"Madame Erica Martin?"

"Yes?"

"Madame Martin this is Inspector Mohsen. Don't speak please. Just listen. I am terribly sorry to bother you at home. I appreciate you may not be able to speak freely. But I greatly need your help. It will take less than an hour. You will not be implicated in any way. We can meet in town at your convenience. I will be in my office all afternoon. Please call me there at: 04.95.77.01.48. That is: 04.95.77.01.48. Again: 04.95.77.01.48. Thank you Madame."

Without comment, Erica quietly returned the phone to its cradle.

"Who was that?"

She smiled grimly. "Those damned French telemarketers. They think people are such idiots, willing to sit through any moronic recording. You know, in the 'States we can register on a 'no-calls' list. I wonder why not here?"

She left the room, headed for the kitchen. There, she would prepare lunch and quickly jot down a telephone number.

After lunch she entered her husband's study.

"I'm going into town. I thought you might enjoy a leg of lamb with some fresh herbs for dinner. Do you need anything?"

He looked up. "No. Lamb sounds good. Oh, maybe roast it with some fresh artichokes?" To her back he muttered "When are you going to hire a cook anyway?"

Erica parked near Place Velleda and walked to a table outside Le Cheval Blanc. Another sunny afternoon, quiet and drowsy, few people about, pleasant in the playful shade of the huge trees.

"A Perrier and ice please. No lemon."

When her drink was delivered she retrieved a phone from her purse and a hastily scribbled slip of paper. Françoise put her through immediately. Apparently her call was expected.

"Thank you for returning my call Madame. I trust you may speak freely?"

"Yes Inspector; and I appreciate your discretion."

"Avec plaisir Madame." [With pleasure Madame.]

"What can I do for you?"

"I would ask you to accompany me to the Coroner's Office in Hyères."

"Whatever for?"

"They are holding the body of a man. We believe he drowned in the recent storm. There is no identification of any sort on the body and we've had no reports of anyone lost. It is possible this man is Charley. I would ask you to view this man and tell me if it is indeed Charley."

"Oh really Inspector, I don't know. Is this really necessary? I don't think I can …"

"This is very important Madame Martin. We can be there and back in less than an hour. We need your help badly."

Erica thought about it. "Alright Inspector. I am in your debt. You've been thoughtful and discreet and I appreciate it.

"Must I be implicated by some official statement?"

"No Madame, this strictly fact finding."

"Okay, I'll do it. I'm presently on Place Velleda at Le Cheval Blanc. Where shall we meet?"

"I'll be right there."

Just Around the Coroner

ALAIN HAD TAKEN many such rides with bereaved family, friends, and witnesses. They were always uncomfortable and awkward. This ride was further complicated by his need to reassure Erica that he sought nothing more than identification.

So as always, he switched his mouth to 'autopilot', allowing it to discuss anything which came to mind. The weather, sports, politics, Paris, family, local gossip. Anything to keep the words flowing and his passenger's mind away from their impending ordeal.

As he parked the car, he turned to her. "This will require but five minutes. I will take you into the morgue. The Technician will present the body. Please understand the sea distorts features, so study it as long as you like …"

"… or as short …"

Alain smiled indulgently. "Yes Madame, or as short. When you've seen enough, we'll leave the morgue immediately and discuss it. Then back to Coirón. Any questions?"

"Will I be asked to sign any official statements?"

"As I said, my sole purpose in bringing you here is to gather information about this body. This aspect of my investigation is strictly unofficial fact-finding. D'accord Madame?" [Agreed Madame?]

She paused suddenly. A secret smile ghosted her face for an instant.

"Okay." She sighed somewhat melodramatically. "Let's go."

~~~~

The body was in fair condition. Extensive bruising, a few cuts. Bloating. And the immutable alabaster pallor attesting to death's ascension. Erica, clearly stressed, peered down at the dead man for about ten seconds, turning away stolidly.

Alain turned to the technician as they walked from the room. "May I have some photos of the cadaver?"

"Certainly Chief Inspector." He extended two prints of the face and chest. "Will these do?"

"Yes. Quite well. I understand there was some sort of jewelry found on the body."

"That is correct sir. A ring."

"May I see it please?"

Alain studied the ring closely. The ring had been cut in order to remove it from the body. Finger joints are the first and most susceptible to the bloating that comes with certain deaths. Yellow gold. BVLGARI. Two beautifully worked parallel ridges ... *the initials AZ precisely engraved inside.*

What goes on here? This makes no sense. Why would a thief steal a man's shoes and clothes ... everything he owns ... and leave an expensive ring?

Alain froze in mid-thought.

Merde! This is the ring of Madame Angela Zaparelli! Mais c'est presque trop facile à être cru. [But this almost too easy to be believed.] *But why would a killer wear the ring of his victim?*

In the reception area, Alain turned to Erica, eyebrows lifted "Well Madame?"

"I know the man."

"Pardon? *You know this man?*"

She responded with absolute certainty. "Yes."

"*Who is he Erica?*"

"Why he's Charley, of course."

Sunset

FOR NEARLY HALF the drive back to Coirón, Alain was too con-founded to speak. When she identified the body he felt her demeanor was nearly flippant. He was sure he sensed a puzzling hint of amusement, per-haps even triumph in her voice. With a single sentence she had closed the case.

There was no reason not to believe her. The cadaver met Charley's description. He was weary of this case and wanted it to end. So in a certain way he *wanted* to believe her. In fact he *did* believe her. Alain was convinced Erica was fundamentally honest. The Zaparelli ring was conclusive, the aggregate unequivocal evidence that closed the book. And so he did.

During the ride, Erica was enchanting. Almost beatific. Alain forced himself to concentrate on the road; and still he found himself spellbound. Captivated by her almost enchanting detachment. A subdued Mona Lisa (*La Joconde*) smile played about her lips when Alain made a glib comment. At other times she was apart and serene, as though she was charmed by some secret vision she alone could see. Never was she complacent, or triumphant. It seemed to Alain she'd discovered something. Perhaps something she'd lost. Perhaps something important.

He walked round the car and held her door. He then took her hand, bobbed his head almost imperceptivity in farewell.

"Merci Madame. You have been … most helpful. I will not impose on your generosity further."

"Good-bye Chief Inspector. You've been most kind. I shall never forget you."

~~~~

The investigation was over now. No need to involve either Erica or Ranny any further. The only remaining task was to confirm the ring on the cadaver had belonged to Angela Zaparelli, although he was certain it was. Then he would simply report the John Doe from Hyères was indeed Charley. He had been identified, solidly implicated in the murders through the ring, and he fit the description. The killer was found and the killer was dead. He could not justify continuing the investigation any further. Dossier Clos [Case Closed].

If he needed corroboration—which he sincerely doubted—well, there was always Paul Bell. He had a wealth of misdemeanors on Paul. Male-prostitution, drugs, illegal alien, working without a permit, and more if he made the effort. He could expect complete cooperation. Probably Paul would substantiate the identification.

Paul was essentially a fine young man. One day soon, Alain was certain, Paul would have enough of this jaded coast, and return home to complete his education. Alain liked him. And Paul seemed to be fascinated with the case. He would cooperate simply out of a sense of duty and well ... fun.

An idea occurred to him. He was going to have a drink with Paul right now. Right now, while he was reveling in a sort of 'school's out' feeling of lightheaded, carefree freedom. 'Case Closed' and he was finally going home.

He stopped briefly at his office for appropriate papers and continued on to St. Tropez.

~~~~

"A glass of rosé s'il vous plait Paul. A Bandol."

"Wine Inspector? No coffee today?"

"Not today Paul. I'm celebrating the end of this case. In fact, I would invite you to join me in a glass? My treat."

"Ah, sure Inspector. Just give me a minute to tell my boss."

Paul returned proudly bearing an unopened bottle of Bandol, two glasses, and a tray of olives, chips and peanuts.

In response to Alain's quizzical look Paul raised the bottle "On the house Inspector. Compliments of Cubana."

Alain looked troubled "Please Paul, I do not accept ..."

"Please Inspector, this is from my boss. Don't get me in the dumper on such a beautiful day."

He paused, realizing this was an occasion that called for gracious acceptance.

"Fine Paul. Please thank him for me."

"Her."

"Pardon?"

"Her. My boss is a woman."

Alain looked thoughtful. This was interesting. "A female superior. With your skills and attributes, I'm sure you're a very lucky young man."

As he opened the bottle and poured, Paul flushed, eyebrows knitting for the briefest moment "Umm yeah. Well, cheers."

"Santé."

"So Inspector, you solved the crime!"

"I'm afraid not. Not this time. We simply found our man. Dead. Drowned off the coast of Hyères, a casualty of our recent storm."

"No kidding. Charley?"

"Yes. I've just returned from identifying the body. Care to see his picture? I would appreciate another confirmation of the ID. Aside from enjoying a drink with you, that is my reason for coming."

"Sure. Did that Erica lady ID him?"

Ignoring his question he extended a photo of the dead man's chest and head. "Here. Take a look."

"Anything turn up on prints and DNA?"

Alain's eyebrows rose slightly. This wasn't the sort of question normally posed by witnesses. But in view of their diffident friendship he elected to answer.

"Not as yet Paul. We've run them through our own files and Interpol, with negative results so far. Charley seems to have materialized out of thin air."

"Mm." Paul directed his attention to the photograph. Then he frowned. "You know, I'm not totally certain this is really ..."

"You must understand Paul. Extended immersion in water bloats and distorts the features, sometimes beyond recognition. Compounding this is the poor quality of the photograph. You have to use your imagination. Reconstruct the face in your mind."

"Yeah ... but ..."

"I would certainly hesitate to reopen this case, with all the surrounding legal complexities, in Coirón, and ..." He extended his arm. "... even here in this bar ..." Alain's face was pleasantly impassive.

"Yeah. I know what you mean about the effects of water. I've seen the same in the lab, in distilled water and certainly in formaldehyde. I can only imagine the effects of submersion in sea water, during a storm, on a human."

"Exactly. So what do you think Paul?"

"Oh it's Charley alright."

"Fine Paul. Would you consent to signing this please? It's a standard statement as to the identity of a corpse, to the best of your knowledge, based on the material presented you. This carries no liability." He extended pen and paper. Paul signed.

"Thank you Paul. Now let's enjoy this fine bottle of wine."

"Good idea Inspector. Cheers."

"Santé."

After a moment "You know inspector, I've been thinking it's about time I got back to the States. I'd like to see my folks again and I want to finish my doctorate before my credits get stale."

"I understand. A fine idea."

"Would the ah ... French Police have any objection to my leaving the country?"

Alain smiled thinly "None whatsoever Paul. I would ask only you to provide me your coordinates in America."

"I'll give you what I can. But I may be moving around ..."

"That would be fine Paul."

Alain left the bar thirty minutes later, shaking hands and wishing Paul the best. He'd made a friend he would probably never see again.

Upon reaching his car he realized it wasn't late, so he decided on a couple of phone calls.

~~~~

"Monsieur le Maire, this is Chief Inspector Mohsen."

"Inspector Mohsen. Ça va? [How goes it?]"

"Ça va bien. [Fine] How are you?"

"Ça va. [It goes]."

"Good. I hope I haven't called too late, but I have good news."

"Not at all Inspector. Any good news is most welcome. What is it?"

"The Beverley Hills Killer has been found and is dead."

"*Wonderful!* Who is he, or rather, who was he?"

"We only know his name was Charley."

"I don't understand."

"We believe he drowned during the storm off Hyères. No identifying marks or documents whatsoever."

"I see. So how can we be confident this man is Charley?"

"We have an eye-witness identification, and we found an incriminating evidentiary item on the body."

"Excellent! And what of biological indicators? Fingerprints, DNA and such."

"All forensic attempts at identification have yielded negative results so far."

"So there will be no trial. You're sure of this?"

This Mayor is a strange fellow. Does he expect us to put a corpse on trial?

"Only a brief administrative hearing is required. We can conduct it in your offices tomorrow morning if you like. We need only yourself, myself, the Procureur Régional [Regional Prosecutor], and the coroner from Hyères. You'll have all pertinent information in my report. I'll be filing the official report tomorrow morning. After that, I plan to return to Paris."

"Understood and agreed. My offices will arrange the meeting. Say 1100?"

"That would be fine."

"Have you made an official announcement?"

"No, nor I have made a press release. I thought you might wish to handle those items personally."

While I escape the ensuing media frenzy.

In his mind Alain could see the smile on the Mayor's face, the sudden brightness of his eyes. He could practically hear his hands rubbing together.

"I appreciate that Inspector. So you are leaving tomorrow. What of Officer Kontz?"

"Officer Kontz?"

That moron is the least of my problems.

Alain chuckled lightly. "Well Monsieur le Maire, I suppose he should return to duty the day after tomorrow. *After* I have departed. When Kontz reports, Officer Thommes will return to St. Tropez. I will brief him. I do believe Officer Thommes should receive a commendation for his work in Coirón. I will submit a nomination from Paris."

"I'm sure you're right Inspector. I will support any recommendation you care to make. Would you have time for lunch tomorrow? After the hearing? A small celebration?"

"Why yes, that's very kind. Thank you very much."

"Good. Then I'll see you at my offices at 1100. A short hearing followed by lunch. *A demain Inspector* [See you tomorrow Inspector]."

~~~~

"Ranny this is Alain."

It felt odd to address her with such familiarity. A warming strangeness.

"I have finalized the case and I am returning home tomorrow. I thought perhaps I might drop by, say adieu, and tell you of the final results."

"I would like that Alain. I'll have the rosé chilled."

"What time shall I drop by?"

"Oh anytime is good for me."

Got to keep it light. Don't let him suspect there's something going on here.

"Shall I call before I come?"

"No. Just come any time."

Stay loose, easy and casual.

"Fine, I'll be by sometime this evening."

"Go round to the pool please, and knock at the kitchen."

"The floors are not dry yet?"

"Ah, 'fraid not."

"Not a problem I'll go round and knock."

"Great. See you soon."

"A bientôt."

Alain strolled the harbor, enjoying the fine, late afternoon. Sun on water, reflecting high into the clouds, glowing on the rustic walls of St. Tropez. Crimson ascending to gold. He decided to dare another glass of rosé, with a sandwich. Such would suffice for dinner. If he followed it with a hot, strong *express*, he should be up for a glass of wine with Ranny as well.

As he sat at the café taking in the summer afternoon, he thought about Ranny and Erica. These were different women, unknown to each other, acting independently, yet they shared some striking attributes in common. Intelligence. Wealth. Sensitivity. Beauty. And the aura of a haunting, possibly common secret. Both so different from the Parisian prostitutes, murderesses and assorted feloness' he routinely dealt with. This alone would inevitably attract him.

They had effortlessly frustrated his parochial police procedures, and moderated his highly disciplined camber to the law. Ranny and Erica had both manipulated him with deft, feminine artistry. In his long career, he had never been so soundly outmaneuvered and outmatched. He knew it was his fault. He'd *wanted* to help these women. He'd liked them and been actually drawn to them in some fashion, however pristine.

The truth though: He had somehow summoned this dénouement. He could have been ruthless. He could have pursued the letter of the law and adhered to exacting procedures. He could have done them injury. Harmed their lives and their marriages. Normally he *would* have hurt them. But this one time, in this precise circumstance, in the purview of these tragic and bizarre crimes, considering the nature and circumstance of these ladies, he decided to spare them futile pain. What was the purpose? He did after all, have substantiated testimony of Charley's death and his guilt.

En Bestia!

"HE'S IMPRESSIVE RANNY. He was actually awake and quite lucid for a time. He drank some tea and I believe he'll be hungry soon. He does have a slight fever. But I think it's only a low-grade infection. Probably a hangover from his river adventure. I don't think it's related to the toxin, so I'm keeping him on the antibiotics prescribed by Doctor Lefebvre."

"He's out of danger?" She held her breath.

"It appears so. As I said though, he could develop some sort of complication in his condition, so he wants watching for a couple of days."

She heaved a great sigh of relief. "Will you stay with me?"

"Of course. I care for David as much as you Ranny. Almost as much as I care for you."

"Thank you Adam."

"And you Ranny. Where do your feelings flow?"

Though she understood, she was unprepared to respond. "Let's go outside and talk."

They sat by the pool.

"Okay Ranny. Talk to me."

"What do you want to know Adam?"

"*What do I want to know?*"

With some effort, he quelled his exasperation and after a moment his voice took on a gentle tenor. "Ranny you attempted to *murder* David. Tell me what this is all about. You didn't do this for *me* did you?"

She looked up fondly at Adam. "No Adam. Something entirely different."

"Please. Tell me."

She drew a ragged breath, a grimly resigned expression framing her features. "I thought David was the killer. The Beverly Hills Beast."

"Mother of God!"

Ranny grew calm, even analytical. "There is no way you could ever understand the terrors which passed through my mind. Believe me though, I had excellent reasons for believing David was the Beast. It turns out I was wrong, thank God. But I wanted to protect David from the horror of confronting the crimes I thought him guilty of. I didn't think he would ever stop killing; and I was sure he would be ultimately caught. Confrontation of his crimes would have destroyed him. I wanted to spare him the nightmare of an arrest, the trial and a life of incarceration. David's a sensitive and intelligent man and he just couldn't handle it. He would suffer unbearably. It would destroy his already damaged mind. I was convinced he would be far better off dead."

Adam considered her words thoughtfully. "I need a drink Ranny. Can I get you something?"

"No. I'm fine."

When he returned from the kitchen "What in the world led you to believe David was the *Beast*?"

Ranny sat at the edge of the pool now. "Several things. No single element was conclusive. But the composite of many things was overwhelming."

"Such as?"

She grimly reeled off the litany of evidence that had convicted David in her mind.

"He also inadvertently dropped the name Charley and then tried to cover it up with a completely false story about topographical wireless survey in Northern France.

Finally, he was in none of the pictures taken outside the villa we discovered on the mailbox. He was never at home when the pictures were taken and I imagined he took the pictures himself and then contrived to find them for some bizarre reason."

"Who did take the pictures?"

Ranny stared blankly at Adam.

She continued. "Even Inspector Mohsen was suspicious of David. And finally ..." She looked up at Adam, studying him closely. "There was the fresh footprint in the tunnel below the villa. Missing the third toe on the left foot. For all these reasons and more, I thought David was ... *Charley*."

"Well Ranny, for that matter, I'm missing the third toe on my own so ... who is Charley?"

Ranny neither spoke nor moved. Only her eyes looking deep in Adam's belied her alertness.

~~~~

Inspector Mohsen glided noiselessly to a stop in front of the Domaine. As he stepped out he looked about, a frown forming as he looked beyond the main entrance.

That BMW was here earlier. I thought it belonged to a stone worker. But not at this hour. Whose car is it? Why is it still here? Something is not right here.

He reached into his briefcase, withdrawing his Saur. He clicked the safety off, checked the load and slid a round into the chamber.

He then looked about the front of the villa. Finding nothing suspicious, he began the slow, tedious task of soundlessly crossing the huge gravel expanse around to the pool, holding his pistol in a classic two-handed, palm-supported, straight-armed extension. In doing so he felt slightly foolish. But knew he would feel far more foolish facing a serial killer, unprepared.

~~~~

"Listen to me Adam. You're a fine man. You're stronger than David in many ways. You know that. So listen. This is the most important thing you will ever hear."

She gripped him by the shoulders.

"It's possible *you* were Charley, Adam. Trust me in this, because I am the only human you *can* trust. I think a diseased part of your mind could have been Charley. But Charley is gone now. Right Adam? Think Adam. Remember Adam. Use your memory Adam."

"Wh-what are you saying? *I* am the Beast?"

"No Adam. No. *Charley* is the Beast. I may be totally wrong and I really don't know or understand, but Charley may have been a part of you. *Charley* may have been implanted in your mind like some poisonous malignancy when you were young and vulnerable—by bad people—monsters really. You remember don't you? Don't you? We discussed this Adam. You remembered. I'm convinced *you* suffer from DID, just as David. More profoundly. More painfully. You've both suffered greatly. Your DID may have summoned the persona of Charley. And Charley, whoever, wherever he is, is the Beast. You bear no guilt Adam. Do you understand? Do you remember?"

A long pause, then a hesitant voice. "Somehow I vaguely recall a time in London long ago. I was very young I think ..."

"Something festered in parts of that innocent young mind having nothing to do with you. It kept you from intimacy with other people for decades. It may have done these atrocities Adam. But not you. *Not you.*

"Adam, If you had been in David's place, or if I thought you too weak to overcome it, if you did these things and were in danger of detection, I would poison you as well. Just as fast." She took his hand. "Gentle, innocent Adam."

Adam was horrified beyond reason. Pulling his hand away, he jumped to his feet, knocking Ranny over, spilling his drink, upending chairs and the table, which fell on Ranny. Terrified he'd hurt her, he hurriedly raised the table from Ranny and then David's voice froze him altogether, clutching the table in mid-air above him.

"Whaatinhells goinon out'ere?"

David stood against the kitchen doorway weaving shakily. After a moment he pitched, slow motion, face-forward into the gravel.

Neither Ranny nor Adam had time to react before a voice rang out from the side of the Villa.

~~~~

"Freeze! Now! Or I will shoot."

The words were so alien to Adam he simply didn't comprehend. Instead he raised the table further to clear Ranny's head, preparing to set it down and assist David.

Alain squeezed off a round. Deafening. A single shot. The report echoed through the hills and down the gorge, fading into the distance.

Ranny jumped. David moaned. Alain charged forward. Adam was violently blown into the pool, a crimson cloud of blood billowing in the crystal water as the wrought iron table dragged him to the bottom.

Fade Tau

"DON'T WORRY ABOUT it. I'm a doctor. A vet actually, but I can certainly tend to a minor laceration like this. Just a grazing wound to my left deltoid. Hurts, but easily fixed. I won't be sailing for a week or so and I'm certainly glad you're not a better shot." He grinned good-naturedly. It was as if the shot had cleared his head—shocked him back to normalcy.

The grin Alain flashed in return was the stuff of pure predation. More of the wolf than the policeman. It was abundantly clear he'd been shot exactly where Alain had intended, probably to the centimeter.

His smile was not lost on Adam. He let it pass, lightly clearing his throat and countering easily "You *could* get me a couple of fingers of cognac though, while I get my bag?"

"Where is your bag Doctor?"

"In David's room. I uh, dropped by to look in on David."

"A veterinary?"

"A concerned friend."

"Mm. So it is your cabriolet in front of this Villa?"

"Yes."

"You have been here for some time I think."

"Yes. I'm a long-time friend of the family and I wanted to ensure David was being properly looked after."

"Madame Woods knew you were here?"

"Of course."

Perhaps these two are lovers?

"I see." Alain looked thoughtful. "Would you like to file a report Monsieur?"

"A report? About what?"

"About the fact that you were shot a few minutes ago."

"Oh no, Not at all. Let's not turn a minor incident into a major scandal."

The Inspector studied him with a whiff of suspicion that Adam of being a little too agreeable about it all.

~~~~

They had fished a gunshot and half-drowned Adam from the pool, revived him and dried him. They had also assisted David into the bar.

"I apologize for shooting you Doctor. I didn't know who you were; and from my perspective it appeared you were preparing to attack Mrs. Woods with a wrought-iron table and you had already done injury to Mr. Woods."

"I realize that." Alain handed him the cognac. "Thanks. I take it you're with the police?"

Alain handed him a card. "The police yes, but not from this area. Chief Inspector Alain Mohsen. I'm on temporary assignment from Paris to look into the Beverly Hills murders, as they are known, among other appellations. May I request your full name sir? I will make a log notation of this incident for your own protection. As and example, should you experience any medical problems."

"Adam MacAfee."

Alain looked up from his notebook. "Middle name?"

"Doctor Adam Bradley MacAfee."

"Address?"

"12 rue de la Plage, Coirón. Telephone 04 94 56 93 42."

"Thank you Doctor. Can I assist with your arm?"

"Yes. Thank you. But that can wait. Let's get David comfortable first."

Alain closely observed as Adam arranged David in an easy chair, bundled him in a blanket, took his temperature, pulse and blood pressure, brought him a glass of tea and a cup of broth, built a fire and helped him drink. He was touched by the concern and affection the man demonstrated.

Dr. MacAfee is disturbingly close to the description of Charley. As in fact is David for that matter. Yet Adam seems totally guileless. No reaction at all to meeting me. He could be Charley I suppose. But he seems ... fundamentally gentle and decent. There is a certain tenderness about him absent in any killer I've ever known.

Ranny excused herself, quickly returning to the bar.

Adam turned, a concerned look on his face "Are you alright Ran?"

Alain was slightly taken aback.

Ran? I like that much better than Ranny. But it seems a little ... intimate. What goes on here?

Did he feel a tinge of ... what? Jealousy? Suspicion? Both?

"I'm fine." She studied Adam intently for a brief moment. *Does he see the danger here?* Then she brightened. "Alain, I promised you wine. Why don't you both get comfortable while I get things arranged?"

Ranny was greatly relieved when Adam excused himself to wash up and complete work on his arm.

She seems in good spirits. Mais c'est pas vrai. [But it is not true.] *She is frightened I think.*

Ranny prepared the wine. "I thought you had news for me Alain?"

"Yes. I did."

"No longer?"

Alain settled into one the bar's generous easy chairs. His had a view into the rest of the Domaine, so he looked about for signs of floor sealants and saw none.

But what do I know of such matters?

He looked out at the setting sun and the valley cascading down to the sea.

"You have security systems here at the Domaine?"

"Why yes, Alain. Why do you ask?"

"They are active now?"

"Yes. At least surveillance systems are active. Alarm systems and motion sensors are engaged at night. But I thought we were going to discuss changes to your report Alain."

"No. No longer. My report remains unchanged."

"… and that is?"

Alain grew quiet, eyes moving from Adam to David to Ranny.

"Alain?"

Alain stared into the fire. "Charley is dead. His body was conclusively identified. It is official: Death by misadventure. He was presumably drowned during the storm. Dossier Clos [Case Closed]. The murders are at an end. Mayor Drôme will issue a press release tomorrow, and I return to Paris."

Ranny raised her glass. "Well, congratulations Inspector."

"I'm not sure congratulations are greatly in order Ranny. A body was found and identified. Which ends it. I don't believe I have exactly covered myself in laurels this time."

"Meaning?"

Alain leaned back. "Meaning a successful case is about the facts and the facts only. Sometimes, very rarely, other factors take precedence."

Ranny leaned forward intently. "Alain, I would think the beauty of your work lies in those *other factors.*"

Alain had a strange look to his eyes. "I'm not sure beauty is an accurate portrayal. I believe I would tend to favor the term *burden.*"

A stark silence ensued, finally broken by Ranny.

"I shall miss you Alain. I will never forget you."

With a nostalgic inner smile Alain thought *Strangely, like my last words with Erica.*

"Neither me, you Ranny." He stared wistfully into the fire.

Adam returned clean and well bandaged.

They regarded one another for a time then he stood.

"It grows late and I have much to do before I depart. So I will wish you a pleasant evening. I hope Monsieur Woods will be fully recovered soon, as well as you Dr. MacAfee. I again apologize for your injury."

Adam nodded pleasantly.

He turned to Ranny. "Désolé Madame. I am unable to report any progress in the mystery of your photographs. Although I suspect the problem was resolved on the rocks of Hyères."

She smiled and shrugged in tacit dismissal. "I'll keep my shutters closed at night. For a while anyhow."

"I thank you for your wine and your charming company. I shall miss both." He shook hands with Adam and Ranny.

With a bittersweet lopsided smile, Ranny nearly whispered. "As shall I. Au revoir Alain."

Alain peered at her with affection. With an air of quiet finality, he responded "Adieu."

He nodded to the two men and took his leave.

As Alain crunched back to his car he thought *She is graceful that one. As was Erica. So many intriguing similarities in this case. And this man Adam ... it was he who was here earlier. And her floors ... they are dry I think.*

~~~~

Alain started the car, shifted into gear and glided around the drive into the woodlands. He drove slowly, almost listlessly. He knew he was hesitant to leave Ranny. He knew he savored the nostalgic feelings she'd awakened in him, but there was more.

Completion of this case had been unsatisfying, to say the least. But there was something. Something else. Something he had overlooked. Something that he had observed this very night and not registered. What was it? A troublesome itch at the back of his mind. He knew from experience how to deal with such dilemma.

Alain replayed the evening in his mind. The car. The crunchy traverse around the villa. Shooting Dr. MacAfee and the bloody plunge into the pool. Dragging him out of the pool, removing his wet clothes, drying him, binding the wound and nearly carrying him into the villa. Then he struggled him into an easy chair and placed his legs on a footrest to ...

Merde! That's it! That son of the bitch was missing a toe! The third toe of his left foot! Alain pulled to the side of the road and slammed on the brakes.

How could I have overlooked such a thing? He could be the killer.

No. No. I don't know that. And I certainly can't prove it. So what do I have? I have a very unsubstantial indication he may have taken those pictures. Beyond that ...

His head was down, both hands on the wheel, eyes closed. ... *and that is all. I have a circumstantial argument he may have taken some harmless pictures. Which I cannot prove. Probably not even a crime considering his friendship with the Woods. Certainly it wouldn't stand up for a minute in the courts. Footprints in a tunnel do not prove a damned thing when the prints are smeared. I know our prosecutors would not authorize prosecution of charges. As to the murders? I have nothing. Could I sweat something out of him, or Ranny? I doubt very much. I could run him by Paul Bell. But Paul has already attested to the identity of Charley's body. He would be most reluctant to change his story now with all that could entail, as with Erica. I could haul the entire staff of the bar in, create a scandal, create much trouble for many people, make a fool of myself, and find my hands were empty and soiled at the end of the day. I truly have nothing, except flimsy suspicions. Sometimes one must simply give it up.*

He drew a long weary breath, put the car into gear to begin the tiring work of preparing for his journey home.

~~~~

Alain's celebratory lunch with the Mayor was surprisingly enjoyable. When not preoccupied with glad-handing, flowers, and politics, the Mayor was actually quite charming and well versed. Alain enjoyed himself more than he had in some time. The food was wonderful and the wine flowed. After lunch they sat on the terrace enjoying the local liquor of the Mauresienne Chestnut, a melancholy remembrance of the unfortunate Evan Lebec.

"Your lunch and your drink have been so generous, I believe I'll require a nap before facing the drive back to Paris, Monsieur le Maire."

"I'm very pleased you enjoyed it. You have done us a great service. You have my thanks."

"You have a fine town here. I am most happy this *cauchemar* [nightmare] is at an end. And now Monsieur le Maire I must start preparations for my trip."

"I understand. Stay as long as you like in your room and don't give a thought to a bill. Again, my heartfelt thanks."

The two men stood, shook hands and departed for their separate destinies.

On the short walk back to his office the mayor reviewed the day's events.

Thank God it's over. Maybe I needn't worry about re-election now and I can get in a little fishing. Mohsen is not nearly the maniaque [tight ass] *I thought he was. He is actually quite likable.*

Peace, quiet and normalcy. How sweet!

I suppose I should call that idiot Kontz now and reinstate him. He's not worth a damn, but we need a policeman on duty, right now.

~~~~

Officer Émile Kontz was far from the sharpest blade in the drawer, yet even his limited intellect eventually realized that suspension wasn't all that bad. Sleep late. Long lunches. Frequent naps and lazy afternoons spent admiring Sophie's long legs at Le Cheval Blanc over a cool glass of wine. Not to mention full pay.

Today however, he was particularly inspired. After lunch he discretely retrieved another of the magic blue pills from the medicine cabinet. Ambrosia for the libidinous. He swallowed quickly, preparing to impatiently await the appropriate interval. After an hour's nap, he called Michelle into the bedroom, inviting her to join, proudly displaying his passion. Michelle was delighted, as was Émile.

Slowly, languidly he caressed her just to the point of consumation, when abruptly his mobile phone rang out shrilly, incessantly demanding.

"Oh merde! I am so sorry Michelle, I must answer. That is my police mobile."

Poor Michelle almost whimpered.

"Allo?"

"Officer Kontz?"

"Oui."

"This is Maire Drôme." Kontz stood a bit straighter, or at least his shoulders.

"Oui Monsieur le Maire. Qu'est-que je peut faire pour vous Monsieur?" [What can I do for you sir?]

"You are re-instated. Chief Inspector Mohsen is returning to Paris and Officer Thommes is returning to St. Tropez as we speak. Therefore you must resume your normal duties immediately."

"I appreciate that sir."

"Do not be too appreciative too soon Officer. I have some serious concerns regarding your recent conduct. We will discuss this tomorrow morning at 0900 in my office. Clear?"

"Absolutely sir."

"Good. Assume your post directly, and I expect to see you at 0900 sharp tomorrow."

"Yes sir. Thank you sir."

Uniform pants, shoes, shirt, tie, jacket … a flurry of clothing … all at once, struggling to dress and report for duty as soon as physically possible.

"Michelle. I am so sorry. I must leave. Perhaps … I pray … later my love."

Her only response was an aggrieved "Ouais, ouais, ouais …" [Yeah, yeah, yeah …]

Fade Omega

AS THE SOUND of Alain's car faded in the hills, David quietly observed: "I'm not at all clear what transpired here. I do know this. I'm grateful to be alive and with you both. I believe something important has passed this night. But there is time to sort it out. And sort it out we shall. Meanwhile, could I have a ham sandwich and a beer?"

A tear escaped Ranny's eye. She stood with a tremulous smile and moved purposely to make David's sandwich, her relief a joy.

Adam wandered out to the pool. For more than an hour he simply sat, unmoving, staring up at the stars. Ranny quietly peered out the door from time to time, trying to penetrate the turmoil roiling through his mind. David took it in, confused, concerned, unable to comprehend.

Finally David and Ranny resorted to simply sitting quietly, studying the fire. When Adam finally appeared at the door he stood somewhat stiffly, an introspective but not altogether glum expression adorning his features.

"I am beginning to remember I think. And I swear by the gods I didn't do it. I'm not Charley. Ran, I owe you my life and my love. I'm innocent and whatever it may have been is gone, were it ever." His face fell into his hands. His breathing labored. "But I'm now having strange visions. Horrible. From the gates of hell itself."

Ranny stood, taking him into her arms. Comforting him.

When he'd regained control, he raised his head and kissed Ranny, embracing her face, looking deep into her eyes with a crooked smile. "I don't know about you guys, but I need a drink." He turned towards the bar.

David sat, transfixed by the scene.

Who the bloody hell is Charlie? Much goes on here I know nothing of.

A suspicious bile of jealousy and anger began choking him. Head slightly cocked, David spoke questioningly, a squinting, calculating, half-smile shadowing his countenance and finely lining his eyes. With some effort he calmly posed a question. "Should I be jealous Adam?"

Adam turned, confronting him earnestly. "Yes. But I think we have greater problems this evening my friend."

Rising on his good hand *"You limy fuck! What've you been doing with my wife?"*

David lunged at Adam, striking out in fury, his vehemence blinding him to his disabilities. As a consequence he tumbled comically to the floor.

Ranny interjected. "David! Stop! This is not you. This is not us."

He whirled on Ranny in a rage of hurt and betrayal.

Surprisingly, she unflinchingly bore his scrutiny, returning only concern and devotion, disclosing neither denial, nor repentance. She slowly moved her head from side to side in mute, gentle castigation.

He was simply too weak to disagree.

Adam carefully helped David to sit up, looking him hard in the eyes. "We're both limy fucks David, in our own way. But no one wants to hurt you here. We've both lived under some very dark shadows all our lives. And we're only now finding our way. And we're doing it together, all three of us. You. If you're going to hold on David, you're going to have to loosen up a bit."

Adam sighed and helped David onto the couch. "Neither of us wants to hurt you, or your love, or your marriage. Do you understand?"

David thought for a time, eye-to-eye with Adam, until a glimmer of understanding slowly banked deep within his eyes.

He adjusted his cast and took a long breath. Then he spoke.

"You and I are about as screwed up as it gets. You know that Adam? The only sane one here is Ranny. And I'm not at all sure about her either." He studied them both closely. Grudgingly affectionate, if and somewhat bitterly resigned. "So you ..." he paused "you bastards ... you're putting the goddamned onus on *me* now?"

Ranny watched both men. Her attention riveted. She dared not speak.

What a desperately fine line we tread this night.

She hardly breathed, fiercely aware she was the cause, the cure, perhaps even the spoils of the troubles passing between these two men. If this fell apart they would all lose and she had no idea where the solution lay.

Adam regarded David intently. He spoke nearly inaudibly "That's pretty much the way it is David." He half-smiled in genuine sympathy. "You can say *No*, and we may all find our way through this. Or you can say *yes*. You'll have your vengeance, and we'll all pay, including you."

A bitter smile in return. "You son of a bitch." His piercing glaze bore through Adam. "So you think you've left me only two options. Yes, or No."

"That's the way it is. I'm truly Sorry Davy. No one wanted this."

He closed his eyes and dropped his head, deep in thought.

After a time he took a deep breath. "Okay. Then I choose *No*." his voice suddenly strong "*Yes* is for Greenies."

Fade to Morning

THEY QUESTED THEIR dawning, if ambiguous concord well into the night. Exploring its un-trodden ways and latent affinities. They talked and shared and confessed. They even laughed at times. Without rancor. Without guilt. Secrets and sickness. Tragedy, death and loss. Lust and love and betrayal.

Adam relived his demeaning childhood. A hapless innocent sickened and corrupted by rapacious perversion.

David recounted his youthful calamity, his time out of mind by the river, and the realization it finally provoked.

Ranny confessed to the attempted murder of her husband, and the many reasons she had for doing so.

Responding to only one item David said. "I understand how you arrived at these conclusions, but there is one point. You didn't realize that there are two France Telecom installations in Charleville-Mézières. The larger one in town provides land-based communications. But there is a second, much smaller facility outside of town that supports wireless and conducts topographical studies in conjunction with RTL in Luxembourg."

Ranny also told them of their respective iterations of DID and the effects they suffered as a result. Forgetfulness amidst the arise of alien persona. Strange symbolism and idiosyncratic behaviors. Some charmingly eccentric, others potentially monstrous.

When the fire finally faded, each knew as much about the other as most humans could, or perhaps should aspire to. They were now consummate friends, lovers and confidants. They had become co-conspirators and compassionate accessories-after-the-fact. Bonded deeply now in a trust formed of interlocking culpability and mutual regard.

Staring into the dying embers David was deeply engrossed in the events unraveling before him. He realized that he did after all sense a complex tangle of jealousy, resentment, even betrayal, deep within, where he couldn't quell his lurid green imaginings. In the march of but a few hours, a single evening, his entire life was now an alien plain. His mind could not help but see a tenuous parallel between the hideous hours on the Isle of Wight and this perplexing night. He prayed the trauma of their dark interplay would not foment similar consequence.

He suspected his enmity would fade with time. He would wait it out. His lurid demons would wither and die and only he would remain, to emerge whole and healthy from the flanks of madness. But he needed time. Time. He must have time.

He glanced up at Ranny and noticed something adorning her neck. He caught her eye and nodded inquiringly at her throat? "What is that?"

"You don't recognize it?" She smiled with a slight tilt of head and hint of frown. She stepped forward dangling the end of the necklace in her hand so he might see it better.

He studied the object carefully. A dark round, swirled stone suspended by a silver chain. Evidently she'd donned the necklace while in her bedroom.

David whispered. "My God. My mother's Ammonite necklace! Where in hell did you find ..."

"Your Aunt Carol gave it to me during her visit." She stood and stepped closer. Partly to allow him a clearer view of the necklace, and partly to hand him something. "She also gave me this." She handed David a fossilized bone.

"I'll be damned." He smiled fondly. "The Tyrannosauroid digit." He looked back to the fire, turning the fossilized bone in his hands, clearly moved. Somehow things didn't feel quite so alien now.

For quite some time no one spoke.

Finally David turned to Ranny and Adam, lips optimistically compressed. "You know, when I'm back on my feet, I think I'll need a little space. I'll leave you two alone, wherever that may lead. I believe I can take it, and *we* can take it. I think you both need the time. I know I do."

All three grew silent again, frowning into the embers.

Adam ventured softly "That's very kind David."

Then Ranny. "Where would you go David? For how long? What would you do?"

With a reminiscent smile "Not really sure how long. A few weeks at least, perhaps longer. I think I'll go back to the UK for a time. I'll get my sister to join me at first. There are a couple of gravesites long overdue for a visit and I believe we need to do some talking. Then I want to do some fossilizing."

Fossilizing. She was pleased David had adopted his sister's flippant moniker. It seemed to signal a lowering of defenses. Acceptance. Perhaps the beginnings of an armistice with his demons and a growing comfort with the past, hopefully the future as well. Although she wasn't entirely clear about his exact meaning.

"Fossilizing?"

"Yes. There's a Cretaceous monster that's been stalking me for decades. *Eotyrannus lengi.*" He glanced at Ranny with a twinkle. "Or *Kittysaurus* if you will …" He gingerly re-adjusted his cast using both hands to change its position, mumbling about an itch promising to persist until freed from its fabric and fiberglass immuration. "It lies about eight meters up a cliff-line on the Isle of Wight. He's been shadowing me for a hundred and forty million years. It's time we met."

Fade to Black

MIDSUMMER. SOUTHERN PROVENCE. Three in the morning. The air warm and sultry. A thousand Jasmines scent the breeze honey-sweet. Ten thousand stars incandesce the heavens. Moonlight so intense it cast brilliant shadows. Razor silhouettes of ebon on pearl.

A man lay unconscious, cushioned soft on pine needles, adrift and alone in a fragrant, resinous forest.

A sudden gust tousled his sandy hair, a blustery harbinger from the north overpowering the night's southerly sea-wind. Come the dawn that wind would herald a howling Mistral.

Dr. Adam MacAfee awoke with a gasp, the sudden, chest-pounding shock thundering life's constancy. Slowly his calm returned. A chill stiffness in neck, back and legs alerted him to his prostration.

As awareness emerged, he peered up to at the night sky framed by pine boughs. Methane-blue needles girding the starry heavens with their bristly contours.

What am I doing here?

Here? Where the hell is here?

Then, befouling the tranquil night, an oily whispery hissing reared and coiled through the darkness inspiring an icy, unctuous dread within him. "Iiiiye brought you heeeere."

Adam instinctively peered upward through the darkness, seeking the source of such malevolence. After a time he perceived a nebulous outline lurking in the moon-dappled shadows. Although the figure appeared repellently androgynous, he somehow sensed it was male. It was tall, shadowy, gaunt and imposing.

It glided soundlessly nearer, insinuating itself close to Adam.

The creature seemed to excrete a close, fetid scent. Adam nearly gagged on the moist metallic and grossly intimate organic odor.

Though it was but an incorporeal wraith he could make it out more clearly now. Its face was gaunt, pale and drawn. Yet it was most definitely male ... and disturbingly familiar.

My God! It's me ... his mind whimpered to itself.

"Good evening Adam. It's me. Charley. You remember me, don't you, *mon petit frère?*" [my little brother]

No ... worse ... much worse! It's Charley. My God! My God, am I Charley? His stomach churned and his skin literally crawled.

Adam sputtered. "Char ... *Charley?*"

"Yes. It's *Ch-Ch-Charley.*"

Adam sprang to his feet and the specter vanished instantly. Although its presence still eagerly attended Adam, as he was loathsomely aware.

Adam was instantly and totally debilitated. He fell to his knees.

I am Charley. I am a monster. A serial killer. I can't continue like this. I must be insane. I must find a way out ... a way to ... die.

"For Christ's sake Adam, find some balls! You're hiding from the truth, as you have for all you wretched life. You always knew I was here, living in the calamitous labyrinth you pretend to be a mind. You just couldn't face it. Now you have no choice."

How ... how is this possible? How can were speak together? In all my years I've never heard of anything like this. MPD sufferers cannot speak with each other!

Adam struggled to his feet as Charley huffed with pride.

"I'll explain it to you brother. Truthfully, I was surprised as well. One day, months ago ... I *discovered* you. Before that I always suspected you existed, or *someone* existed in any event. I wish I'd found someone more worthy. But you'll have to do.

"I knew I blanked out from time to time, so I knew *someone* took control. After an incredible time and terrible efforts I learned how to become aware as well, even when you were in control. It won't do you fuck-all good, so I'll tell you how it's done. But you'll never understand you poor bastard." He paused dramatically.

"You have to learn how to—how shall I say it—breathe in a vacuum." Again he paused. "Then I observed you, the way you live, the things you do and the way you are. And I made a wonderful discovery ..." Charley let the statement dangle, teasing Adam, luring him to ask.

Patiently, warily and wearily Adam relented "What is it Charley?"

"I'm ten times stronger than you."

Adam smiled in distain. "You think so do you?"

"No Adam. I don't think. I *know*."

"Quoting Abbott and Costello: I don't think you know either."

"Very amusing Adam. Now try this."

Adam's entire body dropped to the ground and assumed an incredibly tight fetal position. Every muscle in his body agonized in rock hard spasms and horrific cramps. He feared that tendons would soon snap and bones would crack. Adam nearly passed out from the pain. After long moments Charley released him. Adam could only lie exhausted, raggedly struggling to breathe.

Adam heard the specter of a smile in Charley's voice. "If I can murder women with such skill and relish, do you suppose it troubles me in the least to torture you?"

After a time "My God." Adam whispered.

"In some respects I suppose I *am* your god, Adam."

"How, how is it you don't suffer from my pain, our pain?"

The bitterness in Charley's voice sizzled like sulfuric acid on a sheet of magnesium. "You deliciously stupid fuck, you don't understand anything do you? I don't feel the pain, because I was delegated to hell itself for years. I felt nothing. When I gained awareness somehow, I agonized in a sightless, soundless, zero-sensory perdition. I was driven literally insane. After years of struggle, I learned to emerge and discovered you, you bastard, but I never lost the ability to withdraw, or separate myself from our body. That's why I can totally subjugate you. I've paid my dues in hell. Your bill has now come due. So stand up Adam, and smartly."

Adam drew himself stiffly to his feet, a blossoming fear coldly coursing through his body.

"Tweak your nose Adam. Hard."

He did so. And it hurt, with the freakish pain only a crushed nasal cavity can inflict.

"You understand Adam? We're clear? Now walk over to that oak tree and look about."

Adam listened in wonder. He heard own voice resounding through his head, something perversely akin to a voice-over in the cinema. Beneath the tree he found a leather satchel roughly the size and thickness of a book. A sort of a custom stitched shoulder holster.

"Open it."

Inside Adam found a .38 caliber Smith & Wesson, and a box of bullets. Hollow points.

"What the hell is this you sick bastard?"

Now, amazingly, Charley's voice materialized from his own mouth.

"Tweak your nose again Adam. *Harder.*"

He did so. Again. Harder. Blood ran from his left nostril.

"Goddamnit Charley that hurts!"

"... so lay off the sick bastard talk."

This is insane.

"What hellish abomination are you planning now?"

"I'll explain. It's time we updated our *modus operandi* Adam. You understand?"

"*Your* modus operandi Charley. Not mine. And no, I do not understand."

"That damned frog [French] cop from Paris was getting close, as was that damned girlfriend of yours. Now they believe Charley's dead. Truly, physically dead. Slip on the satchel Adam. Now."

Helplessly, he mounted the holster.

Despite himself, Adam was intrigued. "So you ... you're going to use a new method to ... to ... why does Inspector Mohsen believe you're dead?"

"Ah. I arranged for a suitable cadaver and an irrefutable link to the murders. It worked like a charm. A lucky charm Adam. Mine and yours. Clearly you don't know a damned thing. Don't you read about the papers? Don't you listen to the radio? Talk to people? TV? You're spending far too much time in your lab and on that damned sailboat. We'll change that soon."

"What are you saying Charley?"

"You figure it out." his voice challenging and derisive.

Adam frowned, his eyes nearly closed. Squinting. A look approximating pain dominated his features. "I *do* recall something. A man was found drowned in ... Hyères ..."

"That's right Adam." He chuckled. "You're getting it."

He closed his eyes. Concentrating. Finally it dawned on him.

"You bastard. You fucking bastard! That man 'drowned' after *you* beat him to death and planted evidence on his body!"

"... and afterwards I even administered chest compressions. You don't seem to remember that? I wonder why?"

Stunned. "You administered resuscitation?"

"Well, of sorts. I performed resuscitation as one would for a drowning victim."

"Why in hell's name would you do that?"

"Sort of reverse respiration actually. His head was *under* the water." He puffed with pride. "I filled his lungs with seawater to authenticate drowning. A masterly touch. *Non?*"

Adam could think of no response. He was lost in thought. Willing himself to recall the grisly details of Charley's activities.

"Madame Zaparelli's ring! You placed her ring on the dead man's little finger."

Charley's wolfish smirk slithered across Adam's features.

"You planned this whole twisted deception, from stealing Angela Zaparelli's ring, to sparing Erica Martin and feigning death, to killing that poor drunken bastard in Hyères, to whatever monstrous act you've committed in these woods ..."

Charley grinned smugly. "It worked on Erica Martin and Inspector Mohsen and Ranny Woods. They actually believed I went away. Or *died* as it were." His voice took on a mocking, overly melodramatic throb. "After being reformed by the love of Ranny I became remorsefully suicidal, realizing I was forever unworthy of such a *woman nobly planned* (That's from

Wordsworth as I'm sure you know brother.) ... a wonderful pristine person she ... not to mention a damned good fuck."

"You're not insane Charley. You're *evil*. You've been methodically working this for months."

"Very good. Although, I'm not evil in the least. That, you will never understand. You're the dumb half of our little equation. But you're getting the hang of this nonetheless. I'm proud of you. You figured everything out. And don't think for a second I'll allow you to turn us in, or kill yourself, or any half-assed countermeasure you may dream up. We really are partners now brother."

The thought of Charley as his partner made him nauseous. The thought of Charley as his brother made him suicidal. Adam took a deep breath, ignoring his churning innards, lowering his head deep in thought. Thoughts he hoped Charley was not privy to.

I've never heard of MPD (Multiple Personality Disorder) *manifesting itself exactly like this. It's frightening. Amazing. We actually converse. How is this possible?*

"I'll tell you how it's possible asshole. It took years to struggle from the depths of your tortured mind like some poor primordial creature from the Black Lagoon. When I finally surfaced, I imagine we attempted to combine. We may have actually made some progress. Ultimately though, we must have rejected each other in an orgy of mutual revulsion. So here we sit brother, side-by-side in conjoined hatred, astraddle our impaired frontal lobe and fractured psyche."

Adam spoke introspectively. "Or perhaps we suffer from ACC?"

"ACC. Showing off our fancy degrees are we? What the fuck does ACC mean?"

Lost in thought, David absently intoned to himself "ACC is an acronym for Agenesis of the Corpus Callosum. Essentially the connection between the left and right brains is defective, or non-existent. Were this our affliction, it would be the most unique and acute case I've ever heard of. Perhaps it's a combined syndrome of ACC compounded by MPD. The fact that we do not share certain knowledge, such as the definition of ACC along with Charley's monstrous behavior, would seem to support this."

"Mmm." Charley grinned wolfishly. "I'll have to read up on this. It could be a useful defense someday, if I'm ever caught." Then he grinned more broadly. "And you're not around."

Adam ignored Charley's implied threat.

After a time he spoke. "Tell me Charley, why do you speak to me only now?"

"Well, after our beloved Kitty Day Woods nearly spilled the beans ..."

"Not 'our' you son of a bitch ... 'the' ..."

"Fine. Whatever. I knew you'd uncover me sooner or later. And frankly, I never needed your help before. I should think that would be clear, even to you."

"And you need my help now?"

"Possibly, for a time, yes."

"Why?"

"That's really not your affair."

"... and when you don't need my help any longer?"

"That's really not your affair either."

"*Baisez mon cul.*" [Kiss my ass.]

Charley's voice took on a taunting faux Cockney falsetto. "Cor Blimey! Such talk. And you a scientist and a Doctor and all." Then his tone turned conversational. Reasonable. Almost urbane. "I speak French as well as you Adam; and if I kissed your ass, why you'd be kissing your own ass, wouldn't you? That could be arranged brother. It might even be amusing, albeit painful for you. But you and I are partners now Adam. So be nice."

"If you speak French so goddamned well, *Va t'faire enculer!*" [Go fuck yourself.]

Charley's inflection grew soft and serious and threatening. "One more crack like that and you'll be tweaking your nose so hard you'll pass out from blood loss."

Adam was repelled and fascinated, as one who watches a snake ingesting a rate. "Tell me Charley, when you awoke me, you were a phantasm lurking in the shadows."

"Yes?" Adam could here the greedy anticipation in his voice.

"How is that possible?"

"You figure it out."

Adam thought for moments. "You have the ability to make me hallucinate?"

"Um hmm."

"So you could ..."

"Yes. I could drive you insane. I could make you drive of a cliff, or sink that goddamned boat of yours, literally anything I want. I told you I am ten times stronger than you ... and in ways you can't begin to imagine."

Adam had lost. And he was still losing. He needed a solution desperately. And he had nothing.

"I swear somehow, I'm going to *kill* you Charley."

"As though you could." Adam was shocked to hear himself snicker. "But *I* can kill *you* Adam. You'd exist as I did for years. I can bury you so deep you'll never see daylight again. You'll never laugh, or talk, or work, or sail, or eat, or see anyone, or fuck your pretty little slut again ..."

"You goddamn gigolo bastard I'll ..."

It came from the right, totally blindsiding him.

A thunderous, ear-ringing slap of such force it nearly floored him. It seemingly came from nowhere. He was stunned and amazed. It came from his own right hand.

Head reeling, Adam leant against a pine, calming himself, trying to regain control. Suddenly he clutched at his own testicles, squeezing so hard he screamed and fell to his knees, doubled over in pain and nausea.

A whisper thick with anger and hatred. "You ever call me a gigolo again ... *ever* ... and we both die. You can't even begin to conceive of the pain and the horror and the humiliation ..."

Charley slapped him again. Unbelievably ... even harder. Adam sagged under the blow, wilting to the ground. Then Charley took control. After a long shuddering breath he stood, throwing back head and shoulders, invulnerable to the throbbing ache.

Despite the pain and the fear Adam was intrigued by Charley's reaction. Somewhere in his mind Adam realized he'd stumbled on some sort of key to his psychosis.

"As I was saying brother … I *will* banish you to your own private hell. Forever. And you *will* learn the true meaning of insanity. For now though, you may be useful."

This is hopeless.

Adam looked around, trying to understand what had occurred here, and trying to ignore the wracking pain.

No body. No blood. No other weapons. No villa. No car. Nothing I can see. Thank God.

"Yes. That's right. Thank me Adam."

This was impossible.

"Charley, you know my thoughts. You know how I feel about you and your activities. You know Ranny. You know how you and I became psychologically diseased. You know how you were conceived a monster. Does none of this draw you nearer to something approaching human?"

"Adam, do you have the slightest idea what I could compel you to do to yourself on any sunny Saturday morning in the center of the market on Place Velleda?"

Adam sighed. Exhausted and outmatched.

How did I get here?

"You're going to have to find that out for yourself."

Am I alone?

"*I'm* here you idiot."

What was I doing?

"*You* weren't doing a damned thing. I was."

Unreasoning fear was a vice in his chest.

Good God. What can I do? God help me, what can I do?

His radiant dream of a loving, decent, worthy life had faded into the menacing shadows. His blossoming hopes now a bitter, mocking will-o'-the-wisp. His fear and frustration overwhelmed him. Adam threw his head back wailing, screaming, near howling "No! God no! Please God!"

"*Basta!* [Enough!] You milksop little bastard, you can't do one damned thing. Bloody coward. Pansy little fuck-all-do-gooder!"

Charley was haranguing Adam so vehemently, spittle sprayed from his lips as he snarled.

"*Scientist? Doctor?* Bollocks!" He was screaming now. "You're a *killer*! Just like me. Your hands are my hands and they're drenched in blood. Only you can't face it, or even remotely understand our purpose." His voice became a low contemptuous growl. "*Vous n'avez pas les balles.*" [You don't have the balls.] "And that little slut of yours draws closer to the truth every minute."

Slowly. Imperceptibly. Adam's fingers edged towards the holster under his arm.

Charley's sinister whisper echoed menacingly through his mind. "Adam if you could somehow contrive to draw that pistol, you will be abjectly incapable of turning it on yourself. Instead I will frog-march your chicken-shit little ass into Coirón and we will start killing people, and keep killing until we're out of bullets."

It was becoming impossible to think. Impossible to do anything. Adam was suffocating within his own body.

So he stopped.

He cleared his mind, concentrating on a small pebble at his feet. Smooth and gray. Ovoid and softly luminous in the moonlight. He didn't speak. He didn't think. He didn't feel. He even slowed his breathing. All his faculties focused on the tiny pebble.

Mercifully, Charley seemed to withdraw.

Adam began to pace about. Wobbly legs. Bleary eyes. Aching all over. His mouth as dry as talc.

God what I wouldn't give right now for just some cool water ...

In a sickening flash-back, he returned to younger days. University. Pre-med. Host-Parasite Biology. Vivid memories of loathsome creatures coiled in the hemic darkness of their wretched host's viscera, feasting on unspeakable broths. With odious industry these most foul of nature's vermin writhed and coiled and glutted. He'd wondered then that an alleged deity, purportedly the architect of such marvelous creation, would play the divine trickster, concealing such obscenities within our own bodies. Surely only the random, precipitate advance of evolution would render such loathsome beings. He wondered even more strongly now.

Thus are sown the seeds of doubt. The end of faith unexamined. Perhaps the beginning of wisdom.

Now *he* harbored something far more pernicious. A thing that spoke to him, using his mouth, or hissed serpent-like within his own mind, tormenting and terrifying him. Coiled in dark shadows, a phantom vapor stalking and dogging him. An inhuman malevolence unfolding from his soul much as the long spidery legs of a king crab, grasping out in search of prey. An evil he could not control. A corruption that prevailed over *him*. He couldn't imagine a more wretched fate.

For God's sake ... I'm a doctor, a biologist, a scientist ... I'm not a killer! How could such a monster infest my mind? My soul.

For now though. For the present. He must try to master the malignancy within, and try to understand this grisly invader.

Looking around. Trying to get his bearings. What horror had he and Charley wrought this time? He began to study his surroundings. More carefully this time.

To begin with, he was ... nowhere.

In a moonlit pine forest, near a small dirt road. No one around. No lights. No buildings of any sort. No vehicles. All was quiet darkness.

That's good news at least.

Why was he here?

Damned if I know.

With whom? Some hapless woman?

I pray, with no one. I see no woman, alive or dead.

What has Charley done? What have *we* done?

Nothing. I pray nothing.

What is the last thing he can remember?

I ah ... I was in town ... St. Tropez. I was coming from the boat. I stopped for dinner. Chinese. I was alone. Then I decided to stop for a drink. Where? I have no idea. It all ends there. I wonder how long it's been this time? And that monster is actually talking to me now. And I obey his every command! I must be as insane as he. For God's sake I am he. But I'm aware of my affliction. And that's supposed to indicate sanity. Isn't it?

Aware or not though, the sickness exists, as does Charley, as does my DID, or MPD, or ACC, or whateverthefuck ... as do those butchered women, as does that poor sod beaten to death on the beach.

Jesus God. This is a nightmare. And that bastard won't let me die. I desperately need help ... but from whom?

~~~~

He collapsed on a fallen tree. Trying to clear his mind. Trying to understand. Breathing deeply of the night air, looking wistfully to the sky. Searching the heavens for amnesty, lost innocence and blessed forgetfulness. Peering back nearly fourteen billion years and he was certain, infinitely longer. Gazing into an eternity he prayed was clement and forgiving.

His works in science, nature, medicine and ontology. Exploring the wonder of existence itself. He looked to such lofty pursuits as retreat from the horrors he was forced to confront. A remission of sorts from Charley's heinous misdeeds ... their joint and separate sins.

In some way he hoped his good works might mitigate the dreadful suffering they'd visited upon their victims. Somehow he actually believed in such absolution.

Now aware of the full, ghastly reality of it, he even prayed for it and hungered for acquittal—guilt being man's most abominable burden—the stain that never fades—his hopes tonight frenetic.

Suddenly roused, Charley mocked jeeringly "Hope purrs such fawning promise brother." He chuckled mirthlessly as Adam felt a derisive smirk form unbidden to his face. "And you always rise to its call ..."

Adam whispered, so softly he foolishly deluded himself Charley mightn't hear.

<div align="center">

Nothing
Nothing in this country,
This planet.
This universe.
Nothing in these infinite cosmos ...
Is ever ...
As simple ...
As our hopes ...

</div>

~~~~

Then it came to him.

An inspiration.

Such a sweet, gentle solution.

Great relief and a pulsing rush of hope.

He smiled secretly as he barely breathed the words.

"*Ranny*. I'll find *Ranny*."

~~~~

Charley's blithe flamboyancy resounded an ominous, dark accord—booming demoniacally through his mind.

"An *excellent* idea Adam!"

Adam was instantly defeated, as a monstrous realization dawned upon him. He began to tremble, hands shaking, weakly seeking leniency where none would be found.

"God help me."

"Yes Adam?"

Adam whispered, defeated, with an impassioned rasp. "*Am I truly the author of thee?*"

Surprisingly Charley responded gently ... even kindly. "No. Not you Adam. Not you brother. You poor bastard, our joint damnation was ordained long before you could ever imagine."

It occurred to Adam that his life, for all intents, was over.

Charley's voice grew suddenly commanding and as hard and as cold as carbon-tempered steel.

"Now let's go."

Murder & Missings in the Massif

A prominent resident of the village of Coirón sur Mer, Mrs. Katherine (Ranny) Woods, was found Monday morning by her housekeeper, murdered in her Domaine in the hills above the town. The coroner reports she had been severely beaten, sexually assaulted, and finally shot to death. Her husband, Mr. David Woods, had been admitted three days prior to the attack, into the Centre Médical du Var undergoing remedial treatment for a recent injury. Officer Kontz of the Coirón Gendarmerie stated they had presently identified no persons of interest in the crime.

In a nearby incident, two women from the neighboring village of Cavalaire-sur-Mer, Mme Monique LeHavre and Mlle Susan Remy, have gone missing. They were last seen in a popular nightclub in St. Tropez at approximately 2300. Police have thus far been unable to determine their fate. Any information as to their whereabouts should be reported to the St. Tropez Police at 04.94.97.26.25. Police spokesman, Inspector Henri LeForet stated that there was presently no evidence to indicate the two incidents were related.

Postlude

DAVID LIMPED FROM the taxi and staggered through the front door, groping his way directly to the bar. He tossed his bag and cane aside, pouring himself a large tumbler of Scotch and collapsed. The Domaine was deserted and quieter than he ever remembered. This had been the home he'd always dreamt of. Now it was no more than an empty building.

Two days ago the moronic Officer Kontz had bumbled into his hospital room and artlessly bludgeoned him with the news of his wife's murder. Savagely beaten, sexually assaulted and shot. According to Kontz, the bullet very nearly took half her head away. Thus far there was no indication as to whom the killer might be.

For forty-eight hours David lay awake, tormented with grief, luridly imagining her horror and pain despite his struggle to block such ghastly images. Ranny must have suffered dreadfully in her last moments. Did she wonder who was torturing her, and why? Did she wonder why David was not there to protect her? She must have felt profoundly alone. How long did she suffer? Where was Adam? Was she horrified that her last moments were abased by such a bestial atrocity? Worst of all, he was haunted night and day by the terror she must have endured. David is a profoundly empathetic man by nature, thus he could quite literally feel her terror and pain and degradation. Icy daggers in his gut. His imaginings tormented him with an agony nearly as hideous as Ranny's must have been. Her suffering was over now. Thank God. But his suffering would endure as long as he lived.

He listlessly shuffled through the mail Hélène had left for him on the counter. Any diversion, however prosaic, was preferable to dwelling on Ranny's death. He came upon their weekly English newspaper, *The Riviera Times*. An article on the front page described Ranny's murder.

David observed grimly: *They did a better job reporting Ranny's death than Officer-bloody-Kontz!*

He threw the paper across the room with such force it shattered a large vase.

He poured himself another Scotch.

In less than a breath of a second, everything was gone. His cherished Ranny ... her gentle beauty ... his hopes for their life together ... paleontology no longer held fascination ... the charms of the Domaine and Coirón were lost to him now ... even Adam was oddly quiet, having neither called, nor visited since Ranny's death; a source of puzzlement and even hurt.

His world was suddenly cold and lonely, hateful and dangerous.

This all started when my father was six years old, wrestling with his dog, finding a tiny fossil in the back garden. If I hadn't been stuck in that bloody hospital ... It's my goddamned fault. If I hadn't tried to climb that stupid cliff ... a half-second's poor judgment and my life ended. What is that vapid term? Zero tolerance? God has none.

He threw back the tumbler of Scotch, thirsting after its shock and burn, and the mind numbing release it conveyed. He poured himself another, laying his forehead on wrist, he silently sobbed.

~~~~

Alain was seated in his favorite café, Le Café de Flore, reading his favorite paper, *Le Monde*, jubilant to be back in his native Paris. Home at last.

He balanced a hot *café au lait* [milk-frothed coffee] in one hand with his neatly folded paper in the other. It was a warm, sunny Sunday morning and life was good. Retirement was now scant weeks away and he yearned for it.

A small article on page two of the paper caught his eye.

A Madame Katherine Woods had been savagely murdered and raped in her home in Coirón sur Mer, on the western Côte d'Azur.

Katherine Woods. Katherine?

My God it's Ranny!

The shock of it literally took his breath away.

His career had hardened him to the perverse barbarities humans were so easily disposed to visit upon one another. Yet this was personal and painful.

He was soon lost in thought. It was certainly, even dubiously coincidental that poor Ranny should fall victim to a depraved killer after all that had surrounded her in recent months. In fact Alain had often suspected events surrounded her a bit too closely.

As it had unfailingly for decades, his analytical mind spontaneously self-engaged.

He thoughtfully sipped his coffee, set it down, heaving a long sigh.

I shall genuinely miss her. She was a fine ... Mon Dieu, j'ai été un idiot! [My God, I have been a fool!]

A kaleidoscope of images cascaded through his mind ... a drowned murderer recklessly flaunting the ring of his victim ... missing toes ... Erica's supposed salvation and Charley's alleged death ... a wispy enigmatic smile faintly playing across Erica's lovely features ... Adam intimately whispering *Ran* ... Ranny in intense discussion with Adam by the pool on the night he shot him ... David near-dead from a simple broken leg ... and on and on.

He jumped to his feet, slamming the newspaper down on the tiny café table with such force his coffee cup exploded on the floor, all eyes in the café upon him. He threw money on the table and dashed onto the sidewalk.

I must speak with Erica Martin. Now!

Glossary

A bientôt—See you soon. *A demain*—Parting salutation (See you tomorrow, Literally: at tomorrow)

Adieu—Literally: *To God* Common Use: *Godspeed* Implied Use: *Farewell* with doubt we may see each other again (As opposed to *Au Revoir*)

Affection hépatique—Liver Disease (cirrhosis*)*

Anschauung—To view, or a view with insight, intuition and perception [Gr. *Anschau* to understand]

Au revoir—Literally: *At our next meeting* Common Use: *Goodbye* Implied Use: *Goodbye* and see you again (as opposed to Adieu)

Ausländer—Foreigner [German Ausländer, from Ausland, a foreign country. Old High German, ☐ z, *out* and *land*]

Baisez mon cul—Kiss my ass [Fr. Vulgar]

Basta—Literally: enough! An expression of exasperation [It.]

Boîte—A box or can

Boîte de Nuit—A nightclub

Bollocks—Rubbish, nonsense, drivel, bullshit [Eng. Brit. Slang]

Bon vivant—A taker of pleasures. Literally: A good liver

Boulangerie-pâtisserie—Bread & Pastry Shop

Bloomer—A typical British bread with rounded ends and diagonal cuts atop. The classical bread served with kippers

Bugger Off—Get lost [Eng. Brit. Colloquial]

Bureau de Poste—Post Office

Ça va?—Greeting (how goes it?)

Ça va bien—It goes well.

C'est pas vrai—It is not true.

Charwoman—Char, charlady, or charwoman. House cleaner. Derivative of 'chore woman' [Eng. Brit. Colloquial]

Comme vous voulez Madame—As you wish Madame

Cor blimey—God blind me (British Slang [Archaic])

Décharge d'ordures—Garbage dump

Désolé—Apology (Sorry)

Désole monsieur/ Madame. Je sais bien que vous avez raconté cette histoire plusieurs fois. Mais je prie votre patience et assistance une dernière fois.—I'm very sorry. I know very well that you've told this story many times already. But I ask your patience and help one last time.

Domaine—Estate. A commonly large plot of land dedicated to some purpose beyond habitation, such as wine growing

Dommage—Sadly, or too bad

Donc—Therefore.

Eau-de-Vie—Literally water of Life, a term applied to highly distilled liquors, normally fruit based

Enculer une mouche—Go fuck a fly. (Fr. Vulgar)

Épicerie—Grocery/deli

Êtes vous bien?—Are you alright?

Et voilà!—And there it is.

Femme de ménage—Cleaning lady, housekeeper, or literally lady of the house

Fils de put—Son of a bitch (Fr. Vulgar)

Frog—Pejorative term for a Frenchman (Br. Slang Vulgar)

Gendarmerie—Local Police Station

Gentil—Kind, nice, empathetic

Gens de la campagne—Country-folk

Gens de Provence—The peoples of Provence

Hectare—Metric measurement of land area (1 hectare = 10,000 m2, or 2279.9 yd2, or 2.47105 acres)

Il est bete comme ses pieds—He is as stupid as his feet.

Jugged—a popular method for preparing Kippers by removing heads and tails, placing them into a tall jug and filling it with boiling water. Let sit for six minutes, remove and serve in a warm dish with butter and traditionally, a Bloomer.

Les boîte de nuit—Nightclubs (pl) Literally: 'boxes of the night'

Les Herbes de Coirón—The grasses of Coirón

Les Herbes Intrépides—Idiom, name usage (The intrepid/courageous/strong grasses.)

Kipper—a small oily fish, or whole herring popular throughout the UK. Often prepared by gutting from end to end, salted and cold-smoked

Libeccio—Westerly or south-westerly wind concentrated mainly in Corsica. In autumn, winter and spring, it alternates with *Tramontane* (north-east or north). The word *libeccio* is Italian coming from Greek through Latin. Its etymology traces it to the word for 'Libyan.' [It. Latin & Greek]

L'étranger—A Stranger, or a foreigner, and the title of a novel by Albert Camus

Mairie—Town Hall, mayor's office, city council—also referred to as the Hôtel de Ville

Marché de Noël—Christmas Market

Merde—(Fr vulgar) [Literal translation: shit] Figurative equivalent of the expletive 'damn'

Mas—Farmhouse. Sometimes associated with a large dwelling atop a hill

Midi—Noon. Midday.

Mille-feuille—[mil foej] (Literally: A thousand-leaves) Vanilla cream and multi-layered crust commonly referred to as the Napoleon in the US (purportedly his favorite dessert), is a French pastry. The name is also written as *millefeuille*.

Mistral—Gale propagated in northwestern France, gaining great power as it passes through the vortices of the valleys of the Rhone and the Durance Rivers, roaring south to the sea. The name derives from the Languedoc dialect of the provençal language meaning "masterly." These same gales are called mistrau in the Occitan language, mestral in Catalan, and maestrale in Italian.

N'est-ce pas?—Is it not so?

Notaire—Publically appointed legal counsel/arbiter/administrator

Nôtre Dame des Collines—Our Lady of the Hills

Office de Tourism—Tourist Office

Outré—Outrageous. Beyond the bounds of convention, not generally considered proper

Pastis—A classically Provençal liquor made from anise seed

Pillock—Idiot [Eng. Slang]

Provence—Contemporary legislation has fused the region of Provence, with the Alps and the Côte d'Azur (PACA if you favor acronyms). Precisely stated: Provence now consists of the former province of *Provence*, the old Papal Realm of *Avignon* (known as *Comtat Venaissin*), the former Italian *Sardinian-Piedmontese County of Nice* (known as the *Côte d'Azur*), and the southeastern tip of the former *Province of Dauphine*, in the French Alps.

Quel désordre. Quelle odeur!—What a mess. What a smell!

Qui sait?—Who knows?

Route Communale—Village Road

Route Departmentale—State Road

Santé—Toast (To your health.)

Service d'Aide Médicale Urgente (SAMU)—Rescue Squad

Sod—A pathetic character. (Br. Vulgar slang, derivation of Sodomite)

Syndicat d'Initiative—roughly equivalent to a Chamber of Commerce

Tentative avortée—an aborted attempt

Une Bière—A beer

Vente de Fond—Sale of a Business dissociated from any associated property. When both the business and its premises are for sale it is referred to as *Vente de Fond et Murs* (Business and Walls)

Vin Chaud—Literally 'hot wine.' A winter drink comprised of red table wine steam-heated, optionally seasoned with cinnamon sticks, orange zest, granulated sugar, cardamom, cloves or Cognac, served with sugar cubes on the side, in a tall, glass and silver tea-cup holder

Village de la moyen age—Village from the middle ages

Vous n'avez pas les balles—You don't have the balls. [Francophized British idiom, vulgar]

Wanker—A jerk. Derogatory [Eng. Brit. Colloquial]

Wombourne—A male prostitute [Eng. Brit. Colloquial]

Weltshmerz—[German] Psychological pain caused by the sadness of realization that one's own disillusions and weaknesses are caused by the inappropriateness and cruelty of the world (The term is credited to the German author Jean Paul)

www.ingramcontent.com/pod-product-compliance
Lightning Source LLC
Chambersburg PA
CBHW031656170626
46808CB00005B/1483